The Prion Attachment

By Kathleen Morris
Copyright Kathleen Morris 2013
Amazon Paperback Edition
Rouge Publishing (2nd Edition 2019)
ISBN – 978-1-927828-58-8

License Notes

Warning– The contents of this book may not be suitable for all readers. Some scenes may be graphic in nature and depict violent situation. Reader discretion is advised.

This book is a work of fiction, and any resemblance to a person alive or dead, is purely coincidental.

This book is dedicated to my one-of-a-kind daughter, Renee. Your uniqueness inspired me to write this story and all the imagination that goes with it. You know what I mean.

TABLE OF CONTENTS

Prologue

As the haematologist surveyed the microscope in the faint light of the secret underground laboratory, she finally realized what the anomaly was: *A Prion.*

How could I have missed that? she asked herself. It was simple really.

"C'mere you little bugger," she said as she focused her eyes on the amazing discovery. "Let's see how you managed to attach yourself like that."

As she moved the specimen around, she noticed the folded proteins take on a domino effect. Every single sample she introduced became infected.

That wasn't good.

It explained a lot but not how it got there.

And they said it could never happen. The world scoffed but she had her assumptions all along. It *was* possible.

Yet for some reason, something still bothered her.

The brain sample she examined earlier had mutated within the last twenty-four hours. It was no longer just a causative agent behind mad cow disease they were dealing with here. If that was so, the human form CJD would have proven it by now.

She sighed and put another sample under the microscope, rubbing her tired eyes. It was already 4 a.m. and she needed to get some sleep before her first surgical experiment in the morning.

But they'd never believe her. Not without proof.

If only she could show them this, then they would take her seriously.

All she really had to do was get proof of her Prion attachment theory. But they didn't want to hear about this rebellious little protein. No, they scoffed at her when she explained her fascination for the most amazing biological phenomena in existence.

But then, they hadn't studied blood their entire life like she had.

How could she convince them?

With a tired throbbing head, she went through her research again. Yes, the improperly folded proteins targeted the brain and clumped together causing tissue damage and death but they already knew *that*.

What she had to do was convince them beyond a shadow of a doubt that the Prions were in fact attaching to the very thing they said it never could.

That would explain everything.

Well almost.

If they would only take her creditability seriously instead of merely placing her on staff, she would be able to convince them that this was the greatest threat to mankind they'd ever encountered.

But she'd have to get some sleep first. Her research would have to wait another day.

As the doctor switched off the light and crawled into bed, she heard something outside her door again. *It was them.* She was sure of it.

Usually it was one of her colleagues snooping around trying to find out what she was up to. But not this time.

This time she needed the gun.

Chapter 1

2:00 p.m. San Salvador Airport, Bahamas.

"I told you I don't *want* to!" Nadia screamed as her husband carried her over his shoulder toward the small Piper PA-27 with a grin. It wasn't the first time he had tried to take her for a ride today. The other two times she bolted from the tarmac as fast as she could, and he only had the rental plane for the rest of the afternoon.

She was like a child taking a temper tantrum, kicking and pounding her fists into the back of his shoulder blades in a failed attempt to get away. It was funny really. Why she was afraid of flying he would never know. But he was going to do something about it once and for all.

"Come on Nadia, I promise you'll like it!"

"Manuel, if you don't put me down right now, I *swear* you'll be sleeping on the couch for the rest of our honeymoon!"

"Oh, burn! I think I'll take my chances," he teased, forcing the passenger door open, setting her wiggly body down in the seat as he buckled her in.

"Now, *behave*!" he commanded with a smirk.

She was such a hothead but then that was why he married her. Life with Nadia would *never* be boring.

From the first moment he set eyes on her while ordering a Cappuccino at the Starbucks where she worked, he knew she was the girl for him with her piercing green eyes, flaming red hair, and spirit to go with it. Yes, Nadia Novak was the epitome of hot-tempered redheads if he ever saw one. Only, now it was Nadia Espinosa.

He had to get use to that.

Well, he thought, honeymoon or no honeymoon, Mrs Espinosa was going to see the Bahamas the way God intended.

Manuel raced around to the opposite side of the Piper and jumped in. "Hold on tight, we're flying to Rum Cay Island baby!"

~~~~

A news broadcast interrupted Miriam Novak's concentration on the multitude of wedding photos she was sorting through, but she didn't stop admiring them until her husband Frank turned the volume up on the old television in the kitchen and told her she'd better listen up.

"*At approximately 2:50 p.m. this afternoon a 7.5-magnitude earthquake struck the Haitian capitol of Port-au-Prince. The Pacific Tsunami Warning Center has issued a Tsunami warning for Haiti, Cuba, Dominican Republic, and Bahamas. Please be advised that if you are in these areas an immediate evacuation is underway.*"

The female CNN broadcaster paused for a moment, putting her hand to her earpiece. "*This just in... We have reports of a second earthquake that happened simultaneously 200 kilometres south of Tokyo in the Pacific. The quake measured a magnitude of 7.0 and a 50-centemeter-high Tsunami is headed for Miyake Island.*"

Both Miriam and Frank froze in front of the screen. "We have to call them, Frank!"

"Do you have the number?"

"*I-I don't know,*" Miriam stuttered as she darted to the phone desk in the corner. She leafed through the lavender booklet they kept friends and relatives names in until finally settling on the right page.

"I got her cell phone number."

Miriam pressed in the numbers with her shaky fingers and paused while Frank sat waiting in front of her.

"Well?"

"It's saying it's not in service Frank, I'm worried!"

"Stupid cell phones, I told you they were useless! You never listen to me Miriam! You *never* listen to me?"

"What are you getting all mad at me for? Your daughters out there in possible danger and you have to nit pick! What is *wrong* with you?"

Frank slumped down in his lazy boy with a frown on his face as Miriam grabbed her purse, put her shoes on, and headed out the front door.

"Where are you going?"

"Over to Terry's!" Miriam spit back, "She might know how I can reach Nadia."

"Why don't you just phone Terry?"

"Because I *never* listen to you Frank!"

With that, Miriam slammed the door leaving Frank alone with his thoughts.

~~~~

She was daddy's girl right from the start; her green eyes beaming with that devilish grin she used on him to get her way. But it was the cute little red pig tails that Miriam would put in her hair everyday that made his heart melt the most.

Why did she have to grow up?

Frank liked things the way they were, but then the way they were wasn't always good. There was that time that Nadia was sick. Dads were supposed to protect their children but this was something he couldn't protect her from and it tore him up inside.

It was when Nadia had Strep Throat and they decided to take her to emergency. While she was there, she found a discarded needle poking up inside a washroom sink. It pricked her little finger.

With her immune system down already, they worried about all sorts of things she could contract but mostly HIV. When tests were done on the needle, their hearts were shattered. It was contaminated with Aids.

The events that followed created the worse worry Frank had ever experience. Fear of losing his daughter consumed him for many years afterward as they waited for the virus to show up in her body.

But it never did.

It was just one of those things that people can't explain. Doctors gave her medications and ran tests on Nadia every month for years. She had so much blood taken from her it was a wonder she even grew up at all.

Finally, after so many blood tests, they were told she has a gene called Delta 32 CCR5 It was some gene mutation that was said to give her a rare natural immunity. It was unbelievable really. Modern medicine had come a long way in discovering something like that, yet, Frank still had his doubts.

There was nothing he could do about it though. He had to stop worrying about his daughter and let her live her life. And live it she did!

She was a married woman now and at such a young age. He didn't know how he was going to get his head around that. And now she was in the Bahamas for her honeymoon. Why did they have to go so far away? Frank would never go to a foreign country, it just wasn't safe.

Now look what happened.

A tear streamed down Frank's cheek at that moment. He recalled something his daughter would always say to him whenever he started to worry about her. He needed to hear her say it now.

"Daddy," she'd say, "you don't have to worry about me. I have special blood and God made me invincible!"

Ha! *Invincible?* She was hardly that, yet it was an ongoing joke; the kind that brings a chuckle at family gatherings. But one thing was for sure, she *was* special. She was his little angel.

That thought brought wet eyes this time until the phone rang abruptly, making him choke back the tears. "Hello?"

"Frank, get your shoes on and come over to Terry's, we're trying to locate Nadia and Manuel through their travel agency."

"Thought you were mad at me?'

"Would you just come over you miserable old coot!"

Frank grinned and hung up the phone. Honestly, if Nadia had half her mother's stubbornness, she'd be okay out there.

And that gave Frank the hope he needed, at least for now.

~~~

Nadia was sick to her stomach high in the air above the Atlantic. With Manuel at the controls she felt at ease a bit, but flying was still torture.

"Just relax!" Manuel shouted above the roar of the plane.

"I'm scared!"

"I know *Chica*," he pouted playfully, grabbing her hand.

With him holding her hand, some of the edge wore off but not all. Every time the plane hit hard turbulence she jumped and squeezed it a little tighter.

"You're beautiful!" Manuel shouted.

"Hugh?"

"You're beautiful!"

Nadia beamed a smile at her new husband. At least she was there with *him*. Nobody else would dare drag her on a plane. What a honeymoon. She'd have something to tell their children about.

Children - The discussion had come up a few months ago and they decided they'd try right away. It was something she had always wanted even though she was young. With Manuel eight years her senior they didn't need to wait.

People didn't understand, namely her parents but the way she looked at it, she was the luckiest girl alive to meet someone like her handsome charming Manuel.

It wasn't exactly love at first sight, but close. Manuel kept pestering her at work every day, painlessly making her explain the different types of coffee. He pretended to have broken English and claimed he didn't understand. But he understood alright and he wasn't fooling her. He asked her out for dinner every time he ordered and finally after a month of his persistence, he won her over, but not before she discovered he worked across the street at the fire department and was only fooling her that he couldn't speak English.

That thought brought a smile to Nadia's face.

"What's so funny?" Manuel asked.

"Nothing, I just love you sweetheart!"

She was so content looking into those hazel brown eyes that she forgot all about her fear of flying. Letting her head rest against his broad shoulders, her eyelids fell as she relaxed. *Sleep would be good right now.*

Within moments she was out like a light. The intermittent rocking of the plane cradled her into a long-awaited slumber.

But something wasn't right.

With a jolt, she awakened to the roar of the plane and noticed a sudden loss of altitude. Manuel's attention immediately fell to his instruments.

"What's wrong?"

"The instruments are going all screwy?"

"What do you mean, screwy?

It was broad daylight without a cloud in the sky, yet something was making the plane jump around and the instruments act funny.

"We should turn around," Manuel shouted, "something's wrong!"

Loud alarms were going off in the cockpit and that did not help. Nadia couldn't breathe. It was deja vu all over again.

"Mayday Mayday!" her husband called into his radio but that didn't seem to work properly either.

As the plane started to take a nosedive toward the ocean, Nadia noticed something in the water. It was a large wave and it began to circle like a toilet bowl sucking them in.

Her mind was playing tricks on her again!

And out of the depths of the ocean, a creature stretched its arm, clawing for her as she hovered there helpless and vulnerable.

The plane nearly plunged into the center of the hole but Manuel was able to pull it up as she screamed at the horrifying thing with its black wings and horns at the top of its head.

"Manuel!" she screamed, "get us out of here before it attacks us!"

"I'm trying!"

Sweat poured from her husband's bronze forehead as he tried to gain control of the Piper, until suddenly the plane jolted so hard it nearly made her bite her tongue.

At that point Nadia thought the creature had taken hold, but they were rising. Had the creature caught them as it rose from the water hole?

All Nadia could do was scream as she saw it unfold piece by piece, waiting for the end.

But it wasn't over.

Instead, the plane rose to its proper altitude and they slowly steadied until the threat of crashing was no longer imminent.

Nadia looked out the window again and the creature slowly withdrew to its watery grave. "Hurry," she sobbed, "let's get out of here before it tries to grab us again!"

"What tries to grab us?"

"You know!"

"No, I don't know!"

"You didn't see it?" Nadia shrieked.

"What are you talking about. You were sleeping and I've been flying the whole time. You were dreaming again *Chica*."

Nadia sat there stunned with her mouth open. Embarrassment washed her face crimson red. She couldn't believe it. It was so real.

"Never mind!"

Manuel looked at her with concern. They had perfect flying weather, but even so, his bride was upset and that wasn't a good thing.

"Can we just go home?"

Manuel grabbed her hand and squeezed, "You're *okay Chica*! I'll set the plane down the first chance I get. *I promise!* I'll check everything over and you'll see that we're fine!"

Relieved, Nadia let the lull of the plane's engines pacify her. It would be enough for now, but only for a short time because she knew this was not the end of it.

The nightmare was only getting started!

Chapter 2

Aids research center – Fort Pierce, FL.

The gunmen darted room to room leaving behind nothing but blood and mayhem. The killing spree was deliberate and ruthless, but necessary to the plan they had been hired to undertake.

One million each was not worth the effort John Blake was putting into this project. He kept telling everyone that it was a five-million-dollar job but they all thought he was crazy. He wondered if they thought he was crazy *now*.

As the five military type men in white quarantine suits peppered the helpless Aids patients with machine guns, there was nothing quite like it.

Blood everywhere! But then that was the point.

"Blake!" the commander shouted, "start the collection!"

As if robotic, John Blake did what he was trained to do. He began the tedious job of bleeding the victims one by one. *Knife, slit the wrist, drain into plastic jugs.* He knew the procedure. They were the Bravo, Lima, Oscar, Oscar, Delta team after all.

He prided himself in the fact that he could turn his emotions off when he wanted to. It just got easier for him anyway. This was their fifth and final attack but the euphoria just seemed to get better and better every time. It was almost sad to think they'd be done soon.

"Distribution is next people!" the commander called out, "so hurry it up!"

With everyone dead and the building shut down, there really wasn't much need to hurry, but John knew the final mission and that had to be done pronto. Still, he would take his time and enjoy it, the way he always did. If the commander had a problem with that, he'd give him the shaft himself.

What did John care really? After having three life sentences revoked to take on this mission, he only had one thing on his mind: living in luxury on a small island in the middle of nowhere for the rest of his life...*as promised!*

During his training, he found out there were many teams just like his doing the same thing he was at every Aids research center in the U.S. Now that was huge. To be part of something *that* important made him feel like a king.

It was bittersweet though; distribution would bring it all to an end.

Once the trucks were packed with the jugs of blood, all 1060 of them, they set off for the water treatment plant to dump them.

~~~~

Biological Research Center – Magyarorsza`g, Hungary

Vladimir Chichoffsky clung to the frozen silver vial with all his might. He would not let them get it even if it costs him his life. Too much time and research had gone into this little gem, and with the added LQP-79 ingredient, it should prove the CDC wrong.

His breathing laboured as he tried to catch his breath behind the door to the lab. With the lights being shot out, there was no way he could even see where he was going, but then again, neither could they.

At three hundred and fifty pounds he had not been in shape for running at all. He'd have to figure out a plan fast! If he had to rely on his physique he would soon give out. These men were brutes and they would clobber him before he could turn around. But then Vladimir had smarts.

"We know you are in here you fool!" one of the voices yelled out into the darkness. "Why don't you just give us the vial and we will let you go?"

Vladimir contemplated running, but with his weight, he wouldn't get very far. No, he would outsmart them and play their game. "Okay," he said, "I give up! Don't shoot!"

But as soon as Vladimir made himself visible, machine guns pelted the chest of his white lab coat, speckling him with red polka dot blood.

"You *are* a fool!" the gunman told him.

"No," Vladimir groaned as he lay on the floor in a puddle of his own blood as he attempted to pry open the silver vial, "it is *you* who are foolish!"

"*Get him!*" one of the gunmen ordered, while a solitary shot pierced Vladimir's forehead before he could unleash its contents.

"Grab the vial and let's go!" the commander shouted to his subordinates. "We need to get this stuff in the sky!"

~~~

Center for Disease Control

The loan fax came into the office threatening a terrorist attack using biological warfare. The fax stated the United States was now under attack and would feel the effects within twenty-four hours. All major water sources were now contaminated.

There were no demands; no terrorist groups had claimed responsibility; only one bold red sentence appeared visible at the bottom of the page:

Weed thy Kingdom!

Chapter 3

A whole day had gone by and still no word from Nadia.

The travel agency knew where the young couple was staying but didn't know why they hadn't returned to their suite last night. This was not comforting to Miriam *at all*.

It was all she could do to stay focused at work.

"Why go to work at all?" Frank complained before she left.

"Because someone has to pay the bills. They won't pay themselves you know."

Miriam knew she wasn't being nice, but she couldn't help it. Her nerves were raw. She should have just told him she wanted to go to work so she could get her mind off Nadia, but that would have showed weakness and she couldn't allow that. She was the strong one in the marriage.

Frank crumbled in difficult situations. He was worn thin by a recurring back injury, leaving her to be the bread winner. But she was use to it by now. It was bittersweet really, Miriam liked to be in charge so it worked better that way.

"Do you have anymore toilet paper lady?" a customer asked, breaking Miriam from her thoughts?

"Ahh...*no*," she answered, "I'm sorry sir, as you can see, we've had a rush of customers today so we've run out of a lot of things. We get our next shipment in tomorrow."

"I don't care! Get some more *now*!"

"*Sir...*"

"I want to talk to your *supervisor!*"

Miriam frowned. Maybe she shouldn't have come to work after all. She hated customers who bullied her. It was the worst part of working in retail. Dealing with upset customers never seemed to end.

"I'm sorry sir, my supervisor has a day off today. I'm the assistant manager."

"Look, it's *my* taxes that pay your wages lady so you better fix this right now! I need toilet paper, bread, eggs, bottled water, candles, matches, and flashlights and you don't have *any* of them! What kind of store are you running anyway?!"

Miriam could tell the man was beyond frustrated now. His face was red and forehead perspiring. "No problem..., What is your name?"

"*Oscar!*" the man barked.

"Oscar?" *Using their name always calms them.* "Oscar, I will take a look in the back for you and see if we have those items."

It would buy her some time a least, so the old man would cool down.

"*Fine!* but you better come out with my stuff lady or I'll have your job!"

You can have it! she wanted to say. They didn't pay her enough to put up with this kind of abuse everyday.

Oh, how she wanted to strangle him.

"We've got a live one Tim!" Miriam called out as she entered the warehouse. "Can you do me a favour and look for these items?" she handed him a list, "and see if you can track down security. We might need them today. The shelves are bare *already*. What is going on anyway?"

"It's the news," Tim told her, "haven't you heard?"

"I know about the earthquake and the tsunami warning, my daughter..."

"No... the CDC warning."

"The CDC warning?"

"This morning, the CDC told people not to drink the water."

"Whaaat?"

"Seriously man, the whole city is grabbing stuff off shelves like crazy."

Miriam didn't expect this. It was something completely unusual and she would have to follow protocol and call in the manager for this one, *or close the store.* To heck with grumpy old Oscar!

~~~

Frank tried to drive down 30th Avenue for his doctor's appointment on 8th Street but traffic in Minot was bumper to bumper. It was unusual for a Tuesday morning.

If the car stereo had not been busted out, Frank could have at least turned on some music to pass the time waiting. Being stuck in traffic for over an hour was getting to be boring.

And where was everyone going? It wasn't a major holiday or a weekend, yet people seemed to be going every which way in a hurry.

To the north, Frank could see several Boeing B-52 Stratofortress fighter planes dotting the horizon. It had been a few years since he'd seen one of those babies in the sky but he knew them well...and what they were for. *So, the air force base is on high alert too.*

Something was up and Frank decided his best bet was to turn off his idling motor and exit the vehicle.

"Hi neighbour," he smiled as he greeted the driver of the vehicle in front of him.

"Do you know what's going on?"

"No, do you?" a slim woman in her early forties replied while her teenage daughter fiddled with her iPod connected to the car stereo. "Guess I should turn on the radio."

"No way mom, I told you I'm listening to my iPod," her heavily pierced daughter snapped back at her.

"So, there you have it, the helpless mother shrugged."

"I'll go ask this guy ahead of you."

Frank shook his head. If Nadia had ever been so disrespectful, he would have taken that iPod away. What did the world need with such gadgets anyway? Just adds fuel to a teenage fire. Thankfully his daughter was well behaved.

"Excuse me sir," Frank interrupted the two duck hunters in the camo four-wheel drive ahead of the mother/daughter duo.

"Yeah?"

"Do you know what's going on?"

"I heard the military set up a road block."

"Do you know why?"

"Probably cause of the water."

"Okay, thanks."

Frank kept walking but not back to his car. He figured if the town was flooding again, his car wouldn't get through anyway. Minot has always had flooding issues. The town was essentially a big gully with the Souris river running through it and that meant it would fill itself up like a bowl of soup anytime it fancied.

Miriam's work was nearby anyway, and that was where he would head first.

~~~~

"*Just calm down people!*" Miriam shouted overtop the crowd. "I'm sure the lights will come back on momentarily. We do have backup generators to handle situations like this."

"What do you mean, '*situations like this*'?" a panicked man shouted back.

"Sir please...I don't know anything more than you do."

Shoppers abandoned their half-full grocery carts to listen to the gathering crowd.

Where is security? Miriam wondered, *this was not good!*

"If you would all just remain calm and listen to me for a minute, I'm sure..."

"*Move out of the way!*" a random customer yelled.

The mob became more than Miriam could handle, pushing their way passed her and out the nearest exit with unpaid groceries in tow. "*Come on people!*" she shouted one last time. *It was hopeless!*

An outflow of panicked shoppers escaped into the chaos outside. It was all she could do to avoid getting trampled in the stampede. Customers were beyond panic. One of them pushed her as he tried to raid the cash register but she would not let him near, holding him off with a mop left behind from an earlier customer who decided not to purchase it!

"*Not on your life buddy!*" Miriam shouted as she stood firm with clenched teeth.

The man just snarled at her but really, she should have let him take the money. According to emergency training protocol, she was to give the money to a robber and live. But this was no normal robbery, this was something entirely different.

First, she'd have to try the phones again. If her manager didn't have the common sense to come in after she had left that earlier message, then she didn't know what she was supposed to do.

Panicked, she tried to gather the remaining staff but they were all running out of the store with the last of the customers. She tried to spot Tim. He always had a level head.

"*Tim!*" she called out, recognizing him at the back in mid flight, "*Wait!*"

"Can't! Gotta get home!"

"Tim, I need your help!"

"Cities on evacuation alert! I guess there's road blocks *everywhere!*"

"*What?*" That was absurd! If it was true, she'd have to go home and get Frank.

Miriam started to feel nauseous. She looked out into the parking lot and people were smashing car windows. *Oh no!* That was *her* car!

"Cell phones are out too. *I'm out of here!*" Tim frowned, eyeing the parking lot and opting to take the back exit instead. "Sorry Miriam, but you should go too."

This is crazy. She could feel her heart pounding in her chest. It was time to abandon the cash register and head for the staff room to get her purse and jacket.

Once she gathered her things and high-tailed it out of the office, she searched through her purse until she found her car keys.

Pausing for a moment, she scanned the now abandoned grocery store, eyeing the mess of broken eggs and trampled groceries on the floor. She inhaled a deep breath and dove out of the door to full blown chaos.

~~~~

Frank saw Miriam's car as he approached the parking lot. The situation was grim. The windows were broken and a mob of people were sitting on top of the car rocking it back and forth. His heart started pounding hard.

"*Get off her car!*" he shouted too far away for anyone to hear. All he could see was Miriam slumped at the steering wheel with her head hanging down. *Was she alright?*

As he entered the littered parking lot, he took a b-line straight for his wife's car.

They better not hurt her!

"Get *lost*, you *idiots!*" he shouted, charging like a bull, grabbing anything to scare them off. But they didn't scare easily.

"*We want the car!*"

"Well, you *can't* have it!" Frank shouted back.

"They have the keys Frank," Miriam sobbed.

"If you don't get off her car, I'm gonna hit you with this..." Frank looked at what he had in his hand; Some kind of a broken table leg, "this...*stick!*"

"Oooo a stick," one of them mocked, "I think we'll pass."

They continued to bounce on the hood, all five of them.

"Look..." Frank threw down the stick and put his hands up, "I don't want to hurt anyone. I just want my wife."

Miriam did a double take as she surveyed her husbands meaning.

"Miriam..." he said, "get out of the car!"

"Your wife can go but we get the car!" one of them said.

Frank gestured a head nod to the men, and then to his wife, "*C'mon dear!*"

Slowly she squeaked open the drivers door of the vintage blue Toyota wagon and quickly fled to her husband.

The two of them slowly backed away with their hands up, Frank taking Miriam's arm and pulling her from the threatening situation.

~~~

"Why did you let them have the car?" Miriam scolded her husband as they distanced themselves from the mayhem.

"Because they won't get far with it anyway," Frank told her.

"What do you mean?"

"The military blocked the roads. I had to leave my car a few miles back. I thought it was because of flooding again but I guess not."

"Well there's some kind of evacuation going on. How are we supposed to get out of the city if they blocked the roads?"

"I don't know Miriam! Something strange is going on and we better find out what, because I've never seen it this bad."

Miriam didn't say much after that, she just kept walking in silence. If she wasn't scared back in the parking lot, she sure was now.

And her husband showed a different side of himself, a braver side she hadn't seen before. That in itself was scary.

As light faded on the horizon, the two of them headed on foot. Abandoned vehicles littered the streets in disarray and Miriam realized they wouldn't have made it through even if they *did* have a car. Frank was right.

Hopefully, they would get some answers soon. Heading for their church made the most sense since they were in the area. Surely someone would be there to enlighten them. At best, it was a place to spend the night.

Chapter 4

Nadia held Manuel's hand tightly as Delta 372 came screaming down runway 13/31 at Minot International Airport. It had to make an emergency landing after it and several other flights were forced into a holding pattern for over an hour, draining their fuel.

"What's going on out there?" one of the passengers said as they came to a stop on the tarmac.

"Looks like a zoo!" another one remarked.

Large to midsized aircraft seemed abandoned at the terminal, parked in disarray. It was alarming to Nadia but not surprising. They had been told they were in emergency protocol. They just weren't prepared for what they saw.

They had decided to leave the Bahamas shortly after returning to their hotel room after flying, only to find a frantic message had been left by her mother. Then when they tried to call back, they couldn't get through on the line.

With the Tsunami warning and the vague news reports about a U.S terrorist attempt, it quickly sent them packing. The border shutdown had come into effect while en route to Minneapolis and thankfully they were already in the country.

Manuel was on high alert. He surveyed the tarmac looking very concerned. "Excuse me ma'am," he asked the flight attendant, "why aren't there any emergency vehicles?"

The flight attendant looked out the window, trying to hide her alarm. "Sir...If you'd sit down, I will find out for you."

The entire plane started to stand up, mumbling in a panic.

"*Everyone,*" the flight attendant announced, "please remain in your seats!"

"No way!" some of the passengers called out.

"This isn't good babe!" Manuel whispered in his wife's ear. "Under no circumstances are you to leave this seat. Do you hear me?"

Nadia acknowledged him with a head nod.

Manuel got up out of his seat to talk to the flight attendant when an out of control passenger took a slug at him sending him hard against an elderly woman. Cries from panicked passengers sent everyone into a mob of pushing and shoving.

"*Manuel!*" Nadia called out to her husband as she stood up.

She could see him there in the mess of people slugging each other, and then the flight attendant went down.

Screams filled the plane.

Manuel pushed himself through the wall of angry people back to Nadia. "We're in an exit row and you're the closest. I need to switch with you. *Hurry!*"

Manuel picked her up and moved her petite body to the other side of him as he pulled the emergency exit panel beside the window. A large inflatable yellow slide opened up a passageway to the black tarmac below. "*Slide Nadia!*" he shouted above the screams.

"Not without you!"

"*I have to help!*"

"No, you don't!"

Manuel pursed his lips together and without regret, pushed his wife out of the plane.

"People!" he shouted, "pull the exit panels!"

But nobody was listening. It was dog eat dog as each passenger succumbed to the other's panic-stricken attack.

Piles of people young and old fell on top of each other, trampled by the stampede.

One by one, Manuel grabbed those closest to him, and guided them to slide. If he hadn't had the training, he never would have known to ask for an exit row seat. He always hoped he'd never have to assist but this time he was glad he put his wife next to it.

He couldn't see her below with the growing mob of people he had helped out, that were now cat calling others still trapped in the aircraft to jump.

He could see at least two other emergency exit slides had been opened toward the front of the plane. *That was good!*

As the last passengers slid down the yellow slide, Manuel looked for more to help. It was a gruesome discovery...but the ones that were left were trampled! Had he not opened the emergency shoot when he did, they might all have perished in the havoc.

At least he got his wife out.

Before jumping himself, he went from body to body feeling for a pulse. What did he hope to do, perform CPR right there? *It was worth a shot.*

He lifted an elderly woman from her seat. He recognized her. *The one I fell against.* It was his fault she died. A sadness overcame his chest as he set her back down, noticing a blue blanket under her feet. He pulled at it under her legs, revealing a small infant's lifeless body. It was a little boy. His elfin face bloody, motionless and disturbingly angelic. *How can people be so cruel!*

Tears welled in his hazel eyes as he lay the child back down. There was nothing he could do here. He would have to look for his wife now or he might not find her.

Who knew what chaos awaited him out there.

~~~

Nadia felt herself getting pushed further and further away from the plane as the passengers came down the slide. She couldn't see Manuel anywhere. Had he really stayed to help? *These people didn't deserve help!*

Never could she *ever* attack *anyone* like they did. It was *barbaric!* And Manuel being the fireman he was, always had to help. Where did that leave her? Left on a dark tarmac with a bunch of crazy people.

She tried her best to see the plane's unlit passageway where she came out. If the emergency vehicles had been there like they were supposed to be, none of this would have happened and she would be with her husband, *but not now.*

Tears streamed down her checks as she felt a sense of doom and hopelessness.

"*Manuel!*" she cried out.

With no answer she started walking with the others. Maybe he was in the crowd somewhere and she hadn't noticed he had come down. That was entirely possible because there where so many people blocking her view.

Others beside her were crying as they walked toward the terminal in the dark. One lady with a little girl in tow told her she was suing Delta

Airlines just as soon as she could. *Really?* It wasn't their fault. It was the fault of all those angry passengers. Yet, why wasn't the emergency response team dispatched? That would be the fault of the airport not the airline.

It was crazy anyway. What on earth was going on? Nobody seemed to know. Perhaps once inside the terminal they would get answers, and she would find her husband.

Chapter 5

Souris River Christian Fellowship was a sight for sore eyes by the time Frank and Miriam found their way there around midnight. A single candle burned in the sanctuary window and Frank knew it was his old buddy Pastor McDonald.

"Well isn't this something," the pastor smiled as he opened the door for them. "You have no idea how happy I am to see you. Now quickly, get inside!"

He checked both ways, then blew out the candle and shut the door.

"I only put the candle out for *you*. I was watching you through my binoculars. It was pretty hard to make out who you were in the dark but thankfully the moon is out and I could tell it was my old buddy Frank."

"Why don't you want anyone else to come to the church?" Miriam asked.

"*You don't know?*"

"Know what?"

"The water is making people sick. You didn't drink any, did you?"

"No, but we're parched," Frank answered. "I haven't had anything since this morning except the filtered water in the fridge," he informed. "Did you have any dear?" he turned to his wife.

"No... just bottled at work. Why?"

"According to what the neighbours told me before they evacuated, the military was issuing some kind of antibiotic at the airport. We were all to go there so we could get our dose before leaving for Fargo. That's the safe zone."

"What do you mean the *safe zone?*" Miriam asked with wide eyes. "Safe from what? What the heck is going on?"

"*Biological weapons* Miriam," Frank told her point blank.

"Oh, how do you know?"

"Because I know dear. I read a lot."

"You are full of baloney Frank Novak! Pastor McDonald, please tell him!"

Frank sighed, shaking his head at his wife. She didn't need to embarrass him in front of the pastor like that. His old friend knew him better than she did and that was a shame.

"Now - now you two. No need to bicker at a time like this. I'm afraid Frank is correct Miriam. There *is* something in the water. That has been confirmed. And they don't issue antibiotics to the masses unless there has been some...*biological incident.*"

Miriam's mouth hung open. It was difficult to watch his hard-nosed wife soften like butter. He was use to her demanding, over opinionated, obstinate ways. She could usually handle everything...*everything except this.*

"What do they think happened Pastor?" she asked with tears in her eyes.

"*Terrorism attack.* It was reported on the news shortly before the power left us all in the dark. Been like that for most of the day."

"I know, I was at work," Miriam added.

"I was driving."

"And I was in the study," the pastor sighed.

"So, what do we do now?" Frank asked.

"We sit tight I guess," Pastor McDonald told them, trying to comfort while holding Miriam's hand. "I couldn't get to the airport. I don't have a car you know."

The old man hung his head. He had to be in his eighties by now, but he sure didn't act like it. If he could have kept his license he would have, but his daughter talked him out of it a year ago and made him sell his little blue Toyota Yaris he loved so much. Better to be safe than sorry she told her father. Frank could have just kicked old Tom for agreeing with his daughter.

But then again, picking him up every Wednesday night for bowling was the highlight of his week. The two had become very close because of it, so losing his licence was actually a blessing in disguise...*until now.*

"You would have just been stuck on the road like I was Tom, and that wouldn't have been good for you to walk at your age."

"True enough."

"Okay...so, we wait it out here, and then what?" Miriam asked. "What if we run out of water?"

"We can pray dear...and that's not nothing."

~~~~~

We can pray dear. As much as she loved the old man, Miriam couldn't understand how that could be the only plan the pastor had.

Sure, she understood what he was saying. She sometimes prayed. Less now than before, but she would do it if she had to. Lately though, since her daughter moved out last year she had slumped into a depression and stayed away from Ladies Bible Study and such. She just couldn't do it. She missed her daughter's cherub voice every day.

Up until that man of hers started seeing her, she had Nadia all to herself. It hurt to lose her friendship to a man she didn't even know. And putting up with those other women bragging all the time about their wonderful *Christian* daughters, didn't help matters much. Oh, weren't they so perfect, going off to Bible School after graduation, joining the latest mission group to Africa. Yet, they were the ones Nadia said she caught fooling around with the Youth Group boys. *What hypocrisy!*

It was all *hogwash* in her opinion.

Nadia never did fit in with the other girls and she didn't force her to go to church either like those other mothers. Was it really so bad that her daughter moved in with a man before her wedding? It was only ten months before. They were getting married anyway.

Frank sighed when she told him but smiled and congratulated her anyway. He said it wasn't up to him to judge. "God loved me when *I* was a sinner," he told his wife. Miriam guessed that was probably correct but the church people didn't seem to know that. They did enough judging for the both of them.

Pastor McDonald said to just love her and God would do the rest. Yes, she did love her, but that wasn't enough for all those tongue waggling church ladies. No wonder she hadn't felt like coming to church lately, much to the grief of her husband who went alone.

As the grandfather clock in the foyer chimed twice, Miriam knew she had let her mind wander long enough. She had to get some sleep.

Thinking of Nadia and her new husband made her wonder where they were. Were they still on their honeymoon unscathed from all this, or had they taken a flight in? She hoped they had actually decided to come back. If they were at the airport, they would get their dose of antibiotics and be on their way to the *safe zone,* unlike them, stuck in the inner city with an old man in tow and no way to get to the airport.

What were they going to do?

~~~~

Manuel had searched for a half hour already, but still no Nadia.

With the chaos at the airport terminal, he knew it was hopeless looking for her in this crowd. Yet, he couldn't stop looking for her. And with just a flashlight, it was harder than ever.

"*Nadia!*" he called out as he passed crying children in the corner being hushed by their mother as they lay on the floor in blankets. Trying to sleep he guessed. Now that was a sorry sight.

If he was Nadia, where would he go? *Think man!* She would need a bathroom. Could he find the washrooms?

As he lumbered down the corridors lined with people coughing and crying, he directed his flashlight toward the walls looking for a bathroom sign. *There it is.*

Thankfully a backup generator powered emergency lights so they weren't completely in the dark, but even those appeared to be failing with the constant flicker.

It was hard to ignore all the people who needed his help, after all he *was* a fireman and this was *his* city. He wondered where all the emergency personnel were. It didn't make sense. They had an emergency preparedness program. If not through the city then through the air force base.

Suddenly, through the windows facing the air traffic control tower, Manuel saw a huge fireball at the end of the runway. He went closer to see, straining his eyes, watching until he finally realized what it was.

"*EVERBODY GET OUT OF HERE!*" he shouted to the top of his lungs. It was a plane coming in like a bomb, straight into the airport terminal.

Screams pierced his ears.

Minutes...you have minutes! he told himself.

He pointed to the fireball in the distance. "*It's a plane! Move it people! It's coming straight for us!*"

He tried to direct everyone toward the entrance and away from the control tower but they ran in all different directions like a herd of confused cattle.

"*I'm a fireman and I need you to listen!*"

Suddenly a voice shouted from across the hall. "*Manuel is that you?*"

"*Nadia! I found you!*" he moaned as he hugged her tightly. "*Hurry! Do you see it?*" He pointed to the fireball on the runway, now closer than ever. We have to run as fast as we can?"

The two of them took off hand in hand, Nadia lagging behind her husband almost losing her footing trying to keep up. If she had fallen, Manuel would drag her or carry her, whatever it took to get out of that front exit before the plane hit...*and hit is would.*

"*Stop!*" Nadia gasped, "I can't breathe!"

"*Come on!*"

Manuel swooped his wife up in both arms and ran with all his might. When he got to the entrance, he didn't look back. When he got across the street, he didn't look back. Not even when he heard the loud explosion and knew exactly what it was, did he look back.

Tattered and dirty, sweaty and tired, he ran with his new wife in his arms like she was an endangered species.

One explosion after another, then another until the night sky lit like fireworks. There would be no surviving *that!*

Finally, as his muscular legs gave out about a mile down the road from the catastrophic event, he dropped to his knees still cradling his petite wife. Sobbing against her matted red hair he cried in a passionate embrace.

"*Baby!* I almost *lost* you!"

"I almost lost *you!*" she cried.

They both held each other on the ground, kissing softly as they dried one another's tears. Fire and smoke billowed in the distant ruins behind them forcing them to get up and continue on. They couldn't stay there.

Somewhere, someone had to know what was going on.

~~~~

"*Sir!*" the young Corporal saluted. "You asked for me?"

Corporal Kai Porter had called Minot Air Force Base home for the last two years but he had never dealt with anything so important.

"It's dawn. Your team is up. Hope you're ready because if you're not, you *will* be compromised."

"*Sir!* Yes Sir!"

Kai was waiting for this opportunity. His team was the last to go. The others had flown out the day before leaving a skeletal team to work with. All privates. Expendables he guessed.

"We're leaving at 08:00 hrs and I just wanted you to know that your duty here is appreciated. Private Jackson, Miller, and Grout will assist you. You're to collect as many civilians as you can and take them to the safe zone for assessment. Do you understand?"

"*Yes Sir!* Pleased to do it *Sir!*"

"Well I wouldn't be so enthusiastic son. You know the protocol."

"Permission to speak freely Sir!"

"Of course."

"If we run into trouble, we know the way home."

"Corporal, I just want to be very clear here. If you run into trouble, you are on your own. Do you understand what I'm telling you?"

"I understand that we...."

"*No!* I don't think you do."

"I'm sure I..."

"*Corporal,* if you run into trouble, there *is* no way home! Understood?"

Kai gulped hard pretending it didn't bother him. With a salute and a dutiful nod, he answered his superior back. "*Understood!*"

～～～

As the early morning sunrise glistened through the rear window of the car Manuel and Nadia spent the night in, he could hear shouting in the distance.

Perhaps it was finally some help coming.

"Nadia, wake up," he whispered in her ear. "I hear people."

She yawned like a kitten, stretching her slender feminine arms up to the ceiling of the car, limited to the confined space. It was the only place they could think of to rest for the night. Not quite into the city yet.

"Well, first," she grinned, "I just want to kiss my handsome husband good morning."

She gently kissed him with her dry lips.

"You need some water babe. That's our first stop on the agenda, that and food. I don't know when the last time we ate was. I'm starving."

"Manuel? Do you think my parents are okay?"

"*Chica*...your old man's probably lounging in his chair while your mother's barking orders at him, so don't worry."

Nadia smirked. That thought brought comfort to her as wrong as it sounded.

"But what if they're not?" she sniffled.

"Hey..." he comforted her with a lift of her chin, "just dry those tears. We're okay, we made it out of...*well you know.*"

He didn't want to elaborate so he changed the mood by teasing.

"I'm sure your parents stayed put and are playing bridge or something. As much as I cringe when I go near them, I do think they are smart enough to know how to take care of themselves."

"Hey..." Nadia teased back, "watch what you say about our future child's grandparents.

"So, you think you are then?"

"I don't know for sure. I guess so," she bit her bottom lip. "I've never been pregnant before, but I sure do feel nauseous."

"Well, you better get up then. I don't want you being sick all over me," he grinned as he helped her out of the car. She ran to the nearest tree, holding her hand over her mouth to prolong the vomit.

I have to get her somewhere safe!

Chapter 6

Kai scoured the road in front of him in the military issued jeep. Behind him two large camo supply trucks for civilians followed. They hadn't found anyone yet, but it was still early morning with the sun just up. *Give them time*, he decided.

He had been kept in the dark for the most part. What did they mean he couldn't go home? That was *ridiculous!*

After that incident last year, and his court marshal, his credibility had been damaged. It was supposed to be stripped from his record, but people didn't forget. That was the problem. He had to prove himself now.

C'mon on people. Where are you?

Since yesterday, the majority of the cities population had safely been directed to Fargo, yet he didn't know what good that would do. If his calculations were correct, they'd need a much safer place. But what did he know, he wasn't in charge. Just a pawn to do the grunt work now.

"Do you see anything? *Over,*" he talked on the radio.

"Nothing. *Over.*"

"Copy that."

Garbage littered the streets as they turned the direction of the airport. The explosion last night told him there were no survivors, yet, he'd head that direction anyway.

"Private, do you see that? *Over.*"

"*Hello* civilians! Permission to collect. *Over.*"

"Roger that! *Over.*"

The convoy headed over to two people about five hundred yards away, spotted through the trees heading east into the city. A male and a female.

They pulled ahead of them to stop them from walking any further.

"*Sir...Ma'am?* Come with us."

The tall muscular man stopped, hand in hand with the petite woman half his size looking worn and tattered.

"Are we ever glad to see you," the man said. "I'm *Manuel* and this is my wife *Nadia.*"

"Get in the truck behind me sir," Kai ordered ignoring the introduction. "Private Grout will assist you."

"Can I be of any help?" the man asked. "I'm a fireman for..."

"*No!* Now do as you're told!" Kai scolded, cutting him off abruptly.

"Okay..." the man replied, frowning.

"Please proceed to the vehicle."

The couple quickly did as they were told, obviously not wanting any trouble. That was good because Kai didn't need any trouble. Not like the other teams. He would *not* be compromised.

~~~~

Manuel couldn't believe the soldier's rudeness. He was a fireman. He didn't know how valuable he could be to them?

"Just let it go Manuel," he's probably stressed and tired like the rest of us."

"That's no excuse. *Gringo! Que no le gusta un Latino hermano!"*

"I'm sure he likes you just fine Manuel! Who wouldn't with that charming face of yours!" Nadia smiled grabbing his stubble chin in her hand, bringing him close to give him a peck on the lips.

"Did you see him though? All high and mighty with his blonde hair and blue eyes like some *Hitler Nazi*. This isn't Germany you know. I'm not usually prejudice *Chica* but *really?* Why don't they want my help? I'm more qualified than *he* is!"

"I know," she smiled, swaying side to side, as the large empty truck began to move.

"Manuel, *sweetheart?* Calm down. Usually I'm the crazy one. You're starting to scare me. I need you calm and assertive like you normally are, *please!*"

"*Fine!* But I'm not gonna just sit around doing nothing if something happens."

"*WHAT WILL HAPPEN?*"

"*Nothing!* Just forget it," he said angrily.

Nadia started to cry.

"*C'mere,*" he said softly changing his tone, reaching an arm around his wife. "I'm sorry I scared you!"

~~~~

Manuel scared her sometimes with his macho persona. She forgot how big and powerful he really was. It would be wise for those skinny soldiers to recruit a big guy like her husband, but she wouldn't say anything more. He was too hot under the collar as it was. It did trouble her that they wouldn't even let him talk to them. Maybe that's how the military does things? It probably wasn't anything personal.

The truck didn't help her nauseous stomach as it swayed side to side all dusty and dirty. Her pregnancy made it all the more unbearable. And with everything going on, it wasn't very good timing. Yet, she welcomed her new state and she knew Manuel did too.

"Do you know where we're going?"

"*No, I can't even ask apparently.*"

Poor Manuel, his ego was bruised pretty badly.

"Here, just drink your water," she grinned. "I could drink two of these bottles."

"Have mine then."

Manuel plopped his bottle of water in her lap and looked away. She knew what was on his mind and his melancholy wasn't helping. She just kept silent, guzzled her full bottle too quickly, and belched.

"*Ouch!*" he chuckled.

Nadia giggled and burped again. *Now that's the smile I love,* she thought to herself.

"Sorry, *I'm pregnant,* remember?

"True!" He wrapped one arm around her shoulder and pulled her to him. "You're cute Mrs Espinosa, mother of my child. I think I'll have my water back now or you might scare the baby with your *burping.*"

"Oh, is that right?" she teased, knowing she had finally succeeded in transforming his mood to a better state.

"What do you think about the name Percy?" she smirked at him.

Manuel suddenly choked on his water mid gulp, blowing it through his nose coughing. "*What? NO!* You can't be serious! You're killing me!"

"*Gotcha!*"

"Seriously *Chica* if you're gonna do that, wait for me to finish my water. I got serious backwash now."

Nadia knew she was being naughty. *Naughty*, that's what her dad always called her. It was a silly little nickname most girls with her name had to suffer with. It was cute but she only liked her dad calling her that. At least Manuel didn't use the *'N'* word. Had he tried, she would have kicked his butt.

She hoped her dad was okay. She worried about him a lot since she moved out. Dad usually just sat around the house all day and did his crossword puzzles and watched his game shows. Really, he always acted much older than he was. That was because of his back injury her mom would always say. But Nadia knew it was also because her mother was so hard on him.

Hopefully they would be good grandparents and finally accept Manuel. They didn't really like him much, mostly mom. He had taken away her daughter and that was a *no-no* with her mother.

With everything going on, Nadia didn't know what to expect. She tried to push fearful thoughts from her head, but they just kept popping in. Her parents took her to so many doctors when she was young. Health scares seemed to plague them, but she was fine. *Really!*

This would prove it. She had gotten pregnant and proved that they needn't worry about her health anymore. And the baby would be fine. They would see.

Yet...in the back of her mind, she wondered what would happen now.

With the sway of the truck, her body rocked in motion causing her eyelids to droop. She placed her head comfortably against her husbands broad shoulder and fell fast asleep.

She was flying again, this time it wasn't in the small Piper, she wasn't exactly sure how she was flying but she hovered over the ocean nonetheless...like an angel of sorts.

And out of the depths of the ocean, a creature stretched its arm. It had black wings and horns on its head: A monster trying to grab her.

The ocean opened its mouth, letting the foul creature rise closer and closer to her legs that dangled above. With one arm, it caught hold of her ankle.

No! Let go!

But the creature clung to her, pulling, clawing.

Nadia's leg started to drip blood from the claw marks as they opened up into deep crevices exposing her veins.

It seemed the more she fought, the deeper its claws dug. She was caught in its web, being sucked down into the water. It's teeth were now upon her, ready to take a bite, dripping with saliva.

"Manuel help!" she screamed!

"He can't help you!" the creature cackled, "No one can!"

The creature released its long black tongue and licked her as it held her tightly in its claw. And there, deep in the pit where it rose from, she noticed a chain bigger and stronger than anything she had ever seen before. He was trapped. Unable to exit his grave yet able to hold her, claw her, attack her in any way he desired.

A part of her felt a sense of relief that he couldn't free himself. Somehow, he needed her. Somehow, she was his co-dependant.

"What do you want from me?!" she yelled, struggling to get free.

Then the creature grinned with its yellow blood-stained teeth as a crop of serpents rose from its mouth as it spoke. "I want your soul...and I want the CHILD!"

"Ahhh!" Nadia cried as she woke up to Manuel's big strong arms holding her.

"Your dreaming Chica!"

"My baby!" she moaned as she held her abdomen.

"What is it? Are you okay?"

Disoriented, Nadia whirled her head around. Strangers stared at her as they sat in various places inside the big army truck. They were still driving. She must have been sleeping. The dream!

Panic shot through her like a fierce storm. It wasn't real. It wasn't! But why did she keep having the same dream? What did it mean?

"Chica?"

"No! I mean...yes! I'm fine Manuel. Just that stupid dream again." But she didn't tell him the rest. She didn't want to. It was stupid.

As she sat up, she realized she was the center of attention with everyone eyeing her like something was wrong. "I'm fine everybody. Really!"

A mother sat nearby with her young son, pulling him close to her like she was contagious or something. "I'm not sick if that's what you were thinking."

"Did you drink the water?" the mother asked her loudly over the roar of the truck.

"I drank this water," Nadia answered her as she held up her empty water bottle.

The mother half smiled as if she didn't believe her.

"What?" Nadia asked looking around at the other people sitting with them. She realized she and Manuel were the only ones sitting apart from the group.

"They think we're *sick* Manuel," she whispered.

"They think *you're* sick!"

"I'm not sick everybody. *Really!* And what's wrong with the water anyway?"

The group of people looked back and forth at each other in surprise. "You don't know?" the mother said. "The water is contaminated."

"*What?*" Nadia was shocked. How could the water be contaminated? She just drank it and she was fine. *Wasn't she?*

"Manuel?"

"*Shh*...listen. They'll explain."

The mother began to tell what she knew: "There's something in the water they say. Not the bottled water as far as we know, but some of us here have our doubts," the mother looked accusingly at the man at the end of the row.

"I just said we shouldn't trust the military, that's all," the middle-aged man at the end of the row blurted out. "How do we know they're not trying to kill us all off?"

"Well if they are," Manuel added, "that would be a pretty stupid way to do it. They have guns *buddy.* Why not use them?"

"Hold it!" Nadia interrupted. "*What the heck is in the water?*"

"It's some kind of poisoning," the mother continued.

"No, it ain't lady!" the man at the end said with annoyance. "It's *bugs!* Some kind of miniature ants or something. The Japanese have been working for years on these miniature computer ants that eat us up from the inside. We can't even see them floating in the water."

"*What?*" Manuel laughed. "I don't know where you're getting your information from buddy but you're scaring people," he looked at the little boy clutching his mother tightly.

"*Yes! Please!*" the mother said, "My son is scared enough as it is."

Another man in a tattered business suit butted into the conversation. "I heard that it's *biological contamination*...but we have nothing to worry about because they're taking us to get our antibiotics in Fargo. You see, I work for the government and we have a homeland security program set up for things like this. They *have* to issue antibiotics to us. Our taxes pay for it."

"Let me guess," Manuel mused, "you're a tax man."

"How'd you know? Anyway...I wouldn't worry about it. They just evacuated the city as part of the protocol. We just need to get to Fargo and everything will be fine and dandy."

"Hope you're right," the mother sighed.

Suddenly the truck screeched to a stop, throwing the passengers forward and then backward. The blonde soldier opened the large canvas doorway to a bright sunshiny morning. "Everybody out! *Now!*" the soldier ordered.

Manuel looked alarmed. "Is there something wrong Sir?"

"I don't want any trouble from *you*, now *out!*"

Why were they being so rude? Nadia wondered. This didn't seem right.

The crowd disembarked themselves in a hurry, looking at each other, puzzled as to what was going on. One by one they stepped down without a hand to help them down. The soldiers were standing back like they were afraid to touch them.

"Do *not* touch them Grout!" the blonde soldier told his comrade. "I gave you direct orders! If you would've told me this before, we wouldn't have gone this far. Now I'm going to have to take care of this myself. Line them up private! You too!" he shouted to the others.

"*Wait!*" Manuel pleaded. "Just what do you think you're doing with us?"

"Shut up and spread out!"

A firing squad! Nadia realized. *Nooooo!*

"*Look,*" Manuel pleaded with hands up as the soldiers pointed guns at him, "we're not sick if that's what you're thinking."

"*She is!*" the mother blurted out, pointing to Nadia.

Thanks a lot lady!

"I'm *not* sick!"

"We saw you puking," the little boy tattled.

"*Yeah!*" the tax man added. "*It's not us!*"

The crowd separated themselves from Nadia and Manuel like they had the plague.

"My wife is *pregnant!* That's *all!* It's morning sickness! *Please!*"

"Morning sickness? *Right!*" the blonde soldier guffawed. "Private Grout also saw your wife vomiting. She's *compromised sir,* now *STAND DOWN!* The rest of you can get back into the vehicle. I just need the redhead!"

Manuel's eyes bugged out and his face went mean with anger. "*Oh no you're NOT!*" he shouted. "I Just finished telling you she's *NOT* sick you *IDIOTS!*"

"Grout, hold him down!"

The men struggled until an M-16 machine gun fired in the air and then centered it's sights straight on Nadia.

"Stop now or she dies ugly."

Manuel spit as two soldiers restrained him, "You don't have the guts you wimp!"

"Try me!"

Manuel spit again and pulled hard against his captors but couldn't break free.

Nadia felt the tears well in her eyes. *Was this it?*

"I'll kill you!" Manuel shouted like a wild man. "*I'll SWEAR I'LL KILL YOU!*"

"*Hahaha,*" the blonde laughed, "no, I think not. I have the gun, so I'm the one that's going to kill *YOU!* Now boys...line 'em *both* up!"

Chapter 7

"Good morning Tom!" Frank chided to his old friend as he lay in the recliner with open Bible against his chest. He was slumped there sleeping with his glasses half hanging off his face. Frank had to chuckle to himself. None of them got much sleep last night but he hoped Tom had not stayed up all night praying.

"Oh..." Tom woke with a snort, "I guess I dozed off."

"Tell me you didn't stay up all night!"

"Well I tried."

"You can't do that old man. You need to rest like everyone else."

"True enough, but I think God wants to hear from us at a time like this. One never can get too much praying in."

Miriam interrupted them, sauntering into the kitchen, "I need coffee! *Coffee!*"

"Tom? Got any instant?" he asked on behalf of his wife.

"I don't want *instant* Frank. *Yuck!*"

He didn't know what his wife was thinking. There was no electricity, no way to make the water hot, and a limited supply of bottled water. *Really?*

"Miriam dear, just how do you think you're going to get hot water? Tom can't make it appear out of thin air."

His wife looked annoyed at him but he didn't care. She always seemed to think of herself first and this was one time he was going to put a stop to it.

"Frank...*Shut up,* and get out of my way so I can find the coffee."

Well if that statement didn't infuriate him, he didn't know what would. He felt his neck heat up, more from embarrassment but mostly from her barbed tongue. He just shook his head and stepped out of her way.

"You two!" Tom interrupted. "You've been at each other's throats since you arrived. Do I need to do a marriage counselling session in the midst of a war zone? You need to treat each other better! *Especially right now.*"

Frank hung his head. Miriam kept on rummaging through Tom's apartment as if she didn't hear him. Perhaps it was a good thing his suite was attached to the church because if she didn't find what she was looking for there, she could always try the church kitchen.

"You're right Tom. Sorry." Frank apologized, eyeing Miriam so she would do the same, except there was no answer from her end. *Sigh!*

Tom set the Bible down and eased himself from the recliner. "*Uhhh*...these old bones aren't getting any younger. Let me help you find what you're looking for Miriam."

The old man shuffled along the yellow linoleum floor with his night slippers, trying to help the situation, but for some reason Frank knew it wouldn't do any good.

"Let me see," Tom groaned as he bent over to a shelf below the tea kettle, "I do have instant Miriam...it won't kill you. We can drain the hot water heater a little and make you a cup to soothe your nerves."

Frank just stood back, staying out of her path of destruction. He knew better than that.

Miriam just shook her head and pouted. She closed her eyes as if to cry. This was new, Frank observed.

"Come now," Tom cajoled, "I know there's a soft heart in there somewhere."

"But I *hate* this!"

"We *all* hate this!" Tom said, pulling Miriam into a hug as he winked at Frank standing in awe behind her.

Frank couldn't believe the old man's charms had worked to calm his wife down, yet for some reason he figured they were talking about more than just coffee.

~~~

For years, he watched his own marriage crumble. If he had only shown this kind of compassion decades ago, before his beloved Gail had passed away, maybe she would still be alive. It saddened Tom to think of her at this moment but it was true. Women needed to be nurtured and understood no matter how crusty they were on the outside.

Spending the past twenty-three years as a pastor had taught him a lot. Mostly that people just wanted to be loved. It was simple really. Jesus had professed love. He *was* love, yet so many people, even people in his own congregation thought it more important to judge and beat the sins out of people rather than to simply just love as Christ did. He preached love on a regular basis yet it didn't really seem to do much good.

Still there were church cliques that alienated others, deacons who smeared people's names, self-righteous board members who shun parishioners for things they did themselves, and hurts that caused rifts on a daily basis. Tom knew he couldn't prevent all that, but he was going to give it his best shot. He was going to love enough *for* them because he hated quarrels immensely, especially matrimonial ones.

"*Thank you!*" Frank mouthed as Miriam sobbed against the pastors faded blue sweater.

Tom just nodded back as the woman wailed into his shoulder. It was rather wet now but he didn't mind.

"How bout you say we get that coffee now and dry those tears. Frank, help yourself to some Corn Flakes in the cupboard."

They were going to have to come up with a battle plan. He had prayed all night and gotten his answer. The Lord was telling him they needed to move.

Frank poured a bowl of Corn Flakes for everyone, pulling a jug of milk from Tom's late sixties fridge. He set the bowls on the table and clattered in the utensil drawer fishing for some spoons.

Miriam headed off for the hot water heater with cup in hand.

"How much bottled water do you have here Tom?" Frank asked as he sat down at the table.

"I have about three days worth in the pantry."

"Good, cause we're gonna need it."

Tom sighed and moved a little closer to Frank to whisper. "I didn't want to say it in front of your wife, but...we can't stay here. I mean, we need a plan to get out of here."

"I know, that's what I was thinking. If there's only three days worth of water, we definitely can't stay here for long. And who knows how much tap water has been contaminated."

"*Oh noooo!* Miriam!" It just occurred to Tom that he sent Miriam for *tap* water. Water that had been in the hot water tank, contaminated.

As Miriam entered the kitchen sipping her hot instant coffee, Tom slapped it out of her hand like a wild man. "It's *tap* water!"

The coffee flew in the air, cup conking on the floor, splattering a big brown liquid mess in front of the fridge.

"I'm *sooo* sorry dear!"

"How much did you drink Miriam?" Frank cried.

Miriam darted her eyes wide in alarm. "*I-I drank a quarter cup already!*"

Frank placed palms to temples, shaking his head back and forth.

"*I'm going to die!*" she said.

Tom moaned in disbelief. How could he be so stupid. It would be his fault if she got sick. He couldn't live with that.

They all slumped down at the table. A silence set over them. *Shock.*

"Now lets just think about this for a minute," Frank said. "How long do you think the hot water was in the tank Tom?"

"Well...maybe two days."

"And it's been just about that since the contamination, right?" Frank calculated. "So... the hot water tank may not have been filled since then. Did you take a bath Tom?"

"Well yeah...just before the lights went out."

"That's it, *I'm dead!*" Miriam cried.

"No, you're not Miriam! Stop saying that!" Franks frowned, annoyed. "Doesn't a hot water tank fill from the top?"

Tom's eyes grew wide. "It does...and if Miriam took the water from the bottom, she most likely didn't use the contaminated water at all."

"*Most likely,*" Miriam repeated, not so convinced of their assumption.

"Well it's all we have to go on dear," Tom tried to consol, this time not doing such a good job. "We'll just keep praying."

~~~~

There he goes again. *Just keep praying,* he says, *praying, praying, praying.* She was the one who was going to get sick and die, not them. Praying was no comfort to her at all.

Miriam's stomach churned. She didn't know if it was from nerves or the poisonous water. Probably both.

If someone poisoned the water, she wondered what kind of poison it was and if it affected everybody differently. Maybe she was fine.

"Are you okay dear?" Frank asked her privately while the pastor was in the bathroom.

"Of course, I'm not fine!" she sobbed.

"Look, I know you're scared but...we'll get you to a hospital. They can check you out, give you those antibiotics. If not here in Minot, then in Fargo. I won't let anything happen to you sweetheart. I love you!"

Her husband was a sweetheart and she didn't deserve him. He always knew what to say to comfort her even if she rejected that comfort most of the time. She had been too hard on him for way too long. It was a wonder he still stuck with her.

"I love you too Frank," she kissed him softly.

"I don't know if that was such a good idea under the circumstances but I don't care."

"Oh Frank," she gasped. "I didn't think, I'm sorry. I shouldn't have kissed..."

"Miriam..." he shushed her, "I don't care. If you're gonna die, *which you're not,* but if you did...I would rather die too."

They hugged, pressing their foreheads together.

"Well...I can see you two made up. Maybe I should stay in the bathroom," the pastor chuckled.

"No," Frank grinned, "I promise we'll get a room."

"Frank!"

Her husband was a tease. She'd give him that.

Suddenly, a loud rap on the door caught their attention. Should they answer it? Was it safe? "Just ignore it!" she said, biting her nails.

"I can't just ignore it," the pastor sighed. "This is God's house. If someone has come to seek shelter, then who am I to say no. I've worried about this since the beginning. I don't have enough water for everybody. You know how people get in a panic."

Still Miriam didn't agree. They shouldn't open the door. There could be a mob behind it. Then what would happen to them?

The knock turned into loud rapping. Then a voice started screaming. "That doesn't sound good my friend," Frank cautioned.

"But I can't turn a needy sole away."

Pastor McDonald went to the door and called through it. "How many of you are out there?"

"It's just me Tom," the male voice answered back.

"It sounds like Larry. You know him," the pastors eyes widened as he unlocked the door. "Quickly, come in."

Larry rushed in, shut the door, and stood there looking terrible. His face was white and sickly, and his eyes looked bloodshot...and he had a cough.

Everyone stood back like he was a leper.

"Are you okay Larry?"

"I just have a cold Tom, seriously!

He did not just have a cold!

Miriam grabbed her husband's shoulder and pulled him back to the kitchen table. The pastor turned to them and then back to Larry. "Could I help you with something Larry?"

Ugh! Just get rid of him!

But the old fool didn't catch the hint, or he didn't want to. All that God talk about doing the right thing was getting in the way.

"Uh..." the man twitched, "didn't you hear? We have to leave. I came to get you."

"I appreciate that my friend but I'm here with Frank and Miriam, you know them from Church...we'll, Frank anyway. I think we'll stay a while."

"*You can't!*" he fumed.

"Larry," the pastor said, taking his elbow to lead him to the door. "I am fine! I think you should go though."

Then the man looked confused, his white face turned green as he vomited all over the front of the pastor.

Noooo!

Miriam backed further away, horrified.

Larry dried his mouth with his sleeve and sobbed, "*I'm siiiick!*"

"I know."

There was never a more sorry sight than that. A grown man buckling to his knees, helpless as ever.

Pastor McDonald turned his head to look at Frank as if to get his permission to help, caught in the middle of something hopeless.

"Let me stay here! *Please!*" the man cried. "*Please!*"

"I cannot turn my back on this man you guys."

Yes, you can!

"Not in the Lord's house. Not in this condition!" The pastor surrendered to what he was about to do, showing them they had no choice but to allow the old man his compassion.

"As God is my whiteness," he preached, "I will obey his commands. *'And the King shall answer and say unto them, Verily I say unto you, inasmuch as ye have done it unto the least of these my brethren, ye have done it unto me.'*"

Miriam knew this was not a good idea. Why couldn't he ignore the Bible just this once and do the wrong thing. Now they were all in jeopardy especially the pastor with the man's puke all over him.

"Let's get out of here," Miriam whispered to her husband. "We don't have to stay! We can just leave them both."

"We *can't* Miriam."

But instead of leaving, Miriam followed her husband to get cleaning supplies to clean the mess. What did it matter now?

They were all dead anyway!

Chapter 8

The trouble with these guys was they underestimated Manuel's size. He bench-pressed two hundred and fifty pounds in his sleep.

"*Drop your guns!*" he ordered.

The soldiers immediately dropped their guns, backing up from a very mad Manuel with his burly arm choking one of them. Nadia rushed over to her husband and hid behind him.

"Now kick the gun over to me," he ordered further, eyeing the thin blonde soldier who thought he was a tuff guy.

Manuel picked up the machine gun as he threw one of the men to the ground. "Now don't try anything or I'll use this on you. *Back up!*"

"Sir!" the blonde inched forward. "You're making a mistake."

"I'm not making a mistake. *You are!*" Manuel snapped back, banging on the side of the truck. "*Everybody out!*"

One by one, the mother and her son, business man, and two other men exited the truck again, climbing down the step to the ground. They immediately raised their arms in surrender as they came out to see who held the gun.

"*Now everybody, get over there!*" Manuel directed, motioning his gun to where he wanted them to gather: As far away from him and Nadia as they possibly could get.

"It didn't have to be like this you guys! My wife is *not* sick! There was no reason to panic. She's *pregnant,* that's all," he sighed and shook his head, pulling his wife toward the drivers door. "Get in Nadia!"

With one arm helping his wife up the step, and the other steady on the machine gun, Manuel backed himself up into the truck himself. "Crank the truck over for me *Chica*!"

The big three-ton military vehicle roared to life as Manuel shut the door, hearing the pepper of the machine guns against the drivers side.

"*Go!*" his wife screamed.

Manuel stomped on the gas like a bat out of hell.

~~~~

Kai was not going to let them get away, not if he could help it. He hoped they hadn't seen him hanging on to the back of the truck. It was a big vehicle and he could crawl into the back long before he was spotted.

If he could only get his feet up on the bumper. *Come on Kai!*

Yanking his body up as he grabbed hold of the canvas, he managed to get a foothold. It was now or never. He didn't have time to lollygag. He'd have to be swift and sure.

He decided to climb to the roof and attempted to shimmy his way to the driver's door tossing him back and forth. He held himself there for a moment, gazing forward to the oncoming city. He had to commandeer the vehicle before they got there, then he'd go back and get the others.

But this guy was relentless. He *must* know he was there or else why would he be rocking the vehicle so badly?

Kai decided to slip to one side and kick the man through the open window. Luckily, he had left the window down.

With one swift kick, Kai thrust both feet through the drivers window hitting the big man square in the jaw.

The struggling men fought without concern of the moving vehicle. It rocked side to side, obviously in trouble.

The woman grabbed the wheel to hold it in place, failing as it torpedoed into the ditch.

Kai held on tight!

If he could only just get his whole body inside.

But he was out of time. Ahead, minutes away, was a bridge.

They would all be goners now.

~~~

"Take your foot off the gas!" Nadia screamed to her husband.

It would only be minutes until they hit the river's edge.

The blonde soldier had Manuel in a head lock with his legs. It was inescapable.

He didn't hear her; couldn't respond anyway.

She punched and clawed the soldier's exposed legs but nothing was working.

"Manuel!" she cried.

His face was beet red, he was being strangled.

The truck tossed her back and forth in the cab.

The gun! she thought. *Use the gun!...* But it was at their feet.

No time!

Without warning, the big army truck took flight. *And time stood still.*

Nadia's life flashed before her eyes: *Children laughing, cooing her baby as she rocked in a chair. It was supper time and the smell of roast turkey and baked bread filled the air.*

Manuel was playing, letting the kids ride on his back around the Christmas tree. Mom and dad were there, laughing and taking pictures locked in time forever.

But they were still in mid flight.

In a split second, Nadia's vision of loveliness escaped her. She *was* going to die, they all were!

The big army truck roared as it plummeted fast to the water below, hitting hard!

Then, as if boat-like, it floated for a perpetual instant.

But it was the cold rape of river water that sealed her fate, filling her lungs against her will, forcing her into unconsciousness and awakening the beast of her dreams once more.

"Let me go!" she yelled.

But the beast caught hold of her and pulled her under water.

It was the blue-green Atlantic again, and the underwater Bimini road, the one their scuba guide took them to in the Bahamas.

It was the same with its wall of rock formations, but this time the beast carried her down, down, down the steps where it had no chains to bind it.

They passed coral, schools of exotic fish, and underwater life so spectacular it made her gasp at its beauty. Then, without warning, they arrived at an enormous crack in the ocean floor.

"No!" she cried not wanting to go in there.

"Yes!" the beast replied, "I have prepared a place for you!"

It carried her like its prized possession deep inside the bowels of the earth. Deeper and deeper they went with blackness all around.

Then, in the distance, a glow of red lit the horizon. The water temperature came to a boil and Nadia felt her flesh burning.

"This is the entrance," the beast said. "Now we must rest, for tomorrow you will pay the toll to cross over!"

~~~

Gasping for air, Manuel rose to the surface.

"Nadia!" he cried out.

But she wasn't bobbing in the water. *Where was she?*

Quickly he took another breath and dove back down, searching in the cab of the underwater truck once more.

No sign of her.

He popped above the surface again calling her name, twisting his head of wet back hair in all directions. There was no sign of her, and also no sign of that idiot soldier. He hoped he was dead!

But not his Nadia!

For the first time in Manuel's life he began to pray.

"God," he cried, "please help me find her!"

The river had quite a current and it kept tugging him under even though he was a trained fireman and had been involved in many river rescues. But this time was different, this time he didn't have his gear, didn't have his buddies to help.

He decided he'd better get out of the water before he got sucked under for good. If he had any hope of finding his wife it would be outside of the water. She was a strong swimmer and he knew she'd pull herself to shore sooner or later.

As he raised his dripping wet body to shore, and crawled onto some rocks, he had to catch his breath. It was only for a moment, but he thought he caught a glimpse of someone by the bushes just ahead of him.

"*Nadia!*" he called out as loud as he could.

He knew he only had seconds. He hurried himself over big and small rocks, hoping, *hoping!*

Manuel knew CPR but he also understood its limitations. If he didn't work fast and swift, there would be no hope. That was assuming it was Nadia over there.

Calling her name over and over, he realized the person wasn't answering back. *Not good.* If it was his wife, he'd have to hurry.

If it was the soldier, *he'd kill him!*

Climbing over a few more boulders, Manuel finally had the person in sight. He recognized Nadia's yellow jacket right away and his heart sank.

Chica!

Within seconds he reached her drenched body. He bent to listen for breathing but there was none. She was cold and lifeless, her wet red hair pasted to her freckled elfin face.

Immediately Manuel clicked into work mode. He was going to save his wife if it was the last thing he did.

Mouth against her cold blue lips, he blew breath into her lungs.

Chest compressions followed.

He knew it was likely that he'd taken too long, but he had to try.

"*Come on Nadia!*"

Manuel always thought CPR was easy, but not today; Not when it was someone you loved who just happened to be your entire *world.*

His head ached and his heart beat loudly inside his ears.

"*Come on Nadia!*"

One, two, three, four, five, he pushed on her chest, then bent again to breath in her mouth repeating over and over.

If she died, Manuel didn't want to live either. She was his heart, the only thing that made his life worth living.

Moments went by and then...It was the most amazing sound Manuel ever heard. His wife choked and coughed, arching her neck and back as she hacked some more.

"*Oooh Chica!*" Manuel cried as he turned her on her side to vomit water.

"*The-the toll!*" she sputtered, "I need to pay...*the toll!*"

"*Shhhhhh!*"

Manuel kissed her lips to keep them quiet. What ever she was saying wasn't as important as her life. She was *alive* and he was going to make sure she stayed that way!

But just as he sat her up, he heard pebbles crunching behind him.

The soldier!

Before he even had time to rise, a thwack hit him hard against the side of the head.

Chapter 9

Larry's skin looked white. His temperature was rising and Miriam didn't know what to do for the poor man. How was he her responsibility anyway? If only the pastor wouldn't have opened the door.

The men were visiting and praying in the sanctuary while she had to do all the dirty work. It wasn't fair. Yes, he wasn't vomiting anymore, but now his fever spiked.

Just what were they dealing with?

It was hard to stay positive with all this going on. Were they all going to die this way? And what of her daughter? *Where was she?*

As she dabbed Larry's sweaty forehead, she noticed some foam coming out of his mouth. It startled her. It wasn't puke, it was something entirely different and it wasn't there five minutes ago.

"*Frank!*" she called.

Someone had better come help her because she didn't know what to do and the man was starting to freak her out with his gurgling throat. His voice sounded funny too.

But nobody came to her rescue. They were both so consumed with praying that they forgot about reality. Reality was that God wasn't going to rush in and save them. They were on their own, just like Miriam had figured had happened.

There was no God.

Was this so terrible that she thought this way now? Did it mean she was going to hell? She was pretty sure that wasn't the case, yet, for some reason she felt a sense of loss and lack of comfort that made her truly sad.

Snap out of it! Miriam told herself. Now was not the time to think about such things. What were they going to do with Larry? She wasn't a doctor.

"*Somebody!*" she screamed this time.

But all that did was irritate Larry. He let out a growl of disapproval. *Was that a growl?*

Okay, this guy was starting to scare her.

Miriam got up and decided to head for the sanctuary herself. There was safety in numbers and that was what she was going to do: *Get safe!*

~~~~

"The Lord wants us to trust him right now," Tom told Frank. But it was hard for Frank to see him as a pastor right now. He had always been a close friend and usually only saw him as a pastor on Sunday mornings. This was his buddy telling him this and for some reason he wasn't convincing him.

"So, you're telling me you're not scared like I am?" Frank interrupted.

"Oh, I *am* scared Frank, but I've been through a lot in my day and believe me, God is the only one who has helped me through, every time buddy, every time!"

"We could all die old friend."

"And what if we do?" Tom asked. "Is that the end?"

Frank knew his friend was right. He knew that there was life after death. He knew they were just passing through this world to the next one, yet, he was still scared.

Mostly he was scared of the unknown. The world could get pretty messy without structure and balance and economy and government. After all, they had to live until they die, and the living was what he was worried about the most.

Yet, God had always been there for him. He remembered how scared they were that Nadia would develop Aids as a child. God had protected her from that needle prick even though his daughter and wife didn't like to look at it that way. *He knew.*

But biological warfare was something else entirely. It was unbelievable even thinking about it, yet policies and programs had been set in place since nine eleven. The government had drilled preparedness for years and the CDC had been warning people continuously. Still, people didn't think it would really happen.

"*Frank!*" a voice suddenly shrieked.

It was his wife. She was upset about something. He'd better go calm her down again.

"What's wrong honey?" he asked.

"I am *not* taking care of that man by myself!"

Oh boy, she was in that demanding mood again. That always put Frank on pins and needles. "We said we would help you."

"Oh, a lot of help you two have been. All you do is pray and expect me to do the dirty work. He has a fever and now he's frothing at the mouth. I don't know what to do. I'm not a doctor. You guys leave me there all by myself and he's...*he's*..."

"I'm sorry Miriam," Frank apologized. It was what he did best. He would apologize even when it wasn't his fault. It was the only thing that worked to open the lines of communication. He wasn't a right fighter and Miriam should be thankful.

"Can you guys close that book for just one minute and come and check on him? He doesn't seem right in the head."

"Don't we all," Frank teased.

"What's that supposed to mean?"

Frank looked at Tom for some help but Tom shook his head as if to stay completely out of this one. He'd put his foot in his mouth and he was the only one to get it out.

"Dear," Frank gulped, taking his wife's hand in his and patting it, "just calm down."

"Don't tell me to calm down!"

Wrong words again.

"I'm sorry dear. We're coming aren't we Tom?"

Frank closed the Bible and put it down. He followed his heated wife into the kitchen. Tom reluctantly got up and joined the two of them.

~~~

If those two didn't kill each other Tom would be surprised. It was hard enough being caught in the middle. It reminded him of his daughter. She and her husband always seemed to fight when he was over, completely forgetting he was sitting right in the middle of it.

From what Miriam was saying, it sounded like Larry had taken a turn for the worse. He would say some prayers over him and let God take care of the rest. After all, they didn't know what they were dealing with, and this poison could set into a persons system faster then they realized.

They might be dealing with a death.

"Look!" Miriam pointed to Larry when they arrived at the bedside, "he has some kind of foam coming out of his mouth. It doesn't look normal."

"Of course, it's not normal Miriam!" Frank snapped back, "*It's poison!*"

"Don't use that tone with me!"

"Enough you two, you're like squabbling children," Tom said. "Let me take a look at him."

Tom bent over the pale looking man and heard a low rumble sound in his breathing. He couldn't quite put his finger on it but it sounded like some kind of chest infection. No wait, it was like a growling sound. *What on earth?!*

"This is not good!" Tom decided.

"I told you guys!" Miriam rubbed it in.

Frank came near and listened.

"You hear it?" Tom asked him, sitting on the chair next to the bed.

"I hear it."

Tom didn't want to say it but he knew he had to for their sakes. "Look you two, I've seen this before when I was on the farm."

"What do you mean, on the farm?" Miriam asked with alarm.

Tom still didn't want to tell them but they had to know. "When I worked on a dairy farm in my teens, the owner had lots of dog. Well, these dogs got caught up with a pack of coyotes."

Miriam's impatience got the best of her and she interrupted his story. "What on earth does this have to do with *anything?*"

"Let the man finish!" Frank spit back.

Tom just glared at his buddy. He wished he wouldn't provoke her like that. "Okay," he continued, "so on this farm, two of the dogs got infected. They had *rabies*, and this to me looks exactly like rabies."

"*Rabies?*" both Frank and Miriam repeated at the same time.

"Yes *Rabies!*"

Tom Cringed when he said it. He didn't know how the infected water played a part in getting rabies but he didn't want to find out.

"Now, if my assumptions are correct," he continued, "we need to tie him up...*now!*"

Chapter 10

Manuel's head felt like mush when he regained consciousness.

His wife was sitting beside him holding her knees rocking back and forth. Obviously, they were still on the riverbank. The soldier lay in a heap beside them. Blood smeared his blonde hair and pale face. He was either dead or unconscious, either way he couldn't remember how that happened.

"*Chica*? Are you okay?" he asked.

She just huddled there shaking. *Uh oh!*

"What happened to Mr. Tuff guy?"

Manuel grabbed his throbbing head, trying to focus better. "*Chica?*"

"He's *dead!*" she finally answered. "I *killed* him!"

"You *what?*"

"I killed him Manuel and now I'm going to hell!" she sobbed.

"You aren't going to hell!" he tried to comfort. "You did what you had to do!"

But for some reason he didn't think he was convincing her.

"I killed a man in cold blood," Nadia repeated, rocking in a trance. "I picked up a rock and bashed his head in. He didn't even see it coming. I just snuck up behind him when he was wailing on you with a rock. He was sitting on top of you pounding over and over. I had to do something!"

That's my feisty red head!

"Hey, look at me," Manuel said softly lifting her chin, "we're going to be okay! You had to do it. It was either me or him, do you hear? Now dry those tears and let's get going. We can't stay here. It's getting dark."

Manuel kissed his wife softly, lingering for a moment in hopes to block the days traumatic events from both of their minds.

He pulled her up, wobbling from his head injury, realizing the soldier gave him a pretty good beating. He was fortunate for Nadia's sake that he survived, yet his headache and blurred vision told him he had a concussion.

~~~~

Dusk brought them into a deserted town. Minot had never looked so destitute. The streetlights were out as well as all the other usual lights that were supposed to come on at that time of day.

Cars had been abandoned and vacant with doors left wide open in the middle of the street. Not a soul was around. Not a sound could be heard.

Nadia wondered what had happened. It must have been chaos, trapped in the city like this with no way to escape except by foot. No wonder the military had been gathering them up. Or shooting them like the guys they encountered.

People usually panic under these circumstances, but nobody really knows how they'll react until they experience it. Nadia didn't know how she would react until she was faced with doing the unmentionable.

If someone had told her this morning that she was going to kill a man by the end of the day she never would have believed it.

How could she?

Manuel was right, it was either him or the soldier. And how could she live with herself if she hadn't defended her husband.

But now she faced the repercussions. She *was* going to hell. *'Thou shalt not kill'* was drilled into her head as one of the major commandments. Even though she didn't believe most of the Bible anyway, she did believe that part. The world would be a terrible place if those rules weren't followed.

Nadia sighed, walking silently hand in hand with her wounded husband. Were they in a hopeless age filled with more violence? And what kind of a world were they going to bring a child into?

She thought of the baby inside of her and hoped it was okay. The truck crash had given her body a pretty bad jolt. Had it hurt the baby, she wondered?

The muscle spasms in her abdomen told her maybe.

Under normal circumstances they would be heading to the hospital right now for Manuel's head injury and to check on the baby, but going there was useless. People would have been evacuated a long time ago.

They were probably the only ones left to fend for themselves.

"Manuel?" she asked, breaking the silence, "do you think God is punishing us?"

"*No!*"

"But maybe my dad was right all along. He and his church people always said the day would come when God will avenge."

"Avenge what?" Manuel answered annoyed.

"I don't know," she shrugged, "I guess God wants us to follow his rules and most of us don't. Like *'Thou shalt not kill.'*"

"Nadia! You're *not* going to hell!"

A tear rolled down Nadia's check as she tried to hide it. "If you say so."

"I don't believe God would make a thing as sick as hell anyway."

"If you don't believe there's a hell," Nadia answered a little too quickly, "then how can you believe there's a heaven?"

"There just is! It doesn't mean there's a hell. I believe my *la abuela* is in heaven. She died when I was young and my *el abuelo* always told me stories of her painless life in *el cielo* without the cancer. Don't tell me it was all just a big fat lie! *Ay caramba!*"

"I'm not saying it was a lie."

She knew Manuel was getting annoyed but her dream kept haunting her. "What if there *is* a devil?"

"*Well there isn't!*"

But Nadia knew there was. She saw him in her dreams.

Silence pressed the conversation. It was time to drop the subject, yet Nadia remembered all those Sunday School lessons forced upon her that she so easily dismissed.

Was there something to them?

She thought of all the commandments and how easily she turned from them until now. Deliberately killing someone had a way of eating at a person's soul. Maybe that's what her dream meant? Maybe God was punishing her and he sent the devil to do it?

Maybe this was her toll?

Just the thought of it sent shivers up her spine. *Repentance* rang through her head just like all those summers she spent at Redblue Bible Camp. She remembered the first time.

"Nadia," her camp councillor Tia explained to her one night after the service, "God loves you! He wants you to repent of your sins. We all do stuff we know we shouldn't do and that makes us unclean. Jesus wants to make us clean again."

So, she prayed the sinners prayer that night when she was ten. It was the sweetest moment in her life when all things bad turned good again. The innocence of a child found a way to make sense of this ugly world.

At that moment she felt like her heart had grown too big for her body. She wanted to shout out to the world that she was a *Christian kid* now. She prayed and sang hymns and walked the walk and talked the talk.

Until she got home.

Then, as each summer came to an end and school started, real life set in and her spiritual high always seemed to plummet.

By the time she turned fifteen it came to an end for good.

There was no God! If there was, then why were there so many bullies attacking her daily with their insults? Their exclusion and ridicule left her out of everything including the so-called *Christian* Youth Group.

Mom had sided with her then, pulling her from the Youth Group and all things related to church and Bible Camp.

"Find your *own* friends Nadia," her mom would tell her. "You don't need those snobby church girls anyway."

And so, she did. But the only friends left were the ones that got her into drinking and smoking pot. It was fun for a time but dad soon put a stop to that group.

"We'll move to Minot," Dad decided. But the same thing happened in the Minot school and the new church. *Everybody left her out.*

Sure, moving got her away from the pot heads and the small country school full of bullies, but it left her alone, friendless, until she met Manuel.

Her saviour.

No, she didn't need a God who would turn his back on a little girl when she needed him the most. If Jesus saved people from sins then he didn't do a very good job with her. She was tossed about by the many bullies and *their* sins and those wrongs had never been righted. *She still carried the scars.*

She had replaced Jesus with her new saviour: *Her husband.*

Except now, punishment for that and all her many other sins including her recent one, was to pay the toll.

She wondered what that toll would be.

～～～

They'd have to find some transportation soon before the sun goes down completely.

"Look for a vehicle with keys in it *Chica*," Manuel told his wife.

With his aching head and Nadia's pregnancy, he couldn't chance walking further than they already had. Fatigue was overpowering them both.

His wife's disturbing discussion still lingered but he wasn't about to continue it. It was nonsense, and right now they had to focus on the positive. Manuel was sure things would get better just as soon as they found a safe zone. It would be set up by the military. Hopefully not by the kind of soldiers they had run into. His fireman buddies were probably all there helping out right now. *It's where he should be too.*

"How are we going to get a car out of this place?" Nadia asked as she checked each vehicle they passed, "it's jammed up with vehicles."

"Just keep looking."

Manuel would cross that bridge when he came to it. He wasn't really thinking clearly with his concussion but he was doing the best he could.

As they neared the congested intersection, he spotted a motorbike laying on its side. It looked like it had been rear-ended by the red mini-van behind it.

"Over here!" he called to his wife.

Dodging in and out of the ghost-like traffic jam he reached the intersection and dove to the bike. It was a Harley, one of his favourites. He never expected his first ride on a vintage Harley Davidson Road King to be under these circumstances.

Manuel pulled the mammoth bike to a stance as Nadia rushed up to it.

"Does it have a key?" she asked.

"Hmm," Manuel looked it over, "the keys are in it. *Hop on!*"

With a struggle, Manuel helped his petite wife into the black banana seat and then straddled the monster bike himself.

He turned the key and kicked the bike to life. *Easy peasy!*

As he manoeuvred around the pile of cars, Manuel steered the bike slowly with his wife clinging to his waist. The lights made it easier to see, but it wasn't as easy to avoid the open vehicle doors obstructing their path.

Finally, once they gained momentum and stuck to the sides of the road, they headed south on Broadway Street to the in-laws.

They'd both have a soft bed to spend the night in even if Frank and Miriam weren't there to invite them in.

Ride-em cowboy!

Chapter 11

Larry was not Larry anymore.

No, he had mutated into an animal version of himself and so had they. Tying a grown man up and leaving him in the bathtub was not something human beings did to one another.

But they had no choice.

Larry had all but gone mad. Was that how *they* were going to end up? Frank wondered as he sat rocking in Tom's chair as they discussed what to do next.

"We can't just leave him there?" Frank said.

"Just what do you expect us to do with him then?" his wife snapped back.

"Look," Tom held his hands up in a truce, "I know its barbaric but at this point we have to do what's best and that means to survive. I've prayed over the man and nothing helps. Now, I know it's my fault, I let him in, so...I can stay with him. *You guys go.*"

"Definitely not!" Frank snapped back.

"Yes, we can!" his wife retorted.

Frank just shook his head. He didn't know what to do. His old friend had a mind of his own and if he wanted to stay, there was nothing they could do about it, but he was sure going to try and convince the old man otherwise.

"You two are young," Tom said softly with compassion, "you can walk, I can't. I got these *bunions*. I'm all worn out and plus, he vomited on *me*. We don't know how this thing works. We don't know if it's contagious like a virus or if you get it from a bite or just by drinking the water. If it's contagious, *I'm a goner anyway.*"

Frank refused to hear his excuse, "*No!*"

"Look, If I get sick you will have to tie me up too. Will you be able to do that Frank? How about you Miriam?"

They both looked at each other sadly.

"We can get you to the safe zone in Fargo somehow. They have antibiotics, they can make you well if you get sick," Frank said, hoping his friend would listen.

"I could get sick tomorrow, tonight even. *Then what?*"

"But you said yourself, rabies shouldn't set in that fast," Frank replied, trying everything he could. "You have time. *Please!*"

Miriam just kept quiet. For the first time she actually didn't have anything to say. He knew why. Her silence was working to Tom's advantage but Frank didn't want it that way. *Back me up for once woman!*

"*No!*" Tom shook his head, "I want you two to be safe and you won't be if I'm with you. I could be infected *now!* It shouldn't happen so fast but it did for Larry. I don't know how come. Maybe he got bitten earlier? Who knows what brings it on for sure or what determines the incubation period: age, race, blood type? This is biological warfare. *It's unpredictable.*"

Frank hung his head. The old man was giving up.

"You can leave in the morning," Tom said, "I won't send you out in the dark. Get a good nights sleep and I will pack you up with supplies before you leave. When you get to Fargo, send help for me. I'll still be here."

But Frank knew it would be too late by then.

He'd try one last time to change the stubborn fool's mind.

"*We aren't going without you Tom!*"

"I beg your pardon?" Miriam guffawed her husband.

"*YES, YOU ARE!*" Tom rose, yelling this time. "This is *MY* house, *MY* church, and I don't want you here! Now stop this nonsense or you will leave *tonight!*"

Miriam touched Frank's arm to be quiet. It was decided. They would leave their friend behind.

~~~

Tom couldn't sleep. He tossed and turned all night but his mind kept reeling over his angry outburst, but mostly about Larry. He could hear him growling in the bathroom and it was very upsetting.

What would he do with the man especially when it was time to tend to him?

God help me! he prayed.

He couldn't leave him tied up forever. Eventually he'd need to feed the man and remove the duct tape from his frothing mouth. After all, he *was* still human.

It was unlike any rabies infection he'd ever dealt with. Eventually the man would die from it but then again who knew what they were really dealing with here. It could take days, weeks maybe.

A part of him wanted Frank to try harder to convince him to go with them. Why didn't his friend force him? But it was better this way. *They would be safe.*

If the growling noise wasn't enough to keep him awake, a looming thunderstorm was rumbling in the distance, rustling the leaves and picking up momentum.

He had lived a long life. It was time to be with Jesus. He'd served his church as best he could. Yes, there were times when the congregation almost split apart, but he held them together. Rather, God held them together.

He wondered if God would hold the world together. It's not like history hadn't seen traumatic events before. He'd been through two wars and witnessed plenty of tragedies because of them, but the United States had never tasted the world wars on its own soil like his ancestors in Brittan and Germany did.

Biological warfare was a whole other kind of war.

He thought of Revelations. Personally, he believed Christ was coming to return for his people, trouble was, they may have to endure a great deal of pain before that happened.

Could this be the end?

He needed to study, *pray.* If they were entering what the Bible said was the Tribulation, he needed to get prepared. *He needed to preach!*

Many of his sermons were on the *End Times.* He'd preach it every Sunday if he could. But he found people didn't want to hear it. They were okay with sugar coating it, pretending that part of the Bible didn't matter...*but it did.*

He remembered that sunny Sunday morning when Raymond the head deacon took him aside and told him they wanted him to come to a board meeting that evening to discuss a very important topic.

Well it was important all right.

"Pastor," one of the deacons started to speak, "we just don't feel preaching on the *End Times* is what's best right now. All you're doing is scaring people. Lighten it up, that's all were saying."

Lighten it up? How was he supposed to do that? It was the *Bible!* It angered him even thinking about it.

But he did what he was told. He never preached on Revelations again. He never prepared his congregation for *this* and that was his job. He should have been stronger! He should have fought back! He should have insisted on preaching God's word...*all of it!*

Now where did it get them? They were all unprepared and so was he.

Tom sobbed into his pillow.

An old man with high blood pressure shouldn't get himself all riled up, but he couldn't help it. "*Forgive me Jesus!*" he cried, wishing he had a second chance to preach what he knew he should have years ago. But there were no second chances for a world of sin.

Evil had already come...and it was in his bathroom.

~~~~

Lightening flickered across the dark sanctuary windows as the wind howled outside. Frank sat in silence in the front pew with his head down.

He couldn't pray, he couldn't sleep. He couldn't talk to his wife.

Deep inside, he felt a pain so raw it felt like he was literally bleeding to death. If there was one thing that wrenched his gut it was this: How could he leave his buddy behind?

Tears streamed down his face, channelling a passageway down to his stubble chin. His stuffy nose needed wiping but he didn't have a hanky.

He sighed, sniffling. The storm had begun to pelt hard rain down on the tin roof and it gave him something else to think about. He remembered when they put that roof on two years ago. He'd been up there with all the younger guys, trying to prove he could still do it. But that injured back of his wouldn't let him stay up there for long. Oh how it ached.

That kind of stuff didn't stop Tom though. He didn't go up on the roof but he busied himself down below, fetching sheet-metal screws from the lawn as they fell, handing tools to the men and cleaning up like a busy beaver.

He wasn't just a pastor, he was a friend to all. How could they turn their backs on him now? No, he'd just have to put his foot down and force Tom to come with them. They could send help back for Larry.

Thunder cracked above him as if responding.

God, is that you?

Frank rubbed his tired wet eyes with his fist, listening for what he hoped would be God's audible answer, *yes*.

Instead, a loud shriek cried out startling him immediately. *Miriam?*

It was his wife. Perhaps the thunder scared her but he didn't think so. She wasn't one to be frightened in a storm.

He rushed out of the pew and lit off down the dark hall to the bedroom where he left her. "*Miriam?*"

But she wasn't there.

Another scream echoed.

His heart sank when he realized her screams were coming from the bathroom. Candle light peeked out between a crack in the door. What on earth was she doing in the bathroom with Larry in the middle of the night?

When he flung open the bathroom door, he saw his wife crumpled beside a motionless Larry. She had removed his restraints as well as the tape on his mouth.

"He's *dead F*rank!" she bawled uncontrollably, "He's *dead!*"

"Are you sure?"

"Of course, I'm sure!"

Frank froze in place. He didn't want to go near Larry like his wife did but he knew he needed to check for sure. He placed his fingers on Larry's neck. *No pulse.* Then on his wrist. *No pulse.* He bent over the man's wet mouth. *Not a breath at all.*

Larry lay in the bathtub, crumpled up, cold as ice. He wasn't moving and he was stiff already. Frank wasn't a doctor or anything but he knew a dead man when he saw one.

"I couldn't leave him like this," Miriam whimpered. "When I got up to see where you were, I decided to check on Larry because he wasn't making any noise. That's when I realized he was dead. I felt sorry for him so I took the rope and the tape off because it wasn't right. He-he's dead now. The poor man!"

Frank couldn't believe his wife of all people would care so much. She hid the compassionate side of her quite well surprising even her own husband.

"What's happened?" Tom rushed to the bathroom door.

The old man was in his slippers and housecoat standing there in the candle light with red puffy eyes.

"He's dead Tom," Frank told him.

"*Nooo!*"

"Yes!"

"That's too fast," Tom continued. "Rabies doesn't kill you in only a few hours."

"Well it *did!*" Miriam cried again, bending over the man as she held his stiff cold hand. "Are we all going to die like this? What kind of sickness *is* this anyway?"

Frank didn't have the answers. He knew there was no consoling his wife. How could he console her when he felt the same way? No, he'd let her cry. He'd cry himself.

But there was one thing for sure, they were *all* leaving in the morning.

Chapter 12

By the time the big Harley Davidson Road King rumbled down South Main Street where the in-laws lived, a storm had crept up on them. Getting there had taken too long with the many detours they had to take to get around abandoned vehicles.

The driveway was empty but that was okay. They'd spend the night and then figure out where to go next. Manuel half hoped Frank and Miriam weren't there. That would mean they had evacuated. *At least he hoped so for Nadia's sake.*

Nadia was slumped behind him still grabbing on tightly. She needed to rest, especially for the baby, but first he'd have to get them out of the rain.

"Do you know where they keep the spare key *Chica*?"

Nadia eased off the bike and shook her wet hair, "Under the back-door mat, come on!"

The two of them abandoned their ride and darted toward the back door. The rain was heavier now, drenching them from head to toe.

"I got it!" she said.

As his wife fiddled in the pouring rain to unlock the door, Manuel surveyed their surroundings. Nothing, not a light was on at any of the neighbour's houses, not a dog barked, nothing but the pounding rain reverberated the empty neighbourhood.

Inside, Nadia rushed to the utility closet beside the freezer and pulled out a large flashlight and turned it on. "*Mom? Dad?*"

But as Manuel expected, they didn't answer.

She directed the flashlight through the kitchen to the phone and took it out of it's cradle, bringing it to her ear.

"It won't work *Chica*."

"*I know!*"

He could tell his wife was weary and tired just from her tone. "Let's just get some sleep and we'll figure things out in the morning."

But Nadia wasn't going to rest until she snooped around. She grabbed the answering machine from beside the phone and lifted it up.

"They have battery backup. Look Manuel, the lights flashing. Maybe they left a message?"

"*Seriously Nadia?* Why would they leave us a message? How would they even know we would come here? They probably thought we went home."

"All the way to *Coolidge?* I doubt that. They're closer to the airport."

There was no arguing with her at this point. She was a woman on a mission. He'd let her do whatever she thought she needed to do. He for one was headed for bed.

Even with the lights out, his tired feet knew the right direction. Down the hall and to the left. They'd use that big king size bed of theirs and enjoy every bit of the slumber. He felt as though he could sleep a million years. It was time to kiss his headache goodbye.

"*Manuel!*" Nadia called from the kitchen, "*there's a message! Come here!*"

But he couldn't move an inch. His body resisted any attempt to lift himself up.

"*Manuel!*" she shouted again.

"*Mmmmm,*" he moaned ignoring her.

Then like the trouper she was, she marched down the hallway and put the answering machine right to his ear without giving him a choice.

"*Listen!*"

She pressed the button.

"'*Honey,*" the message said, "'*I'm at the hospital for my blood test, but I still have to go see Dr. Prescott at his office and then I'll be on my way to Tom's for coffee. I won't be home when you get home so don't worry. See you then.*'"

And that was it. Frank only left a message for his wife. No message for them. No mention of the chaos. This must have been left the day they evacuated the city.

"*Manuel!*" Nadia cried, "*do you know what this means?*"

But he had no idea what it meant. Frankly at this point he didn't care. All he wanted to do was sleep. All he wanted was his wife to go to bed. "*Estoy Cansado!*"

"*I'm tired too,* but we have to go to the church!"

"Now? *Why?*"

"Because that's the last place my dad was before all this happened."

"You don't know that!"

"Neither do you! *C'mon!*"

Manuel knew he wasn't winning this argument and he knew she wasn't going to sleep either if he didn't take her. He'd have to roll his sorry butt off that cozy bed and hop on the bike in the rain again. *Absolutely crazy!*

"But it's raining and it's *late Chica!*"

"It's only midnight according to my watch," his wife corrected, "and I'm pretty sure the rain stopped."

Pretty sure? Not likely. Ugh!

"Okay!" he sighed, puzzled that the word even came out of his mouth.

Nadia put a smile on a little to quickly. She was just worried about her parents he guessed. He couldn't blame her for that. But for some reason he felt like she'd just pulled a *naughtia* on him.

"I guess it's back to the bike then."

"Better yet, how 'bout daddy's jeep?" she smiled, dangling keys in his face. "It's in the garage."

Gracias!

~~~~

For the better part of an hour, Nadia rummaged through her parent's cupboards with a flashlight gathering as much food and bottled water as she could possibly find.

At least Manuel could get some sleep for a little while, she wasn't that cruel. His bloody bruised head worried her. Had he forgotten he had a concussion? He wasn't supposed to sleep more than two hours without being woken?

She loaded up her dad's 1983 Jeep Wagoneer inside the detached garage. It was her father's project vehicle. He'd been tinkering on it for the last five years and she never saw him drive it once. Fully equipped with power seats, four-wheel drive, and brown shag rug, Nadia thought it was still the ugliest thing she had ever seen, but at least it would keep them dry in that nasty weather outside.

Bit by bit she loaded the vehicle with groceries and blankets, anything she could find that would help them get to Fargo. It was imperative to check the church before leaving town. If her dad was still there, she'd want to find him quickly. And where her dad was, her mother was never far behind.

Hopefully the Jeep would start. She'd know in a minute but first she'd open the garage door. The wind whistled as pelts of rain hit her head. Man, it was nasty out there. Coming back from the tropics to *this* was not fun! But early fall usually brought the wildest weather in North Dakota anyway.

With a twist of the key, the big engine laboured. *Come on baby!* He probably hadn't started it in a while. The lights were on, that was a good indication the battery wasn't the problem. Then, as she stared at the gauges, she realized it was the fuel. The gas gauge was reading empty. Now she remembered why her dad didn't drive it. He complained many a time that it was a gas guzzler, but he didn't want to get rid of it just in case he wanted to go hunting. *Like that ever happened!*

Dad always stored jerry cans full of gas somewhere, so that wouldn't be a problem. She'd try one more time to turn it over and then hunt for the gas.

Suddenly, the big beast roared to life but it sure took a while. She was thankful her car was fuel injected. These old things were so unpredictable.

As the jeep idled, she looked for the jerry cans. *Yup, in their usual place.* Even though she had moved away, everything was still the same, she had to chuckle under her breath. *Some things never change.*

Nadia dragged two big gas cans over to the jeep, unscrewing the top and pulling the spouts out just like her dad had taught her. She heaved the big can up and started filling the vehicle.

She knew she probably shouldn't be lifting these big things in her condition, *yes most definitely,* but she didn't really have a choice.

The nauseating gas fumes churned her stomach but it wouldn't take long. She'd have it fuelled up and ready to go in no time.

Thunder cracked outside, sending shivers up her spine. It reminded her of Halloween night, spooky and dark. The sooner they were on their way again, the better.

As she clunked the last empty jerry can down on the garage floor, she picked up the flashlight and spied around the garage shelves. *Ah...there it is,* she said to herself, *daddy's hunting rifle.* They would need it if they came across anymore *soldiers.*

She dragged the big thing off the shelf and took a few boxes of shells to go with it.

Now she'd run in and change her wet clothes. Her old room was left as a shrine so she was bound to find something dry to wear. First, she'd turn off the engine. They couldn't afford to waste the gas. It had warmed up enough already.

Inside, she found her old bedroom. Why they hadn't converted it into a games room, or sewing room like normal people, she'd never know. She knew her parents had a hard time letting her go, but this was ridiculous!

The dry sweat-suit she put on felt good against her damp skin. She'd have to find something for Manuel to wear.

As Nadia creaked into her parents bedroom shining the flashlight on to the bed, she saw her husband cuddled in the covers like a baby. *Adorable!* She wondered if that's what their baby would look like.

"*Manuel!*" she whispered.

But he didn't stir.

"*Manuel!* she said a little louder, bending over to kiss his warm lips. "Get up sleepyhead! We have to go!"

"*Mmmmm,*" he managed to moan.

She crawled up into bed and lay beside him, hoping that would help, but it didn't. He just grabbed her by the waist and pulled her down.

"Snuggle up *Chica...just for a minute!*"

Well, he was at least awake. She decided to give him a minute or two to get out of bed, snuggling up to the curve of his body. It was just for a minute, then they'd go.

As she turned off the flashlight, she realized what she had done. Her own heavy eyelids drooped against her will as she joined her husband into a slumber land where she knew she ought not to go.

This time the beast tied her up.

There were others around her. She couldn't make out the faces but they were chained along the fence, unable to move.

"I have no money to pay the toll," she told the beast.

But the beast just grinned its ugly yellow teeth as though it knew something she did not. "Ah but you do!" it said.

Nadia looked around at the flames encircling and realized she was now strapped to the fence with the other people.

"You hold the key my dear."

"I don't have any key."

The beast just grinned again and sauntered away.

She noticed the people chained beside her. Their flesh was burning and they were crying in pain.

Blood formed a pool beneath them.

Then a snake with a human head slithered over to her and hissed. "I know a secret," it said, "If you give me the child, he won't harm you."

"But the child is unborn."

"Exactly!"

Nadia slowly shook her head realizing what the snake was asking her. "No!"

"But I can take it and give it to...hiiim!"

"Oh no you can't!" Nadia cried, pulling at her chains to try and get away.

The snake spit and hissed, laughing as it slithered closer to her. It licked her face and pushed up against her body.

Then without warning, it slugged its large tail into her gut...hard!

Sudden pain shot through her abdomen so fast it knocked the wind out of her as she gasped for air. Blood started to dribble down her bare legs.

"Ha!" it hissed, "it's done!"

"Noooo!"

But the snake just laughed and slithered away.

~~~

Manuel broke out in a sweat and woke with a start. His headache hadn't gone away and his wife had disturbed him with her thrashing.

"*Chica?*"

Nadia ripped off the covers, "*Nooo!*"

But he could tell there was something wrong. "What is it?" he asked.

Light peeked in the master bedroom window filling the room with low beams across the bed. Then, he saw it too.

Blood everywhere!

Bawling she lifted the blankets further to confirm the mess on the sheets.

"God! Oh God!" she panicked.

But Manuel had seen it before many times. His job made him privy to that unfortunately: A *miscarriage.*

"Ohhh!" he moaned, reaching out to his heartbroken wife, *"c'mere honey!"*

He climbed over the big bed and held his wife as she sobbed harder than he'd ever seen her before. Yesterday had proven too much for her petite pregnant body. He should have known better, should have done a better job protecting her.

It wasn't fair.

"I don't know why God hates me so much!" she cried even harder.

"He doesn't *hate* you sweetie!"

"Then *why* Manuel? *Why?!"*

Manuel gulped hard. He didn't have one single answer to give her. The fact was, he didn't know why God would let such a thing happen but he couldn't tell his wife that now. *"It just happens. Nobody knows why,"* he told her rubbing her back as he hugged her.

"Well I know why!" she fumed, sniffling hard as she pulled away from him.

"Don't blame yourself. *It's not your fault!"*

"It's *not* my fault. *It's his!* He's making me pay!"

Obviously, she didn't want to elaborate but Manuel wouldn't push her. He'd allow her to grieve, and anger was very much a part of it. If she wanted to blame God it was up to her. Still, if anyone was to blame, it was *him*. How could he ever forgive himself for not protecting his unborn child?

Nadia grabbed her stomach and curled up into a ball on the edge of the bed. Manuel went to work clearing the bloody covers, gathering towels and washcloths to clean his wife up. It didn't even matter that the whole world had turned upside down. For them, nothing would ever be the same again.

With the truck already packed and ready to go, *something he wished his wife had never done,* he carried Nadia into the front seat and roared the big jeep to life.

She wouldn't look at him and that was disturbing.

"We'll stop at Trinity Hospital for a few things on our way," he said pushing her to respond to at least something he said.

"What for?" she grumbled.

"I need to pick up some things you're going to need."

"And *what* things am I going to need?"

Now she was just plain mad. He didn't like it when she acted like her mother but he'd let it go under the circumstances.

"You need a RhoGam shot...and some meds."

"What's *that?*"

He was not in the mood to argue with her especially with his pounding headache. While he was at it, he'd pick up something for himself. Some T3's or maybe something stronger. Thankfully his clearance at Trinity would allow him to pick up what he needed if there was anyone even there. If not, he didn't have his key-fob so he hoped the ambulance bay would be open.

At times like these he was glad he had also done his paramedic training so he could do EMS as well as firefighting. It was the company requirement when he first got hired anyway.

His wife had just had a miscarriage and he had seen woman bleed to death from that. And she was a redhead and genetically they were more prone to haemorrhaging, not to mention complications from her rare blood type. If she needed a blood transfusion, she'd be out of luck considering the chaos going on right now.

"RhoGam is a shot you need for your blood." And that was all he would tell her. She didn't need to know anymore right now. She didn't need to know it was because she had seventy-two hours give or take before her blood sensitized, making it almost impossible for her to have more children. At least healthy ones.

Sometimes he wished he had her negative blood type, then having kids with her wouldn't be such a risk. The two blood types just didn't mix well. He knew that from his studies. Women with Rh negative blood types that had children with Rh positive men were at high risk to sensitization: Blood mixing. And if that happened and the woman became sensitized, the child would get Hemolytic Disease: A severe life-threatening anemia that causes brain damage and death.

It used to be a real problem in the old days before they invented RhoGam or WinRho depending on what country you lived in. But now he worried that life could easily be set back to those days if war broke out, like biological warfare. It was an ugly realization but one that was at the forefront.

Manuel just shook his head. He didn't want to think about that. Too many other things were going on. Besides, his headache was getting worse. He'd just get the RhoGam, some antibiotics, some T3's, Codeine, and a whole pack of absorbent pads.

As they pulled up in front of the deserted hospital and shifted the jeep into park, he turned off the engine.

"Now, will you be okay waiting here while I get the stuff *Chica*?"

She nodded without looking at him. He knew she was crying again but there wasn't much he could do but get the meds.

She needed some time alone anyway.

~~~

Nadia felt like death.

It was more than she could bear. Her heart ached with sorrow and she sobbed so hard her entire body shook. "*Why Jesus? Why?*"

"*I'm not that bad, am I?*" she asked, using her sleeve to wipe her nose as she sniffled.

"*Why do I have to pay for my sins when everyone else can do whatever they please?*"

The question echoed as she sat in the truck alone. All she wanted to do was run and never come back. But where would she go? She didn't even care that the world was going to pot. *She wanted to die with it.*

It wasn't right to punish Manuel though. It wasn't his fault yet she was so angry with him. She didn't even know why.

She was just angry period.

All she knew was she needed her mom. How could she even tell her about the pregnancy? She would have called them foolish for trying so soon. Her parents would find out she was actually three months pregnant walking up the isle. Something she felt ashamed of and kept hidden even from Manuel: He only thought it was two.

She was supposed to be the *Christian* girl after all, even though moving in with Manuel before the wedding pretty well contradicted her so called status.

She banged her head against the hard passenger window, beating herself up.

Then, in the distance, she thought she saw someone. A man, staggering in the parking lot. She sat up immediately and leaned over to press the auto lock on the drivers door.

But he turned her direction and kept on coming.

Nadia hid, slinking down fast.

Pow! The man suddenly hit the side window with his head.

Great, now what?

His white face pasted against the passenger window, drooling with open mouth and bared teeth like some kind of a rabid dog. His eyes were red and he was obviously sick.

Biological warfare.

Manuel came out of the ambulance bay just then, carrying a large duffle bag. He stopped, dropped it, and grabbed a large stick propped up against the bay door.

This was going to get ugly!

Chapter 13

The wind had stopped howling outside and the sun had finally come up, not that Frank had gotten much sleep. Hopefully Miriam had been more successful. It appeared she had, since she was already up annoying him.

"Come on Frank," she said, "I've been waiting for you to get your lazy butt up. I've filled some old backpacks I found in the Sunday School room for us since we'll be walking. Do you think you can carry the bottled water? I don't think the pastor can do it and it's too heavy for me."

"Sure," he mumbled a little too quickly, forgetting he shouldn't be carrying anything with his bad back. But then most of the time his wife ignored his pains anyway.

"Tom up?" he asked yawning.

"I hope so. We have to go. I don't want to stay in this place one more minute with...*well*...you know."

He knew. He felt it too. There, down the hall lay a dead body. Even though the door was closed it didn't make it go away. Out of sight out of mind actually did help, but still they all knew what lay behind that door.

"I know," Frank answered, changing the subject as quickly as he could.

"I figure we should be able to commandeer a vehicle with some keys in it somewhere. We really can't walk to Fargo."

"And *steal* someone's car?"

"I highly doubt anyone will care Miriam."

"I guess so," his wife frowned busying herself with something else.

He had to give her credit, the tuff old bird. Even though she was crusty and cranky most of the time, she really was a soft marshmallow inside. Most of the time she tried to hide it but he knew. She still had an innocence about her that preserved her soft side. Why would she worry about the ethics of stealing a vehicle for survival unless she really did have a good heart?

"*I love you Miriam,*" he smiled, taking her hand and pulling her to him.

Miriam still held the backpack she was packing in one hand and let him pull her in.

"I know I don't say it enough, and especially with everything going on, but you mean the world to me dear!"

"Even if the world falls apart?" she sniffled.

"*Even if the world falls apart!*"

Frank kissed his wife softly. He was glad they had each other. He would do everything in his power to get her to safety.

"*Ehem!*" a voice in the doorway cleared his throat. "Don't mean to interrupt you two love birds but I thought you'd like some breakfast."

Tom held two bowls of cereal in his hands as an offering.

"*Look,*" he winced, "I just wanted to apologize for how harsh I was last night."

The old man looked as though he hadn't gotten a wink of sleep. His bushy white hair was standing on end uncombed.

"Apology accepted friend," Frank answered. He grabbed the bowls from Tom's hands and set them down on the dresser, giving him a long hug.

"We've all been rattled Tom. This isn't easy for anyone. It makes us say and do crazy things. But

Miriam has everything packed, so we'll eat, and then we're all getting the *heck* out of *Dodge!*"

Tom nodded in silence.

"Now I want you to go put on the best shoes you have Tom. Runners preferably. We need to do a lot of walking and I don't want those bunions of yours acting up."

"Okay, but I'm use to the bunions."

"You may be use to it but walking for a few hours is pretty hard on someone with *good* feet leave alone yours."

Tom nodded again and turned to go get ready for the trip. He returned with a red beavers ball cap, crazy red high-top runners and a red Minot State University jacket to match. "*I'm ready!*"

What a clown!

"Where on earth did you get that getup from?" Frank grinned, "And look at those runners."

"My grandson Riley left them here on Sunday. They're his *kicks*. Like em?"

His kicks! The old man was trying to be a smart-aleck probably trying to lighten the mood as usual. Well it worked. Miriam's demeanour changed immediately.

"Tom you old devil!" she chuckled, "Thank you for that! Just when I needed it the most."

"Why, you're welcome dear!"

Miriam pulled him in for a big hug and then spun him around to help him put his backpack on. "Now hopefully that won't be too much weight for you. You're carrying the food so no munching, you hear?"

"*Yes ma'am!*"

Frank put his own backpack on as did Miriam. They were as ready as they'd ever be.

Now let's go!

~~~~

As Miriam scurried past the bathroom door, she thought she heard something in there. *No, couldn't be.* She shook her head against the ridiculous notion that Larry could still be alive. Yet...*there*...she heard it again.

It sounded like a clunking sound.

"Frank?" Miriam called out.

But the guys had decided to make a quick stop in the sanctuary to pray before leaving.

It was an obvious clunking sound she was hearing and it *wasn't* nothing. Someone was in there. Perhaps the guys had decided to stop in and pray over him first. They had talked about doing that. *But really? Five minutes before heading out the door?*

Still, it was a possibility and it surely made more sense than her crazy assumption.

"*Hello?*" she called through the closed bathroom door. *More clunking.*

This time she decided to knock. "Frank? Pastor? Is that you?"

Did she really have to go inside?

Guessing she better check it out, she eased her hand inside the dark room and flicked on the light.

It was Larry! ALIVE!

He looked like the devil! His eyes were red as blood and his skin as pale as death.

Screaming she tried to pull the door shut again but his long-nailed fingers clawed around the bathroom door preventing it from closing completely.

"Frank! *FRANK!!*"

She couldn't hold the door closed any longer, her hands were slipping.

"HELP!"

Larry pulled and pulled until Miriam's hands lost their grip, sending her backward *hard* against her strapped-on backpack.

"FRANK!!" she screamed hysterically as Larry flung out of the bathroom like a mad man landing right on top of her.

He growled like a rabid dog attacking her as she fought him off, kicking and flailing her arms against his assault.

"Get off!" she grunted, *"GET OFF!"*

But Larry continued drooling on her, trying to bite.

"FRANK!!"

Suddenly from behind, Larry was knocked off his perch. Frank had walloped him a good one with a large metal candle holder, sending him flying against the wall. It had only stunned him.

"Over here!" a voice called.

Miriam turned to see the pastor as he held out his hand for her to come.

The two of them huddled in the corner watching the unbelievable event.

How can this be?

"Frank!" Miriam cried as Larry rose again, *"Watch out!"*

Larry charged at Frank, sending him tumbling to the floor.

"Get my wife out of here Tom!" he shouted as Larry climbed on top of Frank.

Miriam couldn't stand it. She grabbed a stack of hymnals and chucked them one by one at Larry's head. *"Take that!" she yelled.* It was enough to distract the crazy man so that Frank could get away.

"*Come on!*" the pastor called as he and Miriam helped Frank up, "*RUN!!*"

The three of them headed straight for the exit sign, pushing through the double doors of the church. They were outside and away from Larry at least, but something didn't look right outside. People were standing in the street...*people just like Larry.*

~~~

"*Look!*" Manuel pointed as he accelerated the Jeep Wagoneer toward the church, "the *Locos* are here too!"

"So are my *parents!*" Nadia cried, "*Look!*"

Sure, enough it was Frank and Miriam, but it appeared as though they had stumbled into the same kind of trouble as they had at the hospital. The mob had surrounded them as they barricaded themselves up against a white mini-van.

"*Get in!*" he shouted from the window as he swung the jeep sideways breaking hard, separating the *Locos* from his in-laws.

Shocked, with wide eyes, Frank yanked open the back door and pushed an elderly gentleman inside, then his wife, and then heaved himself is as well. "*Go-go-go!*" he shouted, slapping the back of the drivers seat.

The big Jeep Wagoneer spun its tires as it lit out of there immediately.

"*Whoa!*" Manuel shouted, "*That was close!* You guys okay?"

"We're fine!" Frank grunted, out of breath.

Miriam squealed as she leaned forward between the front seats, "*I can't believe you're here honey! How did you know where we'd be?*"

"Dad left a message on the answering machine," Nadia told her.

"Well at least he's good for something. I'm just happy you're okay."

"You too mom, *that was nasty!*"

"Hey, what about me?" Manuel butt in, teasing, "Didn't you miss your son-in-law?"

"*Aaa...Yup,*" his mother-in-law quickly answered, not even bothering to turn to him.

Manuel was probing for an '*I missed you too*' response, but that wasn't it. Even though he was teasing, part of him was serious. He just finished saving the lot of them with not even a thank you. At least she could acknowledge him. His mother-in-law always seemed to leave him out. Nadia touched his shoulder to prevent him from repeating his disgruntled thoughts out loud. It was almost as if she knew what he was thinking.

"We appreciate you Manuel...*and we missed you too!*" Frank sighed, elbowing his wife. "Lucky thing you two came along when you did or else that mob would have gotten us for sure."

Frank, always the peacemaker.

"Luck had nothing to do with it," the old man piped up. Manuel recognized him as the church pastor.

"Oh yes Tom, I stand corrected. It was God who orchestrated that!"

Bible thumpers! They never missed an opportunity.

Manuel had to chuckle to himself. If God had saved them, he'd like to ask why he let this happen in the first place. *Ridiculous!*

"What do you think happened to all those people?" Nadia asked.

"They're sick *Chica*! *I told you a thousand times!*"

"I beg your pardon?" Miriam snapped, glaring long and hard at her son-in-law.

Oh, if looks could kill. He could talk to his wife any way he pleased and it was none of her business.

Okay, so he was annoyed at the fact that whenever his wife was around her mother she turned into a bubblehead. *She knew*! He had explained it in depth along the way. The *Loco* that tried to attack her at the car, acted the same way. Manuel had no choice but to take a few swings at his head. *It wasn't pretty.*

Still, *she knew!* Didn't everyone know by now?

"*Sweetheart!* They have rabies!" Miriam told her.

"They have a whole lot more than rabies," the pastor added, "When you have rabies you die. You don't do what *Larry* did!"

Manuel looked puzzled as he eyed the white-haired gentleman in the rear-view mirror. Now he caught his attention. "What do you mean?"

Frank shushed the old guy immediately.

They knew something.

"We have to tell them," the pastor whispered, "How can we *not?*"

Nadia looked interested now. "Tell us what?"

Frank was beside himself. Manuel had never seen the man so upset before. Usually he was the calm one and his wife was irate.

"Sorry Frank," the old man apologized, "but kids...there seems to be some re-animation involved here. *They come back to life.*"

"*What? HAHAHA!*" Manuel couldn't stop himself from laughing. That was the silliest thing he'd ever heard. "*Chico!* That's impossible!"

Then the pastor told him Larry's story and it *was* compelling. But still, reanimation? *Please!* They had probably mistaken the man for dead. Happens all the time. People think they know how to read someone's pulse but they don't.

"Only medical professionals should pronounce someone dead," he told them, "otherwise...*we make mistakes.*"

"It *wasn't* a mistake," Miriam snapped back at him.

Easy!

Frank's face was red. He started shaking his head. "*NO!* He-he was cold. He was *dead!*"

"We're sure of it," the pastor added, "he had already gone stiff."

This whole thing annoyed Manuel, and his headache was pounding harder than ever. Obviously, these people believed what they were saying. He just didn't happen to agree.

"Okay, so let's assume you're correct. That would mean we're in big trouble. You're talking about a world-wide epidemic here. What appears to be the flu from contaminated water, manifests itself as rabies and gets passed on with a bite. Or so we assume. One person can infect a whole lot of people...and then if they don't die...the world as we know it is pretty well gone. How do we even fight them?"

Manuel was starting to scare himself. It had to be wrong.

"What about the antibiotics?" Miriam piped up.

"Yes!" Frank added, "We'll go to Fargo and get treated. My Jeep will make it. I bet you that's where everyone is. The military has gathered everyone and we were left behind.

"The military is a *joke!*" Manuel snapped back.

"*Whaaat?*" Miriam guffawed, "The military is no joke young man! I'll have you know my grandfather was is the war and..."

"No... Mom!" Nadia interrupted, "he's right. They tried to kill me."

"*What?*"

Nadia explained briefly as she darted her eyes over to her husband and then back to her mother. At least they were all on the same page now. Sort of anyway. But obviously they were still going to drive to Fargo. Manuel had his reservations about that but he was outnumbered. If he had his way...he'd head straight for the border.

As they drove into the blue noon sky, Manuel decided he'd stay out of the conversation from now on. It didn't matter what he said. Nobody was listening and he had too much of a headache to care right now.

So much had gone on in the last forty-eight hours for one man to comprehend. He'd concentrate on driving and that was going to be a challenge at best. The road was cluttered with garbage and abandoned cars.

As he numbed his brain to the chatter in the back seat, he set his thoughts on their silly theory. Could there really be something to it after all? He hoped not all the water was contaminated? If it included river water then he and Nadia had swallowed mouthfuls.

It was only a matter of time before they joined the ranks of the *Loco*.

Chapter 14

Gala Silverton tried not to let it bother her, but it did. How could treating a million people with a placebo possibly help? *It was shameful!*

The Department of Defence had deliberately sabotaged their own relief efforts. *Why?* Even her colleagues hadn't caught on. Left out of the loop again, but not for long. She'd hold a meeting with the staff just as soon as she was done with line up 155 in group 'B': Her designated relief sector.

A young woman with her two children stood in front of her, waiting for their turn to be next. Trust beamed from their eyes as they hoped for an antibiotic injection to protect them from contamination. *But it was all a lie.*

"Now, look away from the needle," she told the little girl, "you'll just feel a pinch."

The little girl began to wail. She was only three and Gala's heart sank when she had to inject it. Next, she'd have to take a blood sample to confirm she was blood group 'B' positive. "I'm almost done sweetie, we just need to prick your finger."

Within moments, the test confirmed her blood type was correct. Gala stamped her hand with a 'B' plus and asked her older sister to take a seat.

"I don't know why you have to do this," the girl's mother complained, "I already told them both girls are 'B' positive when we came in. I'm the only one that's an 'O'."

Gala nodded and didn't answer the mother's question. She continued administering the needle and then confirmed the same blood type as her sister.

"Wait for mommy over there," the mother told her young daughters, "It's my turn now."

Smiling, Gala lifted the woman's sleeve. "You said you were an 'O'?"

"Yes...but I had to stand in this line because of my girls. I hope that's okay. Or...should I go to the 'O' sector now?"

"No, I can test you here," Gala assured her, looking around to make sure military personnel were not eavesdropping again. Others had tried to do what this mother did but were not allowed. Someone always directed them to the proper sector. But she would squeeze her in if nobody was looking.

"Why do they need to know our blood types anyway?" the mother asked.

"Just procedure...so that we give you the proper antibiotics," she lied.

It was surprising that the Department of Defence wanted to type their blood. What did it matter anyway? Yet...Gala had a sneaking suspicion this whole ruse was all about blood typing. The placebo was just a cover to get blood type information. But then, she couldn't be sure. The only thing she was sure about was the placebo wasn't an antibiotic. Her private analysis proved it last night when she questioned the dosage per weight.

"No need to adjust the dosage," she was told, "everyone gets the same."

Like beans, everyone gets the same. She hadn't been studying medicine for thirty years for nothing. How could she give a baby the same dose as an adult male? *It was ridiculous.* That's what prompted her to investigate.

Gala held a cotton ball to the mother's arm and pasted the band aide over it. "Now, the blood test should only take a few more minutes."

"You definitely are an 'O'... *oh wait...*" Gala whispered, "you have no *Rhesus Factor...ummm!*" Gala looked around trying not to get caught. She hadn't expected the woman to be a negative. The military took all negatives away for some reason...and they hadn't gotten any 'O' negatives in the last twenty-four hours. The last one was taken away kicking and screaming.

"What does *that* mean?" the mother asked, parroting her whisper to Gala's.

"It means you have to go to sector 'O' after all."

"*NO!*" the mother shouted loudly, "me and my girls have been here *all day!* This is ridiculous! I can't put them through that *again! I WON'T!*"

Gala wished the woman had not done that. She was only bringing attention to herself and that wasn't good. Now the guards were heading her way.

"We got a problem over here?" one of the soldiers asked, readying his semi-automatic machine gun.

No! Gala wanted to say, but the woman wouldn't let her.

"Yes officer! She tells me I have to join the line up in sector 'O' and I've been here all day with my little girls already!"

"What's her type?" he asked bending over Gala's results.

The soldier immediately blew a whistle, motioning other soldiers to come. "Ma'am, you're going to have to come with us!" he said, pulling her arms behind her back and handcuffing her like a criminal.

"*No...my GIRLS!*" she cried frantically.

"Check them!" another commanded his comrades, observing the girl's stamps on their hands. "Just 'B' positives," the one said discarding the children like they didn't matter. "Someone will take your girls to sector zero and you can join them later."

But Gala knew that was another lie. There was no sector zero. *What the heck was going on?* "Girls," she tried to calm them, "go with the officers and your mommy will come get you later."

It killed her to add to the deception that was going on, but for the time being, even though the girls were still sobbing, she could tell the situation had been diffused. *Sad!*

Could they be needing blood donors? Perhaps that was what was going on here. 'O' negative blood types were the universal blood donors after all?

It was probably that, but why such brutality? Couldn't they just ask without traumatizing people? But then, that was the government for you.

One thing was for sure, she was going to snoop around some more and find out the truth...*because this was not right!*

~~~~

"The place looks like a concentration camp if you ask me," Ebenezer Hofstein whispered to the distraught woman who had done nothing but bawl for the past two hours.

He had been handcuffed and brought here the same way as she had. They had all been taken from their families against their will; held hostage by people that reminded Ebenezer of his youth; his days in the Warsaw ghetto.

As far as he could tell, they were only after one thing: *Blood sucking Nazi vampires!*

"What is your name dear?" he asked as he sat his old bones down beside her.

"Yvonne," she sniffled.

"Now that's a pretty name."

"Thanks...*I guess.*"

At least the woman had stopped her awful bawling. Now he could at least have a conversation, find out what was happening on the outside world. He'd been trapped in there for two days. And the numbers were growing. "Do you know if they're still giving out antibiotics?"

"Yes, my girls both got them. But then they took *me* away. I don't know why?"

"They want your blood."

"What? *Why?*"

Ebenezer didn't have any answers to offer. He wished he did. The only thing he knew was the medical staff came in and took two vials of blood from each person three times a day. That's why they were all laying down on cots he presumed. Forcing them to give blood was exhausting not to mention *barbaric.*

"As far as I can tell, they are only interested in people with Rhesus Negative 'O' types. Let me guess...that's what you are Yvonne. Am I correct?"

"Correct!'

"I've been noticing they don't care what age, colour, or creed we are...as long as we have the right blood type. But there are more of us that are white, than any other colours. In my day, it was the Jew they singled out."

"In your day?"

Ebenezer flashed his numbered tattoo from Warsaw. It always spoke volumes.

"*I'm sorry,*" Yvonne looked away.

"Don't be sorry! Being there just helps me recognize when something isn't right. Like now. These people are animals. I don't care what anybody says. They can't keep us here for whatever lab experiments they want even if it's stamped with the U.S Department of Defence's approval. It's a human rights violation."

"And so...what do we do about it? We can't fight the government!"

"That's dangerously similar to what was said in Warsaw," Ebenezer frowned, knowing all too well the memories were already flooding back to him. "*We just do!*"

But before Yvonne could reply, machine guns peppered the crowd outside the chain-linked fence that segregated them.

"*What on earth?*" Ebenezer didn't know if he should run or hide under his cot. "*They're shooting people out there!*"

"*Get down!*" Yvonne shouted, pulling him down to the hard cement floor. It was a waiting game. Then more gun fire. *Warsaw...he was running with his mother. She was shot...falling. Left on the dirty ground with a bullet in her back.*

Stop it Ebenezer! He told himself, shaking his head to get rid of the disturbing memory. But only dizziness prevailed.

One by one, they watched the assault as helpless people clung to the fence, dropping, hanging in response to the terrible firing squad he knew all too well.

It really *was* the end this time!

Gala heard it, but she couldn't believe it. Everyone was going mad. She had to get out of there before the mob made it impossible.

She turned toward the exit sign, but it was one of *them*: A sick person. She knew it would happen sooner or later. In the last hour alone, guards had to restrain what appeared to be sick feverish individuals with some sort of delusional response that was very similar to rabies. *They were biting people!*

And the military was shooting back!

"Over here!" her co-worker yelled, holding a hand for her to come. But it was too late, he was attacked from all sides by a biting, clawing, mob.

She ran through the large warehouse, passed by crying children and injured people laying in her way, until she reached the outside. The bright sunlight hit her like a bomb. It was hard to see anything; hard to find her way.

People were screaming...*biting*...shooting!

They were *all* savages!

"Over here lady!" a voice called from behind a fence.

She squinted, stepped over the dead, and darted unnoticed to the other side where an elderly man and the young woman they had handcuffed earlier, were hiding.

The two were the only ones left in a room full of empty cots. It appeared to be an old airplane hangar with chain-linked fence surrounding it.

These were the guinea pigs.

"We can't stay here!" she told them, "They're everywhere!"

"We can hide!" the old man whispered, "Come!"

Against her better judgement she went with the old man and the young woman. They brought her to an old walk in freezer that had been converted into a storage closet. They pulled the big metal door shut with a thud and locked themselves in.

"*There!*" the old man said, "we're safe...*for now!*"

In silence they all slumped down against the wall and waited in the dark, panting and breathing hard. The young woman switched on her cell phone illuminating their surroundings.

"This is a bomb shelter I think," Yvonne presumed. "Look at the food! And here's an old oil lamp. Anyone got a light?"

The young woman pulled out a lighter as her cigarettes dropped to the ground. Thank heaven she was a smoker. Under normal circumstances, as a doctor, she would have scolded her...but not now.

"Thank you..."

"*Yvonne*...you can call me *Yvonne.*"

"Yvonne," she repeated while lighting the wick of the oil lantern, lowering the glass. "I'm Gala...and you are?" she asked the old man.

"Ebenezer."

"Pleased to meet you both. Wish it was under better circumstances. Now, do any of you know what's going on?"

The man nodded, "Warsaw lady...*all over again!*"

Chapter 15

The four-hour drive to Fargo was taking longer than expected. They had stopped far too many times for bathroom breaks and stretches not to mention dodging obstacles on the highway like the bus that overturned a mile back. It blocked the highway causing Manuel to do some off-roading. Luckily, they were back on the highway now heading south about an hour north of Fargo. They'd be there soon, hopefully before the sun went down.

It was a long trek with a headache, yet he refused to give up the wheel. Between all five of them, he was the most experienced in emergencies and who knew what they would encounter on the way. He had to be prepared for anything.

So far, they were the only vehicle on the road. Manuel didn't know if that was a good thing or a bad one.

But he kept on.

For the most part, the group had been sleeping but now they were all wide awake except for him, though he wasn't about to tell them that.

It was his wife that he worried about the most. Losing a baby was a big deal. Anything could happen. He'd done everything he was trained to do to take care of her, yet for some reason at the last pit stop he wondered about the diagnosis. He followed his wife into the bathroom and locked the door.

"Don't be embarrassed babe," he told her. "I need to check to see what's going on down there."

"Manuel! *Jeepers!* No!"

"C'mon I'm a professional. I need to check for haemorrhaging. I do this all the time."

"Well not on me you don't!"

"*Please!* I'll be quick."

"*Fine!*"

And so, he got his way, and what he found didn't make sense. There was no blood at all. Could she still be pregnant? He knew of many cases where a woman bled for a while but remained pregnant.

"*Chica*, there's nothing there."

"What do you mean *nothing?*"

"I mean, you're not bleeding anymore...*nothing.*"

"What does that mean?"

Manuel wanted to give her hope but he didn't know if he should. He decided to be as professional as he could.

"*Well*...just how far along do you actually think you were?

Manuel could tell she was getting upset but he didn't intend that. Tears started forming in her eyes as she sobbed, "*Three months.*"

"*What? Are you serious?*"

"I didn't want to tell you. I didn't want anyone to find out."

"Oh *Chica!*" he pulled her into an embrace, "you should have told me!"

"I didn't want my dad chasing you down the isle with a shotgun!"

Well that made him laugh, yet, he did feel a little hurt. Still, he understood. They would have to work on better communication skills in the future...if there still was a future.

"So, the two weeks before our wedding and the two weeks we spent in the Bahamas you already knew for sure?"

"*Yes,*" his wife sheepishly answered, pouting her bottom lip out.

He loved when she did that. How could he be mad at *that?*

Breathing heavily with a sigh, he just continued to hug her. "*K*...in the future, I need to know these things *Chica*. I'm part of this you know."

"*I'm sorry!*" she sobbed, "It doesn't matter anyway. *There is no baby now!*"

"Not necessarily."

"What do you mean?"

He told her there could be a chance, *a small chance,* that she was still pregnant. The bleeding had stopped completely and that was a good sign.

"How do you feel?'

"*Terrible!* No cramps, but my stomach has been nauseous the whole trip."

"Well that would be a good sign."

Nadia stuck out her tongue in fun. "*For you maybe.*"

He was glad she was her playful self again. That told him she was getting better from whatever trauma had caused the bleeding. At least they could continue on without him worrying of her haemorrhaging.

Maybe there was still a chance he'd be a father in a few months. *Six* to be exact. *Should have picked up a pregnancy test from the hospital numskull!*

Excitement washed over him...and then a doom so heavy he had to turn away from her. *They could lose it all if they were sick.*

All the more reason to push on to Fargo.

~~~~~

Tom reached for his backpack and pulled his Bible out. He was glad he had Frank put it in there at the last minute. They would need it if his assumptions were correct. And what he was thinking was, they could be entering the tribulation period mentioned in prophecy. He didn't know how far into it they were, but it was definitely the End Times.

Oh, he'd never tell anyone *that*, but he would share a very interesting verse with the group. "Listen to this you guys," he said, flipping to the right page, " I found a verse in the Bible that speaks about the crazy people."

"You mean *Locos?*" both Nadia and Manuel corrected in unison and then smiled at each other.

They seemed to like giving the crazy people a name. "Locos then," he said to please them. "Now listen...In Zechariah 14:12 and 13 it says, *'And the Lord will send a plague on all the nations that fought against Jerusalem. Their people will become like walking corpses, their flesh rotting away. Their eyes will rot in their sockets, and their tongues will rot in their mouths.*

"*'On that day they will be terrified, stricken by the Lord with great panic. They will fight their neighbors hand to hand.'*"

"Is that not *something?*"

The entire vehicle was struck with silence. Had he said too much? Only the hum of the big tires on the pavement answered him.

"Well?"

"Pastor, I don't think it's a good time to be reading the Bible," Miriam piped up.

Everyone else in the vehicle remained silent.

"You're scaring people *el abuelo!*" Manuel frowned, eyeing him in the rear-view mirror shaking his head.

"Better to be scared than unprepared," Tom snapped back. "We need to be prepared people! Larry came back from the dead! His eyes were sunken...I *saw* them...and he was a walking corpse...*because of this plague!* What's wrong with everyone? Don't you see what's happening here?"

"Tom!" Frank shushed him, putting his hand on the Bible, "another time."

It was maddening! They didn't want to listen to him, just like his congregation, just like the board. Now, when it mattered the most, they wanted...no *chose*, to be in the dark. He didn't understand it at all.

Well...he wouldn't say another word. They were probably thinking the same as him.

Stupid old man!

~~~

Nadia thought perhaps she was the only one in the vehicle that wanted to hear more of the sermon but she didn't dare say so. She knew the Bible verse had merit and sounded like the all too familiar evil that lingered in her dream.

She tried to keep her eyes open but succumbed to her nodding head and an unwanted slumber that would match the chaos around them and then some.

"You can't have it!" she shouted, standing there in chains. "I'm keeping my baby!"

"Then we'll find another way!" the serpent hissed, slithering off to the hot coals where it came from.

She was glad it was gone. But next to her, chained by hand and foot, she saw the others.

Corpses, all of them. Their eyes rotting, dripping with maggots and blood. The stench was horrible.

Teeth peeked through a fleshy decomposed jaw as a chained-up corpse snapped back at her. At least it couldn't come any closer.

Suddenly, a light shone in the distance; the kind of light that people always talk bout in near death experiences. Was she going to die now? Maybe she already had?

Slowly, it came closer until it hovered right in front of her.

"Leave me alone!"

But the light wouldn't leave her alone. A human form stepped out of the light and spoke to her. "Come with me."

"I'm chained up!" she answered as she tugged.

"Break the chains that bind you, and throw off the ropes that hold you down."

But Nadia didn't know how she was supposed to do that. "You ask me to do the impossible," she cried, "I can't!"

"With man, this is impossible, but with God all things are possible."

"Are you God?"

Then the form suddenly turned sharply, as the beast returned with a vengeance.

"Leave this place!" the beast shouted as it charged the light, missing its target completely.

"This is my blood of the covenant," the light replied.

"She is NOT your blood!" the beast snapped back.

"I bought her with a price! I will fight to the death for her!"

"So be it!" the beast charged, grabbing a long silver sword. The light held its ground as it hovered in front of her to protect her.

With one swing of the blade, the sword pushed through the light, through the human form that stepped out of the light, and right into her own heart.

A pain so immense, so unbelievable, crushed her chest as it heaved against the horror. "I don't want to die!"

"You have died with me Nadia," the light said, "now shall you live!"

"Not if I can help it!" the beast growled again, grabbing her by the throat as the light disappeared, leaving her to suffer alone. "You are still mine!"

Nadia screamed as she awakened suddenly. *It was just a dream! It was just a dream!* She put her hand to her fast-beating heart to feel the blade...*nothing!* Breathing hard, she turned to Manuel at the wheel, still driving the Jeep down the highway in the dusk.

"*What?*" he asked with wide eyes, "another dream?"

All she could do was node, throwing her head back against the head-rest as she squeezed her eyelids closed to the salty tears that channelled down her cheeks.

"Wanna talk about it?"

She shook her head *no*, hoping she hadn't woken the others up in the back seat.

Was she sick? Was she going to turn *Loco*? Was she going to come back to life and bite people too? All these thoughts throbbed in her head like blood pulsing through her veins. *And what about the baby?*

She wished these dreams would stop plaguing her.

"*Uh oh!*" Manuel suddenly interrupted her thoughts as he made an announcement. "You guys better wake up. *We got trouble!*"

Nadia noticed they just passed the entrance sign to *119 Wing, Air National Guard.* They must be at the Fargo base. Ahead, rather than the usual military personnel at the gate, a mob of hungry *Locos* charged their way.

Chapter 16

Yvonne the young woman, held her hands over her ears so she couldn't hear the screaming people outside the bomb shelter. Gala on the other hand, had to listen for her own sanity. Perhaps her tolerance level was higher. After all, she'd worked as a Haematologist for years and knew trauma first hand.

The government had rushed her to the base the moment the incident happened, supposedly to help with distribution of the antibiotics. But a placebo? That was an insult. Her research apparently meant nothing: A total waste of time. Nurses could give boosters. They didn't need someone who studied blood to distribute a placebo.

Yet considering the screaming chaos outside, they were definitely dealing with a blood born virus. The contaminates in the water sample she'd been studying implicated some sort of HIV mix with unknown elements. It was unlike anything she'd ever studied. She'd wanted to do more tests but was shut down immediately when she probed for more info, especially when she mentioned the similarities to Creutzfeldt-Jakob Disease.

No, she didn't think they were dealing with CJD but is sure made her wonder. Yet, with all her research, none of it mattered in the end anyway. They didn't even consider her advice or expertise, dismissing her like she was some silly intern.

They seemed to be fishing for something she hadn't even considered: A blood type connection. It made no sense, yet it fascinated her at the same time. Could there be certain people who had natural immunity like those resistant to HIV and Smallpox? Historically the odd person survived the Bubonic Plague too and nobody knew why. Could it be they carried Rhesus negative blood? Could that be the case now?

Light bulbs went off in Gala's head as the screaming started to diminish. Maybe they wouldn't have to stay in the bomb shelter for long. It was getting hard to breathe with the fumes of the lantern hovering in the air. Obviously, there was no ventilation. They would have to find a new place to hide, either that or blow out the light and sit in the dark.

"Are you okay Yvonne?" she asked the sobbing, chest heaving woman.

"*No, I'm not*...and you shouldn't be either! *We're all gonna die!*"

"Now ladies," Ebenezer interrupted, "let's calm down. I think we should take a look outside. It's getting quieter out there."

Gala shook her head, agreeing with the old man. He had been through a lot more than both of them put together. At least there was someone she could rely on. Yvonne was a loose cannon.

"Okay!" Gala grunted as she stood up, "I'll open the door a crack and peek out."

"*I don't think we should!*" Yvonne complained.

"I'm just going to crack it an inch. I'll pull it closed the moment I see anything dangerous. *I promise.*"

But Yvonne began to sob even louder.

"Sweetheart!" Ebenezer sighed, trying to comfort, "It will be fine...but you need to hush or they will find us. *Please!*"

The old man shushed her like a child as Gala blew out the lantern and set it down with a hollow clunk on the cold cement floor.

Rattling the lock, Gala opened the creaky door, clenching her teeth as if that would help the noisy door be quiet. She peeked her eye through the one-inch crack she made in the door. Luckily the emergency generator still had a few lights on in the hangar.

But what she saw was unspeakable.

Bloody bodies everywhere; children, women, old, young...torn like ravenous wolves had killed them for sport. It turned her stomach as a child lay in front of the doorway, blocking their exit.

In a moment that seemed to last forever, Gala surveyed the young lifeless child in front of her. She couldn't be more than six years old. It was hard to make out the face with her blood-matted blonde hair stuck to her features. She was the victim here, attacked by those carrying the virus. Bite marks assaulted her bare arms and blood oozed out of her perforated neck. Gala had to turn away.

From what it looked like, it was all but deserted out there. Only the carnage remained.

Gulping hard, she shut the door and rested her forehead against it. What should she tell them about *this?*

"What did you see?" Ebenezer asked immediately.

"Nobody left." *Nobody except the dead.*

"Good! then let's get out of here."

"I don't think that's such a good idea!" Yvonne sobbed.

Ignoring her, Gala helped the old man up and guided him to the door. Yvonne shuffled behind him in the dark. "Now, follow me no matter what you see," she told them both.

"*Why?* What will we see?" Yvonne whimpered.

Gala just sighed. Luckily, they couldn't see her own teary eyes. She'd let them discover the horror themselves. There was no way she could prepare them for *that!*

"On the count of three, I want you guys to push this door hard! *Ok?*"

All she could hear was Yvonne repeatedly asking, *why?*

"*One...two...three!*"

The three of them heaved forward, pushing what Gala knew was a young body away from the door so they could get out. What she wasn't prepared for, was Yvonne's reaction once they exited the bomb shelter and discovered the child.

"*Mindy! BABY!*" Yvonne suddenly shrieked in horror. It was *her* child.

Oh nooo!

The distraught mother bent down on her knees and held her dead child, wailing so loudly that Gala was sure the whole world could hear them!

~~~

It was heartbreaking! Flashes of memories assaulted Ebenezer's clouded judgement. *Warsaw!* Children were dead and dieing in the street: *His friends!*

He could hear his own heart beating loudly in his chest as his ears muffled the screaming sounds around him. His vision blurred with the bloody horror before him but he couldn't even move his frozen feet!

"*Ebenezer!*" a muffled figure called in front of him.

But he couldn't recognize who it was.

"*RUN!*"

This time he felt a tug at his arm. She was pulling him, slapping him!

"*Ouch!* That hurt!"

"Good! Now *RUN!*"

And then...there in front of him, he realized the devil himself had come. The little girl who had been dead a minute ago had now risen to attack her own mother, biting her blood pulsing neck.

What in heavens name...?

Numbness grew as he felt his body being tugged away from the bloody scene. There was no escaping what was happening here: *Humanity had failed!*

The two of them now hop-skipped backwards as they tried to escape, running as far away from the mayhem as possible.

"*STOP!*" he finally said, pulling his arm away from the middle-aged woman.

All he wanted to do was rest for a minute, but he knew a minute would be all it took for the sick people to catch up to them and attack them.

Without breathing, he let Gala pull him again. This time they'd duck behind an abandoned vehicle to catch their breath.

"*Did you see that*?" he panted.

"*Shhhh!*"

Gala crouched beside him bug-eyed in silence.

It was a game of cat and mouse. And they were the mice; the Jews. Once again victims of the Nazi regime; the flesh-eating Nazis.

Suddenly he heard soldiers running, then machine guns pepper the dark night. If they were able, they should escape the ghetto now before the Germans trapped them in.

"Ebenezer?" Gala's whispered, "are you okay?"

Ebenezer just nodded, but he knew he was somewhere far away, somewhere she couldn't understand. He wanted to stop his mind from spiralling but he couldn't. The *Gestapo* was coming! *"Hurry!* We need to find *Yahbez!* He will know what to do!"

"What?"

She didn't understand. She was a foolish girl. If they caught her, he knew what they would do. And worse, he would also be gassed. No, they would have to sneak through the sewers like rats. It was the only way out of Warsaw. The streets would already be cordoned off.

But Gala wouldn't co-operate. She stood and waved at the Gestapo like an idiot. Now they were dead for sure! *Schlub!*

~~~~

As soon as they saw her, the soldiers headed their way. "Don't shoot! We're *not* sick!"

With hands up Gala stepped out in front of the car she and Ebenezer were hiding behind. Yes, it was risky but what else could she do? The old man was paralyzed with fear and no use to her at all.

"Who else is with you?" one of the soldiers asked behind the barrel of his semi- automatic machine gun.

"An old man! *Don't shoot!*"

She pulled Ebenezer up by his jacket; he was so resistant. He didn't understand they were safe now with the soldiers...*If she could convince them they weren't a threat anyway.*

With arms still in the air, standing next to the shaking old man, she explained herself. "I'm Doctor Gala Silverton and this is my patient."

They didn't seem to like that much; guns steadied only on Ebenezer now. *Ops, wrong choice of words.* "*No no no!* he isn't sick. He has a Rhesus clearance. I need to get him to the lab! Can you help us?" *It was mostly a bluff but it would do.*

"*Ma'am*, the whole base has been compromised!"

"I know, but what about the lab?" *They knew what she meant.*

The group of soldiers talked amongst themselves for a minute, obviously deciding their fate. Hopefully they would take her to the top-secret underground research lab. It would've gone into lockdown the moment the outbreaks started, but she had enough security clearance to bypass that.

"*Please!* I have the pass code! I can get you in too." *Well...she only hoped they'd let the soldiers in.* She wasn't in charge of the lab as it was so rudely pointed out to her several times since her arrival.

"Fine! Come with us then!"

Gala practically dragged Ebenezer over to the soldiers. His eyes had a wild look in them. It was obvious he didn't' trust them at all. But it was either trust them or get attacked by a mob of sick, flesh eating, people who didn't stay dead.

After a long trek across the tarmac in the dark of night, protected by military *SWAT* personnel with machine guns, they finally arrived at their destination: The entrance to the underground facility that most people didn't even know about.

Once inside, the soldiers carried out protective stances, searching around doorways for sick people.

"Clear!" they informed, motioning Gala and Ebenezer to follow.

"It has voice recognition software and retina I.D," she told them as they all waited for the big metal door that guarded the research lab to let them in. All eyes were on her.

Gala spoke the pass code clearly into the computer, repeating her name and then bending in for the eye scan. The door beeped and unlocked, opening at once. Gala repeated another pass code so it would lock them in.

But behind the door, a new group of people were waiting: White coated professionals, her colleagues, and they were *not* happy.

"Drop the weapons!" the man said, speaking for the group of white coated doctors who were also armed. It looked like around twenty male doctors had decided to protect the lab and prevent anyone from entering.

"*George? P-Peter?* You all know me!" she stuttered.

"You might as well march right back up those stairs Dr Silverton!" Peter ordered, "because we're not letting you in! We'll shoot you *all* before we ever let that happen."

The soldiers had lowered their weapons and looked angry. "Don't bother! We'll go!" one said, "Just back off and let us take our guns."

"I'm not going anywhere! I *work* here! Remember?" Gala spat back.

"Fine!" Peter agreed, nodding his head, "get the soldiers out of here then!"

He let them slowly back away, weapons in hand. Gala was told to let them out the same way they came in. *It was ridiculous!* The soldiers had helped them and this was the thanks they were getting. "I'm sorry!" she apologized, as the last one left.

Once Gala returned to the two doctors who remained behind to wait for her, she realized she had left Ebenezer with them.

"Where's the old man?" she asked.

"The other doctors took him inside already. *He told us his secret.*"

"What secret?"

"I think you know," the armed doctor snapped back. "Why didn't you tell us you had another lab rat?"

"A what?"

"A *negative* Dr Silverton. Don't play dumb with us."

So, there is a definite blood connection.

Chapter 17

They were on top of the Jeep now!

For the last half hour, Tom watched in horror as soldiers shot down the many devils. But still, they kept on coming and now they were rocking the vehicle, trying to get inside.

The women and their continuous screaming didn't help matters much. It was hard to think, hard to pray. *God! Help us now in our time of need!*

If this was the end, he was ready. He'd lived a long life. But this was not exactly how he pictured meeting his maker. They were sitting ducks. His instinct was to fight back even in his old age. *"Can't we do something?"*

"Like *WHAT?*" Manuel shouted back.

"I don't know!"

The rocking motion became unbearable. *They were going to turn them on their side!*

"Grab a weapon!" Manuel shouted, *"They're pushing us over!"*

"I packed daddy's gun," Nadia shouted, "But it's under all the stuff in the back."

"Too late for the gun," Manuel bellowed again, *"Just grab anything!"*

Tom grabbed what he could find but figured they didn't stand a chance against the crowd that surrounded them. At least he'd go out fighting.

As the vehicle moaned to its side, the front and back passenger windows shattered. He and Nadia were trapped against the cold pavement and broken glass. It was only a matter of time before they righted the jeep and crawled in the broken windows.

Manuel clung to the steering wheel, trying to hold himself in the seat so he wouldn't crush his wife. Frank and Miriam were already crushing *him*. It was hard to breathe.

Then Tom felt the *Locos* assault the vehicle once more, rocking it back to four wheels with a thud and more shattered glass.

"You are my refuge and strength," he prayed with tire iron in hand. Ironic, that it had come to this: saving himself instead of allowing God to fight his battles as he'd always preached. But this was something entirely different. *Forgive me God!*

He swung the tire iron against the foul creatures trying to get inside, beating them one by one. Manuel and Frank did the same, protecting their windows.

But if they lost the front window, they would all be goners.

Nadia wasn't doing too well. She had chosen a floor matt as her weapon, batting it against the intruders without much success. He tried to help her, but it was too late. They were pulling her from the vehicle.

"NO!" Manuel shouted, looking over to her, unable to help. But they kept pulling at his wife. Then in the distance, he heard the sounds of the welcome Cavalry. Machine guns peppered the air and started taking down one *Loco* at a time until the threat was completely gone.

"Are you people Okay?" the soldier said rushing up to them.

Everyone was still in the vehicle except Nadia.

"My wife! *Where is she?*"

"*BABY?*" Miriam cried.

They all got out and found Nadia under a couple dead *Locos*. She was still alive.

Manuel rushed up to her immediately, "*Chica?*"

Tom saw the love he had for her...and the pain. It was unbelievable. Her parents were sobbing as well. His heart was also crying at the carnage he now saw around him. *How could God allow this?*

"*ARE YOU BITTEN?*" Manuel shouted, frantically searching her body.

Then they all saw it: Flesh had been torn from her shoulder and neck.

"Sir!" a soldier commanded, pointing the gun at Nadia now. "She's been compromised! *PLEASE STAND BACK!*"

"*NO!*" they all cried.

"You are *NOT* going to shoot my wife!"

"Then you'll *all* be shot!"

Manuel stood up to fight. Miriam dropped to her knees. Tom began to pray. "Lord in heaven, stop this *horror!*"

Frank picked up Tom's tire iron and threw it to Manuel. "You *won't* shoot *my* daughter!"

But the soldier held his ground, aiming his weapon at Nadia. His comrade held his gun steady on Manuel, and the others aimed ready to shoot anyone who tried anything.

"You guys can't save her! *She's infected!*" the soldier explained. "It's too late! I have to kill her before..."

"Just try it *Chico!*" Manuel snapped back in anger, slapping the tire iron into his left hand ready for a fight.

Then in the distance, an army jeep roared toward them blinding them with its high beams. A doctor with a long white trench coat stepped out of the vehicle. "*Please!*" he said, holding up his hands in surrender, "everybody lower your weapons. There's been enough killing. I'm looking for survivors. *Now please!* Has anyone been bitten?"

"Doctor, this one has!" the soldier told him right away, pointing to Nadia as he and the other soldiers lowered their weapons.

"How long?" the doctor asked, checking Nadia's bloody neck.

"Minutes only," Manuel answered hopeful. "Can you help her?"

"What blood type is she?"

Manuel crinkled his forehead, "What does *that* matter?"

"Oh, *it matters.*"

"She's an 'O'," Miriam blurted out.

"Good...we need 'O's."

"Look, I'm a fireman *and* paramedic and she doesn't need a blood transfusion, she just needs the antibiotics we came for...and she can't give blood either," Manuel looked suspiciously over to Miriam as if he had a secret. "."

"Of course, she can!" Miriam blurted out again.

"*NO!* Miriam...she *can't!*"

The two of them obviously had a hidden vendetta against each other but this was not the time. "Miriam shhh," Tom stopped her and touched her arm. He shook his head and pulled her back to him and Frank. "Let her husband deal with this."

"Does she have a condition that prevents her from giving blood?" the doctor asked.

"*Yes!*" Manuel replied looking over to her parents.

"And that would be...?"

"*Umm...*" Manuel raked his hands through his hair, "I'd rather tell you in private."

"You can tell me *right now!*"

Manuel looked uneasy and bent down to whisper in his wife's ear. "Fine...*She's three months pregnant.*"

Tom heard the awful gasp from Miriam as he stood beside her. He thought the woman was about to faint. This was obviously *not* something she knew about *or* wanted. He guessed it was more like a shock to both parents.

"*Sorry mom...dad!*" Nadia bawled into her hands.

The doctor checked her vitals and continued asking questions. "So, what are you *not* telling me?"

"She's...*been spotting,*" Manuel choked, "...we thought miscarriage but..."

Miriam gasped again. Nadia just kept sobbing.

"And what medications? What have you been giving her?"

"I stopped at the hospital and got her some antibiotics and some Tylenol. But does this really matter?"

"Yes! Now what else did you give her?"

Tom wondered why he had to question them *there,* and why he was being so mean about it. The poor girl had already been traumatized enough as it was.

"Well?" the doctor continued to probe.

Manuel shook his head trying to think. "Um...I guess I gave her a shot of *RhoGam* as well but..."

"*WHAT?*" the doctor interrupted with surprise.

The way he answered didn't sound right. Something fishy was going on.

"*I'm taking only her!*"

"Over my dead body you are!" Manuel snapped back, "*I'm going with her!*"

The soldiers immediately aimed their weapons on Manuel again. "As you wish!"

"*No Manuel, Don't! I'll be fine!*" Nadia pleaded as she got up and went with the doctor, showing them that she was capable.

"The rest of you can go with the soldiers," the doctor told them as he helped Nadia into the vehicle, "they'll see to it that you have somewhere safe to stay."

But for some reason, Tom didn't trust him. It was written all over his face.

~~~~

They were taken underground to a room at the end of a long empty corridor. It was large, white, and an elderly gentleman shared the room with them. At least they had heat but this place gave Manuel an uneasy feeling. Lately everything gave him an uneasy feeling. It had been three days and he still had no word about Nadia.

His mother-in-law wasn't speaking to him but at this point he really didn't care. He sat in a corner by himself sulking.

"*Why didn't you tell us?!*" she screamed at him the first day.

"Because I didn't know!"

"*What?*" Miriam attacked even further, "Then you're an *incompetent fool!*"

"Miriam, stop!" Frank said trying to control his wife.

"No Frank, *I will not!* You know you're just as upset as I am. I'd like some answers. What was all that talk about starting a family after the wedding, when my daughter was already pregnant walking down the isle? *You jerk!* Did you just marry her because you knocked her up?"

"*NO!* Didn't you hear me? *I said I DIDN'T KNOW!*"

"*Baaah!* I don't believe you. You're an *idiot,* just like I thought!"

So, the truth comes out! He knew she hated him from the start. Well that was fine with him. He didn't need them. They could sit over there in the corner talking with the two old farts all day and he would be better off! *Gringos!* All he cared about was Nadia anyway. He married *her*...not her stupid family!

Manuel recalled the many unpleasant conversations that followed, mostly from Miriam. It was a direct attack on him and he had asked to be put in another room, but the doctor always said no. When he asked about his wife, he was always told the same thing: Sorry, it's restricted information. *What's restricted about his wife?* Is she dead or alive?

Hopefully they had given her antibiotics for the sickness in time. At least she had a chance here but the place was driving him nuts. It felt like a jail. They couldn't keep him there against his will.

Again, he banged on the metal door and again there was no answer.

The soldiers had been summoned to hand them over to the doctors shortly after Nadia was taken away. He had hoped they were taking him to his wife after all, but the quarantine room was in a deserted wing of what appeared to be an old underground military hospital, and he was told Nadia wasn't in that section of the hospital anyway. And who knew how big the place was. He couldn't even find out. From what he could make of it, the computerized locking system prevented any means of escape.

The only time the doctor came in was to deliver their rations of food for the day, that and take samples of their blood. He didn't see how that was quarantine procedure. Didn't they have to give them antibiotics and tests? Why just the blood samples? Where was the vaccine?

Manuel sunk his head in his hands, sighing. He rubbed his stubble face, then looked at the stamp they pasted on his hand with some kind of ink that didn't wash off. 'O' positive it said. Yeah, he was an 'O', so what! It was what was on the other hand that made him scratch his head.

With his daily walk-a-bout around the room to stretch his legs, he deliberately tried to annoy his mother-in-law by walking as close to her as possible, glaring at her without saying a word. It was then that he noticed she had the same blood type as him, and so did Frank. The pastor had 'A' positive and the old Jewish man had the same blood type as Nadia: 'O' negative. Then she noticed his in-law's other hand had been stamped with the word *Allele,* same as him. What did that mean? He tried to recall from his paramedic training.

As far as he could remember it was some blood term. He wished he could remember for sure, but he couldn't. What were they up to? For some reason he didn't believe this was a real quarantine. Were they using them? *For what?*

One thing was certain: He wasn't sticking around to find out.

~~~~

The green military cots in the quarantine room were very uncomfortable. How was anyone supposed to sleep on them? Yet, with the loud snoring going on, Miriam figured at least some people could, namely the old Jewish man Ebenezer. He was quite the character, unshaven with his own unique scent.

Ebenezer had hit it off with Frank and the pastor early on. She was glad they had each other to pass the time with. That good-for-nothing son-in-law of hers could snub them forever if all she cared. She just couldn't believe how rude he was being. He only knew Nadia for a short time, *they* knew her for a lifetime. Who did he think he was, thinking he was the only one who cared about her? It was driving her crazy not knowing where her daughter was or how she was doing but you didn't see *her* acting like a baby sulking in the corner. *It was childish!*

Miriam figured if there was anyone that had a right to be angry, it was her. How could her own daughter not tell her she was pregnant...and for three months already. She blamed that on Manuel. Nadia had never deliberately disrespected her own parents until *he* came a long.

Look at him over there on his cot, she told herself. He couldn't sleep, just like her. She didn't feel sorry for him, not one bit! Yet, what the pastor was trying to teach her today still nagged at her conscious.

"You need to love your son-in-law Miriam," the pastor told her, "He loves your daughter! I've seen it!"

But she couldn't love him. How could she love someone that lied to her? Yet, looking at him now slumping on his cot like a little boy made her think of Nadia. He really does love her. And... she supposed if her daughter could love him, so could she.

"*Can we talk?*" she whispered to him as she sat on the edge of his cot, surprising herself that she made the effort to go talk to him.

"*No!*"

"*Look!* Maybe I over-reacted."

"*Maybe?*"

Now see, this was why she hadn't talked to him earlier. He was *ridiculous!*

"*Fine!* I over-reacted then," she sighed, "I'm just...I'm just worried sick about Nadia."

"And *that's* an apology?"

He was a tough cookie. He didn't let her get away with a thing. Perhaps there actually was some substance to the man after all.

Miriam sighed and dropped her head, continuing to whisper. "*I'm sorry! Please!* Let's bury the hatchet...*for Nadia's sake.*"

"Heck, why not?" the mockery flew from his tongue, "*For Nadia's sake*...yeah! Lets everyone just pretend."

"*What?* What do you mean?"

He didn't care to elaborate but Miriam could tell he had actually been crying. A great big lug like him. He wasn't the only one. Her heart crushed. "*You've given up!*"

"Why not? It's going on the fourth day now and they won't tell us anything about her. That usually means..."

"*Don't you dare say it!*"

"She's *dead!*"

"My daughter is *NOT* dead!"

Miriam wanted to argue, fight with every breath she had, but something stopped her: The sad look in his teary eyes. He was in more pain then she realized. Her motherly instinct set in immediately, just as if he were her own son. "*C'mere!*"

She pulled his big muscular body to her scrawny frame and just held him. They both sobbed into each other's arms. Their pain was a shared pain, yet she knew his love was different than her own. She'd die if anything ever happened to her own spouse. She supposed that was where Manuel was at now.

"You can't give up. Look how far you've taken us."

"But my..." he swallowed back tears, "my *Chica...*"

That silly nickname struck a nerve. Him saying that brought more tears to her eyes then she expected. She wiped her runny nose with part of her sleeve.

"My daughter is still alive! I feel it...*here!*" she touched her heart. "*A mother knows!*"

Manuel just sat there, eyes wide, believing like a little boy.

God, let her still be alive.

"Then we have to get out of here and find her Miriam!" he whispered.

"But how?"

"I'm not sure, but I have and idea that *might* work."

"Well tell me about it! Maybe I can help."

Miriam listened to the man's plan for the next hour. It had merit. "We'll try it in the morning. The guys can help. We'll follow your lead...and just so you know, we're not leaving a soul behind, *not even Ebenezer.*"

Manuel chuckled against his tears, "I don't know if I can stand the smell of him."

"I know," she mused, "but some people can't control their body odour."

They both burst with giggles. It was good to see their smiles return with a glimmer of hope, even if it was over something so petty.

"Now let's get some sleep *son*. We're going to get your wife back tomorrow."

As she left his side, she returned to her own uncomfortable cot.

Frank's eyes were beaming. "Thank you!" he mouthed as he blew a kiss goodnight.

Miriam swelled with pride. All was well if only for a few short hours.

Chapter 18

Gala was assigned to Nadia as soon as she was brought in. It was her job to keep an eye on her. She'd been bitten several times and not expected to make it through the night. But she had made it through three days already and there were no explanations, at least not any she was privy to. "Just monitor her," they told her, "we'll do the rest."

Insulted, she complied anyway. It was madding that they didn't let her in on the research especially since she was probably one of the more experienced staff members, but whatever. At least she wasn't out *there!*

"How you feeling dear?" she bent over the young girl in the low light.

"Better!" she answered tugging at the handcuffs.

It was a matter of precaution they told her the first day. They had to keep her restrained. "You'll get a fever, then start to turn. We've had others but they haven't made it this far."

"I feel fine! My neck is healing already."

Gala wanted to give the girl hope, she'd made it through so far, but they still didn't know what they were dealing with, so really, anything could happen at this point.

"What about the baby? I keep asking and nobody tells me anything."

Yes, the baby! She was told not to check, *not to care.* There was no hope for the child so why bother. Well, she *did* care. It wasn't right to deny the girl at least a peek of her unborn child. She'd made it this far, it might give her reason to fight whatever this was.

Gala peered around for the other doctors but it was 3 a.m. Who would still be up? She could sneak the ultrasound into her room and hook it up. She'd be done before they even realized. It was the only right thing to do.

"Okay Nadia! *Shhhh!*" We're gonna take a look at the baby. But if they catch me, I'm done, do you understand?"

The young girl nodded with tears in her eyes, she threw her head back and began to sob silently. "Thank you, Dr..."

"Dr Silverton...but like I said from day one. My friends call me Gala, and you're my friend *sunshine.*"

"Thank you, Gala, and thanks for treating me like a human being. Why are the other doctors so mean?"

"Well dear, some doctors have no bedside manner, *but I do!* Now let's sit you up a bit." She raised the electronic bed, thankful for the many generators that powered the underground facility.

"I'll be right back with the ultrasound machine."

With the low light in the hall to conserve the generators at night, she found it hard to find the right equipment. But there it all was, stuffed in a corner unused. How hard would it have been for Peter to do this the first day when she had asked? *Really!*

As she wheeled the monstrosity to Nadia's door, she accidentally bumped into the doorframe on her way in, making a loud noise. "Oops," she smiled, pausing, "we better not do that again or we'll wake everyone up."

Then, another sound reverberated through the hall in one of the far rooms. So, she wasn't the only klutz awake. Still, she'd better be careful. Someone was on the prowl.

Once the machine was warmed up, Gala asked the girl a few questions just as if she were at a regular doctor's visit. She'd give her that at least. It was probably her very first child considering how young she looked.

"So, how far along do you think you are?"

"Probably three months or so."

"Or so?"

"It's been crazy," the girl frowned, "I really don't know what's happening. I thought I lost it but my husband...Manuel, he's a paramedic, he says I might be fine because the bleeding stopped."

"So, you had some spotting then?"

The elfin-faced redhead bit her lip as she shook her head, confirming that she had.

"Spotting can be normal you know," Gala winked to re-assure her.

She really hoped she had some good news for her. She wasn't aware there had been any spotting. Nobody told her that little tidbit. Perhaps she would have reconsidered the ultrasound and let nature take it's course. But still, she had the ultrasound with her now and she wasn't about to waste it.

As Gala removed the girls blankets and lifted her medical gown exposing her warm bare abdomen, she saw a bulge. *Now that isn't three months.* "Three months you say? Looks further along than that."

"Well I can suck it in pretty good so it's probably just blubber. You know," she chuckled.

"Yes dear," Gala chuckled, even though the girl was very skinny compared to her own paunch, "I've got that problem too."

"Okay, lets have a look-see," she said, squirting the warm gel on Nadia's tummy and then on the probe as it rolled around on her belly. The monitor spoke right away.

"Now you hear that?" Gala beamed. "That's your beautiful baby talking to you. It's the heartbeat...and babe sounds wonderful!"

"Really?" the girl squealed, "*I can't believe it!*"

"Well believe it! That's your baby," she told her pointing to the monitor screen. But there was something else there. "Wait a minute..."

"What is it?" the redhead asked, biting her lip again.

Gala was quiet now. She wanted to be sure before she said anything.

"There's...*two* in there!"

"*Whaaat?*"

Gala smirked, "Yup! You're having *twins!* Do they run in the family?"

"*No.*"

"Well then, you are *doubly* blessed," she told her, happy to give her some good news. She wanted to make sure the second one had a strong heartbeat like the first one and it did. "Listen, this is baby number two."

Nadia paused...listening, then giggled with wide eyes.

"Looks like you're about seventeen weeks. Already through your first trimester."

"*Really?*" Nadia beamed, "I didn't think I was that far along."

"*Yup!* No doubt about it my dear.

Hope seemed to be restored as Gala pointed out the heart and the backbone and the feet and hands of both babies. It was refreshing to see such beauty in amongst the ugliness of the last few days. Surely everything would be okay and the young girl wouldn't become infected. She'd do everything in her power to help her.

"So that's it!" Gala announced, turning off the machine. I have to put it away before anyone catches me. "*Congratulations sweetheart!*"

"Thank you *SO* much!"

"My pleasure! We need a little happiness around here."

The girl smiled and then it waned a bit as she touched her bandages, obviously remembering why she was there. "*I hope I'm okay.*"

"You're okay! You made it longer than anyone I've seen. I'd say you're in the clear." Now, lets get this thing back where it belongs."

But before she could get it out of the doorway, Peter blocked the way. "And *what* do you think you're doing?"

"*Oh!*" He scared her half to death.

"Yeah...*Oh!*"

"Help me roll this back."

"Why, so you don't get *caught?*" Peter scolded her. "I gotta report this you know."

"No, you don't Peter!"

The two of them rolled the ultrasound machine back into the empty room and left it there. "Now Gala, you owe me big time."

"You name it, just please don't tell on me."

"Fine then, you're assisting me with surgery tomorrow."

"*Surgery?* What surgery?"

Gala gulped hard. She knew there were only a handful of patients in the facility: Ebenezer in sector 'C' whom they had been experimenting on, and the four others. One of which was the twins father. And then there was Nadia the primary focus of their entire research, and it had better not be her.

"They want *fetal* tissue."

Gala's eyes went wide. "*I beg your pardon?*"

"Don't look so surprised Gala. She's sick anyway. We're aborting the baby."

Babies! And there's no way in hell that's ever gonna happen!

~~~~

Nadia went to sleep with a smile on her face.

It was such a relief to be told her baby...*babies*, were fine. She couldn't believe she was having twins.

Yet, her joy was replaced with a sudden assault to her body that made her scream in terror. She was back at the fence, chained as before.

"Leave me alone!" she shouted at the serpent.

But it wouldn't, it just kept digging into her chest with it's tail. "I told you there was another way! I cut an entrance to your heart, and now it's mine!"

Nadia was gasping. She couldn't fight the beast. The pain was unbearable!

"Get out of me!" she cried again.

"I will have all of you!"

"NO!"

"Then I will dig out the twins?"

Blood ran down the side of her mouth as she tried to call for help. The other prisoners around her were hanging by their chains in a dead-like state yet they were still moaning.

"God! Come back!" she called for the light.

"He can't help you now!" the serpent spit back.

"GOD!"

And then the light appeared again. It hovered before her unnoticed by the serpent as it continued the assault.

"Call in my name and I will answer!"

"I DID! I don't know what you mean?" she cried, confused.

"I am the Christ! You know my name!

"Jesus?"

She said the name with tears in her eyes. Then she was suddenly a little girl again, sitting in Sunday School with her fancy Christmas dress remembering Jesus like a long-lost friend...and the promise she made to him so long ago to love him forever.

He reached out his arms for her to run to him. "Oh, how I have missed you my child. Come unto me!"

With arms wide open, she ran to his embrace.

Then she heard the church choir singing her favourite song: 'Create in me a clean heart; and renew a right spirit within me'. And she suddenly realized what she had to do.

Without warning, the serpent withdrew from her body, spitting her blood out like it was poison. "WHAT HAVE YOU DONE?"

Smiling she raised her head with pride and repeated, "God is my refuge and strength, a very present help in trouble. Therefore, I will not fear!"

And with that, Nadia woke happy from her dream for the very first time. God was watching over her, just like the doctors were doing right now.

"Wake up Nadia! We need to prep you for surgery."

~~~~

By the time Gala was roused from her slumber, it was already mid-morning and Peter was calling her. "Come on sleepy-head! We have the patient prepped and ready. I need you. *Remember...you owe me.*"

Oh no! She forgot! How could she stall this procedure? There was no way she was going to allow them to abort the babies. It was barbaric and she would have no part of it. Yet, as a physician, and under these uncertain circumstances, she was obligated.

Torn with what she had to do, she decided to try and stall. "Don't start without me Peter!" she pretended to be enthusiastic about the surgery. She'd come up with something to ensure they postpone the surgery. *Something!*

With the generators at full capacity again, she switched on the bathroom light and turned on the tap. A rush of water burst through as she splashed it into her tired eyes. Thankfully their water supply was untouched by the terrorists. Even so, it was flushed and replenished with a private source just to be sure.

Her mouth tasted like stale milk. Grabbing a toothbrush, she rushed the paste through her mouth in a hurry and spit, sloshing some water to rinse. Her reflection didn't please her at all. Grey mousey short hair was not very attractive but it would have to do. What she would give to have that lovely red hair her patient has. Ah youth, it had escaped her so fast. She didn't even have time to blink let alone find a husband.

There was a time that she hoped to have her own baby. She thought these feelings had left her but seeing Nadia's ultrasound last night had awakened that urge again. It was too late for her, but not for that young girl. She had made it this far with positive results, how could they deny her the right to bear children? *It was wrong.*

Why they wanted fetal tissue was beyond her. Perhaps they had found something? Nadia was 'O' negative. That meant her babies could be negatives as well, but only if the husband had no Rhesus factor. That was unlikely being only 7% of the worlds population carried the 'O' negative blood type. But if he had an *Allele,* there was a small chance.

Gala mused at that thought. Could they really be that lucky? The 'O' blood type was the purest of blood. It was the most sought after for transfusions; thought to be the universal blood type until they discovered the Rh factor: Blood that contained no protein factor. Then it quickly became known that 'O' negative blood was the new universal type and soon became the number one stocked blood in every E.R worldwide.

Blood typing had been a leading fascination in her field of research for decades and still they couldn't crack the Rhesus negative code. When they had a breakthrough with blood substitutes, they all basked in the glory. But the stubborn negative blood was the only type that couldn't be cloned. It was unreal, almost as if a higher power prevented it from being tampered with. They called it the *Blood of the Gods.* Gala always scoffed at that statement because she didn't believe in a higher power, but what else could design such a wonder? *Aliens maybe?* They had even found the gene that linked them to monkeys through all the other blood types, but not Rh negative. Their blood contains no monkey protein at all. So much for Darwin's theory that we evolved from apes, even though that's what she was taught and still believed to this day. Evolution probably resulted from another species other than ape. They just had to find the link. The Rh factor seemed to contain that missing link. There were so many questions that fascinated her.

Like why on earth is the Rh-negative blood type the only type that can't procreate with it's own species. That always puzzled her. Before modern medicine came along, babies would die from *Haemolytic Disease* because of cross contamination with negative and positive blood. RhoGam prevented that nowadays. It was always a mystery that blood from an unknown source was floating around in the world, foreign and untamed. *Where did it come from?*

Perhaps that's why they wanted her fetal tissue? It was because of the blood purity. If 'O' negative was the purest blood in the world, then an unborn child who had that same blood type would have *pure gold* running through its veins. All the virus's in the world would not have touched it yet, unpolluted from mankind. A very valuable resource. Of course, they wanted *that!*

She didn't have it all figured out yet, but what she did know, was she was going to be late if she didn't hurry now. She flung on her white lab coat and blew breath into her hands to check for that stale milk smell. Good enough, she guessed.

When she got to the prep room and started washing up for surgery, she peered through the large glass at the already assembled staff.

Rats! They were about to start without her.

Chapter 19

When Frank was told of the plan once he awoke, he immediately went over to Manuel to make amends. Miriam had worked her magic. She had the ability to either make someone really hate her or really love her. It was usually the former, but she did surprise him from time to time.

Once he hugged his son-in-law and got through the awkwardness of it all, Manuel's plan sounded pretty good. "Okay then," Frank agreed with Manuel, "I'll distract the guard when the doctor comes in. Miriam can watch the door."

And so, they did. Manuel pulled the doctor aside and told him his headache had returned and he felt funny like he wanted to *bite* someone. *It was genius.* Immediately the doctor took a step back. "*Guard!*" he called, "get your handcuffs...*Guard?*"

But the guard didn't hear him with the coughing fit Ebenezer was faking. He didn't even notice Frank stealing the handcuffs from his belt. *It was working like a charm.* The guard bent to check on the old man, and then they had him. Ebenezer helped Frank use his own handcuffs on him and then took his keychain with the fob to the door.

Manuel had already kneed the doctor in the gut as he doubled over in pain. Tom had the straight-jacket ready that he found earlier. Together they wrapped him like a mental patient and threw him in the corner with the guard, tying their legs together.

"*Now tell me where my wife is!*" Manuel shouted out of breath.

"She's *dead!*"

Manuel stepped back. "You're lying!"

"Don't believe me then!"

Manuel proceeded to kick the doctor over and over as he lay there on his side.

"Okay *okay!*" the doctor moaned, "*Stop!*"

"*Then tell me the truth!*"

"I don't know where she is! I don't know where *anyone* is this morning. They don't tell me much. *I'm only an intern.*"

Manuel blew like a bull as he continued his assault. He was madder than Frank had ever seen him before. If he didn't stop soon, they'd have to pull him off the doctor.

"Then tell me where the generators are! *We'll flush them out like rats!*"

"*Fine!*" the young intern pleaded, "just *stop* already!"

Manuel paused to give the man a chance to speak. "Okay, I'm listening."

"Down this hall," he said, lifting his chin in the direction, "turn left on 'D' wing, and then straight down to the end of the hall. Take the steps that lead to the basement and you'll find the generators."

"If you're lying *Gringo*...and we don't find it..." Manuel spit with anger, "I'm coming back to *kill* you!"

The intern just nodded in disgust.

Manuel bent down to the guard and unbuckled the man's gun. "And we'll take this too!" he said, eyeing it as he checked the clip and stuck it in the back of his pants. "*C'mon team, lets get the heck out of here!*"

~~~~

Miriam was proud of her son-in-law. He got the job done successfully and they were headed down the basement steps to the generators already. Ebenezer and the pastor had a great deal of trouble getting down the steps fast so Miriam gave them a hand. They needed to stick together but Frank and Manuel were a few yards ahead.

Once they were finally down, Manuel handed them all flashlights. He had already scouted the loud room with working generators inside. "We're looking for the shut off valves," he shouted to them above the roar. "See if you can find the main one."

Miriam didn't know exactly what she was looking for, but she would try.

The system looked to be highly computerized with exhaust ventilation systems...But the shut off valve? That was going to be a chore. There were so many valves and she didn't know where to begin. It was probably all controlled by a computer.

The two old men scurried about but didn't find anything. "I need to sit," Ebenezer informed her, "I'm not as young as I look."

Miriam smiled at him. He was sweet. *Smelly,* but sweet. His long white hair stood on end and he had an uncanny resemblance to Albert Einstein, moustache and all. If she had met him on the street, she would've thought he was a pan-handler. She was ashamed of that fact and didn't know why she had the bad habit of judging people. It was time to stop, and realize they were all human beings...well...except the *Locos* outside.

Suddenly the lights went out. Miriam started to panic.

"*I found it!*" Manuel shouted in the dark, "The key fob controls it!"

Glad they found what they were looking for, Miriam pointed her flashlight toward Ebenezer hunched on the bottom stair. "Are you alright?'

"I'm fine," he said, "just tired."

"Can you make it up the steps?"

"Well, I think so. You might have to carry me though," he winked.

There he goes teasing her again. She mused at the fact that he still had a sense of humour after all he's been through. He was one tuff old man. His stories of Warsaw impressed her and left her in awe each time. And she thought *she* had a hard life.

"Come on," she chuckled, stretching out a hand to help him up, "I can pull you but I ain't gonna lift your sorry butt up *those* stairs. Now move it!"

"Yes *Balabusta!*"

She wondered what that meant, but from the look on his face he just poked fun at her in Yiddish. She shook her head and laughed. But as she pulled him upright, she noticed him wincing in pain, and that was no joking matter.

Something was definitely wrong with Ebenezer.

~~~

"Come on! Let's move it!" Manuel shouted, wishing they hadn't *all* come down the stairs. It was hard enough sneaking around with two people, leave alone a group consisting of two old men and a woman. What was he going to do with them? Miriam didn't want to leave the old men and so that was out of the question. But they had to move fast.

"Look," he whispered to Frank privately, "me and you gotta do this. We need to get the others somewhere safe until we find Nadia, or else we'll get caught for sure."

"*I know.* But where do we take them?"

Manuel scratched his head trying to think. "Let's just get everyone up the stairs first and then we'll figure something out. I don't want them to think we're abandoning them."

"Right," Frank agreed.

As they struggled getting Ebenezer up the stairs, Manuel remembered seeing an exit at the end of the wing. But where did it lead? He'd have to run ahead and check it out.

Once everyone was up the stairs, they huddled in the dark with only their flashlights to guide them. "Okay, you guys stay here a minute. I gotta check something out. Stay with Frank and try to keep quiet."

"But they will be coming to turn the generators back on, won't they?" Miriam said.

Right. He didn't think of that. Even though he broke the keypad so they couldn't turn it back on, they may still be able to override it somehow. They'd be coming fast and furious. "Okay then," he sighed, "follow me and *hurry up!*"

It they were lucky, they'd reach the end of the hall before *Christmas!*

Bounding down the hall like a herd of elephants, they reached their target and huddled beside it. There was a door with a computer key-pad that controlled the locking mechanism. It wouldn't be dependant on the computer anymore. He tried it but it still seemed to be locked.

Emergency lockdown might flip from computer to key entry. He'd try the keys. "Frank, I need the fob. It has keys on it as well."

Frank threw him the keys and he went to work on the door. "*Got it!*" Slowly he eased the big grey door open, beaming the flashlight into the next room. It was an empty cement foyer that lead to a stairwell that he presumed went up and out of the facility. It would be key-locked as well. A perfect place to stow the others until he got back.

"Okay," Manuel urged, "*go go go...Inside!*" He pushed the group into the foyer one at a time until they were all safely through the door and closed it behind him.

"Now listen everyone," he said, "Frank and I are going to find Nadia. We'll be right back. I'll lock the door behind us as we go, and you'll be safe here until we get back."

"*You're dumping us?*" Miriam snapped.

"Miriam *please!*" Frank blurted out, "it's easier with two people."

"She's *right*," Ebenezer agreed. The pastor did as well.

She didn't like it but she nodded anyway. "Okay, but hurry up! Anything could happen down here. What if we get *attacked?* Or *sick?* What if you forget about us?"

"We *won't!*" Frank told her, giving her a kiss goodbye. "Don't worry!"

Now he knew where Nadia got her worrying from. *It was genetic.*

"Okay, let's go Frank!" Manuel sighed, impatient to get going. He fingered the gun stuffed in his waist and pulled it out, checking the clip once more to make sure the safety was off. He'd need it. "And bring a couple flashlights! You're gonna be my eyes."

They eased open the door, made sure nobody was coming, and pulled it shut again. Frank jingled the keys and locked the others inside. "Follow me Frank! We have a lot of ground to cover."

"Right behind you *son!*"

The two of them crept slowly and quietly through the long hallway heading north. Every room in the corridor was completely vacant. Finding Nadia was not going to be easy, but Manuel knew he'd either find her...*or die trying.*

Either way was fine with him.

Chapter 20

"*Scalpel,*" Peter asked his attending as he reached with his gloved hand. Gala was told she could only observe. Yet another insult, but she was use to it by now. They ganged up on her because she was late. It wasn't easy being the only female doctor on staff. *Too much testosterone!*

She'd observe but she was not about to keep quiet. "And why through the abdominal cavity doctor? Why not just a traditional abortion?"

"Dr. Silverton..." another responded, "please *just* observe!"

But they hadn't even started yet. If she kept this up maybe she'd be lucky and they'd cancel or postpone the surgery altogether. *Not likely.*

As the knife was about to slice, Gala started coughing. She would play hardball if she must. *Never underestimate a woman!*

"Gala *enough!*" Peter sighed through his surgical mask. "What are you trying to do? Sabotage this?"

"*No!*" she lied, "go on!"

Manipulation was her specialty.

Peter lifted the scalpel again and glared at her. If looks could kill he'd be a murderer already. There was no way he was winning this one. "*Hachoo...!*" she sneezed this time. Fake as the last attempt, but ever so convincing.

"Alright...*OUT!*" he pointed, red as a beet.

Jerk!

But she was *not* giving up. They would have to drag her out kicking and screaming.

"You can't throw me out!"

"Wanna bet..." another doctor snapped back, grabbing her by the arms yanking them behind her back. Her mask fell down and glove came off in the struggle.

"See, you contaminated the O.R. You'll *have* to reschedule."

"GET HER OUT!"

But before they could drag her from the room, the lights suddenly flashed. *Perfect timing!* A power outage. In the dark room, she fought off her captors and pulled herself out of harms way. They were mad and looking to blame her.

"I didn't have anything to do with it!" she cried, trying to escape their wrath. "*Honestly!*"

"*Leave her!*" John ordered the others, "we'll have to postpone. Gala can clean up the mess since she's obviously to blame for all this! You can baby-sit the patient too. That's all you're good for anyway!"

Yeah, no problem you buffoon!

"Let's go fix the generators," Peter told the other physicians as they bumped into each other like idiots in the dark. *Yeah, you can all go.* She didn't need them anyway. How many doctors did it take to screw in a *light bulb* anyway?

Nadia would still be sedated for another half hour. That would give her time to get her back to her room, dressed and ready to get out of this place. She'd put her in a wheelchair and roll her to the nearest exit before anyone came back. It would take them that long to figure out how to turn on the generators anyway.

Hopefully Nadia would be coherent enough to make it up the stairs by herself because there was no way she could get her up in a wheelchair. And who knew what they'd face on the outside. But at this point, they both had run out of options.

Time to move!

Hurrying, she searched in the dark for the emergency flashlights. She stumbled to the cupboard next to the door but found nothing. Great, they took them all. Guess she'd have to rely on her memory. There were a couple wheelchairs down the hall. She'd quickly go get one even though she didn't like to leave her patient unattended.

Ugh! It was dark.

Now she knew what it was like for a blind person. Even the smallest things were hard. She'd have to feel her way against the wall to find the chair.

Owe! She bumped right into them. At least she found the wheelchair she needed. Rolling it, she hurried back to the O.R. kicking something in her path. *A flashlight.* The buffoons must have dropped it. Or maybe someone left one on purpose. *That would be the day.*

She clicked it on and beamed it in Nadia's direction. She was still there, laying on the operating table like an eerie corpse. The sooner she got her out of there the better.

Within minutes, Gala had her in her room and started dressing her. It was quite a chore but without her clothes she'd never make it out there in the cold fall wind. And then what? Gala wondered what the next part of her plan would consist of. Surely the military had organized things outside enough to gain control over the base. *Surely!*

It was a chance she'd have to take.

~~~

Nadia stood outside her body and hovered over it. Was she dead, or just asleep?

She peered at her surroundings but it was still burning hot with explosions of volcanic lava bursting in the distance. It hadn't changed and she thought it would. She'd have to try and escape this underworld but it wasn't going to be easy in her hypnotic dream state. Obstacles were repeatedly thrown in her way, and Jesus had left her to her own demise.

"I am with you always," he told her in spirit, "remember that!"

And she tried to remember, but why couldn't the light follow her where ever she went? Why did he have to keep leaving? She needed him. Wasn't he supposed to stay?

"I am with you always!"

Sobbing, she felt numb all over like the serpent had drugged her. The thing was coming back soon, she knew it. Even though her chains had miraculously broken and she could pull herself free from the fence, her feet would not move. She was stuck.

The rotting bodies hanging next to her were calling out, but not to come, to go. She wanted to, but she needed help. She turned around and saw herself in a mirror but she was thirteen years old this time, and she was crying.

They didn't like her, none of them. The stupid bullies! They called her names, and she wanted to die. Jesus didn't save her. He made her endure this. How awful! If he was really God, he would have made them stop.

Yes, it was then that she started questioning God.

It burnt a hole in her heart the day she turned away. But really, she was just angry. If he didn't care, then neither would she.

"I am with you always."

But thirteen-year-old Nadia felt it was just a lie. She hurt so bad and nobody knew, not even God. She had no choice but to endure her life of misery and cave to the pressures of her friends. Little by little she became polluted, unclean like a festering sore, victimized by the growing plague. She wondered how God could help. He certainly wouldn't save her now.

"'...and when I see the blood, I will pass over you and the plague shall not be unto you to destroy you.'" the voice said. But what did it mean? Her grown up self was confused, ashamed.

"Ah ha!" the serpent grinned, "I knew you couldn't leave me. You smell like rotting flesh. You belong to me, you and your filth. Your legs are numb because you don't want to leave. We are the same as you, and you need not feel ashamed. Stay with me and I will turn your sorrow into pleasures beyond your dreams."

But Nadia felt sick to her stomach, guilty she hadn't already tried to run. The serpent made perfect sense and was very enticing... and right! She was filthy and unclean.

"'You have redemption through my blood, even the forgiveness of sins!'"

Nadia felt torn. She didn't know who was telling the truth. She knew she had a choice to make. But which one? She remembered hearing about the father of lies? He was either on her right or her left. She was confused and didn't know which way to go.

"'The son of man shall be seated at the right hand of God.'"

Or was it the left? She couldn't remember for sure. All she knew was that she was being bullied by both sides. Right? Left? What was she supposed to do?

She felt out of control, like someone was pushing her against her will.

~~~

They were coming!

Gala could see the flashlights illuminating the hallway about five hundred feet ahead of them. She was stuck between two corridors and she didn't know which way to push the wheelchair. On the right she saw flashlights beaming the halls. On the left she saw the same thing. They had surrounded her.

What was she supposed to do, run right into them?

It was now or never. She'd ducked into the linen closet, pulling Nadia's chair backward. She manoeuvred the chair as far to the back as she could and left her there, crawling to the edge of the crack in the door to peek out.

Now please Nadia, don't wake up. Not yet! They had to stay quiet until they passed.

But suddenly a crowd of men gathered in front of the closet door.

"Did you hear that Peter?" John said, searching with his flashlight. "I thought I heard something."

Gala tried to control her heavy breathing, trying not to make a sound.

"Just your imagination."

But then, suddenly from around the corner a voice shouted, "*Hold it right there, Gringos!*" The man meant business by the tone of his voice. Perhaps there was still hope.

The doctors immediately stumbled backward when they saw the gun. They set their flashlights down and raised their hands. "Now just put the gun down buddy," one of them said, "we're not the bad guys here."

That's what they thought.

Another man stood a distance away from the one with the gun. Gala had never seen either of them before but the only explanation she could think of was they were the prisoners in quarantine. They must have gotten out. That meant the young man with the gun was probably the baby's father, and if she was lucky, *she'd have her way out.*

"Where's my wife?"

Yup, she was right.

"Who?"

"Don't play me like a fool," Nadia's husband shouted back, raising his gun to a steady aim. "*I wanna know where she is RIGHT NOW!*"

Gala thought of stepping out and telling them all she was right there but that would be insane. She wasn't about to risk everything.

And then one of the doctors made a move, thrusting his body against the gunman. Shots rang out. Men pummelled each other...more shots. Bodies falling...running as the gun continued to hunt them one at a time.

"*Go get the guns George!*" one of them shouted. The other doctors dispersed as fast as they came, leaving only two men and one dead body on the floor with a pool of blood.

"Frank you okay?" Nadia's husband spoke.

"I'm hit."

"Where?"

"Shoulder."

Gala wondered if now was the time to make her appearance. What would she tell them? *Hi, I saw the whole thing. By the way, I have your wife?* They would shoot her too.

But she had to do something.

"*Pssst!*" she whispered, "*in here.*"

The man spun around startled. He picked up his flashlight and gun and aimed it at the door. "Who's there?"

"*Don't shoot!*" she said. "I'm in here! *Quickly!*"

The men pointed their flashlights into the closet and shut the door. What they saw made them gasp. "*Chica!*" the man said, rushing to his wife. He dropped to his knees and held her limp body. The older gentleman who was grabbing his wounded shoulder started sobbing. *Now she had to explain why she was unconscious.*

"What happened to my wife?

"I'll explain later," Gala told him. "We don't have much time if I know these guys, they'll be back with a vengeance."

"Come on then, we're headed to 'D' wing."

Gala went along with them just to get out of there, but 'D' wing was not the place to go. It was a dead end, literally. They had a breach there a couple nights ago and they had to seal off the exit. Nothing left in that direction but the infected or the dead. But she'd tell them that little detail later.

For now, they'd have to *run!*

Chapter 21

Tom couldn't understand Ebenezer's babble. He didn't make any sense at all. It seemed the moment they got locked in there, his mind went back to Warsaw. It wasn't good.

"*The Gestapo are just beyond those stairs,*" he pointed like a crazy man.

Miriam just sighed and said nothing.

Tom decided to play along, hoping it would help. He knew a thing or two about senile old men. "*They won't come Ebenezer! We are safe down here.*"

"No, we're *NOT!*" Ebenezer continued even more upset.

"*God is with us!*"

Ebenezer grunted, "*Aak!* Don't give me that *nonsense.* God has forgotten his people."

Uh oh! Now what did he get himself into? Tom wasn't sure what to say next.

"Tom *shhh!*" Miriam whispered.

He guessed that was his queue to be quiet and let the old man be.

"*Yitzy* and *Mootka* were gassed this morning so don't tell me your *God* is coming. He has turned his back and we're all going to die in the chambers like the rest of them because we're too stupid to get out of the ghetto," Ebenezer continued to moan.

Tom couldn't stand this. And he was supposed to be quiet? Even in this delusional state, he had to help the poor old soul.

"Eb!" he blurted out, "we're *not* stupid. We have to wait here for the others."

Miriam just guffawed. He looked at her dull expression that told him she was very annoyed, but he didn't care. He had to help.

"They're coming back as soon as they find Nadia."

"And they will find her gassed as well," Ebenezer blurted out.

"*Enough!*" Miriam shouted, "*Please you guys!* It's hard enough to wait here in this cold dungeon and stay positive, *so both of you just shut up!*"

Ebenezer started to cry. This time Miriam said something. "Ebenezer, you are *not* in Warsaw anymore. That was a long time ago. You're an old man now."

"Not too old to understand," he sobbed. "I know what's going on."

Whether he did or didn't wasn't apparent. Tom only hoped that was the last of the old man's trip down memory lane. He'd try to get them both focused on something positive from now on.

"Hey, I got an idea. I'll tell you both a story...."

"Can't we just be quiet," Miriam sighed.

"I want to hear your story *Pastor.*"

Tom relaxed against the cement wall and decided to appease Ebenezer and not Miriam so he told one of his favourites. "'*For God so loved the world that he gave his only Son, that whosoever believes in him shall not perish but have eternal life.*'"

"That is not a story my friend," Ebenezer corrected, "that is a Bible passage and I don't follow the Bible, I follow the Torah...or I use to anyway."

Tom frowned. He had a purpose for reciting that scripture.

Miriam just signed and didn't contribute to the conversation. That was okay with him, but Tom was going to preach anyway.

"But you believe in God, right?"

"Well, I had my doubts many a time."

Tom continued, hope rising in his chest. "I am the same. I've wondered why God allows suffering. Why he lets bad things happen. I shake my head at all the wars and violence...and this *incident* right now."

"And the *Holocaust*."

"Yes of *course!* But one thing I do know is that God loves us. We are still here and that's not a coincidence. He sent us the messiah and his name is, *Jesus Christ*."

Ebenezer choked. "My people received no help, and this Jesus you speak of was nobody. He wasn't the messiah, just a man. I know that much from my Torah."

This was not going to be easy, Tom thought to himself. He'd go on with the story anyway since it may be his last chance, and Miriam...well he knew she heard it all before. She was just too stubborn to apply it.

"Well I believe that Jesus Christ died for my sins," the Pastor continued, "and I'm not perfect. I sin...I admit it. I need help just like everyone else. But Jesus is my helper. He went to hell to cast my sins into the pit of fire so that I don't have to go there."

"*Hogwash!* the old man spit.

Perhaps this wasn't a good idea after-all, and Tom wondered if it was the right place. His timing always seemed to be off.

"It's not hogwash. It is my *life* sir!" Now there he went getting defensive again. *Lord help me!* "I also went through the war...*two wars*, except I fought in the trenches with brave God-fearing men. I watched them die to save another. I killed many in the name of war and I had to ask forgiveness. It tore me apart for the better part of my life. Caused me to strike out against my wife in anger."

He turned to Miriam and frowned. "*Yes!* I'm sorry, I'm an awful sinner saved by grace. Jesus was my only hope, especially back then. I don't care if you don't agree Ebenezer, but I needed a saviour and his name is Jesus Christ the *messiah*. He helped me to turn from all that and become the man I am today. He can transform the *vilest* person."

Ebenezer just cleared his throat and let him finish.

"People go around ever day saying Jesus Christ was not who he said he was, but I know differently. It is *personal* with me. He is my *best friend*. It's not about which Bible you follow or even what the scriptures mean or don't mean. Man has been trying to interpret scripture since the beginning of time to no avail. But believing is a whole different thing. I believe; therefore, I am promised a relationship with him and forgiveness of all the stupid things I've done...and specifically right now...I'm promised if I believe in him, I will not *perish* but have eternal life."

Miriam fidgeted and Ebenezer sat there stunned. Perhaps he'd said too much.

"So, you're saying if I *believe*, I won't be infected like the others?" Ebenezer mocked.

"No, I'm saying if you believe in Jesus Christ and profess that he is God, you will not go to hell for eternity but will be with God forever. *Let the biters come,* let them destroy us. But if we have God...we will *not* perish. Even in death we will live in happiness forever with God. There are more ways than one to die."

"Oh, that much I know my friend, *that much I know.*"

"Yet you refuse to hear me," Tom added, shaking his head.

"I hear you. I just don't believe you. I've heard it all before in the ghetto and all those people died."

Tom frowned at what the man must have gone through. "Yes, but perhaps they are now living with God? Their bodies may have died but how do you know God abandoned their souls?"

"Point taken! I guess I didn't think of it that way."

Bingo! Tom's heart rose. There was hope for this man yet.

"Then would you pray the sinners prayer with me my friend...*and believe?*"

"*No!*" Ebenezer snapped.

"But why?"

"Because it's too late for me."

Tom scratched his head, puzzled at what was going on in Ebenezer's head now. Was he out of his mind again or did he seriously think it was too late for him? "Eb, it's *never* too late."

"Oh yeah?" Ebenezer said as he pulled himself to his knees with great pain and difficulty and started to lift his shirt. "Look at this. You tell *me* Pastor. Can your God transform *this?*"

Miriam gasped as Ebenezer exposed his stomach. An infection brewed so foul, they all stepped back in fear.

"*Ebenezer!* What on earth is *that?*"

"Their *experiment!* They injected me in the gut several times a day before I ran into you people. It itched at first and then I saw the lesion start to form. I asked them about it but they said it was normal. A side effect of the antibiotic they were giving me. Antibiotic ha! *I was their guinea pig!*"

Tom had to hold his nose to look closer. It smelt like a dead body and looked like gangrene had set in already. His entire stomach was one big festering sore. *The smell*...it was *this*, not his body odour. Tom immediately felt ashamed.

"And you've had this the whole time?"

"Well it gradually got worse, *but yes!*"

Tom didn't know what to say. His mouth wouldn't move. He couldn't believe the severity of this man's infection. It was unbelievable.

"Well Tom?" Ebenezer grunted as he pulled down his shirt and sat back down. "Do you have any fancy Bible verse for me *now?* Hmmm?"

"I'm sorry," he said, speaking softly. Tom could see the obvious pain in the man's sad eyes. *Lord give me the words to comfort him.*

But no appropriate words came.

"Frank and Manuel will be back with Nadia soon," Miriam said. "We'll get out of here and find someone to help you Ebenezer."

"Who will help? *Surely not God!*"

Tom sighed. Was it really too late? What were they dealing with here? Was it some kind of flesh-eating disease? It struck Tom with the harsh reality that maybe they were all going to die like this.

"God is *still* with us, even in the darkest hour!" Tom finally found the words. Not that it did much good to comfort Ebenezer now. He just looked away sadly and said nothing.

Silence set in after that. Nobody wanted to talk. But from what Tom had seen in his life, he was sure God was bigger than even this and he could help if only the man would let him. There was nothing more *he* could do.

I surrender him to you Jesus!

~~~~~

Miriam sat there silent in the dark for quite some time between two flickering flashlights. The batteries were about to die and then what? Would they sit there forever waiting? Would they freeze to death in the cold stairwell? Even now they could see their breath fogging in front of them. They couldn't stay there much longer.

The pastor was down right mean to poor old Ebenezer. Couldn't he save his preaching for the pulpit? Did he have to always sprout it at the most inopportune time? *Really?*

It was bad enough he was suffering with such a painful infection. She didn't know what to think of *that*. Perhaps it was better not to think at all. If anything, she would focus on what to do if Frank and Manuel didn't return. They couldn't wait there forever.

"I'm gonna climb those steps before our flashlights die out," she said breaking the silence. "If I don't do something, I'm gonna go mad."

Neither Tom or Ebenezer answered her. They both just sat there pouting.

Miriam rose against her cold numb legs and stretched the kinks out. She grabbed a flashlight and shone it over to the first step and saw the twisted stairwell. Then she focused the light's beam in every corner of the little cement room they were in. It was full of dusty old cobwebs, bugs, and who knew what else.

Here goes.

With one shaky foot, she started the climb and rounded the corner. Her foot hit something punky beneath her, but she couldn't make it out in the low light.

Then with her flashlight, she peered down to see, and the shock almost sent her tumbling down the steps. She jumped back against the railing. "*Nooo!*" she screamed. *It couldn't be.*

But sure enough, it was the bloody head of a dead woman, hair matted in a knotted glob, mixed with dirt and brain matter. Her face was half ripped off. Miriam couldn't look at it without nausea consuming her.

"What did you see?" Tom shouted.

But how could she tell him? How could she even describe it? "Just a mouse," she lied. It was easier that way.

Above the rise, she beamed her flashlight higher to reveal where the head had come from. Two bodies lay there in a heap in front of the exit door. One had no head, and the other was what? *Moving?*

Like Larry.

Slowly and without a sound, she backed away hoping it didn't see or hear her. But it did. It charged down the stairs like the devil, grabbed at her, growling like a rabid animal. "*Help!*" she screamed to the men below.

Tom beamed his flashlight in her direction immediately as he starting up the step, but it was too late. The thing grabbed her ankle, clawed at her until she tumbled to the bottom of the stairs, crashing head-on into Tom.

"*Get him off of me!*" she screamed. The *Loco* was trying to bite, just like they all did. Miriam kicked and fought against him.

Tom kicked like a schoolyard bully in a fight. Ebenezer stood frozen in place.

"*Hit him with the flashlight Tom!*"

"*I am!*" he cried, ramming it over and over into the attackers scull.

Miriam managed to pull her body from underneath as she heard the skull cracking. It was then that she knew they had won. "*Enough Tom!*" she scolded him, retreating into a curled ball in the corner like a small child.

Was this murder?

She began to sob uncontrollably. Tom continued to beat the man longer than he had to until the head was clearly severed. Finally, he stopped and sunk to his knees and cried, "*God forgive me! Oh God...forgive me!*"

"*Pfft! You and Hitler are the same!*" Ebenezer scoffed. "There is no forgiveness for those who gas *innocent children!*"

"*Shut up you old fool!*" Miriam cried. *Not now!*

"Are you okay Tom?"

But he didn't answer. Miriam would take that as a no. The truth was, none of them were okay. Yes, they were alive but none of them would ever be okay again.

~~~

Tom wanted to die!

That was the most horrible thing he had ever had to do. *Had to do?* Did he really need to crush the man's scull to the degree he did? And was that even a man?

He moaned deep within his soul, hidden from Miriam, from Ebenezer. Hidden even from God.

Could he hide such a thing from his maker? He didn't think so. *No!* God saw the actions of man and it repulsed him. *He, repulsed him.*

You and Hitler are the same! Yes, that was probably true. He was a beast; a cruel monster and he knew it. He knew it when he shot his first German, when he knifed his first soldier in the gut as he looked into his dying eyes and saw him take his last breath.

Tom was an abuser, a gentle man who became corrupt with sin and beat his wife. He was out of control then and he was out of control now. His wife was the innocent party. She never deserved his attacks. He flung his fists at her until her pretty face was bruised so badly. Oh, but he'd never let her out of the house until she was healed. He didn't want people to know. But they knew anyway. They hated him, *he hated him.*

And to think he thought he had left that all behind. He *was* forgiven, but not any more. No, *there is no forgiveness for those who gas innocent children*, or abuse their loved ones, or beat a man to death.

But that wasn't a man!

"Tom!" a voice called him back to reality.

But he couldn't answer her now, not in his self-pity.

"*TOM!*" the voice yelled this time. It was Miriam. "*Say something!*"

But he tried to form the words to no avail.

Then, heckling in the background, he heard another voice. "*Hitler was ridden with guilt also. That's why he killed himself.*"

"Ebenezer would you *SHUT UP!*" Miriam snapped. "I'm worried about him."

Tom felt a hot tear run down his cheek. He looked at his bloody hands in the dimming of the flickering flashlight and began to cry. *"I-I couldn't stop!"*

"Tom, you didn't have a choice!" Miriam tried to comfort.

But he had always had a choice.

"You-*you* saw it! I killed him with my bare hands!"

"Tom, you're in shock!"

"I'm in *hell!*...and I deserve it!"

Then he saw her bend to hold him. She held him as he wailed, as she patted his back, as she tried to comfort his God forsaken soul.

Useless!

"Tom," Miriam explained to him, "you saved me! If it hadn't been for you, I wouldn't be here right now so snap out of it. God knows your heart."

"My heart is *dead!*" If she only knew the kind of man he really was, she wouldn't even bother to comfort him.

And then she slapped him...*good and hard!*

"I *need* you Tom McDonald, now get over it!"

Her hand-print stung as he held his aching face. *"I-I'm sorry!"*

"*Stop being sorry* and help me with Ebenezer! We gotta get out of here and I can't do it alone. There are a lot of steps to climb...now *come on!*"

He shook his head and realized he had to snap out of it, if not for himself, for her sake. And Ebenezer's, though he sure didn't feel the same about him after his cruel Hitler remark.

The two of them guided Ebenezer up the stairs one step at a time. It was tedious and slow but the man was in obvious pain. Each step took a toll on him and Tom wondered if he'd even make it to the top.

Once they got to the middle of the stairwell, they paused to rest. "The flashlights are almost dead," he announced. "They're so dim."

"All the more reason to keep going," Miriam told him. "Are you okay to go on Eb?"

The old man just nodded that he was ready.

Tom took an arm and continued up. But suddenly a bright light assaulted their eyes above. *Was it God? Was it judgement day?* Tom squinted at the light.

A lone dark figure stood in the open doorway.

"*H-Hello?*" Miriam whispered cautiously. But nobody answered.

Tom shushed them both, then paused to listen. *Did he just hear a growl?*

Chapter 22

"And *I'm* telling you we *CAN'T!*" Gala agued with Manuel.

He wasn't about to listen to a total stranger. The rest of their group was depending on him returning for them. He'd left them in the lions den unaware and if anything happened to them, he'd never forgive himself.

"I'm going to get them no matter what you say! You can come if you want," Manuel told her point blank.

"I'm coming with you. My wife is there," Frank sided.

"But I'm telling you," Gala argued again, "It's not safe!"

"*Lady...*"

"I told you my name is Dr. Gala Silverton and *please*...listen to me!"

But Manuel refused to listen to the woman. He was a man of his word and that was that. The others were depending on him. Then again so was his wife. Could he really put her in danger again? It was either stay and be hunted down by the doctors, or take a chance and go to 'D' wing to be attacked by *Locos*.

What a choice!

"Okay," he decided, giving Gala a chance. Her caring eyes told him to at least hear her out. "What would you suggest then?"

"*Thank you!*" she paused before giving her suggestion, "I know this place like the back of my hand. If we go to the generator room, there's a little stairway that leads up to an emergency exit.

Without power, the door won't be coded, but it has a back up locking mechanism. We could try to pick it somehow or use something to break the latch."

Manuel dangled keys in front of her. "Like these?"

"*Yes, like those,*" she smirked. "We won't be able to take the wheelchair up so you'd have to carry your wife, but I think it's doable. Then once we're outside, we should be able to come around the other side of the 'D' wing entrance. If your friends are still...I mean, if they're in there, we'll have a fighting chance to get them out. Coming from the top is always a better position than coming from the bottom."

She actually made sense. Manuel was starting to like this woman. "Okay, lets move then, we're wasting enough time. *Vamos!*"

The three of them ran down the dark hall, wheelchair rolling as fast as he could push it. He had stuck his gun in the back of his blue jeans and gave his flashlight to Gala. She and Frank beamed the light in the direction they were going. All he cared about was getting his comatose wife to safety.

Emergency lights flickered as they neared the end of the hall.

"Okay," Gala puffed out of breath, "this is it!"

Manuel recognized it from their earlier sabotage so he knew the woman wasn't steering them in the wrong direction. Her idea was sound.

"Let's take her out of the Chair," Gala advised, labouring as she helped Manuel get his wife to a standing position so he could swoop her into his arms.

If only she could see him now, carrying her like he did when he put her into that plane on their honeymoon. It seemed like a lifetime ago.

Thundering down the stairway in a flash, they reached the bottom. Same generator room as before, but he felt uneasy with no way to reach his gun. "Frank," he ordered, "Pull my gun out. We might need it...and give your flashlight to Gala."

"Right," Frank nodded, tugging at his beltline for the gun. The man was obviously not use to holding a weapon. The weight of it pulled his arm down immediately.

"You're our protection now Frank," Manuel told him, "Make us proud!"

Frank sighed, and pulled the gun to a ready stance behind Gala, who led the procession with her flashlights beaming straight ahead.

"Follow me!" she whispered.

They crossed the main generator floor and headed to the north west corner. Manuel saw the door. "*Keys!*" he called out, motioning Frank to go after them in his pocket. "Sorry man!" Fishing in another man's front pocket was something guys cringed at but it was better than the lady doctor doing it.

"Got em!" Frank said, jingling the keys to find the right one.

"Here," Gala offered, "let me try."

She found the right one and unlocked the door leading to a narrow stairway no bigger than one you'd find in the attic of an old two-story home. "Up there fellahs!" she pointed with her flashlight.

All they had to do was follow.

~~~

Frank was not use to playing cop, but right now as he followed Gala up the dark stairwell, he was the only one that could.

They stopped at the top. Gala was jingling the keys, he was in the middle with the ready gun, and Manuel was behind them with his wife in his arms.

It was nothing for the big brute to carry his daughter up a flight of stairs even as narrow as it was. Frank knew his son-in-law was built like a tank. Unlike him, and his scrawny arms. His one shoulder had already been taken out of commission with a bullet wound. It stung like hell but he wasn't about to let on.

"I got it!" Gala whispered, clicking the door open to the bright sunshine.

A cold wind whipped at them as they all exited the building and clung to the wall. Now what? He'd been the gunman but he was ready to surrender that job.

"Come on!" Gala continued, "follow me to the 'D' wing entrance. And Frank, keep your eyes peeled. The biters can come out of nowhere."

Great! He readied his gun again.

Manuel shifted Nadia in his arms, following behind. They clung to the building's red brick wall until they reached the corner. Growling in the distance told him the *Locos* were gathered around the entrance...and it was open.

Miriam?

Silently they all withdrew, clinging to the cold wall.

Frank was not about to take pot-shots at them. He'd miss for sure and then they'd all come after them. No, he looked at Manuel for help.

"Don't look at me," Manuel told him, seeming to know exactly what he was thinking. "You have the gun *Chico*, I have your heavy daughter...Wanna trade?"

"Here," Gala held out her hand, "*gimme the gun!*"

The doctor surprised them both when she explained, "*Physician's Gun club champion of 2009,* now hand that baby over."

Frank's mouth fell open. "Be my guest lady," he said, handing her the gun immediately.

Before he had a chance to even collect his thoughts, Gala pulled the trigger repeatedly, picking the *Locos* off one by one.

"Let's go!" she called them. Frank felt like he was following *G.I Jane* into battle. But instead of battle, she had led them straight through bloody *Flanders Field.* The mess lingered in the doorway, smelling of rot and decay.

"If they're still alive, you'll find them down there," Gala pointed down the open doorway to a stairwell.

Frank gulped and grabbed the gun.

Time for *him* to be the hero.

~~~~

And now...someone was carrying her.

Nadia felt light as a feather as she continued her dreamlike state. Perhaps she was actually flying? Or maybe she was a marionette puppet led by somebody.

She couldn't make out the face but she was sure it was someone she knew. He was carrying her in his arms, about to kiss her. No wait. He was biting her.

She felt the flesh being gnawed from her bones. He set her down and continued to rip away at her neck.

"Stop!" she tried to speak, but only small squeaks came out of her mangled throat. He was eating her like a ravenous dog.

She kicked and flung her body against the assault, but it was no good. He was hungry and sick. All she could do was moan in agony.

Then in the distance, a light shone radiant, scaring the assailant.

"'Your flesh is my flesh,'" the light said. "'The clean cannot bind with the unclean.'"

Once again, Nadia didn't know his meaning. She tried to ask but gurgles of blood filled her windpipe.

I'm dying! She wanted to say.

But the light read her mind and answered her. "'You have already died my child. Now LIVE! You are flesh of my flesh and blood of my blood. It is the blood that will set you free...the BLOOD!'"

Then, as she looked at her attacker again, she realized she did know him. Manuel? is it you? How could you do this to me?

Angry, she rose with all her might, pushing against his muscles to free herself.

He laughed at her like the devil he was, pointy teeth and all. "You can't get away from me, you're too weak!"

With all the strength she had in her, she kicked and flailed her arms pulling herself toward a bucket. It was filled with her own blood.

With one swift move, she chucked the blood at his face, sending him screaming in pain. How could her blood hurt him?

But then, not only was he screaming, he slowly started to disintegrate. The blood ate at his entire body like acid.

He cried out to her, but before she knew it, he was gone. Only a remnant of ash remained, that and a pool of blood that gave off her own reflection as she looked into it.

Her reflection was relieved. For the first time in a long time she felt as if there was actually hope. She didn't know why.

All she knew was she had to open her eyes.

Chapter 23

They had successfully fought off one *Loco* that had come down the stairs, but now two more stood at the doorway. Miriam wondered if they could trip them too. The *Locos* didn't seem to see well with this sickness.

Soon the one she'd tripped would come up from behind. It lay at the bottom of the stairs still hissing and growling.

Then she heard it: *Gunshots from above.* Was someone out there?

She saw two *Locos* from above drop from the gunfire, then one more.

"*Help!*" she cried. Ebenezer and Tom shouted as well.

A lone dark figure stood at the entrance again, Miriam couldn't make out who it was, but the voice was familiar.

From behind her, a low growling caught her by surprise, but she kicked it away as she held onto Ebenezer, who now clung to the rail. Tom was above them ready to charge whoever or whatever was coming through that doorway above.

Their two dead flashlights tumbled down the step, crashing and thudding against the concrete. Miriam just held onto the rail now, just below Ebenezer's hand. She kicked against the darkness and growling with every ounce of energy she had.

"*Hurry! Up here!*" the voice above called out to them like the cavalry.

Tom pulled Ebenezer from beside her and helped him slowly upward, Miriam was still busy kicking at the *Locos,* waiting impatiently behind the men for her turn to get out of there. It was taking forever and she didn't know how long she could fight this one off.

"*Come on you guys!*" she wailed.

By the time she got to the top doorway, she turned backward and looked down at the *Locos* illuminate face in the sunlight. The evidence of a sickness beyond her understanding revealed itself with rotting bloody mouth and dark sunken bloodshot eyes. *This man was the devil himself!*

It lashed and clawed at her pant leg, ripping away a portion of fabric. It took a bite of her lower calf but thankfully she had worn her long leather dress boots and it couldn't bite through.

Miriam was on her butt now, crawling backward out of the sunlit doorway. Above her, holding a gun was her husband. He pressed the gun to the *Locos* temple and pulled the trigger. A shower of red speckled her clothing, and the ground beneath.

She kicked the bloody head away from her with her heals. "*Frank!* What took you so long?" she sobbed.

Frank just bent down and held her. "I'm sorry," he said, "Are you hurt?"

"*No!* Where are the others?"

"Right behind me dear."

~~~~

"Let's move! Manuel shouted, still carrying his wife in his arms. "We have to find somewhere to hide. I see other *Locos* staggering around. It's not safe to stay here. Gala do you know where we can go?"

"Well..." the women paused, "I know an old bomb shelter. Ebenezer and I hid in there when we first got overrun. It's on the other side of the compound though."

Manuel didn't care, it was either stay there like sitting ducks and be eaten, or take their chances with Gala's suggestion. He had carried Nadia this far, a little further would have to do. "Okay, you lead the way."

Through the bright sunlight of the day, the group headed past burned out vehicles, dead bloody bodies on the ground, and littered streets. It wasn't exactly a walk in the park. They had to be careful not to attract attention, but more importantly they needed a way out. This military base was not the haven they once thought it was.

They came to an old airplane hangar as Gala led them inside to what appeared to be an old walk-in freezer. Bodies of mothers and children lay scattered, lifeless and bloody. Manuel winced as he pressed on. He noticed the others did as well.

"In here!" Gala motioned as she opened the door, urging them inside.

At least this would give him some time to figure out a plan, Manuel thought. And hopefully Nadia would start waking up soon. The fact that she was still unconscious alarmed him. He'd probe Gala for some answers soon.

Gala grabbed for a lantern once she opened the door and took out a lighter from her back pocket to light it. They all herded in behind her and locked the big door from the inside. It was a perfect hiding place...*for now.*

The small room, no bigger than a mid-sized utility closet, was lined with shelves of food. In the flickering lamp light, Manuel set Nadia down gently. She was fully clothed but for some reason it didn't look like she had dressed herself. His wife would never wear her shirt with the tag on the outside. No, she was too meticulous for that. Someone else had dressed her.

"Okay," Manuel puffed as he stood upright and stretched out his back, "Gala, I need to know what's happened to my wife. Why is she like this?"

Gala looked around as they all began to bombard her with questions. "Stop!" she said, "One at a time. Please! And lets just sit down!"

As they all took a seat on the floor around the small lantern, Gala began to explain what had happened to his wife. A huge sadness grew in his belly for what Nadia must have gone through down there. *But why was she prepped for surgery? Surgery for what?*

Manuel couldn't help thinking the doctor was leaving something out.

"I did an ultrasound last night too," Gala smirked.

Manuel tried to read her face but it confused him. *Ultrasound? Surgery?* "So, is she still pregnant then?"

"I'll let your wife tell you that," she smirked again, "look, she's starting to wake up."

Gala rushed over to her side and grabbed Nadia's elfin face in her hands to observe. "Nadia? It's Dr. Silverton. Wake up sweetie?"

Manuel liked how caring this doctor was. She had done nothing but help and that goes far in his books. She'd be a good person to keep around, especially if a baby was on the way. And if his assumptions were correct, *she was still pregnant.*

"*Chica?*" he said, kneeling down beside her, "open your eyes!"

Her parents knelt beside him with wide eyes, watching.

"Where-*where* am I?" Nadia groaned as if awaking from a bad dream.

"It's okay baby! You're safe! We're all here. You're parents too."

She looked around bewildered. It made Manuel's heart skip a beat. Her face looked so helpless like a small child. He would keep her safe even if that meant sacrificing his own life. And the life of his baby?...well, he'd do anything!

As they sat there holding each other, Manuel swore to himself that they were never going to be separated again. They'd stay together at all costs. He was not losing his wife again! "*I love you Chica!*"

~~~

The man's love and adoration for his wife moved her so much, she fought back the tears. Never had Gala ever experience that kind of love. In a way, it broke her heart to listen to him. *Why couldn't she find someone to love her like that?*

They were young, so very young. Gala thought of herself at that age. She closed her eyes and fought against the tears. She had set aside boys right from the start. They were not getting in her way. All her other friends had become distracted with boyfriends. Some of them even dropped out of medical school for a guy. *Not her.* Not Gala Silverton. She'd succeed no matter what. And so, she did. Now what did she have to show for it? *Nothing.* No job anymore, no life, no ring on her finger, and nobody to love her like these two young people in front of her.

Gala couldn't help but feel alone, *so, very much alone.*

She gave the family some privacy and decided to take a seat between the two older gentleman a few feet away from them. Ebenezer she knew, but this Tom she had been introduced to, he reminded her of her own father. *A character full of mystery.*

And obviously religious, from his steady praying as they made their way over here.

"So, Tom!" she decided to break the silence between them," what's your take on all this? *Is God punishing us?*"

Why she asked that question was beyond her. Probably to change the atmosphere. She needed a distraction from feeling sorry for herself that she had never experienced love. And the opposite of love was hate, and hating religion was one of her past times. It made no sense to a practical medical professional.

"You don't want to ask me," Tom mumbled.

"Sure, I do?" Gala answered immediately, "I heard you praying. You obviously believe in prayer for some reason. What are you, a preacher or something?"

"*Was!*"

"Well that doesn't sound good!" The man sat silent in a huff. She could tell he was either scared or upset. *Probably both.*

"Look, if it makes you feel any better, you don't have to preach to me. I don't believe a word of it anyway. God is just a poor man's crutch. *Seriously!* Think about it. Most of us who make an honest living...*made*...an honest living, are *not* Jesus freaks. We know how to make it on our own. I don't need anyone but myself." *And maybe a man.*

Old Tom eyed her with disgust. *Uh oh. That didn't go over well.* It was too late to take her well rounded opinion back. Leave it to her to open a can of worms. She'd gotten herself into trouble with her big mouth many a time. Right now, was no exception.

At least it was a distraction.

"Do *not* talk to me!" Tom snapped, turning his head away.

"I-I only meant that you seem to be a pretty *cynical* preacher." *Now she'd done it.*

Then he turned back to her and got loud, so loud the others stopped what they were doing and listened. It was embarrassing.

"*You have no right to judge me!!!*" Tom shouted.

Okay this was uncalled for. All she wanted to do was have a conversation not get a lecture from some old fart. "*I'm not judging you!*"

"Then what are you doing?"

"I-I was just..." she looked around at the others and then back at Tom and decided to apologize. It wasn't worth the bother. Tom was obviously brewing about something that had nothing to do with her. "I'm sorry. I didn't mean to make you lose your temper?"

The man's face turned red then as he continued his rage. "*I am not losing my temper!* If I lost my temper, you'd know it! I would beat you until your head falls off! I'd rip your body apart like...!" Tom cried in horror, "like I did to all those...*people!*"

Sadness came over Gala then as silence filled the little room. She recognized what was going on. "*I'm sorry Tom,*" was all she could say.

Then the one they called Miriam, Nadia's mother, came over and sat beside Tom, shoeing her away. It was insulting. How could she have known what he'd been through? *She didn't know.*

They'd all been through so much trauma in the last few days. He wasn't the only one, yet they made it out to be so. But she'd keep quiet for now and not speak until they spoke to her. After all, she was apparently the outsider of the group. She'd have to earn her wings if she wanted to stay with these people.

Tom Sobbed in Miriam's arms as she tried to console him. Perhaps it was the fact that he was an old man that made him so emotional. He wasn't as strong as the rest of them. Not even Ebenezer, yet she had heard him break down as well, just in a different way.

Speaking of Ebenezer, he had been pretty quiet. No more Warsaw stories or delusional episodes? She'd go check on him.

"Eb?" she whispered as she went over to sit with him, "Scoot over!"

Ebenezer's eyes were red and glossy, alarming Gala immediately. "You okay?"

Sweat beaded down his forehead telling her he wasn't. "What's wrong?"

Miriam must have heard and rushed to his side immediately. Tom would have to suck it up like the rest of them. A doctor always had to prioritize and right now it was Ebenezer who needed medical attention the most.

"He's got an infection!" Miriam blurted out, "he's had it for a while."

Gala's eyes went wide. "*Infection?*"

"They've been experimenting on him."

Yes, she'd half expected it. Her colleagues were responsible for this. "Lay him down flat and bring the lantern. Let's take a look at what we're dealing with here."

"I can help," Manuel told her, "I'm a paramedic."

"Yes, I heard you were. I could use your assistance then!" At least someone was on her side.

Manuel helped her lay Ebenezer down. They removed his jacket and tried to lift his soiled shirt to no avail. It was stuck to him, to the infection. They'd have to cut it open but they'd need a pair of scissors or a knife.

"Anyone have a knife?" she asked around.

Manuel pulled a knife from under his pant leg, hidden in a leg holster. *Oh, he was prepared.* Gala liked this Manuel. She could tell he had a head on his shoulders. Where could she find another one of *him?*

"Hold him still and I'll cut the shirt," she told Manuel.

Then as if opening a rotten can of tomatoes, Ebenezer's belly became exposed. Infection had gone beyond hope. It was gangrenous and bloody. He didn't have long.

Gala just eyed Manuel as if speaking silently from one professional to another.

They'd give him hope even though he had none.

"You'll be fine Ebenezer!" she said biting her lip and shaking her head, "just fine!"

Manuel hung his head in silence.

All Gala knew was they'd better get that preacher doing his job and quickly. Ebenezer deserved someone to give him his last rights after all he's been through his entire life. She only hoped Tom was up for it because it definitely wasn't going to be her.

Chapter 24

"'Yea, though I walk through the valley of the shadow of death,'" Tom repeated, *"'I will fear no evil: for thou art with me; thy rod and thy staff they comfort me.'"*

Tom repeated that more for himself than for poor Ebenezer. *It was fitting.*

"You have nothing to fear," he told the old man as he bent over him with the others. But they had everything to fear. They were stuck in a closet-sized room in the middle of some kind of an epidemic and who knew what awaited them outside.

Death was everywhere and they were definitely in the valley of the shadow.

It was times like this that he wished he had his Bible but it had been discarded long ago with their escape from the underground facility. *God give me strength*, he prayed to himself. He needed it to go on and to pray over this man who was about to die.

He'd let his weaknesses consume him far too long. After all these years of strength and all the garbage God had pulled him through, this was how he reacted? It saddened him more than anything. He would not let Satan win. No, he had to be strong, if not for himself then for the others who may be strong in character but weak in spirit. He was God's chosen one like Moses. Unfit but called anyway, and he would do what God wanted even if that meant his own death. Yes, that was Pastor McDonald talking, giving *him* some spiritual guidance of his own.

Correction, that was *God*.

"Okay," Tom forced a smiled and gathered his courage, "It is time to say goodbye my friend." He held the old man's hand that was shrivelled and worn from age. Much like his own. Except this man had been through *Warsaw*. Tom didn't feel he had a right to question his morals but the poor man was without faith, and that was his job to try and change that.

"Ebenezer, I don't know if you can still hear me," Tom continued, "but please listen if you can." Tom looked around in the dim light of the lantern and everyone was listening with wide eyes. They all needed this and God was working here.

"Life doesn't always turn out the way you want," he went on, brushing a tear from his cheek. "We screw up. I've screwed up. Sometimes people screw it up *for* us: Hitler, The Gestapo, an abusive spouse, divorce, crummy jobs, poverty, poor health, you name it. We don't always have control of what comes our way. *But God does.*"

"I know you said you don't believe that Ebenezer, and some of the rest of the people here say that too, but when push comes to shove, people always speak of praying. Praying when a tragedy happens is usually the first thing people tell each other to do. I've seen it time and time again. Even those people that say they don't believe."

"If you can get a prayer out my friends, you believe. You *believe!*" Tom felt privileged to speak a sermon. He was being used by God again and that was thrilling. More importantly, people were listening and that made it all worth it. Well *almost.* He didn't want to be that satisfied.

"Now Ebenezer, I can't take away your sorrow. I wasn't there when your friends and family were killed in the gas chambers. A great pain aches inside of me when I think of the things you went through. Life is not easy for any of us, but especially those who suffer," he nodded to the others around him.

"Only God can take away your suffering. We think the ideal time to take our suffering away should be when we are alive, but God's timing is perfect. Our brains can't fathom the vastness of him. He made the universe. There is more to us than just the life we know. We have a *soul*, and that *soul* lives on. You will live on. It is only a question of *where*."

Tom wondered if he should continue. The next part may offend but perhaps they needed offending. They were living in the end days. It was now or never.

"You see, when you die, your soul travels. It will go to heaven, or it will go to hell. It all depends on you. If you believe, you will live with Jesus Christ in a place free from sickness, suffering, and pain. You will never again have to experience the hardships you did in this life. All the storms will be over and you will live in peace for all eternity. It's hard for us to understand that, but we must try, for if we don't, and we shrug it off thinking it isn't true or doesn't matter, we will be sadly mistaken.

"There is a place called hell. I know some don't believe that but it's true. I had a woman tell me she didn't believe in hell, but the Bible says that even the demons believe in hell. I truly believe the Bible is God's word, so why wouldn't I believe what is written in it? I've seen Satan's destruction...and it's nasty! The Bible says God threw Satan into a pit and chained him there. He cannot harm you unless you place yourself within his grasps. *Some have*."

Did he dare go on? They were all so quiet, Ebenezer more so than anyone else, though his chest was still breathing up and down. Even if he didn't have his eyes open, Tom knew he was listening and that was good enough for him. Nadia on the other hand just leaned in more intently at the mention of the pit. *Something was up.*

He'd go on indeed.

"The Bible doesn't tell us where hell is exactly. I know there are some that believe it is hidden in the bowels of the earth. Some say it's located in the *Bermuda Triangle* in a large hole in the bottom of the ocean. Some even say there's a portal to another dimension if you dive down the *Bimini Road* to what was once said to be *Atlantis.* Some say it's in another galaxy altogether."

"I don't know if you can believe all that folklore but the Bible clearly says there is a hell, and I don't want to go there. They say you experience death over and over. It's a life of living fire."

Nadia gasped, and put her hand over her mouth. Manuel consoled her and then continued to listen. Tom would have to talk to Nadia next.

"So...my point is," Tom went on, "that you have a choice. Ebenezer, you have a choice, and the rest of you do as well. You can choose God, or you can choose Satan. Heaven or hell. It's up to you."

"I know where I'm going. I was promised that if I asked Jesus Christ to forgive me for all the awful things I did in this life, and I had many," he looked at Miriam's sad face and felt a tear escape his eye, "then I could be forgiven of *my* sins and have eternal life...and I would receive a helper: *The Holy Spirit.*"

He bent as he spoke into Ebenezer's ear, "This is what I want for you my friend," he eyed everyone around him in the flickering lantern light that illuminated their accepting faces. *All except the doctor.*

Tom thought to ask Gala what she felt but this wasn't the place. This was for Ebenezer. She wouldn't take that away from him. He wouldn't let her have a chance.

"If you can hear me Ebenezer, and you want to pray the sinners prayer with me, just squeeze my hand. If you can't do that, then push with all your might to pray it silently with me."

Tom thought he felt a slight squeeze of the hand, but he couldn't be sure. He'd ask the rest of them the same question. He'd have to be blunt because they'd simply run out of time for politeness. *This might be their last chance to repent.*

"Is there anyone else that wants to say the sinners prayer with me?" he asked. "We've all been through...*stuff*...and we are all sinners. Not a one among us is exempt. You may have said the sinners pray a long time ago and fell away. That's okay. God has a forgiving heart. He wants you to come back home."

"*Anyone?*"

"I hate to be one of those pastor's that puts people on the spot, but frankly, you might not make it out of this. God wants you to break the chains that bind you now. Put up your hand if you're with me."

Nadia suddenly burst into tears, she sobbed into her right hand and lifted her left. "I'm with you Pastor!"

Then Miriam burst into tears and lifted her hand as well. Frank followed, raising his hand in silence. Manuel sat there staring into space. Tom wondered what the big man was thinking. Perhaps God was working on him, perhaps not. Maybe this was the first time he had heard a sermon like this.

Regardless, it had to be his own choice. He wasn't pushing anyone. God didn't work like that, and neither did he.

Suddenly, Manuel sighed, lifted his arm like he was stretching, and then rubbed the top of his head and scratched. Tom could see the visible struggle he was having. Manuel was fighting his demons right there in front of them. Then, suddenly, the big man's arm shot up strong and stayed there. "Count me in too," he nodded with a quivering bottom lip as he looked at his wife with tear filled eyes.

Everyone looked in Gala's direction. All she did was hang her head without looking up. To Tom's disappointment, the woman wasn't ready. That was okay. All in God's timing.

"So, let's begin," he said, squeezing Ebenezer's hand and lifting his own in surrender.

"*With all my heart, I accept you Jesus Christ as my personal saviour. I repent of my sins and, by faith, accept Christ's mercy and forgiveness which he bought for me on the cross of Calvary.*"

"*With the help and power of the Holy Spirit I want to be a faithful Christian from this day onward, no matter what comes of this world. In Jesus name...*"

"And all God's people said...?" Tom smiled, looking around at their warm faces.

"*AMEN!*" they repeated in unison.

Everyone except Gala.

~~~

They were all nuts, every single one of them! Gala thought to herself.

She had heard many a preacher, even been to different churches, and never had she *ever* felt so embarrassed! He didn't have to put her on the spot. No, she was too stubborn for that. *He was not changing her!*

And what were they talking about anyway? They might be these so-called sinners, but she definitely wasn't. Everything she did in her life was for a reason. She didn't go around hurting people, on the contrary. She had devoted her life to helping people and saving lives. *If that was sinful, they were insane.*

Yet, one thing she did envy, was the way they seemed so content now. It was as if all their burdens had suddenly been lifted. She could only wish for that. She wished they'd snap out of it. Someone had to care that Ebenezer was dying right there in front of them. Perhaps they did, but they sure didn't show it.

"Oh, for goodness sake," she said pushing the group aside, "let me check Ebenezer. You could have a bit more concern for *him* instead of yourselves."

She checked his pulse, thready at best.

Gala smoothed the old man's wild white hair along his sweaty wrinkled forehead. He'd lived a long life. She had only briefly known him, heard about his adventures and traumas and yet, she felt a closeness to him. She always felt this way when taking care of a dying patient. It was hard to detach, but necessary. She'd better prepare herself for this one.

Then suddenly he gasped as if choking for air,"

"Eb?" she called one last time, but he was gone. She kissed him on the cheek and sniffled. *No tears, no tears!*

"Well, your *God* took him now, didn't he," was all she could say. But in the back of her mind she knew who was responsible. And they were running the show down in the research center. He was experiment number twenty-two. Just a number to them. She wondered if she would ever see those physicians again.

She found a wool blanket on the shelving unit beside her and covered the body up. There was no sense leaving him exposed for all to see. Who knew how long they would have to stay there. Hopefully it was only going to be a few hours because Ebenezer already had a bad odour. They wouldn't be able to stand what came next.

"Frank, you had a shoulder wound?" she asked after finishing with the blanket. "Let's take a look at it before you become the next casualty."

She may as well flip into doctor mode. Nobody else was going to. Reality told her that no *God* was going to fix a bullet wound.

"It's just a graze," he said, holding the area, "It's not really bleeding much."

"Still, I should look at it. I'm a doctor."

"Manuel did already...and he's a *paramedic*."

Oh, so did that mean she wasn't needed in this group? Were they snubbing her now because she didn't believe? Typical Christian people, all they do is judge. Well, she wouldn't stick around and be picked on, or harassed, or disrespected. No, she'd be better off on her own. She'd beg her colleague's forgiveness and they'd let her back into the research center. She'd be able to finish her secret project and prove that they were dealing with a *Prion* after all. She would be appreciated *then*.

"Oh, well *excuse me.* I guess I'm not needed here after all!" she blurted with hurt.

Nadia came up to her then and put her arm around her. "Gala, you mean *everything* to me. I *need* you! You helped me when nobody else would. *You saved me!* Don't ever think we don't appreciate you!"

Then an actual tear did come. Just a little one. It rolled down her cheek and she immediately brushed it away as fast as it came.

"When you did that ultrasound," Nadia smiled, "you showed a part of yourself that I've never seen in anyone. You helped me in spite of yourself. You could have gotten into a lot of trouble."

"*I did,*" she mused, brushing away another tear.

"Well, *seeee..,*" Nadia consoled, trying to make her feel better. Gala sure liked that little red head. If she would've had a daughter, she would've wanted her to be just like Nadia. *Sweet, so very sweet and innocent.*

"You guys," Nadia said, calling the group together, "in all the excitement, I never got a chance tell you the good news. Gala helped me through a lot of stuff when I was in the research center. One of those things was this," she smiled, grabbing her husbands big hand, placing it on her little bulging tummy, and Gala immediately melted. *She still hadn't told them?*

"I wanted to tell you *first* honey," she looked at her husband with warm eyes, "but...I guess there's just no time...*or privacy.*"

"What is it *Chica?*" the handsome Spanish man took her hand and kissed it. That man had charisma. A real gentleman to say the least.

"You already told us you are pregnant, sweetheart," Miriam blurted out as she teased her daughter, "and we *already* forgave you."

"Mother *stop!*" Nadia cut her off, giving her a teasing evil eye back.

Now what was this about?

Frank lightly slapped his wife on the arm as if to shut her up. All the hidden drama was coming out, Gala suspected. This was kind of interesting. They weren't all saints after all. That was a breath of fresh air to Gala. She had to smirk at how the tiny girl put everyone in their place.

"Listen," Nadia continued, "and *don't* interrupt me again *mom!*"

Then she turned back to Gala. "Dr. Silverton...*I mean*...Gala, gave me an ultrasound and showed me the most precious gift of all: I saw *two* heartbeats."

Nadia turned to Manuel and smiled widely as she held both of his hands.

"*Two?*" he asked with hopeful eyes.

"Two!"

Manuel kissed his wife long and softly making Gala's heart melt. Those two are special. She didn't know about the other three, but one thing was for certain, she wouldn't be leaving them anytime soon. *Nope.* She was sticking to them like glue.

"I can't believe it!" Miriam mumbled, "we're having *twin* grandbabies Frank. I still think you're too young, but twins are fine with me. I can put them in identical dresses."

"Oh, *nooo* mom! We don't even know what sex they are."

Gala piped up then, "Yup, grandma can dress them in the same dresses. They are identical twin girls."

She didn't know if she was supposed to give the gender away. She'd intended to keep it a secret, but under the circumstances, they had a right to know what she did.

The family hugged in a circle, leaving Gala and Tom as outsiders. But she didn't mind at all. It was a welcome happiness that sent a chill up her spine. In amongst a world of chaos and death, something good remained. A hope for mankind, safely tucked away inside the womb of a young girl. *A special girl.* Gala couldn't quite put her finger on it, but she knew that Nadia had something most people didn't.

Perhaps it was God, but Gala wanted to write it off as a pregnancy glow at least for now, at least until she figured it out. She was, after all, the lone survivor of a biological contagion and she wanted to know why.

For now, she'd let them be happy.

Chapter 25

The sun set on the littered, torched, and mostly deserted 119th Wing. Only a handful of soldiers were left. Parrington Dawson the Third was one of them, or use to be anyway. He usually went by First Lieutenant Dawson up until about a month ago before his medical discharge. But he could still fly just about any bird in the sky. His specialty was the C - 140 Cargo Plane and only because that's what he was trained on when he was stationed at Fort Bragg last year. Safest plane in the sky he'd say. Frankly it was the only one he trusted to get the job done, just like his favourite hooker.

She was always reliable when their chutes deployed from the static line. He'd seen a lot of mishaps with other planes so it was a stipulation of his transfer. She had to go with him and so his plane was quickly nicknamed *Dawson's Hooker*.

And there she stood, all primed and ready. But he'd lost most of his buddies; got separated from those he was with earlier in the day. He'd go alone if he could but he needed someone to do the dirty work. He couldn't get near his woman right now anyway. Those things were on her like a dirty scrap of toilet paper.

He called them *'things'* because they weren't real people anymore. They were more like rabid animals now with their growling and hissing and biting. It was a riot to shoot them down with his buddies just like opening season. He usually always pulled in the biggest buck because, after all, he was Parrington Dawson the Third.

Man, he should have been in the sky hours ago. *This was ridiculous.* He hadn't seen a real person for a long time now, but then he couldn't see much of anything since the sun went down, and it was getting colder. He could already see his breath.

He huddled in the corner, hidden behind the wooden cargo boxes as he crossed his arms against the shakes. He'd have to find somewhere warm or he'd freeze to death.

But where?

Parrington looked around for someone, not the animals, but for someone that even resembled a human being. Or, was he the last man standing? *He hoped not.* Surely some of the *old boys* had made it too.

Surely.

Then, out of the corner of his eye, he caught a light flickering. Just for a minute, and then it vanished. It was across the way in the abandoned airline hanger next to him. He was sure he saw it. He'd wait for a few minutes to see if he could see it again.

Yes, there is was. It was coming from the *rabbit hole* they called it. Someone was inside. He made his way over, slowly, quietly, and very carefully.

Parrington didn't have a weapon, that was his only disadvantage. He wasn't allowed to have one. And hand to hand combat didn't seem to work very well either, so that was out of the question. All it took was one bite and you were a goner.

He wasn't going to make the same mistake as that *retard* Jarvis. He'd keep low and quiet until he reached the rabbit hole. Then he'd knock and hope for the best.

When he finally reached his destination, and stepped over the mess of bodies that lined his path, he stopped and waited just outside. He'd listen first. If they were human, he'd knock. If they were animals he'd leave as fast as he came. But then, animals didn't need light to see in the dark and they definitely had a light in there. He'd seen it a few minutes ago. Someone must have opened the door a crack.

Then he heard a voice. *It was human alright.* His heart jolted. Come on Parr, he told himself, rap on the door and get yourself some rabbit tail. He loved his corny sense of humour.

One, two, three, he counted to himself, rapping on three.

He paused for a response.

Surely, they could hear that. He would pound louder if it wasn't for the *freaks,* they were everywhere. He knocked again, this time a little louder and longer.

"Who's there?" a man's voice whispered.

"*First Lieutenant Dawson,*" he whispered back. "Can you let me in?"

Then a low creaking sound of the familiar rabbit hole door eased open. A big *Mexican* goon pointed a gun at him. Not exactly his favourite people. *Stupid wetbacks!*

"*Please,* let me in and I'll help you get out of here," he lied.

The man opened the door and pulled him in with a sudden jerk. Before he knew it, he was inside. They had the lantern on and there was about six of them.

Parrington raised his hands to show them he was unarmed, *unfortunately.* "I'm not sick," he told them.

"We know you're not sick buddy," the goon replied with an accent, "we wouldn't have let you in otherwise. *You alone?*"

"Umm yeah," Parrington replied, "I lost my buddies this morning. I've been trying to make it to my plane ever since, but it's almost impossible without a weapon."

The goon lowered his gun. "Names Manuel," he introduced himself," raising a hand to shake. "Sorry for all that, but we had a run in with the military a while back, and they were not so nice."

Riiight!

"Got it! I'm Parrington."

"You said you had a plane?" Manuel asked immediately.

"Yes! In the next hangar. *She's all mine!*"

"Can you fly us out of here?" Manuel asked again.

"I can."

But I won't!

Then it hit him. The stench was so rancid Parrington almost passed out. "What the.," he covered his nose with his arm. "What is that awful smell?"

"We have our own problems in here as you can see. He died," the goon pointed to a body in the corner that was covered with a blanket.

Immediately Parrington stepped back, "You can't keep him in here!"

"*He's dead!*" he told him again.

"Not for long. Don't you know? They ain't all the way dead!"

The goon filled him in, "We know, but this one won't come back. He wasn't infected with the virus...*well he was*...but not like *that*."

Parrington looked around at everyone else, they had a little smirk on their faces. *Retards!* This wasn't funny. They should have dragged him out a long time ago. Either they do that or he's turning around and heading right back out that door. First, he couldn't stand the smell one minute longer and secondly, he didn't need a bunch of *idiots.*

"I'm sorry," he said, squeezing his nose, "I'm leaving."

"Hold on a minute!" the goon grabbed his arm, "you're not going anywhere!"

"Manuel don't!" a small voice from the background spoke up. It was a teeny-bopper with long red hair. Must be his little sister or something, though, he'd never seen a white-faced Mexican ginger before.

"If he wants to leave, we can't stop him," the ginger continued.

The goon huffed, and removed his hand from the door. "*Go then!*"

Parrington looked back at the other people sitting on the floor. He shook his head. They were so stupid. They would all be infected by morning but that wasn't his problem. Still, maybe he could use them somehow, at least the big goon. "Look," he said before opening the door, "let me help you drag the body out."

He'd be nice for a change. It would pay off.

The goon sighed again, "*Fine!* We've been trying to do it ourselves except every time we try, another *Loco* comes around."

"*Loco?* What's that?"

"The sick people," the Mexican told him.

Parrington couldn't believe how stupid the name sounded.

"Oh *okay,* I see what you mean. Can't seem to peck em off fast enough," Parrington mused, "I just call them all *animals, freaks,* you name it."

Parrington just smirked and tried to make light of the situation. Perhaps he could get something out of these people if he tried hard enough. He'd have to work on getting them to trust him. The big one was definitely worth his weight in grunt labour and that's what he needed. He'd struck a gold mine here. Plus, they had a weapon.

They each grabbed a leg as it poked out of under the blanket. The smell was so bad, Parrington could hardly breathe. One of the old farts peeked out the door and told them when the coast was clear.

When he nodded, he smothered the lantern until it was completely dark. Then they dragged the smelly man about twelve feet from the doorway and left him there. *Good riddance!*

"Are you coming back inside?" the goon had the nerve to ask him point black.

"Well I can't very well stay out here, now can I?"

He was led back to the door and brought inside to the warm ambience. Finally, he'd found help to do what had to be done. *He'd con him somehow.*

~~~

As they lit the lantern again, Manuel began to interrogate the soldier. It wasn't that he didn't trust the man, it was just that he needed some answers.

"Sit," Manuel motioned for him to take a seat on the floor. "Tell me everything you know. Is there someone in charge here or are we it."?

"We're it man."

Manuel squinted, observing the strange man. This *Parrington* was less than half the size of Manuel, mid forties, with a baby face and glasses. Not a typical looking man by any means. He was completely bald and scrawny. But he was a soldier non-the-less, a Lieutenant of all ranks, and proved himself valuable: *He had a plane.*

"So," Manuel continued to drill him, "do you know how far this virus has spread?"

"Last I heard," Parrington cleared his throat, "the entire U.S."

Manuel frowned, as did the rest of the group. It was what he suspected but he still hoped it wasn't true. Who would have done such a thing? Done what though? They didn't even know what exactly happened. Maybe Parrington knew.

"Do they know what happened?" Manuel threw his next question at him.

"Well, it *was* classified, but I guess since we're practically *family*, I might as well share the info," Parrington told him. "They said the CDC was notified that a biological weapon was released into the United States water supply. They don't know exactly what it was, a mixture of some kind of crap, but it wasn't airborne, that much they know. You have to chug it or get bitten by someone who has it. It works kind of like rabies and there's some weird re-animation involved. Don't ask me how that works but it's pretty darn freaky if you ask me. I've never seen anything like it. The doctors on the base were supposed to be working on some kind of vaccine, but that bombed, I guess. I don't even know if they're still kicking."

"Oh, they're still kicking," the doctor piped up, "you're talking to one. I'm Dr. Gala Silverton and we just spent the last few days trying to get away from them. *Don't ask.*"

The weird man nodded hello.

Manuel changed the subject back to the contagion. "So, is it just the U.S then? Is any other country affected?... because we flew in from the Bahamas and there was stuff going on there too. They had an earthquake...and a Tsunami warning. We were sent back to the U.S pretty fast. I wonder if they suspected something was going on?"

Parrington looked puzzled, "*Don't ask me!* All we were told about was the U.S. I don't know anything about the Bahamas. I guess the earthquake was just a freak coincidence that it happened at the same time. Canada, last we heard anyway, wasn't affected. That's where I'm headed. I'm going to take the bird to a base I know there in Moose Jaw, Saskatchewan. Buddy I use to know from Fort Bragg lives up there. He's retired now but he'll give me clearance or I'll kick his butt."

"Canada shut it's borders on the ground and in the air. They won't let anyone in without clearance. Can't get a hold of my buddy Rigs right now, but that's understandable since the entire U.S has no way to communicate with the outside world since the power grids went down. Only way to contact is in the sky *baby.* Once I get to the border, I can get him on the horn pretty darn quick."

Manuel decided the man's plan sounded trustworthy. Could he really get them into Canada though? That was the question. He guessed they didn't have many options. It was either stay and be *Loco* bate, or take their chances with Parrington. He knew which one he wanted to pick and it was safer in the sky than the interstate, *that was for sure.*

"So, you'd take us with you then?" Manuel asked.

"Yup! *No problem!*" Parrington grinned.

The man didn't even struggle with the decision. That in itself told Manuel the Lieutenant was someone he could trust. Not like those other soldiers he and Nadia had come across on the road a few days ago.

"Then we'll go with you in the morning," Manuel decided for everyone.

The rest of the group nodded in agreement, all except his own wife.

"I am *not* getting on another airplane *Manuel Enrico Espinosa!*" Nadia argued with him, "I can't do it again!"

"*Chica!* You're killing me!"

"*Please!* Don't make me fly!" Nadia begged him, sulking with her arms crossed.

"I won't let anything happen to you! *Yo prometo!*"

He'd carry her kicking and screaming if he had to but they were *all* getting on that plane no matter what. It was the best shot they had.

"We'll go!" he turned to Parrington, "My wife just has a fear of flying but she'll be fine. Won't you *Chica?*"

He beamed smiling teeth at her. She refused again, so he blew a kiss at her. Then she sighed and gave in, matching her nod with his, "*Okaaay.*"

"*Whoa!* I thought she was your sister for a minute buddy," the Lieutenant laughed, clicking his tongue, "she's so...*young!* What are you...*sixteen darlin'?*" he winked.

Okay, that ticked Manuel off but instead, he laughed, trying to ignore it. He couldn't afford to get on the wrong side of their ticket out of there. He just eyed his wife and could tell she was also ticked off at the Lieutenants comment. Hopefully it would work to his advantage. Nadia always flew easier when she was mad anyway.

"See dear," Miriam piped up, always at the wrong time, "we're not the only ones that think twenty is too young to be married."

"*MOTHER!*" Nadia gave her the evil eye.

Now he'd better change the subject or there would be a cat fight for sure. "Just calm down you two. Let's get some sleep or we won't be doing anything in the morning. Grab some blankets from the shelves and turn out the lantern doctor."

Gala grabbed a stack of wool blankets and tossed them to everyone as they tried to find a comfortable position on the hard concrete floor.

"Not the easiest place to sleep with a bad back," Frank moaned.

"Oh, be quiet!" Miriam snapped, "we all have aches and pains."

Manuel chuckled to himself. Those two were characters. He hoped he and Nadia could stand each other when they got as old as them.

He snuggled up to his still fuming wife and pulled the blanket over them. Then with one hand he tickled her in the ribs. Immediately she jolted, and pushed his hand away. *Yup! Still mad.* Good, drag it out until we get on the plane. *Please!*

He smirked at her as he kissed her goodnight. She did *not* kiss back.

"You can turn down the lantern now Gala," he told her, "we're all ready, aren't we?"

Everyone answered in unison.

"Oh, just wait," Parrington added, "I forgot to mention something. I have one little problem with our plan tomorrow."

Here comes the deal breaker, Manuel thought to himself as he rolled his eyes. The guy was full of it. He probably wasn't even a pilot.

Parrington popped his bald head up, "We have no fuel."

Oh Great? How were they supposed to fly out of there with no fuel? "And just how do you supposed we fly *Lieutenant?*"

"We need to get the fuel truck," he gave a sheepish grin. "They blew up four of them already. We've only got one left on the base."

"And where might that be?" Manuel asked, knowing there had to be some catch.

"Half across the base," he said impishly, "under lock and key, of which I don't have. And it's in a place I can't really get a plane near, so we need to go get it first. But my plan was to try and taxi the plane as far as I can go and then get the fuel somehow."

Somehow indeed! He wanted to scream at the man for getting their hopes up. *Ay carumba!* He knew it was too good to be true.

Chapter 26

Morning came to Frank with an awful pain shooting through his lower back. Sleeping on a cold hard concrete floor was the worst thing he'd ever done. He was going to pay for this big time.

Miriam was still snoring...*loudly.* He was surprised that the others were able to sleep with it. He'd always worn earplugs at home.

"Miriam," he whispered, poking her, "move over, you're blocking the door and I have to take a leak."

She suddenly made a snorting sound and jolted right up. "*Hugh?*"

"You're blocking the door," he whispered again.

"Frank! *Jeepers!* Quit waking me up," she growled, rolling in the opposite direction to go back to sleep.

Man, she could be cranky sometimes. At least he could sneak out of the door and relieve himself without waking anyone else up. He'd be back in a flash. His bladder was about to burst. Slowly, he eased his aching body to a sitting position. At least his back wasn't out. It didn't feel like it at least. The cold floor seemed to act like an ice pack; a good thing, he supposed, but *oooh* the stiffness was unbearable.

Straightening against the pain, he silently unlatched the door. The hinges moaned a bit as he opened it a crack but not for long. The sun was just rising and he could see the chaos of bodies scattered in disarray. *Ignore it! Just ignore it,* he told himself.

Once outside, he carefully stepped around the bloody mess to a clearing and unzipped his fly.

Ahhh the relief he felt to finally pee. He'd waited as long as he could and there wasn't a place to do it inside. Well he could of, but that wouldn't have been appreciated. It was bad enough they had to endure the smell of old Eb...he had a hard time just thinking about the man. Was he *really* gone?

Once he was done and zipped up, his eye caught the terminal next to them. It was a short distance away, but he was going to investigate. The Lieutenants claims seemed fishy to him. Was there even a plane there at all?

Well he was going to find out. He needed to stretch his back out, and a bit of a walk would do the trick. There was nobody around anyway. It seemed all the *Locos* from the night before had cleared out.

He'd be back before anyone even noticed he was gone.

<p style="text-align:center">~~~~</p>

Nadia's dream had transformed.

She was no longer in the burning place, she was running in a meadow full of lush green grass and she was chasing something.

"Come back here," she laughed, "you are not getting away this time."

What was it exactly that she was after? She couldn't make out the shape of it but it was something human anyway.

She was carrying something in her hand but she couldn't make that out either. Her eyes were blurry. She rubbed them but still couldn't see much at all. It didn't seem to bother her though. She was happy.

It was almost as if she was playing a game but there was a purpose to it. The rules were vague but she was determined to catch something.

"Come out, come out, where ever you are," she chided.

But no matter how hard she ran, she just couldn't catch what she was looking for. Then suddenly she turned, and caught a glimpse of another one. Oh, they were sneaky, the two of them!

She crouched down and waited in the long grass.

Silently she hushed her heavy breathing and waited with that thing in her hand. What was it again? She listened for their footsteps and then heard them in the rustling grass. One of them behind her, and the other one in front. Was she trapped?

They are definitely not playing by the rules.

But then there were no rules. It was every man for himself out there, and Nadia wondered if this was a game of tag or something more serious.

Suddenly, a face shot through the grass.

"Ahhh!" she screamed

She wasn't ready for that.

Then they both revealed themselves: Faces of rot and blood draped with weeping flesh, hung off their bones. One of them tried to bite her. This was no game!

"Take that!" she charged forward, knowing exactly what to do. It had all been planned out from the beginning. She had the weapon, and the weapon thrust into the first ones neck, then the second one.

It was finished. She had won.

Finally, when she wiped her weapon off and put it back into her pocket, she felt a hand on her shoulder. It was ANOTHER!

A face with bulging eyes coming out of its sockets, snapped at her, biting, BITING!

~~~~

Her daughter screamed in her sleep again!

She had always had those nightmares but this time she had woken the whole group up. Nadia was hunched over sobbing in Manuel's arms as Miriam observed in the low light of the lantern Gala had just lit.

"It's okay!" Manuel told them all as he continued to console his wife. "She just had a bad dream. Go back to sleep."

"Who can go back to sleep now?" Miriam snapped. "What time is it anyway? Does anyone know? Frank?" she reached for him but only found his discarded blanket. "*FRANK?*"

"Where's daddy?" Nadia immediately cried in alarm.

"I don't *knooow?*" Miriam wailed. "I think he went out to go to the bathroom earlier but he should have been back by now."

"An you *let* him mom?"

"It's not *my* fault! He doesn't think sometimes."

Why did she always get blamed for Franks stupidity? It was like taking care of a little child. He drove her crazy, but if anything happened to him, she'd never forgive herself. She should have stopped him. He could have peed in a bucket or something. He didn't have to go out there. Oh, she shuddered at the thought of him stumbling around out there with the *Locos. God help him!* And yes, that was a prayer.

"I'll go find him," Manuel charged to the door. "Why didn't he just stay put? I hope he didn't go far."

"Take the gun honey!" Nadia nagged.

"I have it," he grumbled, "just everybody else stay put. I don't want to end up looking for the rest of you. Eat something while I'm gone. There's plenty of food on the shelves and some bottled water over there. Hopefully when we get back, we can all make a run for the plane...*together!*"

Manuel opened the door and shut it, leaving a silence afterward that Miriam figured she'd fill. "*Welp,* who's hungry?"

Suddenly Nadia heaved into a bucket and wiped at her mouth, "*Sorry!*"

Great! Now they all just lost their appetites. It was going to be another long day cooped up with these people. Her daughter she could tolerate, at least when she wasn't puking in a pail, but this Lieutenant guy was making strange noises with his nose and mouth and trying to hork something up. *Gross!*

"You just about finished?" she asked the man.

"I have sinus problems," he told her, "sorry bout that. I thought it was the perfect time to do that since your daughter was making all those gagging noises; you know what I mean lady."

"No, I don't know what you mean sir." Wasn't he just the most annoying man ever? If they didn't need his plane, she'd kick him out right now.

"Thought you said she wasn't sick," he said.

"I'm not *sick* already," Nadia burped in anger, "I'm *PREGNANT!*"

Miriam could see her daughter didn't like the man either. There was just something about him that was annoying. He reminded her of *Steve Urkel* from that show in the 80's she hated so much: *Family Matters*. Her daughter wouldn't even know what she was talking about if she mentioned it, so she'd keep that comparison quiet. But good grief, he was annoying with his whiney voice. It wasn't masculine at all.

"The old man knocked you up hey?" Parrington snickered without a bat of an eye.

"Okay...*Mom?*" Nadia spit back in anger, "would you *please* shut this guy up! I can't take this right now." She puked in her pail again, and this time she didn't hold back.

"*OUT!*" she pointed Parrington to the door, "You don't insult *MY* daughter and get away with it!"

"I wasn't!"

"*Leave!*" she said again, pointing. Either he'd go on his own or she'd drag him out by his scrawny neck.

"Enough you guys!" Gala interrupted, "he can't go out there. It's not safe. *Please!* Stay Lieutenant! Just watch what you say next time."

"I didn't say anything," he grumbled. "Are you all on the *rag* of something?"

"*I beg your Pardon?*" Gala stopped short. She looked at Miriam puzzled and Miriam looked at her, and then Nadia puked again.

This was not happening. Was this man raised in a barn or did they just talk like this in the military. It was down right insulting.

"Okay look," Tom piped up, "obviously we all got off on the wrong foot fellah. These ladies are not to be talked to with that kind of vulgarity but we don't want you to leave. I'm sure we can all get along with each other. Lets just try and be civil."

"*No,*" Parrington sulked, "I know when I'm not wanted. *I'll leave.* You people can find your own plane out of here. *You're not going in mine!"* He charged out the door and slammed it hard.

"*Great!"* Tom fumed, "now I'm going to have to go after him. *Thanks a lot ladies."*

"No Tom, stay here! *Please!"* Miriam insisted, "It's not safe, you'll get bitten. You don't even have a weapon."

"Manuel told everyone to stay here you guys," Nadia told them, drying her face with a towel now, looking a lot better then before.

"She's right Tom," Gala told him, "you can't go out there. Hopefully Parrington will come back. He's probably just blowing off steam. But seriously you guys, we didn't need to chase him away even if he was acting like an idiot. *We needed him.* He was our way out of here. I hope for your sake he comes back."

"Why?" Miriam countered, "you think my son-in-law is going to blame me for this one too? It's bad enough my husband is out there. You think I want that silly Lieutenant on my conscience as well?"

Miriam couldn't control her anger. She could feel her blood boiling. She was sick of people blaming her for every little thing. Mostly she was just sick of all *this!*

"Miriam!" Tom butt in, "*let it go dear!* Just let it go." He held her tightly in an embrace like her father use to do. She wanted to scream but somehow, he calmed her down, just like at the church. He was good at it. He was a pastor. He was *her* pastor. Why hadn't she ever utilized that before?

She sobbed in Tom's arms. Hopefully the Lieutenant would come back. Hopefully Manuel would find Frank.

Hopefully he was still alive!

Chapter 27

Frank saw the plane but he couldn't believe it, it was full of *Locos*. The door was open and they were definitely inside. How were they going to use it? The Lieutenant said nothing about having to take over the plane. He knew the man's plan sounded like a bunch of malarkey.

But now he was stuck between a rock and a hard place, surrounded on all sides. Tom was right, they were walking corpses just like the Bible predicted.

God help me now! I've gone and got myself into trouble, he prayed.

He figured his best bet was to hide but he couldn't do that forever. Frank had left the plane and the hangar he'd found it in an hour ago, and he still wasn't able to get back to the others. He'd already been kneeling behind some old welding equipment far too long. His knees were raw and aching to the point of numbness. All he needed was to lose the use of them. He had to get up and stretch. *Stay or go Frank?*

He'd go! But he'd make it quick.

Just as he managed to stand up, he noticed he'd been spotted. *Here they come,* he braced himself looking around for a weapon. Luckily, there were rusty metal welding rods laying sporadically on the ground. He picked two of them up, one for each hand, and started swatting with them.

He felt lethal as he sliced through the air ready for an attack. It was now or never. He was ready for anything even though his back ached and his legs were numb. He wasn't too old to defend himself.

Yet, he questioned what he was even doing out there.

Too late to ponder, they were almost on him.

"Take that, you ugly thing!" he shouted, poking a rod into the *Locos* head. It dropped to the ground gushing with blood.

Not bad!

Another one was on his left already. He swiped the rod backward but missed. Then more *Locos*. Was he losing the battle?

As if he had two machetes in his hands, he worked them both together but didn't do much damage. They kept on coming, grabbing him, clawing him. It was too late. *IT WAS TOO LATE!*

Then a gun shot rang out.

Someone was shooting. Someone was there for him but he couldn't see anything underneath the dog pile. It hurt, *it hurt bad!* Blood sprayed his face as they bit through a main artery in his neck and wouldn't stop. *They were eating him!*

It was his time to leave this awful place; he knew it. *But God was still with him.* He was in the *light* and someone was calling his name. *"'Come with me my good and faithful servant,'"* the voice of God told him, *"'I will give you rest.'"* He reached out his hand through the bloody attack and found solace there, but that meant he'd never see his wife and daughter again.

Goodbye my loves!

Goodbye!

~~~

Manuel was too late. His father-in-law was gone and it broke his heart. He saw the bloody mess as the *Locos* rose from their feasting. *It was barbaric.* Only savages could do such a thing. And savages they were, with their bloody dripping mouths.

He'd be next if he didn't get out of there fast.

Manuel turned tail and ran out of there as fast as he could. Not one *Loco* stood in his way. He could feel his heart pounding in his chest. It was more from the shock of seeing Frank being eaten alive, than his own fatigue but he couldn't stop to collect himself. No, he'd keep going for Nadia's sake. *Nadia,* how would he even tell her?

It was going to be the most difficult thing he ever did!

Rounding a corner, he realized he was back in the old hangar and almost home free, if you could call it that. The hideout was just a few feet away.

Just then he heard a whistle. It was Parrington. *What was he doing outside?*

"Over here?" the Lieutenant called.

Manuel looked both ways and then ran quickly to meet the man. "You should be inside; It's not safe out here."

"I know. I was just out for a *stroll.* Thought I might find you and give you a hand."

A stroll? In these conditions? The man was a nut.

"I don't need any help."

But for some reason, Parrington didn't seem to realize the danger. Under normal circumstances Manuel wouldn't care, but he had a plane and they needed him. He was too valuable to let anything happen to him. "C'mon! Let's get back inside."

"I'm not going back there with those *witches!*"

What?! "Excuse me?" Was he serious?

"Well, I could call them something else but you wouldn't be too happy."

237

He wasn't happy now! He was going to hit the man if he didn't shut up.

"They've been harping on me since you left buddy. I don't know how you can stand them, all menstrual and everything. And your little *'B'* is barfing her cookies all over. "

Shut up! Shut up! Don't react Manuel!

He chose to bite his tongue, as difficult as it was. Even though he was boiling mad, he would not let it show. *He would not let it show!* The man was a fool and had a red-neck mouth obviously, but he had a plane. *He had a plane!*

That made it all worth it, didn't it?

~~~

Parrington gave himself a pat on the back. What a clever guy he was, finding the leader of the pack. Now he could get him to do his dirty work without having to deal with all those *stupid* women.

It was what he wanted in the first place. He didn't need the whole group, only the big lug. Then he could be on his way, *solo.*

"How bout we take a look-see at my plane bucko?" he told the big wetback. He'd be able to clear those animals out in no time and all he'd have to do is stand back and watch. It almost worked last time with that other guy he brought over to do it, but they killed him before he got the job done. If the same thing happened to this guy, it was no sweat off his back. He'd just find another guinea pig.

Parrington hoped he was capable though. He really wanted to get out of there. Then there was the fuel problem. If the brute succeeded in clearing the plane, he mused to himself, he'd be able to do the rest no problem. And finishing the guy off in the end would be exciting to say the least. No need to take him to Canada anyway.

Just a dirty old wetback.

Chapter 28

"Pastor McDonald? Can I ask you a question?" Nadia broke the silence as they ate.

"Sure can sweetie, but you don't have to call me Pastor McDonald, Tom is just fine."

"Okay, *Tom*. I've been having these dreams..." She wondered if she should even mention it. They seemed so stupid now. "Do you think God speaks to us through our dreams?"

The old man looked worn. He scratched his head and rubbed his stubble chin. Nadia hadn't paid much attention to him over the years. He was just the pastor of the church she'd hardly attended. Her dad's pastor really. But now she was curious.

"Well, you know, I've heard so many different things about this topic," he said. "A lot of pastors would say no. But I think dreams can be very prophetic. God spoke through dreams in the Bible. Why wouldn't he now? That's my take on it. What were your dreams about?"

Nadia eyed her mother and didn't know if she should give the graphic details. She didn't want to scare her. "Um, they were kind of scary."

"Nadia has always had bad dreams," her mother said, "even when she was a child. I don't know why. We always wrote it off as a wild imagination."

"Well, is it a repeated dream?" the pastor asked.

"Um, yeah."

"I see."

She didn't know what 'I see' meant, but his tone didn't sound good. Perhaps she shouldn't bother him at all. It wasn't the right time or place, yet, they had to do something while they waited for Manuel and her father to get back. The waiting was driving her crazy and she assumed it was driving her mother crazy as well, with her incessant nail biting.

"Is a repeated dream bad?" Nadia asked shyly.

"Not necessarily," the pastor told her, "my personal opinion is that God is trying to tell you something. Usually our dreams are our subconscious mind trying to work out our lives. Our dreams kind of tell us about ourselves. I know people who are so into dream interpretations that they become obsessed with it and they forget about God. There are entire websites dedicated to this kind of thing. But I think we should pray and ask God's guidance more so than a silly website. But I believe we need to pay attention to recurrent dreams though."

Nadia's eyes widened, "What do you mean?"

"Well, I'm just saying we should pay attention. What were your dreams about if you don't mind me asking?"

There was no way she was going to tell him the gory details, but Nadia figured she would give him the sugar-coated version for her mother's sake. "I kept dreaming that something was grabbing me. I was hovering in the air and it pulled me under. I thought it was the devil."

"Oh honey," her mother chuckled, "when you're pregnant you have wild dreams sometimes. We all do. But it will pass."

"Mother...It's not *that!*" Nadia was miffed now. Her mother always said something annoying about her feelings. Her dreams were not because she was *pregnant*. They started long ago.

"Now wait Miriam," the pastor held up a hand, "we can't just write this off. Did the dreams stop? Or are you still having them?"

"Well, they got better for a time, and now they are about...*this* stuff."

"What do you mean *this* stuff Nadia?" the pastor probed.

"You know...the *Locos*."

Her mother laughed again. She usually laughed when she was stressed but Nadia wished she would be quiet for a change. Her dreams really bothered her and she wanted some answers if anyone had any.

"You mean to tell me you foresaw all this?" the pastor asked.

"I don't know if I would put it that way, but I saw dead people in hell."

Nadia regretted it the moment it left her mouth. She looked at her mother and knew exactly what she was thinking: Her own daughter was nuts. Now everyone else would think the same thing. Why did he have to ask? Why did *she* have to answer like *that?*

"Okay, I've had enough of this young lady," Miriam shrieked, "There will be no more talk of this nonsense. Do you hear me?"

"*Mother...* I am *not* a child anymore!" Nadia countered, "You can't dismiss what I feel or think. *Jeepers mom!* You've always done that to me. I'm not your little puppet that you can make me do or think what you want anymore. *I'm sick of it!*"

"Well..." Miriam cowered.

"Now just wait a minute girls," the pastor got between them, "there is no need to attack each other. We're all on edge. Now Nadia, I want you to explain to me in detail what your dreams have consisted of. If your mother doesn't want to hear, we can go in the corner and whisper. But I think this is fascinating dear, and not just a coincidence. God has spoken to you. You have a gift and you must use it."

Nadia didn't know what to think. At this point she just wanted to shut her mouth and never open it again.

"*No!*" Nadia said point blank, "I'm not telling anybody anything anymore. I haven't even told Manuel. Judging by the looks on your faces, I shouldn't have said what I said to you. And if I have any more dreams, I'm certainly not telling *anybody*. Got that mom?"

Miriam just scowled at her, not saying a word. But Nadia knew that look. She gave it to her father on a daily basis. It meant I'm right, and I don't even have to say it.

Nadia sighed, and pulled the covers over her head.

"I'm done," she said.

~~~~

"You know," Gala piped up, "I happen to know a lot about psychiatry. I did my dissertation on dream interpretation and the subconscious mind, and you might find what I know quite fascinating."

"Do we have a choice?" Miriam bit back.

"No, you don't *mom!*" Nadia shouted from under the covers, poking her head out to listen. She glared at her mother as if warning her not to say a word.

Gala knew far more than any of these silly people did, but she would try to put it into layman's terms so they would understand. Hopefully she wasn't overstepping her boundaries, but anything at this point would be helpful. She was tired of hearing them bicker.

"And what makes you the ultimate authority on this subject?" Miriam continued even though her daughter was glaring. Gala was glad she didn't have a mother like that. She would've put her in her place a long time ago.

"Years and years of schooling ma'am," Gala answered right away, annoyed that the woman even asked. Did she not know she was a doctor? "I've gone to school longer than you've been raising your daughter, to put it bluntly. I know what I'm talking about."

"I doubt that," Miriam mumbled.

"I beg your pardon?" Gala flipped back, deciding to continue despite the negative comments. "Firstly, dreams are not biblical. I have studied Sigmund Freud's theories on where dreams come from and what they mean and according to him, dreams are repressed memories from childhood."

The pastor wiped his sweaty brow, obviously irritated by what she just said. "I beg to differ," he said. "These are just theories from some philosopher who used to live a long time ago. He hasn't proven anything nor has any other philosopher out there."

Gala was taken aback with his statement, in fact she was quite annoyed. "I can't believe you just said that. Sigmund Freud was the father of psychoanalysis. And I'm sure he has done far more studies than you and I ever will. Now just hear me out before you dismiss what I have to say."

"Dreams are kind of like a persons subconscious way of dealing with unexpected things in life. The unfulfilled wishes and thoughts of a child usually get repressed in childhood because when we're little we don't know how to voice our opinion; thus, we suppress our feelings. It's really quite simple."

"When we go to sleep our subconscious mind stays active and the suppressed feelings show up as images or scenes from our lives. It's a way to bring these things to consciousness so we can deal with our past and move on."

Miriam and the pastor began to laugh which irritated Gala even more. "What, you don't believe me?"

"It's not that we don't believe you," the pastor tried to explain, "It's just annoying when people dismiss the fact that God has anything to do with it. If what you say is true, and dreams are just repressed memories from childhood, and it's a way to deal with our past, then who do you think made us like this?"

"I'm not discounting God, though I have my own viewpoint on that; I'm just stating the facts."

"Well they aren't facts," the pastor pleaded, "that's what I'm trying to say. If you want to discuss theories then fine, let's discuss theories. But God's involvement should at least be considered. Theories are not facts my dear so please don't pollute young Nadia's mind by saying so."

"You guys, *just stop!*" Nadia interrupted, "This is ridiculous. Just forget I even mentioned my stupid dream."

Gala felt her blood boil. Sure, Nadia wanted to close the conversation but she did not. No, she was just getting started. "You know, Artemidorus of Daldis was despised by diviners just like you, and I can see nothing has changed since the second century A.D."

Gala could see she was losing them with that last statement. It was evident by their confused faces. She'd have to explain herself with this one, but at least she'd have the opportunity to explain now that she had their full attention.

"Artemidorus of Daldis was a great philosopher from the second century. He believed that dream interpretation was non-biblical and there were only two types of dreams: Thematic, meaning dreams that meant exactly what you see, and Allegorical, meaning dreams with imagery."

"And then there's the philosophy of Aristotle, and he was also against biblical explanations in dream interpretation. In fact, Aristotle argued that if God were the source of dreams, why would he send them to the average person?"

"Why would he *not?*" the pastor countered his attack, "we are *all* God's creatures."

Gala just guffawed under her breath. Once a diviner, always a diviner. "And I suppose you call those *things* out there God's creatures too? Well I'll tell you what they are: they are definitely *creatures* alright, I'll give you that. But I highly doubt God had anything to do with it."

The pastor's face just went blank. He opened his mouth without saying a word and then closed it again. He obviously didn't have anything to say to that. But honestly, Gala was getting tired of this debate. She didn't really know what had gotten into her. Perhaps she shouldn't have been so judgmental. Perhaps she shouldn't have come on so strong. Usually she was opinionated but this was a little bit over the top. She could tell she had made everyone in the room uncomfortable, and this was as good a time as any to stop.

"Okay, that was too much," Gala admitted, "I'll shut my mouth now. I'm sorry I got carried away. You guys can believe whatever you want and let's leave it at that. We've all been cooped up here a little too long and under the circumstances I'll just let this go."

Gala scratched her head and looked around at the frowning faces. Nobody said a word. They all needed to get out of there.

The guys should have been back by now.

Chapter 29

Manuel decided to follow Parrington as much as he despised the guy. He was leading him to the plane and hopefully the guy was on the up and up. If not, he'd head back to the others and ditch the idiot. If he gives him any trouble, he'd use the gun without hesitation.

In the distance, Manuel caught a glimpse of the plane. It was bigger than he thought it would be, but that didn't matter. As long as it got them the heck out of there, it was good enough for him.

The two of them paused, hiding behind a stack of crates. Parrington was out of breath from running; obviously not the trooper he had professed to be. Manuel hadn't even broken a sweat.

"If we're headed over there," Manuel pointed as he whispered, "you'd better arm yourself with something. Here, take this."

Manuel reached down and pulled a large crowbar from a tool box that spilled it's contents on the concrete floor and gave it to the small man. He didn't know how much help he'd be, but at least now he could defend himself. And there was good reason to be armed. *Locos* were wandering everywhere.

"How bout we trade," Parrington suggested, "I should have the gun. You could do more damage with a crowbar than I could. One swipe and you'd take those animals right out. Me on the other hand, I'd probably just drop the thing. And besides, I'm the one that's trained with a gun. My eyes are 20/20 and I've got perfect aim. Seriously, I was the top of my class."

Against his better judgment, Manuel handed the scrawny imp his weapon. At least he'd have his back. Swinging a large crowbar was a lot easier for someone who actually had muscles rather than little girl arms. "Fine," he frowned, "cover me then. You do know how to do that don't you?"

"Of course," Parrington guffawed.

"On the count of three we'll head for that pillar over there," Manuel pointed. "We'll go pillar to pillar until we reach the plane."

"*One... Two... Three... Go!*"

The two men bolted toward their destination, Manuel leading the procession with crowbar in hand, and Parrington following. One after another Manuel swiped his crowbar against the oncoming *Locos,* taking off the head of one and the arm of another. Blood spat everywhere as they pushed on.

"*C'mon, hurry up!*" Manuel shouted, hop-skipping behind the large pillar. They had made it to one pillar. Five more to go and still that silly man hadn't used one shot.

"You can use that thing anytime you know?"

"I will! I'm just waiting for the right time," Parrington told him. "I know what I'm doing. I'm *not* an idiot."

Manuel thought otherwise, but he didn't dare say so. If this *nincompoop* had his way, he'd make *him* do all the work. What a coward!

They made it all the way to pillar five without much of a problem, but Manuel was shocked when they got near the plane. "It's open," he said surprised.

"What do you mean?" Parrington answered as if he didn't understand.

"*You knew it all along you idiot!*"

"Nobody calls me an idiot!"

Manuel could see the man's anger in his red face, though he had no idea why he would be so angry. If anyone should be angry it should be *him*. He had been doing all the work. He was the one who killed all the *Locos* to get to the plane. Now what were they supposed to do? An open door meant there were *Locos* inside, and if there were *Locos* inside the plane, there would be no safe way to clear it unless of course he wanted to commit suicide.

"You *are* an idiot," Manuel argued with the little man, "if we go in there, we are not making it out. *Do you understand that?* We don't know how many are in there. There could be a horde of them for all we know?

"If you keep calling me an idiot I am *not* helping!"

"*Helping?* You haven't been helping *anyway!*" Manuel snapped back at the man more frustrated now than ever, "I've been doing all the work. You haven't shot off one single bullet yet. Guess you're still waiting for the right time I suppose? When *is* the right time?"

"Right now, you dirty stinkin' *wetback!*" Parrington snarled aiming the gun squarely at Manuel's jaw, "Now, you're going to do *exactly* as I say."

Oh, you've got to be kidding.

Manuel couldn't believe it. He was right all along. *Stupid!* Why did he give him the gun? The guy was a fraud, worse, *a lunatic!*

"Now pick up that crowbar you greasy dirt bag and clear out the plane!"

"*Come caca!*"

"What was that?" Parrington asked, cocking his head while shoving the gun further into Manuel's jaw. Don't try any of that *spic crap* with me. It ain't gonna work."

"*Boca de pedo!*" Manuel mumbled quickly under his breath wishing he could use the word he really wanted to say. But *fart face* would have to do, just in case he spoke Spanish. He didn't want to make things worse by aggravating him. The guy was a nut and looked capable of doing anything. It was evident that Manuel had no choice but to comply.

"*Ease off buddy!*" Manuel tried to say. The gun was pressing so hard into his jaw that he could barely speak.

"Not until you start moving!"

Manuel picked up the crowbar and readied himself for the daunting task. He should use the crowbar on Parrington instead, but the gun was still pressing hard against him, so there wasn't much hope of that happening.

"Get going," Parrington said, shoving Manuel into the open. "Over there," he motioned with the gun. "I'll have this thing trained on you the whole time now get up those stairs and get to work. I don't have all day."

This was nuts!

A couple *Locos* came at him before he could even get there. He took both their heads off with just a couple swings of the crowbar. Actually, it was quite an effective weapon. He'd use it on Parrington the first chance he got, but first he had a steady line of *Locos* to contend with.

"*Um, a little help here God!*" Manuel mumbled under his breath.

One by one, bloody disfigured men and women loped toward him while Parrington hid behind the pillar holding a silent gun. If this was how Manuel was going to go out, at least he would go out fighting: Like a courageous man. *Not some wimpy Come caca!*

Getting up the stairs and entering the plane was a task in itself. The *Locos* just kept coming out knocking him down the stairs. But they weren't very fast, and definitely not very smart. That worked to his advantage.

Once Manuel made his way inside the plane and looked around, he knew he didn't have a chance. There were about twenty or thirty of them inside. It looked like an infestation of savages with bloody faces and decaying flesh, but he swung anyway.

Manuel moved forward an inch at a time, swiping his crowbar as if it were a machete. A few days ago, this would have been traumatizing, but now it was just a natural reflex, a means of survival. All he knew was that he had to keep fighting. One pause and they would bite, *and one bite would be the end of him.*

~~~~

Parrington wondered what was taking the guy so long. He couldn't even clear a plane properly. *Good for nothing Mexican.* If this didn't work, he'd have to think of something else because he needed that plane. It was the only way out of this hell hole.

He'd give him a few more minutes and then sneak up to the stairwell for a look-see. At least he cleared them away from *around* the plane. That was more than the other guy did.

Parrington could see the plane rocking back and forth so he knew the big brute was still alive in there but he couldn't help snickering to himself. It reminded him of an old joke he and his buddies would tell: *If you see it rockin', don't come a-knockin'.* He wished that was the case now. But sooner or later he'd have to come knocking.

"*C'mon spic,*" he mumbled to himself, "hurry your ugly butt up!" He's going to waste the whole day at this rate, and they still have to get the fuel.

As Parrington surveyed his surroundings, he realized he loved this stuff. He couldn't remember the last time he had so much fun. The dead body parts in front of him excited him beyond words. It was straight out of his videogame, and now he could finally prove himself to the world.

As soon as the Mexican clears the plane and gets him the fuel he needs, he'll fly for the border in the blink of an eye. Then, he'll re-create himself. He could be almost anybody. The president, a doctor, or maybe even an axe murderer. Better yet, he'd be *Ramson Carnage* from his video game. *Awesome!*

He had to give his head a shake though, now was not the time to be thinking about that. He had a lot of work to do still, and he had better focus otherwise the Mexican could screw the whole thing up on him.

He looked at his watch, almost noon already. What was taking that idiot so long? Parrington was growing impatient by the minute. If the guy would hurry up, they could taxi the plane to the fuelling station, get the truck and fuel up, and be in the air within the next two hours. That would put him in Canada by nightfall. That is, if he didn't run into any trouble. Trouble meaning that group of witches and the old fart back in the rabbit hole. He should've strangled them all with his bare hands before he left. Then he wouldn't have to deal with them again. Of course, he could just tell the big brute to go fetch the witches by himself while he waited in the plane, and then fly away without warning. *Flying away without them was the plan anyway.*

There was no way he was bringing them with him. He was flying solo even if he had to slit each and every one of their throats. But wait, he had a gun now didn't he. A simple bullet to the temple would do the trick nicely.

Parrington smiled at his brilliance and then let out a sigh of impatience as he looked at his watch again. Okay, it's been too long. Maybe that Mexican didn't make it after all.

He'd better go check.

Inch by inch he tiptoed toward the entrance of the plane, readying his gun, making sure he didn't make a sound...because there were *animals* nearby...again. The plane had stopped rocking and Parrington wasn't sure what that meant.

He got to the step and thought of calling out to the Mexican but didn't want to draw attention to himself just in case the animals had overpowered the brute. He managed to slink inside the plane without making a sound.

Then, as his eyes adjusted, he saw the devastation. It was amazing actually. Body parts lay hacked here and there. Blood speckled the entire cargo area as if somebody had just painted a fresh coat of red paint in there. *It was exhilarating.*

Fully charged, Parrington proceeded with caution. He tiptoed to the front of the plane where a pile of dead bodies lay. It didn't look as though the animals had won, but he also couldn't find the Mexican.

It didn't look good.

Nobody could live through this, especially not a stupid dirty wetback. He had better hightail it out of there before he got trapped inside, himself.

Obviously, the Mexican was one of the dead, perhaps even at the bottom of the pile. He wasn't going to hang around long enough to find out. No, the plane was unusable now. *He wasn't going to clear it.* And finding another guinea pig to do the dirty work now was virtually impossible. There was nobody left except for the people in the rabbit hole. And the old man certainly wouldn't be able to do it. The witches were a joke, and so he'd have to move on to *Plan B.*

He'd go back to the rabbit hole; use them as human shields to get to the chopper deck. There had to be a way to get that bird in the air. He had tried a couple times before, but the third time is always the charm.

Better not waste any more time, he decided, scurrying out of the bloody plane as fast as he could. As long as he had a gun in his hand, and his wits about him, he'd make it back without a fuss. After all, he wasn't a big noisy Mexican that attracted every animal within 100 yards. He was a surefooted, sly Fox, that could tiptoe around the carnage like a pro. Yes, he was *Ramson Carnage,* conqueror of the underworld in 3-D.

Onward to slaughter! he cheered and roared to himself, raising his gun to victory like some small child playing cops and robbers in the bushes.

He stopped for a moment, observing a cracked bloodied skull at his feet. Bending, he poked at it for a minute, enjoying the squishy sound. Then, he raked his two fingers through the bloody mess and swiped them across his own forehead and cheeks like a savage.

"*OohRaw!*" he roared, all psyched and ready to go!

Chapter 30

Parrington was back at the rabbit hole in a flash, knocking profusely at the door. "Let me in! *Let me in!*" he shouted.

The stupid people. They better still be inside.

Suddenly the door slowly creaked open as he barged forward impatiently. "It's me!" he spit and sputtered, annoyed that they were so pokey opening the door. *Jeepers, he could've been attacked in the time it took them to open the door. Stupid broads!*

Huffing and puffing, he collapsed to his knees and wailed. "Look at me," he sobbed, "I must've killed at least twenty of those stupid animals, and they still kept coming. We didn't have a chance."

"What do you mean *we?*" the young babe asked, "Where's Manuel?"

Where's Manuel?...he mocked silently to himself.

She was *his* now. *No more Manuel.* He wanted to put his hands on her immediately but thought better of it. No, he had to wait, play the game, or he'd be the next one slaughtered. They didn't call him *Ramson Carnage* for nothing.

"*He didn't make it!*" Parrington wailed even harder, putting on a real show. He had to be believable if he wanted them to trust him.

"*Nooo!*" the women cried.

"Are you sure?" the old man asked.

"*Am I sure?..* Of course, I'm sure! How do you think I got this blood on my face? I tried to save his life but there were too many of them. They overpowered us."

That's when they *all* started to cry. Why oh why did they have to cry? It was the most annoying shrieking sound he'd ever heard and he had to put a stop to it quickly or he'd have to put a bullet in them right there and then.

"*Stop!*" he insisted, "We don't have time for this. We have to get going right now, or we'll be surrounded by those things. It's what Manuel wanted. *Please!* Let's go!"

"I'm not going without my husband," the old witch barked, "*Where's Frank?*"

Oh brother! Not her too. He had to think on his feet now. He didn't really know exactly how Frank had ended up dead, but he certainly could make up a believable story so they wouldn't go looking for him. Time was of the essence.

"*They ate him!*" he sobbed again, trying to make it more believable, "Yup! And there ain't nothing left. You should've seen it. Those animals were hungrier than a pack of wild wolves. I jumped on their backs even, trying to get them to stop, but Frank was a goner right from the start."

"*I think that's enough son!*" the old man ordered.

Parrington just glared.

The old bat screamed louder than he'd ever heard a woman scream before. Okay maybe his explanation was a little over the top, but it did the trick.

"*Come on people!*" he interrupted the crying wailing women, "we don't have time for this. *They're gone.* They're *both* gone and there is nothing we can do about it. You have to come with *me* now. We need to get to the chopper deck."

"Chopper deck?" the old man asked, "Wait a minute. I thought you said we were going on your plane."

"They overpowered the plane. There's no way we can get inside now. It's unusable. Am I gonna have trouble with you *old man?*" he asked, pointing his gun to make a point.

"*No,*" the old man raised his hands and stopped short. At least he knew when to back down from a gunfight.

"Now let's go," he motioned them with the gun, "I don't mean to be harsh. I don't want to have to use this thing but I will. It's for your own good; I'm trying to save your lives. You guys are like a bunch of *scrawny little chickens.*"

"Just put the gun down and we'll do whatever you want," the doctor piped up.

Parrington realized he'd have to be careful with this one. She seemed to have all the smarts, but she wasn't going to outsmart him. He'd lower the gun to appease her, to appease them all, but there was no way he was going to holster it. One wrong move from any of them and he wouldn't hesitate to shoot them, *human shield or not.*

"Okay, okay," Parrington smiled as he lowered his aim, "I guess I'm a little on edge. You would be too if your buddies were slaughtered in front of you. They're everywhere, those animals, and we need to be cautious. We need to be on our guard at all times."

"We get that," the doctor replied, "now what'd you want us to do?"

Parrington silently mused as he stood there glaring at their big bug eyes. This is fun, he thought to himself. None of his video games had ever been this intense, not even live combat, though he hadn't seen much of that.

"It's simple," he said, "old man, you can lead the group. Take a stick or a piece of something for a weapon and head up the front. I'll bring up the rear and shoot anyone I see that tries to attack. Ladies, you get the middle. Try not to fall down and scrape your knees."

"Funny," the young babe snapped back.

"*WHAT?*" Parrington eyed her.

"Nothing," she mumbled almost immediately. Yeah, she better shut her *gob hole* if she knew what was good for her. Parrington was not putting up with insubordination. And the *little honey* had better watch her mouth in the future or he'd shove a gun in it...*with pleasure.*

~~~

"Just do as he says," Gala whispered to the group as they set out on foot, eyeing the silly little man behind them sporting the gun like he was a hit man. "We don't want any trouble from him. If what he says is true about Manuel and Frank, we have no choice but to do what he says. Staying alive is on the top of my list right now and it should be on yours too."

"Yeah, never mind that he's *completely* insane," Nadia said.

"He may be insane, but he's the one with the gun right now," Gala answered, holding a pitchfork in a ready stance as she walked. The garden tools they found in the corner were a complete surprise. Nobody even knew they were there until they tripped over them while searching for weapons. The other two women had shovels and the pastor carried a rake. Not as effective but it would have to do.

"All I can say, is that man better hold on to his gun pretty tightly because I'm going for it the first chance I get," Miriam told them, "*He's a nut.* For all I know, he's the one who killed my Frank."

Miriam began to sob.

"*Stop it mom!*" Nadia whispered, as she glanced nervously back at Parrington, "Don't you think I want to cry too? My husband and my father are *both* dead but we don't have time to cry. Not with that lunatic behind us. Who knows what he's capable of."

The group set themselves apart from Parrington. He followed them at a distance which made Gala think he only had one thing in mind: He was using them as a shield. It didn't take a brain surgeon to figure that out. If they stumbled upon any *Locos,* they would be the first to be attacked, leaving good old Parrington unscathed. Well, Gala was wise to his tactics. The tables would be turned soon enough. It was every man for himself out there, and there were no exceptions for lunatics.

Locos didn't play favourites.

~~~~

Being the leader of the pack was not easy. Tom held his rake as if it were a gun, but all he could do was think of how he was going to use such a thing. *Could he possibly rake somebody to death?*

Perhaps he should have chosen a different garden tool, but all that was left was a *whipper-snipper* and he didn't think that was as effective as a rake. Hopefully he wasn't going to have to find out. As far as he could see, the base was deserted. They hadn't seen one single *Loco* since leaving the hangar. But now, half across the compound, he realized he'd have to use his makeshift weapon sooner or later. He thought he spotted someone staggering about five-hundred feet in front of him.

"Hold up everyone," he turned to tell them as he held up one of his hands and pointed, "thought I saw something over there."

The girls stopped and huddled behind him, quietly observing the person in front of them. They looked back as Parrington caught up to the group and loudly informed them that they either keep going or he'd use his weapon on them.

"*Son...*" Tom whispered, "lower your voice or the *Locos* will hear you."

"Firstly," Parrington squinted, "I am *not* your son, so quit calling me that, in fact, don't ever call me that again. And secondly, you do as I say! *I'm in charge here, not you!* Got that?"

Tom just shook his head. He wasn't even going to answer. The guy was on some ego trip and he didn't want any part of it. He was going to get them all killed if he didn't shut his mouth.

"Look, Parrington..." Gala piped up, "give the old man a break. He said he saw something and we need to be cautious unless of course you want to be the next meal."

Parrington just scowled at Gala, giving her the evil eye. He completely ignored her and turned to the others. "*Get up and get going, all of you!*" he said usurping his authority. "*Don't be such cowards.* If you need to fight them, then fight them. It ain't that hard. Like I said, I slaughtered a good twenty of them myself, *so move it!*"

The crazy runt flung his gun around like he was a gunfighter from the old West. It was apparent to Tom that he was full of it, and that made him nervous. If they were supposed to head toward that *Loco* in front of them, they were bound to meet up with others and that was worrisome.

He'd fight to the death for those women, but not for Parrington.

*God help him...*not for Parrington.

~~~

The group moved forward against her better judgment. But what could they do? The man was obviously delusional, psychotic even, and Gala knew they were headed for trouble. If they met up with *Locos,* she would defend herself and the others as best she could but she had made up her mind that the first chance she got she would take Parrington out. *It was unavoidable.* He was not right in the head, and she had to protect the others somehow.

Suddenly, a bloody walking corpse jumped out at them as Tom turned and thrust his rake into its stomach, driving it away from them. She noticed Parrington darting behind a vehicle right away leaving them exposed and vulnerable. He had no intention of fighting. He was the coward, not them.

The corpse charged again, this time toward Nadia. She jabbed her shovel into its ribs and cried, *"Take that you bloody son of a..."*

"Nadia, watch out!.." her mother yelled, *"behind you!"*

A second corpse flung itself at the girl, missing its target and landing on its knees.

Gala spun around and walloped the *Loco* over the head with her shovel allowing Nadia and her mother a means of escape.

The pastor had problems of his own. Just as he fought off one corpse, another one filled its spot. The poor old man didn't have a chance.

"*Get out of here!*" he shouted to the women, "I'll hold them back as long as I can."

"*No!*" Miriam cried, "I'm coming to help you!"

Two or three of the corpses had already bitten large chunks out of the pastor's forearms, while he held his ground, shoving the rake hard against them like a barrier. He looked back with tears flooding his eyes and said, "*Just go!* I'll be okay. *I'll be with God.*"

Both Nadia and Miriam started screaming and crying and moaning. Gala could see their struggle. They wanted to help him but they knew it was too late. If they wanted to live themselves, they had to listen to the old man. He was trying to save their lives and he didn't have much time. Sooner or later the *Locos* would overpower him.

And all the while, Parrington hid like a coward.

"*Go!*" Gala shouted, pushing the two women as hard as she could in the opposite direction until they were safely away from the scene. If Parrington could hide behind a vehicle, so could they. But not for the same reason. They had done what they could for the old man. Parrington had not. All it would have taken was a few bullets. *The pastor didn't have to die.*

As soon as she got her hands on that little coward, she'd give him his own medicine. How could a man just idly stand by and watch an attack like that? Especially if he had a weapon more powerful than theirs.

She shook her head and was never more disgusted with the *idiot man* as she was right now. The three of them sat in horror as they peeked over the hood of the Jeep they were hiding behind. Suddenly they saw the unbelievable horror: *a dog pile, clawing, biting...and the screams of a gentle man who was now being eaten alive.* Gala shed tears of her own, and that was a rarity. But this she could not bear. She had to turn away, and she made the other two turn away as well. *"Don't watch,"* she sobbed. *"Just don't."*

Gala gulped hard at the reality of the situation. The three of them were now alone, left to their own demise. Even if Parrington still intended to use them for sport, it meant they were in grave danger both from him and the *Locos*. And, if he had already taken off, they were defenceless and exposed in a world that was unsafe and unpredictable.

She honestly didn't know what to do next.

If she was a God-fearing woman, she'd pray right now. But unfortunately, she wasn't, and so she'd leave it to the two women who were.

Chapter 31

The noonday sun shone brightly through the cockpit window. The realization of what had happened appeared evident by the bloody mess.

The stink of rotten flesh was unbearable.

Body parts, blood, and entrails lay heaped in a pile where military cargo used to be. The site was straight out of a horror flick. Actually, it looked like a bomb had blown up an entire town, except this town was *Loco*. This town was *not* human.

Small groans were still audible and they were coming from the pile of the undead, because they didn't die without a beheading. That was a certainty. They kept coming and coming, sinking teeth into flesh to feed.

Groans became growls now and there was only one question that needed asking: Had he become one of *them?*

Manuel heaved the smelling carcass off of him and surveyed his bloodied hand, moving his fingers to check that they were still intact. Yes, he realized, he was in fact alive...*and not Loco, as far as he could tell.*

With every muscle in his body, he yanked himself from under the pile. The smell of the dead wafted with such a stench it made him gag immediately. The task at hand was unlike anything he'd ever encountered as a fireman. Even the worst fire or traffic accident paled in comparison.

Manuel wondered where his crowbar had gone? If he was going to get out of there in one piece, he'd need that thing. He looked around in a panic as he eased his aching body to an upright position. Then, there at his feet he spotted it.

He also spotted the big lumberjack who was on his feet again. *Go for the head this time Manuel*, he told himself reaching for the crowbar, swinging at the big *Loco* for the umpteenth time. This was one hard sucker to put down. He resembled a four-hundred-pound wrestler and that was not good.

"Okay *feo!*" Manuel uttered in Spanish, "time to die *sucker!*"

With one swoop of the crowbar, the head severed from its body and plopped to the floor. *It was over.* He could rise from the ashes undefeated and get the heck out of there. The plane was unusable.

As he made his way to the door, he could hear the groaning and growling again. Obviously, he had not fatally wounded many of them. They would rise again and kill someone else, *but not him.*

Once Manuel exited the plane, he looked around for Parrington, hoping to find his scrawny neck so he could strangle it. Lucky for him he wasn't there, but he'd find him, and when he did, he'd wish he was never born.

Quickly, Manuel rushed out of their. He'd make his way back to the others and figure out what to do next. If Parrington had the nerve to be there, he'd feed him to the *Locos*. But most likely the guy was long gone.

Within minutes, Manuel was back at the hideout. The door was open and everyone was gone. *Now what was he going to do?* They could be just about anywhere? He thought of shouting their names but that would attract the *Locos*. Instead, he leapt out of there into the open sunlight. If they went anywhere, they would have left some kind of a trail.

Think Manuel, *think!*

The place was deserted. He looked around to survey the overturned vehicles and littered streets but there were no signs of them, only dead bodies. Should he go to each and every one of them to see if it was his wife? Panic struck him as he thought of doing just that.

Perhaps he'd take a moment to look over his own body first, he thought to himself. He had just been through the battle of a lifetime and was limping pretty bad. Not only that, but every inch of him ached, and the question that nagged him since he pulled himself out of the plane was now front and center: *Was he bit?*

Wiping his sleeve across his sweaty brow, he sighed and sat down on the cool asphalt, resting his back against the exterior wall of a building. He rolled up his sleeves and looked at his forearms, bloody, dirty, but no bites. Then he rolled up his pant leg, nothing on his left leg, but the right leg hurt so bad he couldn't stand it. Guess that's why he was limping.

He took another breath and rolled up his right pant leg. The front shin looked okay but it was the ankle at the back that got his attention. The tendon was torn and hanging off the ankle, just above his shoe. It probably looked worse than it was. He could've done that to himself or it could be a bite. He just didn't know.

If he had been bitten, wouldn't he have become one of those things already? he thought to himself. His head was so full of questions but he didn't want to answer even if he knew. He'd just wrap the ankle and hope for the best. After all, finding Nadia and the others was his main priority right now.

Manuel squinted in the sun, looking around for something to use as bandages. He limped over to an

Army Jeep turned on its side and opened up the glove compartment. A small first-aid kit jumped out at him. It was old and looked as if it had been there for many years, but surely there was something he could use to wrap his ankle.

Once he finally got the silly box open, he realized it had been picked through and there was only one small tensor bandage left. Well, he thought, it would have to do. He whipped off his shoe and started wrapping the bandage around his heel and ankle, forcing his shoe back on once done.

There, he decided, good to go.

Manuel stood scratching his head now, realizing he needed another vantage point. If he could get higher, he could see further. And if he could see further, he might just be able to see where his wife and the others were.

Could he be so lucky? Maybe luck had nothing to do with it. Maybe it was time to pray. *God, please help me find my wife. Please!*

He climbed his way up on top of the Jeep. It wasn't high enough, but it would do the job. From there, he could see clear across to the other side of the compound. It looked like a war zone but he tried to focus on anything that moved. Trouble was, nothing was moving.

Nadia...Chica where are you?

Then, suddenly, as he stood atop the Jeep, he thought he heard some birds. At first, he squinted in the sun as he looked above him, but realized there were no birds in the sky, only skiffs of white puffy clouds hanging in an autumn blue haze.

On any other fall afternoon like this, duck hunters would be out, and you could hear the distant pop of the shotguns in the fields. But not now, not today. Today bore the evidence of a new form of hunting.

Manuel shook his head, trying not to think about it.

As a slight breeze whipped across his face, he heard the bird sounds again. But this time, he skirted the horizon. The sound wasn't coming from above, it was coming from across the compound. It was ahead of him, and it was a definite start and stop. No, that was no bird, that was a chopper. He could see the propellers whirring around in the distance. Someone was trying to lift off, and he knew who that someone was.

Parrington!

Not on your life buddy! *Not on your life!*

~~~~

As soon as she heard it, Gala knew they had to get to the chopper. It was their only hope. Obviously, Parrington had gotten there first and was trying to take off. If they didn't get there quickly, their chance of getting out of there would be gone.

None of them knew how to fly a chopper on their own, but maybe they could work out a deal with Parrington. Not that she wanted to, but she didn't see any other way. If they could just get the gun, they might be able to force him to fly them out of their. But first, from the sounds of it, she was pretty sure it needed fuel.

"Do you hear that you guys?" she asked, "We need to get to that chopper!"

Nadia and her mother perked their ears to listen, and agreed.

"But what happens when we get there?" Nadia asked, "He's got a gun and he'll use it this time. And he's the only one who knows how to fly a chopper."

"We can convince him he needs us," Gala suggested. "If he doesn't want to work with us, we'll take the gun. There's three of us and one of him, and he's pretty scrawny. Seriously, we have to try. And how hard is it to fly a chopper anyway? Surely not that hard. *Surely!*"

"What are we waiting for?" Miriam piped up, "let's go get the stupid jerk!"

The three of them darted from vehicle to vehicle making their way to the helipad. They weren't very far away, but they had to be cautious because of the *Locos.*

Once they had the labouring helicopter in sight, they shrunk down beside a platform and waited.

"If we all go," Gala told them, "he's liable to get spooked. So, I'm gonna go over there first. I'll knock on the door and simply have a little chat with him. He listens to me, or at least I think he does. I'll make him come to his senses somehow and see what he says. Okay?"

Nadia shook her head, "No! We're all in this together. We should all go."

Miriam shook her head, agreeing.

"No, you guys," Gala insisted, "I can't jeopardize the group. And besides, all this running around isn't good for you Nadia. You're carrying two babies, remember? Just stay hidden, and you can rest a bit. If you see him shooting me, definitely don't reveal yourself. But that won't happen anyway, so don't worry. *I'll be right back.*"

The two women agreed and watched with wild eyes as she snuck with pitchfork in hand, to the helipad where Parrington was sitting inside the chopper, still trying to get it started.

Gala rapped on the chopper door and waited.

It was now or never.

Chapter 32

"What the?..." Parrington mumbled to himself. Was that a knock, or was that just his imagination? He looked around baffled. Surely those dumb broad's didn't make it all this way. They were too simpleminded for that.

Still, it was a possibility.

Rap-rap-rapping, again at the door. Where was his gun? He had to find his gun before he opened the door. It could be one of those animals, or it could be *them.* He had to think, prepare himself, before he even thought of opening the door.

The rapping continued, and he could see the top of her head. Perfect vantage point to shoot her, but then he'd have a hole in the door. Didn't want that. No, he slowly opened it, and aimed the gun. Wait, perhaps she was still of use to him. He needed fuel, and he needed a guinea pig to go and get it for him.

Opening the door, he put on a good act. "Doctor," he grinned, "I am so glad to see you! I wasn't sure if anyone made it out of there. I got attacked too. Those animals crept up on me while I was hiding behind the truck, and so I had to run. I wanted to help you guys, but I seriously couldn't. *Seriously!"*

The silly pug woman just stood there with her arms crossed and a smirk on her face. He didn't really care if she believed him or not. As long as he could convince her to get the fuel for him, he didn't care. She was expendable anyway, with her ugly mousy grey hair; her and that other old bat. The only one he really wanted was the redhead.

"I suppose you fought off some twenty *Locos* again, hey?"

Make fun of me all you want you little witch, but I'll get you!

"I don't have to explain myself to you, now get out of my way and let me take off," he fumed, trying to make her feel desperate. It was that desperation that he wanted. Make her feel like she was being left behind, and she would do anything for him. That's how all women were; every single one of them.

"*Now just hold up!* I know you need fuel, so why don't you let me help you?"

Thank you! Parrington wanted to say, but instead he just grinned. She was playing right into his hands.

"But I don't need any fuel," he lied. *Make her think it's all her idea.* Master manipulator *Ramson Carnage* strikes again.

"I know a little bit about choppers," the woman argued, "I've been airlifted off of many helipads in my day and I can tell you it's stalling out because it needs fuel. Now do you know where to get some or what?...because we're wasting time."

All he needed was someone to go get the crew cab with the portable JP8. There was no time to get the larger truck. It was still locked up anyway. But a chopper didn't need as much fuel as the plane did, so the crew cab would suffice.

The old bag could go get it herself and drive it over to him. Make her earn her keep. If she got bitten in the process, who cares. At least he'd have the fuel.

"See that old white crew cab over there?" he asked, pointing, "that's the portable. It's full of helicopter fuel, but I don't have the key. I don't suppose you know how to hotwire a vehicle."

The woman scratched her head and looked back and forth from the crew cab to him. "I don't know how, but I'll give it a try. Let me have the gun and I'll go get your fuel."

Oh, she was sneaky but there was no way he was doing that.

"I don't think so," he said, "I'll just keep trying to start this thing, and hopefully I'll be able to jump it over there. How about that. *How about I don't need you at all.*"

Whoops, he better not play too hard to get. He actually needed her to help.

"*Fine,*" the woman fumed, "I'll just go without the gun. I just thought it would help the situation."

Right you did.

"Well you have the pitchfork, that's good enough. *C'mon...flex those muscles.*"

Parrington loved it when he won an argument. It made him feel superior, and rightly so. The old bat on the other hand didn't look too pleased, but he didn't care.

The woman shut the door and stormed off toward the crew cab, mumbling under her breath like some complaining old wife.

Man was he glad he wasn't married to her!

~~~~

She was only doing it to appease the stupid man so he'd fly them out of there, she kept telling herself. *Grin and bear it Gala.* And if he didn't comply, she'd stick him in the butt with her pitchfork and enjoy it thoroughly!

As she neared the rusted old crew cab about five-hundred feet away, she only saw one *Loco* that needed to be taken care of before getting in the vehicle. Luckily the door was wide open.

Take that, she charged toward the sickly thing, piercing it right through the forehead. She withdrew her pitchfork in a manner that even surprised her. It was quite easy to kill these days and that wasn't necessarily a good thing.

When she got inside the truck and banged the door shut, she searched around for keys. Parrington said he didn't have any, but maybe whoever had left the truck had left the keys as well. But nope, they weren't in the ignition.

Perhaps the floor? She bent down to look, but didn't see anything. Even the glove compartment was completely empty. That was not good. Something she did notice though, was an old license plate on the floor mat of the passenger side, and beside it lay a yellow flat-head screwdriver.

Hmmm, she thought, the truck was an old 70's model and if her assumptions were correct, she'd be able to try an old trick her dad taught her on the farm: Stick the screwdriver in the ignition and crank her over.

The old crew cab came to life no problem. Thank you, dad,

Lucky she knew how to drive an archaic old *stick-shift* as well. Funny how her upbringing had finally paid off. She used to be so embarrassed, telling people she grew up on the farm. But today she was very thankful.

Gala shifted into first, and slowly removed her left foot from the clutch, pressing her right foot hard on the gas. Chugging, the old thing crawled as she put it through the gears and headed toward the chopper. She was doing this, and they'd be out of there in no time.

She pulled up alongside the helicopter and brought the truck to a stop. Parrington jumped out of the chopper with a frown on his face. *Well, didn't he want fuel?* she puzzled. The unappreciative jerk. But Gala kind of figured it was probably *her* that he didn't want. *Well too bad.*

He grabbed the nozzle and started filling the helicopter immediately, pushing her aside. He was not going to leave without them. And that was the vibe she was getting.

"How many people fit in the chopper?" she asked.

He didn't answer of course.

Gala bit her lip, wondering if she should make her move now. Instead, she motioned the two women to come over but her mistake was letting Parrington see.

"*They're* not coming!"

"What do you mean?"

Parrington looked nervous, jigging up and down, looking at his watch, trying to mentally make the thing fill faster. He obviously didn't want to explain himself, but he had a lot of explaining to do, and the other two had just arrived so he could start any minute now.

Miriam and Nadia stood quietly behind her, waiting for her to say the next word. "Get in the chopper ladies!" she commanded the two of them.

"*NO!*" Parrington spit, pulling his gun from the back of his pants, aiming it at all of them. "Nobody's going anywhere!" he said all shaky. His hands palsied as he tried to steady himself. *The silly man.* He had no nerve at all. What was he thinking?

They could overpower him no problem.

"You owe us!" Miriam spit.

"Yeah!" Nadia agreed.

"I don't owe you stupid broads a thing, now get out of my way!"

Suddenly a large click sounded and they all realized it was the nozzle stopping the fuel because it was full. The chopper was ready to go, and Gala took that as a sign. As Parrington's eyes darted to the nozzle and away from them, she jumped him, forcing him to drop the gun.

Miriam pulled Nadia away as Gala and Parrington rolled on the ground, but Parrington somehow found the gun and regained his advantage over her by giving her a hard slug to the abdomen, knocking the wind out of her.

"*Now back off,*" he panted out of breath, "*all of you!*"

The little man was stronger than she thought he was, and that sent terrible pains through her stomach as she buckled over, spitting blood.

"*Please!*" Gala begged, "take us with you! You *can't* leave us here!"

"*I can, and I will!*" Parrington stood up, gaining composure.

Miriam and Nadia just held each other and sobbed.

If they would have only taken their garden tools with them this may have had a different outcome, Gala thought to herself. Even her own foolishness had caused this. There was no way she could grab the pitch fork she put in the back of the crew cab now.

They had lost the battle. A tear came to her eye as she sat crumpled on the helipad.

Parrington pulled the nozzle from the chopper and hopped in, bringing the big bird to life. The chopper blades came to a steady whir as the evil man grinned through the window, waving goodbye.

As the wind blew hair in their faces, the three women ducked out of the way as he lifted off. *They had been defeated.*

All hope of getting out of there was now leaving with the chopper.

Chapter 33

Manuel catapulted himself as he leapt off the top of an overturned truck at the edge of the helipad grabbing hold of the chopper as it took off. He caught the right landing skid with one arm and dangled there as it lifted higher and higher.

Swaying, he managed to force his other arm to grab hold, feeling the chopper lean to one side with the added weight.

This was his advantage. Obviously, the silly man knew nothing about flying choppers, or he would have compensated for his weight by now. But the lean was good. He'd crawl into the passenger door.

The chopper started to spin and Manuel knew he only had minutes to gain control of the bird or they'd crash.

As he opened the door, a gunshot ricocheted past his head.

Okay scum bag! You're dead meat now!

With one swing of his body, he was inside the cabin. He kicked the gun out of Parrington's hand before he even knew what was coming. The runt wasn't so tough now. But he was fighting back, and that surprised Manuel.

He clawed at him like a girl, and scratched Manuel's face, drawing blood.

The chopper whirred, and spun out of control.

"Let me have the controls!" Manuel shouted.

"NO!"

"We're gonna crash!"

"Good!" Parrington grinned against the struggle.

Suddenly, the little man punched a hard pointy knuckle into Manuel's temple, sending him reeling in pain. He shook his head with the throbbing pain and countered with a punch to the nose, sending Parrington backward against the cabin door, forcing it open.

He hung there upside down, blood pouring from his nose.

"*I give up!*" he cried as the chopper spun round and round.

A foot was the only thing holding him inside the fuselage. His shoelace was tangled around a raised bolt on the floor and it was beginning to untie.

Manuel reached for the shoelace, stopping it from coming undone further. He could hold it tightly, but the chopper would crash before he pulled the stupid man inside. He could let him go, but he was no murderer.

God! Help!

Manuel had an idea. He'd tie him in with his laces. But just as he tried to make a knot, the man's shoe popped right off, sending him plummeting. All Manuel could hear was the faded scream as he watched him fall to his death.

And the Locos were waiting below.

Manuel hadn't noticed they were there at all, but gaining control of the chopper, he hovered there and watched the devastation with a sadness he didn't think he'd feel. Parrington held up his bloody hand in surrender as a pack of wild *human* wolves ravished his body.

It was a sight straight out of a horror flick, as blood squirted everywhere.

God forgive me!

He didn't mean for the man to die...especially like that.

Manuel moved the chopper away slowly as he caught sight of the women at the opposite end of the helipad. A sudden hopelessness overcame him as he contemplated what had just happened. He was a *rescuer*, had devoted his entire life to saving people, not this.

Definitely not this!

And with a moments notice, he had set the chopper down, motioning the women to hurry over and get inside before the wild pack of *Locos* reached them as well.

~~~~

"*Manuel!*" Nadia screamed as she jumped into the passenger door. She held his face with her shaking hands and kissed his warm lips. "I thought you were *dead!...He...He said you were dead!*"

"*Oh Chica! I should be!*"

"*No no no...don't say that!*" Nadia tried to sooth him, but there was no soothing what had just happened in front of them. Even though they disliked Parrington, it was painful to see him die like that.

Perhaps they were all in shock.

Miriam and Gala quickly climbed in the back of the chopper as Manuel lifted off the helipad. The *Locos* were still preoccupied with their feasting as the helicopter rose high in the bright blue sky.

The panoramic view of the military base was breathtaking. From their vantage point they could see all the overturned vehicles, garbage littering the streets, bodies in pieces scattered beneath them...*and all the dead...walking.*

Nadia wondered only one thing: *Where was her dad?*

She was afraid she knew the answer, but she just needed to hear it.

"*Where's Daddy?*" she shouted over the roar of the chopper.

Her husband didn't look at her, nor did he answer, he only worked his throat.

"*WHERE'S DADDY?*"

Suddenly Miriam burst into tears. She sobbed into her hands in the back seat. It was their answer. The silence spoke volumes. If that was all the explanation they were getting, the details were too horrific. Even picturing it in her head was too much.

A single tear escaped Nadia's eye as she brushed it away, refusing the emotion completely. There was no time for that. The world had changed in the blink of an eye and there was no turning back. The horror she had seen in the last few days had numbed her. There had been too many losses. And now Daddy.

Goodbye Daddy.

A heavy gloom consumed Nadia as she let the whir of the helicopter blades sedate her, tuning everything out, withdrawing, as she stared out of the cabin window to the autumn landscape below.

Where are you God?

~~~~

Gala observed the three exhausted people she was flying with. Miriam was next to her, silently sobbing to herself. She wished she could do something for the woman, but there was nothing to do. Her husband had just been killed like so many others.

Surely there was some way to end this nightmare.

Perhaps they could fly to another facility where she could continue her research, but if every place was like this, there was not much hope. Still, there had to be a blood connection like she had first thought. After all, Gala had Nadia: the only known survivor of this epidemic. Her recovery from the virus was unique. The connection was her blood type, she was sure of it.

They watched her carefully when they first brought her in, and she didn't even appear to have the physical signs of sickness like the high fever other victims had.

Speaking of fever, Manuel didn't look so good. His face was almost white, except for the smears of blood from an obvious battle.

She kept an eye on him as they flew. He started coughing, and Gala watched as the sweat beaded down the sides of his face.

He was sick.

Leaning over his shoulder so he could hear her, she shouted above the roar of the chopper, right into his ear, "*Manuel, are you bit?*"

"*No!*" he shouted back at her.

"You look sick."

Nadia heard them and stared at him with wide eyes.

"*I'm not sick!*" Manuel shouted.

Gala reached over and felt his burning forehead, but he brushed her away quickly. "*Stop it!*" he shouted again, "*I'M NOT SICK!*"

"What is that?" she pointed, still leaning over his shoulder like a busybody.

It was a bandage wrapped around his right ankle. It was bloody and alarming. She needed to know what that was, *for all their sakes.*

"I had an injury!" he told them.

It was hard to hear over the chopper blades, so Gala remained perched right next to the big lug's shoulders. If he had been bitten, they needed to land *immediately.*

"*IS IT A BITE MANUEL?*" she shouted again.

Men, they always had to hide things. Why didn't he just tell her.

Manuel sighed, frowning at his wife, "Look," he said, talking as loud as he could, "I had a plane full of *Locos* to fight. That idiot Parrington put me right in the middle of it. I made it out alive, but later I realized part of my tendon was hanging off. I wrapped it as good as I could. I-I don't think I was bit...*but I could have been.*"

Nadia looked at her with a worried look on her face...and then began to cry.

Gala knew they didn't have much time; the man was going to *turn... and soon!*

"*SET THE CHOPPER DOWN...NOW!*"

Chapter 34

They set down in the middle of a marshy field near an abandoned farmhouse. Gala decided it was the best place to find supplies. If Manuel was in fact bit, she would have her work cut out for her. It was finally time to test her theory.

"Should we check to see if anyone's home first?" Nadia asked them.

"Or if there's any *Locos?* Miriam added.

Gala was frustrated trying to help Manuel hobble inside, and answering questions at the same time. *Yet, they were right.*

"Don't worry ladies," Manuel chided, "I found the gun in the chopper and it's still fully loaded. Let me go, so I can scout out the place. *Jeepers!* I'm not an invalid. I'm pretty sure I'm okay. You guys are just overreacting."

Gala guffawed, "Well I'd rather overreact than get eaten alive. Who knows how long you have before you become one of those things."

"*Ay carumba!* I told you...*I'm fine!*"

But against her better judgment, Gala let him go. He whipped out his gun and limped over to the doorway, knocking loudly.

"*Anyone home?*" he shouted.

No answer.

Slowly he turned the knob, surprised it was unlocked. "You guys stay outside," he whispered, "Let me check things out."

And into the doorway he disappeared.

They waited outside for what seemed like hours before he finally came back out. They hadn't heard a shot so Gala assumed they were in the clear.

"We got food, and we got medical supplies ladies," he smiled, poking his head out of the door, "now get inside and do your thing so we can get the heck out of here."

Gala wiped her brow in the warm sun and took a deep breath. She hoped they would let her do what she intended to do.

A blood transfusion was not going to be easy.

~~~

"Now, before I start, I have to explain exactly what I want to do," the doctor told them all as they gathered around after she cleaned his wound and told him there was evidence that he had clearly been bitten at the ankle.

He didn't feel that sick, except for his cough and sweaty brow. *That could be anything.* But maybe the doctor was right, and it was just a matter of time before he turned into a flesh-eating monster.

"What do you have in mind?"

"*A blood transfusion,*" Gala explained, "I would need Nadia's blood. If we transfuse it into your body, I'm hoping you will take on her natural immunity to the virus."

Manuel began shaking his head violently, "*Not on your life!*" he fumed, "You will not be doing any such thing with my wife's blood. *She is pregnant.* I don't need to remind you what that means doctor. I've seen this out in the field, *personally,* and it is far too dangerous for the average person...*leave alone someone who's carrying twins.*"

"I would be careful!"

"*NO!*"

Manuel was not going to let this woman put his wife in jeopardy, and he certainly wasn't going to let her put his *twins* in jeopardy. Nothing would make him change his mind, not even losing his own life.

He knew that if she gave blood, *that much blood,* she would become anaemic and may possibly haemorrhage or miscarry. It was definitely out of the question. The doctor would just have to find another way...*or let him die.*

"Manuel," Nadia sighed, "I want to at least try. I can't lose you!"

"*It's nonnegotiable!*"

"*Please Manuel!* I'll rest right after, *I promise.*"

"And there's enough food in the house to replenish her iron supply," Gala informed. "We'll even stay here a couple days until the both of you are ready for travel."

Manuel wanted to throttle the doctor. She was overly persuasive, but he figured he didn't have the energy to keep arguing with her. She was going to do this transfusion whether he liked it or not. His wife was obviously convinced, but she didn't know the full extent of the risk. If she did, if she'd seen what he'd seen, she wouldn't even consider it.

"I don't think we should do it," Miriam piped up.

Finally, a voice of reason, though he never thought he'd be saying that about his mother-in-law.

"Mom, I have to...*or Manuel will die.*"

"I won't die! *Ay carumba!* I've just got a mild fever, that's all!"

"This virus affects everyone differently Manuel," the doctor tried to reason. "I've seen numerous cases that happened very quickly. I've also seen others that take much longer for symptoms to show up. Be reasonable. Think of what would happen if you don't recover. Think of where your wife and your babies will be without you."

"*Fine then!* Just get it over with." But he wasn't happy. He knew the risks and he wouldn't be able to live with himself if something happened to Nadia or the babies because of him. But if the only one that was on his side was his mother-in-law, perhaps he should reconsider.

"I don't want to lose my daughter too," Miriam began to sob.

"*Oh mom!*"

The two of them hugged each other in the middle of the living room. Manuel felt like second best? He knew he meant the world to Nadia, but obviously his mother-in-law still didn't care much for him. After all, the only potential loss she could see in this situation was her own daughter, *not him.*

But that wouldn't be the first time.

Yet, since praying with the pastor, he had hoped that would change things with them. But then, some things never change. It would shock him completely if she ever did put him first.

"*C'mon...enough of the mushy stuff already,*" Manuel complained, hoping to change the mood in the room. He felt silly with so much *female* emotional stuff going on. "Just get a move on before I change my mind."

~~~~

Gala was thankful they found this particular farm house to break into. It had a large medical supply in the bathroom. It looked like whoever used to live there had some sort of health problems, and by the surgical smell of the house, its inhabitants were most likely elderly, or sick, or both. A hospital bed was even set up in one of the rooms.

She couldn't believe that they would have such luck, yet, something told her that luck had nothing to do with it at all. Perhaps there was something to this faith they spoke about, yet Gala refused to let her mind go there.

Right now, she had to focus on the task at hand.

She'd use the hospital bed for Manuel and the twin bed opposite it for Nadia. She'd found enough surgical tubing amongst the medical supplies, and the syringes that would work perfectly, now all she had to do was begin the procedure and hope for the best.

Once Manuel was on the hospital bed, she decided it was safer to tie his arms to the metal frame of the bed, just in case the procedure didn't work and he became violent like the dead people...*like the Locos.*

"Is this really necessary?" Manuel complained.

"It's necessary," she answered, "You're a big man, and if this doesn't work...we will have our hands full."

Not that she thought it wouldn't work, but her many years experience of being a doctor had taught her to expect the unexpected.

"Now Nadia," Gala instructed, "I want you to eat all the eggs that your mother just fried up for you, before we even start this procedure. *Be a real pig.*"

"*Haha...okay.*"

"She doesn't know how to be a pig," Manuel shot back with a teasing eye, belching so loudly it echoed across the little bedroom.

"*Gross!*" Nadia guffawed, screwing up her face, "It looks like somebody is enjoying his fried eggs."

Miriam just stood in the doorway scowling with her arms crossed.

Gala could tell the mother was bitter. Losing her husband had taken its toll. She'd been very quiet since they arrived. And when she asked her to fry up as many eggs as she possibly could, her response was just a shrug. She didn't even know if she'd actually do it until she came back later with two large plates full.

She could see how a risk to her daughter would send her over the edge, but it had to be done. *It was the only way.*

Once they were both finished their meals and the young couple said a prayer between them, Gala inserted a syringe into Nadia's arm with a makeshift rubber tube attached. She got the blood flowing and then crimped the tube. At the other end she inserted a syringe into Manuel's arm, and let Nadia's blood flow through to him.

As night fell on the little farmhouse, and dark shadows filled the room, Gala monitored by their bedside. "Just cuddle up with the blankets and go to sleep," she said, "In the morning you'll both be as good as new."

Now it was just a waiting game.

Chapter 35

Her dreams were wild and crazy, but this time somewhat different.

They were in a traveling circus, and the circus was out of control. Nadia had brought the children there with her mother, but the animals had escaped and were on the prowl. A lone Tiger sauntered in and out of the seats looking for its next meal.

"Run!" Nadia screamed at her mother. But her mother couldn't move, she was stuck to the seat with cotton candy.

Screams were heard everywhere.

Then from a trapeze wire from above, Manuel came swinging to the rescue like Tarzan. "Grab my hand Chica," he said.

But it wasn't his hand after all...it was the hand of a clown, an ugly clown.

The clown wasn't just ugly, it was evil. It had bloody rotting flesh falling off of its cheeks. You could actually see its skeletal eye sockets.

But the clown reached out again saying, "Take my hand Chica," as if he were Manuel.

Nadia wondered why the clown had pretended to be Manuel. It looked like him from the distance, but up close its ugly rotten clown face shocked them all.

"Had he turned into a clown all of a sudden?" she wondered, "or had he been a clown all along and she didn't even notice?"

How could she not notice?

The twins where screaming and she didn't know what to do. The tiger was almost near, and her mother was stuck on the bench. Nadia felt a panic *rise in her chest. Her heart beat loudly. It was do or die.*

She could either take the hand of the evil clown in hopes that it was just a mask, and Manuel was really behind it, or help her mother who was about to be eaten by the tiger.

It was an awful predicament.

Then suddenly, fireworks went off, and behind the cloud of smoke a wizard appeared that looked like Gala, except she was tall. Very tall.

"Abracadabra," the wizard spoke, "Don't be afraid, this is all just an illusion."

But it wasn't an illusion. It was real.

The tiger roared and told her that he had reached her mother. She turned to try and save her but it was too late. It swiped its big paw against her back.

"MOM!" she screamed.

~~~

"I'm right here sweetheart," a voice whispered.

"She'll be okay," someone else spoke.

Between two blurry half-closed eyelids, two figures moved about. It was hard to tell who they were. It was hard to figure out where she was, but she couldn't shake the doom she felt.

"Mmm-Mom?" Nadia finally focused.

"Yes honey, it's me."

"W-what's going on?"

Nadia recognized the room, the room her husband had shared with her, but he wasn't there. Panic immediately set in. *"Manuel?"*

"He's fine!" Gala interrupted, moving Miriam aside. "Here, let me check your vitals. You've been out for two days. We were quite worried about you my dear."

"Yeah that's an understatement," an angry voice came from the doorway. She recognized it to be her husband's right away. Boy did he sound mad.

"We told you to stay out!" her mother ordered.

"*NO!*" he snapped back, "I told you not to do this. It was too much for her!"

"*She saved your life*, you should at least be grateful!" her mother attacked, pushing past him, crying as she stormed out of the room.

"*I would have rather died!*"

Nadia wanted to stop them from arguing but she didn't have enough strength. All she wanted to do was hold her husband. He was alive. *He was ALIVE!*

They embraced, holding each other long, and as tightly as possible.

"I'll leave you two alone," Gala smirked, turning away from her bedside.

"*Wait...wait,*" Nadia stopped her, pulling at her pant leg, "I want to know...how are my babies? Did I... *lose them?*"

"*No,*" Gala grinned with arms crossed, "those two troopers held on for dear life. I think the rest was good for them. In fact, I'm pretty sure that's what got them through."

"No," Manuel corrected, "*It was God.* I prayed the whole time you were playing God. It was the *real* one that was watching over her and the twins, not *you.*"

"*Manuel!*" Nadia scolded.

"Well it's the truth *Chica!* She almost killed you."

Nadia watched the camaraderie. The two of them must have been going at it the whole time she was out. The three of them actually. Poor Manuel, he was only just scared he'd lose her.

~~~~

By evening, everyone had made amends.

Nadia was doing better, getting stronger, and eating like a horse. It was good to see his wife up and around. Manuel didn't know what he would have done if she had died. The silly doctor had risked far too much and he was still a little bit mad, but he decided to let it go. After all, she *did* save his life.

He was feeling back to normal to, and it would soon be time to get out of there. He figured he'd head for the Canadian border. He calculated the amount of fuel they had and it should be enough, or at least he hoped so. The last time he flew a chopper had been many years ago, and he admitted he was pretty rusty.

But the way he figured it, they didn't have much of a choice.

With the map spread across the kitchen table, Manuel pointed to their destination. "If we can make it over the border, and set down somewhere around here," he said, "I figure we can get the help we need. They say Canada hasn't been infected, but who knows. We have to be prepared for anything, so that's why I spent the last couple days stocking up the chopper with emergency supplies. Were headed into unknown territory and winter's on our doorstep, so I got jackets for all of you, boots, blankets, you name it, I got it."

"But don't you think it's wiser to set down here Manuel?" Gala pointed on the map. "I have friends that have been to Regina, and they say it's pretty big. Wouldn't it be better to set down in a large city? We would have more opportunities there: policing, hospitals, grocery stores. I just think the chances of a small town having what we need is pretty rare. I've never heard of this *Moose jaw* before."

Manuel was starting to get annoyed. Why did he feel like a minority here? Because he was. He was the only male in amongst three panicking females and that made his job harder than it had to be. *Why didn't they just listen to him?*

His wife and mother-in-law agreed with Gala, and he didn't like it one bit.

"C'mon you guys, you're killing me," Manuel whined, "Moose jaw has a military base for the umpteenth time. Their country would've been placed under martial law the moment they got word that the U.S was under attack. They close the borders and that's naturally what happens. At the very least, the Canadian military would have been put on high alert. I think our best chances are going there," he pointed a solid finger to a place on the map just northwest of the North Dakota border.

"And what if they don't let us into their country?" Miriam asked.

"That's what I was thinking," Nadia told her mother.

Manuel was up against a rock and a hard place. He'd have to step it up.

"Were going to *Moose jaw* and that's that ladies," he commanded, "and we have a radio in the chopper, so we can let them know that we're in distress. I'm sure they'll allow us to at least land. They can check us out when we get on the ground. You guys are making it bigger than it has to be. I think Moose jaw is the best place to go and I'm in charge, so I don't want to hear anything more about it. *We go at first light.*"

Chapter 36

Morning came with a vengeance. The wind had picked up, and freezing rain pelted against the kitchen window as the four of them sat sipping coffee they'd reheated on the wood stove from the night before.

"I guess we're not going anywhere then?" Miriam asked.

"We can...wait for a bit," Manuel answered in between sips. "As soon as the fog lifts, we should be able to go. Wind isn't really a factor, and neither is the freezing rain. It's not like we have to drive on the highway. I just need to see in front of me."

"But Manuel," Nadia sighed, "shouldn't we just wait till the storm passes? It's getting pretty bad out there."

Manuel was once again being bombarded by three panicking women. He was going to have to do something about this or they'd never settle down.

"Look," he half grinned, "I know from my training that you can fly a helicopter in almost any weather. They're pretty durable. But this fog is alarming, I must admit. I do need to see where were going, so the only thing stopping us is zero visibility. If we wait for a few hours, the fog will probably lift, then we can go no problem. But the danger is, if we don't get going soon enough, and this freezing rain turns into an all-out blizzard, we may be sitting here for a few more days. And days turn into weeks, and weeks turn into months. Then we'll be stuck here all winter, and we don't have enough food."

He hoped that was plain enough for them.

"We could hunt?" Miriam suggested.

Manuel wasn't even going to go there. There was no *we*. He would be the one that would have to do all the work, not them, and hunting wasn't much of an option anyway without a rifle. A handgun would only last so long. And as far as he could tell, the old farm house didn't have any weapons, not even a pellet gun.

Most farm houses were equipped, but this place looked more like a hospital than anything else. Obviously, whoever lived there was very ill for a long time, and someone was coming in and out of the house to take care of the person. Sad really, but Manuel had seen it far too many times.

No, hunting was out of the question. They needed to get out of there as much as the women wanted to stay. Yes, it was warm and cozy in there with the wood stove burning, especially on such a miserable cold grey day, but they couldn't stay there.

"We have to leave!" Manuel ordered, "and soon!"

The three women sighed, and said nothing.

"As soon as you three are done, I'm going to give a little lesson on parachutes."

"*Parachutes?*" Miriam snapped, "What do we need with parachutes? We're going in a helicopter."

"I want you to put them on anyway," Manuel explained, "I want you to know how to use them. If something happens, I want there to be an option."

"*Option?*" Miriam shrieked, "Just what do you think is going to happen out there?"

"*Mom calm down!*"

"*Don't tell me to calm down!* I'm not going if we have to jump out of a helicopter. I didn't sign up for this. *I don't know how!*"

Miriam stormed out of the room, bawling again.

Nadia glared at Manuel, and went after her mother.

"I guess it's just you and me then," Gala mused. "You can certainly show me how to use a parachute. I know as well as you do, that anything can happen out there."

Manuel forced a half-smile, and went to go get the parachutes. Little did they know that there were only three of them. Someone had to go without. For all he cared, he'd take Miriam's parachute. But most likely, the miserable woman would end up going anyway, especially if his wife had anything to do with it.

He was already the odd man out.

~~~

Nadia wished her mother wasn't so emotional.

God, help me talk to her, she prayed.

It wasn't easy dealing with her father's death. She couldn't imagine what her mother felt like. It was probably the source of her unpredictable emotional state right now, that, and the fact that their whole world had been turned upside down.

"Mom," she sighed, "Manuel is trying to do everything he can. Don't be so hard on him. He means well."

"I don't care if he means well. I don't care about *anything* anymore. I don't *want* to go! I want to stay here! I want to stay...*with your father!*"

"*Oh mom!*"

Nadia felt the hot tears escape her eyes. She hugged her mother as the two of them sobbed against each other's shoulders. There had to be a way to get her to listen.

Jesus...please!

"Look," Nadia sniffled, holding her mother, "If you don't come with us, you will break my heart. *What about your grandbabies?*"

Miriam just sniffled, wiping her tears.

"I need you mom!"

"Your father needed me too, and I let him down."

Nadia moaned and shook her head, "No mom, you didn't let him down."

"*I did to!*"

There was no consoling her. The grief was too much for her to bear, too much for Nadia even. Perhaps the best thing to do was to leave her alone for a while.

"Why don't you take some time for yourself mom? Just pray about it."

The moment it left her mouth, Nadia realized it was the wrong thing to say. As far as they both had come in their faith, it wasn't enough for her mother to accept it right now. She could see it written all over her face.

"*Just pray about it? How dare you!* After all we've been through together, after all that miserable youth group stuff, after all the times that I tried to get you to come to church and you wouldn't, after I stayed home with you Sunday after Sunday because you were hurt, *after I let it destroy my own faith*...you tell me to just *pray* about it. You have no right! You don't know how I feel. *You still have your dimwitted husband so just leave me alone!*"

Nadia's mouth hung open. She didn't know what to say. Her mother's lashing out was expected, but it was still very painful to hear.

She left the room without another word.

~~~~

Manuel attempted to explain the workings of a parachute to his wife, his very upset wife. He didn't know what went on in there, but it was obviously not good. What were they thinking anyway, it wasn't the time for them to be fighting. He'd seen it so many times before and he'd always have to undo the damage his mother-in-law did to his wife. *Well not this time!*

"Why do you let her get to you like that *Chica?*"

"She's just *grieving.*"

"Well she'd better get over it quickly because the fog is lifting, and if she's not coming, I need to know."

"She'll come," Nadia spit out, "*I'll make her!*"

Well, Manuel didn't know how she'd make a stubborn woman like that listen, but he gave his wife credit for trying. He couldn't imagine leaving his mother-in-law behind, but in the end, there was a decision to be made. They'd have to go without her if she refused, and no amount of convincing would change that.

He helped his wife get into her parachute, and prepped the two women to be ready to leave in the next fifteen minutes. It was already mid-afternoon and they had wasted too much time already, waiting for the fog to lift. It was now or never.

Manuel figured it was time to have a chat with his mother-in-law, but when he knocked on her bedroom door and opened it, the woman was nowhere to be found.

"*Miriam?*" he shouted as he went room to room.

No answer.

"What's the matter?" Nadia stopped him mid stride.

"*Your mother's missing!*"

Panic struck her face as her features fell to despair.

"We have to find her!"

"*We*...aren't doing anything! I want you and Gala in the chopper *now!* Everything is ready to go, and we're leaving in *five* minutes with or without your mother!"

"*I'm not leaving without my mother!*" his wife cried angrily as she squirmed to get away from him.

"*I'll find her, I promise!* Now go with Gala and wait in the chopper!"

~~~

It was hard coaxing the girl into the large helicopter, especially without her mother, but at least they were both safely waiting inside while the freezing rain drizzled across the windshield.

Gala sure was glad she wasn't the one running around in a frozen wet marsh like Manuel had to, but it looked like he had found her in the bushes about five-hundred feet away. It was her red jacket all right.

"Look Nadia," Gala pointed, "he found her! *Over there!*"

Nadia bent forward and peered out of the window, sighing without saying a word. The girl was still melancholy, but at least she had stopped crying.

With the awkward silence, Gala decided to pass the time doing a mental inventory to make sure they hadn't forgotten anything. She was glad she insisted on bringing as many medical supplies as possible. The trip was supposed to take about eight hours but there was a lot that could happen between now and then. Preparedness was something she and Manuel had in common.

The food was neatly tucked in the two boxes at their feet. Not much, but it would have to do. They had flashlights, a flare gun, and matches. The extra jackets were propped up against the side windows for comfort to sleep against, and they both had a wool army blanket on their laps ready to go.

Last-minute, Gala grabbed the third parachute from the kitchen table. She wasn't exactly sure who would be putting it on, but bringing it with them was a must. It bothered her that there was no fourth, but then she figured Manuel knew there were only three.

Hopefully they wouldn't have to use their chutes anyway.

"C'mon already," she said out loud, shivering in the cold as she watched her breath puff in front of her. The temperature had dropped dramatically since the day before, and sitting idle, freezing as they waited, wasn't something she wanted to do for long.

Manuel grabbed Miriam by the arm and started pulling her toward the chopper. It was obvious she didn't want to go, but he was making her.

It was amusing actually. Gala couldn't help but smile.

"*What's that?*" Nadia turned in her seat, pointing at the bushes to the left of the house as the fog lifted from the area.

Immediately, Gala turned as well...seeing the group.

"*Oh noooo!*" they both moaned.

Locos!

Chapter 37

"You can't make me go with you!"

"Wanna bet?"

Manuel had tried to have patience with the woman, but she just kept refusing. Finally, he had to take her by the scruff of the neck and practically drag her.

Patches of fog lay here and there as he thrust his mother-in-law in front of him toward the helicopter, hoping he wouldn't have to carry her. *One way or the other, she was getting on that chopper.*

They almost ran into a small bush hidden from low-lying fog, and stopped short. "Did you hear that?" Manuel asked, cocking his head to one side to listen. "I thought I heard something. Is someone calling us?"

"I don't know," Miriam paused to listen, "Sounds like Nadia and Gala. What are they yelling about?"

"*C'mon! Let's find out!*"

The two of them ran side-by-side toward the helicopter. Nadia was hanging her head out of the door yelling for some reason, but Manuel couldn't quite catch what she was trying to say.

They made it to the bushes beside the house, and suddenly a large man dressed in hunting gear jumped out, grabbing hold of Miriam's arm.

"*Locos!*"

With one swing, Manuel punched him hard in the side of the head. He went down to his knees and got right back up again.

"*Go go go!*" he shouted to his mother-in-law, "Get to the chopper!"

Miriam took off in a flash.

A second *Loco* came at him, then a third, and a fourth, all meeting the same fate as the first. Manuel just kept swinging until he finally got away.

He followed Miriam, but when he got to the chopper, there were two more *Locos* clawing at his mother-in-law.

She spun around, batting them off.

Immediately, Manuel swung, sending one careening to the ground. He opened the door of the chopper and tried to heave her in, but she fell to the ground. He picked her up, punching every *Loco* with one arm, until they were all down.

"*Get in!*" he shouted, heaving her up through the door like a rag doll, slamming it shut, then running around the chopper to his side.

With one jump, he put himself into the pilot seat and slammed the door.

Locos clawed at the windows outside.

The girls were both screaming, "*let's go!*"

The whir of the chopper blades started up, lifting the bird inches off the ground. But Manuel had to rock the chopper just to lift off. The *Locos* were hanging on.

"*C'mon c'mon baby!*" he cried, "*get up!*"

The girls screamed and yelled while the chopper spun around with one *Loco* left clinging to the side of the helicopter. It banged on the window as it pressed its bloody rotten mouth against the glass, slipping away as the chopper rocked.

"*They're gone!*" the women cried.

But the chopper was spinning out of control, and Manuel had to stop it or they'd be right back down on the ground where they started.

He grabbed hold of the cyclic stick and tried to steady it, pressing his foot against the tail rotor pedals, trying to even it out. Manuel knew he had to increase the tail rotor speed to compensate for the torque from the main rotor, if he was going to regain control of the helicopter.

He increased the main rotor power and then tried to match it with the tail rotor until the bird stood sure and steady. The whir of the blades made a beautiful sound as they hovered over the chaos below.

"*Adios amigos!*"

Whistles and cheers bounced off the walls.

Now they could get the *heck* out of there!

~~~

The rain streamed down the chopper windows against the low hanging storm clouds that still lingered in the air. But at least they could see where they were going now. The fog had lifted enough, but it had taken the better part of the day.

The dreary weather made a fitting ending to the devastation they were fleeing from, yet, Gala wondered what lay ahead. It could be worse somewhere else, but she was glad to be in the sky anyway.

Her mind *whirred* with the deafening sound of the chopper blades. Surely there were some more helmets with built-in headphones somewhere. "*My ears!*" she yelled to Manuel, motioning that it was deafening her, and pointing to the ones he and Miriam already had on.

Manuel grinned and handed her a couple helmets.

That's better! "Thank you," she smiled back. At least she wouldn't have to yell to be heard, or go deaf like the first ride they took in the chopper a few days ago.

Gala joined in the conversation through the intercom that joined them. At least she could hear herself think now, except for the argument that was going on between Manuel and his mother-in-law. She supposed that's what the grin was about.

Was there a way to turn it off now? she wondered.

At least it was interesting.

"I don't care!" Miriam argued, "I am not putting it on!"

"You're more stubborn than I am, you know that?"

"I *am* not!"

"You *are* too!"

Manuel grinned from ear to ear. He was liking this, Gala could tell. *Strange man.* Yet, it was kind of humorous, but not to Nadia. Once she caught wind of what was going on, she ripped her helmet off immediately and slumped down in her seat frowning as she shook her head.

"I just don't want to wear that stupid parachute *Manuel.* I am *not* jumping."

"I didn't say you *had* to! Just put it on to be safe."

"I *am* safe!"

"No, you're not!"

"*I am too!*"

"*Ay carumba!* Don't put it on then! See if I care!"

Miriam sat there beside him, stunned, with her mouth open, then ripped off her helmet like her daughter did. She said something else after that but nobody heard her. Gala assumed it wasn't something very nice.

"*Okay then...*" Gala mused, "That was interesting."

"You liked that did ya?" Manuel answered her, "I get that all the time. Doesn't matter what I do, it's never the right thing where my mother-in-law is concerned. I think she's just scared. Heck, we all are."

"*Ain't that the truth!*"

"Sorry you had to hear that."

Gala nodded with a smile, "Don't worry about it." She could see the man was genuinely sorry. She actually felt bad for him, but he was right. Miriam was scared...and from what she learned of the woman so far, she didn't do well under stress. She leaned over from the back seat and put a reassuring hand on the woman's shoulder, but she pulled away immediately.

Suit yourself, she frowned and turned back to Manuel. "So, you think the trip will take about eight hours?"

"Give or take, depending on the weather I guess."

"How is it?"

"*Getting worse!*"

~~~

Nadia dozed on and off for the last few hours while the storm intensified. The affects of the argument between her husband and mother still lingered in her mind and she couldn't quite shake the anger she felt. Why did they have to argue all the time anyway? she thought to herself, fuming underneath her breath.

After all they had been through, they were still at odds. And now as the chopper bounced around with the inclement weather, she figured it was the best time to pray.

God, she said to herself, *don't let us crash, and don't let me strangle my mother or my husband even though they are driving me insane.*

She smirked under her breath, and hoped that God had a sense of humour.

Her stomach was starting to churn with the up-and-down motion of the chopper. The wind was throwing them around with a lot more force than she had expected. And being pregnant didn't help. The nausea was rising in her throat.

"I'm gonna be sick!" she cried, but nobody heard her without her helmet on.

She pulled at Gala's arm, hoping a doctor would know the signs. Immediately Gala grabbed an empty box beside her and shoved it her way fast.

Heaving the contents of her stomach, she held the box tightly, hanging her head as she waited for more to come out.

It was most of her lunch and breakfast, *great!*

"You okay sweetie?" Gala asked, smoothing strands of hair from her sweaty face.

All she could do was shake her head in silence.

But now Manuel had heard through Gala's helmet intercom.

"*Chica?*"

He turned half around in his seat with a worried look on his face, "What's going on back there? *You okay Nadia?*"

"She's fine! Just turn around and fly this thing without crashing us please."

"I'll be okay Manuel," she managed to squeak out, but again nobody heard her.

Feeling a little better, she grabbed for her helmet and put it on. "There, now I can hear everyone. I said I'm fine. I always feel better after I puke. *Sorry.*"

Manuel reached a hand to his wife as he blew a kiss and gave her a sympathetic look with furrowed brow. Nadia could tell he was still worried. But as far as she was concerned, the only thing he had to worry about right now was flying. And it was getting pretty hard to do that at the moment.

Miriam joined in the conversation now by putting her helmet on. "*I want you to set this thing down Manuel!*" she ordered, "*You're going to crash us!*"

"Mom, *stop it!*" Nadia immediately defended her husband, "We're not going to crash...*are we babe?*"

Manuel focussed on his instruments and didn't answer. Everything was beeping. The snow made it hard to see and it was already dusk. Perhaps it was a good idea to set down somewhere and start again in the morning.

"*Babe? Are we okay?*"

Manuel still focused on the instruments and didn't answer.

Gala leaned forward sitting on the edge of her seat. "Maybe you'd better get that parachute on Miriam?" she spoke against the shaking helicopter.

"*Gimme it!*" the frantic woman ordered.

Gala reached beside her seat and pulled out the parachute, handing it forward.

"I'll just hold it in my lap. I can't put it on right now anyway."

The helicopter tossed about, bumping and shaking against the violent wind. The entire instrument panel was flashing and beeping with alarms going off.

"*What's happening?*" Nadia cried

Suddenly a large bang hit the side of the chopper, sending them careening sideways.

Everyone screamed!

"What was that?" both Gala and Nadia wanted to know.

"*WE'RE UNDER ATTACK!*" Manuel shouted.

What on earth?

Suddenly a voice invaded the radio. "*This is Echo Charlie Six Six Five Tiger. You have entered restricted airspace. Please identify or we will shoot you down. Over.*"

"*Answer them!* Miriam yelled.

"*I can't!* I don't know who we are."

"*What do you mean you don't know who we are?*"

Manuel frantically searched the cockpit. "What are our numbers? Find something that identifies us! *Quickly!*"

Who shoots first and asks questions later? Nadia wondered.

"Are these them?" her mother pointed to a series of numbers under the *GPS* display on the instrument panel.

"*Yes...YES!*"

Manuel immediately hailed the greenish-brown and black calico coloured chopper beside them. "*Roger that!*" he said, "*This is Bell Alpha Hotel One Zebra Viper Bravo. Over.*"

"*Roger that!*" The foreign voice answered, "*Where did you come from? Over.*"

Manuel paused, biting his bottom lip, "*Fargo Air Force Base. Over.*"

"*Roger that Viper. We have a compromise; I repeat we have a compromise. Fargo Air Force Base is under quarantine. We cannot let you* proceed. *Turn around or we will shoot you down. Over."*

"Whaaat?" Gala gasped.

Manuel punched the side of the chopper and shook his head, *"I don't think so buddy.* Brace yourself girls. *We got guns too!"*

Chapter 38

"Requesting confirmation! Over." the voice echoed for the second time.

Manuel knew he had to respond sooner or later, or they would carry out their threat. But he also knew that he'd have to buy some time somehow.

"Roger that, Tiger. Confirming turnaround. Over."

"Roger! We'll escort you back to the U.S border. Over."

"Copy that."

Great! Manuel fumed. How were they going to get out of this one?

"I don't get it," Miriam whined, "I thought we were going to fight them."

"We are," Manuel answered back, "just not now. We'll let them follow us back to the border and wait a while. We still have plenty of fuel. We'll prepare ourselves, come up with an attack plan, and then hit them when it's dark."

"But that sounds dangerous," Miriam frowned.

The whole darn thing was dangerous but they didn't have any other choice. It was fight back or die, and that wasn't exactly comforting. He'd have to come up with something good to prevent the rising panic from taking over.

"It *is* dangerous, but doing nothing would be more dangerous," he warned them. "We have to try. And besides, by the looks of this chopper, *it was meant for combat.* That's not nothing."

His wife sobbed in the back seat while the doctor held her. He was glad she was back there confined with someone who could keep her calm while he flew the helicopter, especially with her fear of flying. It was his mother-in-law co-pilot that was a loose cannon, and that didn't bode well with him since she was right next to him. Maybe he could calm her down if he put her to work like a real co-pilot.

It was worth a shot.

"Miriam," he said, "I need your help. I need you to find everything you can about our armament. Do you think you can do that while I fly?"

"*Armament?*" she asked, "*What the heck is armament?*"

"Our weapons. I need you to find out what kind of guns we have and how to use them so we stand half a chance."

"*Oh,*" she snapped, obviously embarrassed.

"Don't worry, you can do this!"

"I'm not a good navigator. Frank always did the navigating?"

" You got this," he tried to reassure her, "Just look for an information booklet. There has to be one."

"*I CAN'T!*" she bawled, "*Why me?*"

"*Because I need you.*"

"There's too many computerized gadgets, *I CAN'T!*"

Obviously, his plan to keep her busy was not working, and he could use a *real* co-pilot right about now.

Nadia continued to sob even more now.

"*Chica please!*"

"Don't push her so much Manuel," his wife bawled, "*she's upset...and so am I!*"

"We're *all* upset, but I need someone to at least find the book for me."

He couldn't do everything himself. He had to fly the beast and it wasn't easy with his limited flight time in a chopper, and the looming snow storm. He needed someone with a level head.

"*Jeepers!* I'll find the darn book then!" Miriam grumbled, "but that's *all* I'm doing."

That was at least something.

"Give the book to me when you find it," Gala piped up, "I can help him."

And that would be the level head he needed.

"Thank you, Gala! Ever play video games?"

"*Some,* Why?"

"*Cause you're gonna be my Gunner?*"

~~~~

"*Haha,*" she grinned, "well, I have four brothers and they're all gamers. I use to think they were a little odd to still be playing video games at their age, but I'm sure glad they taught me a thing or two. I'll do my best, but I must admit, Miriam is kind of right. All these computer gadgets are pretty daunting."

Gala observed the colourful monitor screens in front of her, and the clear visor attached to her helmet that displayed maps and charts and targets, just like a video game. Except this time, it was all real.

"Did you find the book yet Miriam?"

"Is this it?" Miriam asked, handing her something, "It says, '*Bell Helicopter - A Pocket Guide.*'"

"That would be it."

She flipped through the information booklet and observed the many diagrams, and realized it would take her years to master this.

"Gala, I want you to read me the information about the Armament," Manuel told her, "Don't worry about the rest of the stuff right now. I need to know what guns we have, and how to use them."

"*Got it.*"

She leafed through the beginning of the book and found the table of contents that read, *Weapon Systems*. "It says we have *guns, rockets, and whoa...even missiles.* I don't think we'll be needing all that."

"You never know," Manuel chided, "Go on."

"It says that the pilot can shoot too, as well as the Gunner. All I have to do is look through these eye things on my control panel, and press the red button. Sounds simple, but it looks pretty complicated from back here."

Gala dropped the booklet with a sudden jolt of the chopper. The wind was pretty bad outside still, and the sun had finally set. Even the Tiger chopper that had escorted them had left. They were finally alone and she had better hurry up and find out how to work these gadgets before they turned around again.

"Sorry girls," Manuel cut in, "I'm trying to keep this beast level but it's pretty hard in this wind. And it looks like we lost our buddies...*finally!*"

"Yup, they're gone," Miriam added her part.

Gala was glad the woman had calmed down a great deal. She wasn't helping matters with her panic. Nadia had calmed down as well, and that was a good thing. Perhaps she could help her with the *Gunner* duties somehow.

"We should all have some duties," she suggested.

"That sounds like a good idea," Manuel added, "but before we settle on duties, I just wanted to point out the dual controls in the co-pilot seat. Miriam, since that's your seat, you should know that you can control the chopper like this."

He showed her how to use the hand controls, and alternating foot controls.

"*Don't show me that,*" she snapped, "I don't want to know how to fly it."

"Well, if anything happens to me, you should know since you're sitting there."

"*Well I can move!*"

"*No!* I need everyone to stay put. *Miriam,* I'm sure the least you can do is be my eyes," he told her. "You don't have to do anything, just tell me when someone gets close to us. *You think you can handle that?*"

"Don't patronize me," Miriam snapped back, "*Of course I can.*"

Looks like there are still hurt feelings in the air.

Manuel smirked. Gala guessed he knew his mother-in-law better than he let on. At least he could handle her.

"Nadia honey," the big man turned to his wife, "I want you to be the second Gunner. Looks like this bird is equipped with a dual Gunner seat. You don't have controls but you will be Gala's eyes. *Okay?*"

"Okay," she half-smiled, trying to regain composure.

"And you ladies know what I'll be doing: I'll try to keep us in the sky. I'll shoot what I can when I can. And Gala, you do what you can. If something goes wrong, you know how the latches work. Open them and jump out. Pull your shoots when you're clear of the chopper blades, and we'll meet up on the ground."

"*Jump?*" Miriam squawked.

"Yes *jump!*...so you better get that parachute on Miriam."

"Nooo! I'm NOT jumping, I told you that!"

Oh, not again. The woman was relentless.

"Mom, *get it on!*" Nadia groaned, "*Please!*"

The woman was about to open her mouth again but looked at her daughter and obeyed. She wrestled around with it and pulled it over her shoulders and fastened it up. "*There!...Satisfied?*"

Everyone clapped and cheered, lightening the mood a bit.

"Nice to see I'm the subject of everyone's amusement, but what about you Manuel?" Miriam asked, "Where is *your* parachute?"

"I don't need one; I'm flying the helicopter, remember?"

"*You still need one babe,*" he wife said sadly.

"There were only three chutes Nadia, nothing I can do about it. We probably won't need them anyway. Now let's turn this bird around ladies. The weather is getting worse by the minute, so brace yourselves. It's gonna be a bumpy ride, but we ain't gonna let that stop us, now are we?"

"*Nope!*" Gala beamed at the man's contagious charisma. He should've been a motivational speaker.

"*Yippee ki yay mother...nature!*"

"Oh brother! Gala chuckled.

"Sorry, he gets like this some times," Nadia snickered.

Miriam frowned, and fidgeted nervously in her seat without saying a word.

At least the three of them were focused and calm, and they'd need that in order to pull off an outright assault on the very people they were tying to seek asylum with.

It was too late to turn back now, anyway!

Chapter 39

"Yea though I walk through the valley of the shadow of death, I will fear no evil..." Nadia spoke aloud. It was the only Bible verse she remembered off the top of her head, as she caught sight of the Tiger chopper approaching them fast.

"For thou art with me..."

Manuel readied himself with the weaponry and Gala had her thumb on the trigger.

"Thy rod and thy staff they comfort me..."

And the assault began.

Bullets pinged the side of the chopper as it danced to the right, shaking profusely until Manuel regained control.

"Take that you bugger!" Manuel shot back.

Gala looked through the eye binoculars on her dash, and then pressed the red button on her hand control. *"WAHOO!"* she yelled.

"There's two of em?" Nadia cried out, "Look...*to your left.*"

"Oh, my lord," Miriam screamed.

Bullets peppered the side of the chopper again, but this time Manuel held steady. "I can't see anything with all this snow! *I'm pulling back and taking her around.*"

Gala let off another missile but it missed its target. *"Whoops!"*

Their chopper was running, with the other two in hot pursuit behind them now.

Ping ping, went the bullets.

"Turn around Manuel!" Gala yelled, "I have one in my scope!"

Manuel hovered for a minute and turned the beast around. "*Give her all you got!*"

Gala pressed her thumb down and out came the missiles one after another, lighting up the sky as it reached its target.

Cheers resounded as they watched the explosion flash before their eyes.

But through the thick smoke and snow squall, the second chopper attacked with a vengeance.

Ping ping ping, went the machine gun, ripping open the co-pilot window.

"*MOM!*" Nadia screamed.

But no answer.

Ping ping ping, again.

Suddenly smoke billowed from the engine, sirens went off in the cockpit.

They were going down!

"*Gala, take my wife and jump out!*" Manuel cried, "*Miriam, you too!*"

Manuel desperately tried to hold the cyclic stick steady but the bird wouldn't co-operate. It was shaking and spinning out of control.

Gala opened the door and tried to pull Nadia over to her side, but the space was too confined.

"I can't get her," Gala cried.

"Just jump then," he said, "I'll see what I can do."

But there was nothing he could do. Gala slid out of the chopper as she was told.

~~~~

Miriam's head was dizzy. All she could see was blood. Blood on he hands, blood on her face, and the moment she let go of her neck, more blood pulsed out.

"*MOM!*" Nadia cried, "*you're hit!*"

"I'm fine!" she lied, "*Just get out of here!*"

"No, Miriam! Take your daughter's hand and jump together!" Manuel ordered, holding the chopper steady for the time being.

Miriam couldn't see the Tiger Chopper at the moment, but she knew it was out there somewhere in the dark blizzard sky. She knew they only had minutes before it found them again.

And then she said something she never thought she'd say.

"I'll take over the controls," she told him, "You go with your wife!"

"*Absolutely not!*" Manuel fumed.

"No way mom!" her daughter cried.

"Now listen to me you guys, we don't have time for this now!" she said with tears in her eyes as she held her bloody neck. "*Do what I say, and for once in your life, don't argue with me!* I'll jump last. I have a parachute, and you don't son. *Remember?*"

Manuel paused for a moment, and looked at her with sad eyes. "Fine, but you jump right after! *Do you understand?*"

"I'll just hold the bird steady until you get out of here, and then I'll be right behind you. *I promise.* Now get my daughter...and twin grandbabies, *out of here!*"

Manuel squeezed through the narrow passageway between the front and back of the cockpit, and lifted Nadia out of the helicopter window. The two of them jumped together, leaving Miriam to hold the cyclic stick steady as the chopper began to spin again.

Then, from the left, the Tiger chopper revealed itself and headed toward her.

Ping ping ping, went the bullets hard against the metal frame.

God help me! she cried.

~~~~

Manuel held her tightly around the middle, as the two of them plummeted into the dark night. The whipping wind and blizzard conditions took them a safe distance from the chopper, well enough away for the chute to deploy.

They rose instantly as the parachute opened, hovering as the chopper spun round and round, completely out of control now.

The Tiger chopper was in full attack, almost on top of the other.

"*MOM!*"

"*She'll jump Chica! She'll jump!*" her husband tried to comfort.

But just as he said it, the two choppers collided in midair with a bright fireball in the sky, exposing the two of them as they sheltered their eyes from the burning wreck.

"*MOM! NOOO!*" Nadia screamed.

She sobbed so hard she felt as though the whole world could hear her. There was a nothingness left inside of her.

Her mother was gone.

"*Manuel?...Baby?*" she cried out to him, but he didn't answer.

She grabbed him quickly because he wasn't holding on anymore, and she didn't know why. He went limp without any warning at all. She tried to hold him up, but he was too heavy. *What was happening?*

"MANUEL?"

She held him under the arms, but she couldn't hold on for long, and she couldn't let him go either: The ground was still too far away.

Then, a horrible reality set in: *He had been shot!*

"Wake up!...MANUEL!!!"

Her arms ached!

She couldn't hold him.

The wind tossed them about in the blizzard night!

And he slipped away.

Chapter 40

Nadia lay on her back with her eyes open, watching snowflakes land on her nose. She had touched down a while ago, and now lay on a pile of torn-open round bales. All she knew was she was in the middle of a barren field somewhere, with remnants of her parachute flapping in the wind.

It was the loneliest place she'd ever been.

Without Manuel, there was no point.

Without her mother and father, there was no point.

She might as well give up and die.

All she could hear was the howling of the wind in her frozen exposed ears. And she had lost her helmet. She wondered how long it would take to freeze to death. Ten minutes? Two hours? She really didn't know, but she was going to find out.

There was no point to this anymore.

Then, as if by impulse, she held her abdomen and felt something flutter. Perhaps there was still something to live for, but she didn't want to care.

Tears flooded her eyes.

How could she go on without him? There was no way she could've held on to him longer, but she should've tried harder. She should've been stronger. If only she had held on for a few more minutes...her husband wouldn't have fallen to his death.

Where was he now, lying dead from the impact, from his wounds?

"*Aaaaaaaaa!!!*" she screamed into the stormy night.

It felt like her heart had ripped right out, yet she could still breath, still move her limbs. *It wasn't fair.* She should've been the one to die, not her precious Manuel.

God had not been fair. He took the love of her life away.

"*Why God?*" she sobbed.

Nothing but the wind answered her back.

The snow was starting to cover her face now. She licked the bits of snowflakes from her mouth and blinked away the clumps of ice that blurred her vision.

It was only a matter of time now.

Nadia looked up into the night and tried to find the stars one last time, but all she could see was a myriad of snowflakes dancing every which way above her. She pretended the snowflakes were tiny angels, dancing and skipping in the wind like little children. Perhaps like the twins she would never hold.

Tears blurred her icy vision once again as she gulped hard.

It wasn't fair.

After all the dreams she had...after God revealed himself in such an odd way, this was the result. It was all for nothing.

Pointless.

Perhaps it was a punishment for all the sins she'd done.

Yet, something told her otherwise, and she just couldn't shake the feeling that she'd been in this situation before. But it didn't make sense. Why was she feeling this *deja vu?* It was as if she could see herself lying there dying, and her older and wiser self kicking her and telling her not to give up.

But she wanted to give up.

Perhaps an angel was standing in front of her.

Yes, something was obviously there...and it was talking to her.

"You have a purpose!" the voice spoke, "Get up!"

But she shook her head against the tears, "*NO!*"

The voice continued, "*You're not done yet!*"

"*I am too!*"

She was as done as anyone could be. How could God ask any more of her?

"'*You are flesh of my flesh and blood of my blood,*'" a second voice said.

Two figures stood above her now, encased in a glowing light. *It was an illusion.* Her brain was slowly starting to freeze, and nothing made sense anymore.

If this was God, and he was bringing her to heaven, that was what she was waiting for. She would be with her family again instead of alone.

"*Just take me now,*" she mumbled with a frozen mouth.

"*NO!*" both voices shot out.

"*Aaaaaaaaaa!*" she screamed out of sheer frustration, "*WHY NOT?*"

"*Because you hold the key!*"

"I don't know what you're talking about!" she cried again, rubbing her blurry frozen eyes. Maybe she was imagining this?

"*You shall lead the way for my people like the days of old. Like that of Noah I have called you to salvage my creation. Like that of Moses you shall bring the multitude unto me. Like Abraham you have been proven worthy. You are the chosen one,*" the illuminated voice spoke in the wind.

"*Not me!*" she retorted, "*I don't deserve anything. I'm not special!* Why would you pick someone as useless as me?"

"*Because you can cleanse the people,*" the voice told her. "*There have been many who were thought unworthy whom were called in my name. I choose the pure of heart. You are one of them my child. Now get up before it's too late!*"

"It's already too late!" she cried.

Full of self-pity, she closed her eyes against the two illuminated figures in front of her, and willed her body to die. "*JUST GET IT OVER WITH!*" she yelled.

But nothing happened. Only the wind answered her back.

"*Aaaaaaaaa!*" she screamed again as if doing so would make everything stop.

But the wind howled, and the snow pelted against her frozen form...and darkness hovered over her.

The two illuminated figures disappeared and left her to her own demise.

Nadia could feel a numbing sensation flood over her. She wasn't cold anymore. She was actually starting to feel cozy like her own warm bed.

Closing her eyes, she forced a smile. *This wasn't so bad.*

In minutes, it would be over.

"*Here I come babe,*" she whispered with a raspy voice.

Then, without warning, she felt her body rise.

Was she standing now?

Was she finally dead?

But then, a figure moved in the shadows, and she felt a sudden pinching pain in her arm. No, it was more like something grabbing her hard.

Pain shot through her legs too as she moved them.

But how could she walk if she were dead?

What kind of a corpse does that?

Then, as if everything suddenly made sense, she realized...there was only one kind of dead man walking.

And it wanted to eat her.

Run, she instinctively told herself. But her body wouldn't co-operate. She was numb all over, yet...something picked her up and carried her against her will.

Then suddenly, a loud roar echoed in the blizzard night, shining two blinding bright lights at her.

A shot rang out. Then another.

She was being ushered into the beast against her will.

Then a door slammed.

Hugh?

The familiar slam of a truck door made her realize she had been placed inside a vehicle. Yes, the wind had suddenly stopped, cocooning her inside.

The slow-moving grind of the gears, told her she had been rescued.

But by whom?

A warm blanket was thrown around her shivering body as someone held her close, someone familiar. His smell was like that of a hospital room.

Oh, how she wished her eyes were not so blurry. It was frightening not knowing who was in front of her. What if he meant to harm her?

But then her own mind answered: *He saved me.*

But he wasn't Manuel.

"You okay sunshine?" the masculine voice asked her.

But her mouth wouldn't work right, and all she could do was shiver and grunt in a frozen mute response.

"That was a close call," the voice in the drivers seat spoke again.

The two men on either side of her held her shaking body, draped in a blanket. They didn't say a word, leaving only the driver to speak again.

"Let's go home!" he said.

Nadia continued to shiver, hearing the swishing pattern of windshield wipers against the three men as they spoke to the driver now, whispering something in familiar voices she thought she heard before.

There was one thing that came through crisp and clear, and Nadia heard that with clarity, "*Stupid weather!*"

Then laughing.

"*That's Saskatchewan for you!*"

"Yeah, pretty much like Fargo."

"Can't believe the idiots almost blew her up."

The driver chuckled again, "Oh well, it worked to our advantage anyway. At least we got her back, and she was right where Dr. Silverton said she'd be."

"Now let's get her to the lab."

###

**BE SURE TO CHECK OUT BOOK TWO IN THE
'BLOOD WAR TRILOGY'
BLOOD PURGE ON AMAZON.COM.**

Here is a sample of BLOOD PURGE.

Prologue

High in the sky, the January sun shone down on the western prairie landscape.

It was a fine place to live, secluded from the rest of the world. It didn't matter if everyone teased them and called them survivalists.

They were the dummies now.

Sure, at first they tried to knock down their doors, but they persevered and held them off. The firepower they had was second to none. Kevin made sure of that.

It was a little unorthodox to live off the grid at first, but worth every minute of it. The kids got use to it, and Kiki didn't seem to mind.

It was a breath of fresh air really.

No cell phones, no laptops, no tablets, just pristine fresh air. It was their private oasis at first. But now, when everything went dark, they were all in the same boat, except they were one-up on everyone else.

Just like Kevin said they'd be.

Her husband was a genius, and the kids knew it, their neighbors knew it. Kiki was just glad to call the place home. There wasn't a reason for her to even venture out.

Not with *them* out there, anyway.

They'd come crawling around in the night, but they couldn't get in. Sometimes they sounded like mice in the walls, but that's when Kevin fortified the perimeter fences, and adopted the security rotation. Another added bonus.

Their protection.

But not now, not since he left. Was he ever coming back? Kiki wondered when the food would run out. She wondered what the fuss was all about. Why did he have to protect her from it?

She should have been more prepared for the monsters, instead of being naive. If she knew the real threat, she would have demanded training as well.

Now it was too late.

It was only a matter of time before she turned into a monster herself.

Chapter 1

Nadia Espinosa awoke to chopping sounds.

In her blurred vision, she hadn't realized she was the only one sleeping, tucked securely into the warm sofa. Even the howling winds couldn't move her from her slumber. No, she would stay there in a half-conscious state as the storm brewed.

In front of her, a large figure moved.

"Yup, she's breathing!" The deep voice huffed. "Get *Sleeping Beauty* up! We got chores to do."

Then, someone pulled her body to an upright position. She rubbed her eyes to see, finally focusing on a familiar woman. It was Gala, which brought her back to reality. They were still in the hunter's cabin, and they were still held hostage by Peter and his sidekick.

It wasn't their original destination, but when they found her, they told her they were going back to the med lab on the base. That was before the bombing. Rebels attacked the base the same night she parachuted to the ground, the same night her husband and mother died. It was a thought that saddened Nadia and she held her swollen belly, now eight months along.

"Can't you leave her alone already?" Gala shouted back at one of the doctors. "It's not like she can help you chop that wood. *She's pregnant!*"

"We know she's pregnant!" The man answered sharply. "She's the reason we're here. She's the reason we're stuck in this old man's smelly cabin for the winter. You think this is fun, Dr. Silverton? We were ensured a spot in the med lab for tests. We can't exactly do that here, now can we? We have no choice but to let her carry to term, eating all the food up like a pig. Now she can make *us* some food, so get her up!"

"It's not her fault the base was attacked," Gala defended. "You should thank your lucky stars you weren't there at the time. Actually, you should thank Nadia."

The doctor rolled his eyes as he held his axe like a weapon.

"Oh, big man," Gala fumed. "What do you think you're going to do with that?"

Nadia didn't know what to think of the argument, so she shut her mouth, and left it up to Gala, who had been her protector ever since the doctors captured her. She explained the night they found her, that she wasn't part of the doctor's elaborate scheme to abort her twins for experimentation. Gala sobbed when she told her this. She hadn't expected them to put a tracking device into Nadia's skin. That's how they found her.

Why they didn't come get her at the farm house in North Dakota, where Gala performed a blood transfusion with her and her husband a few months back, she'll never know. Perhaps it was because they were waiting for her to come to them, or at least that's how Gala put it. It still sounded fishy.

They had simply headed to the nearest military base north of the Dakotas. It didn't take a brain surgeon to figure out where she'd turn up, but it was heartbreaking just the same. To think they would have aborted both babies just to find out what made her blood immune to the infection. Well, they weren't getting them. Neither she, nor her babies, were lab rats. If Manuel would have survived, he'd have kicked butt long ago.

Thinking about him made her sad, angry actually, mostly at herself. He had been shot, and she couldn't hang onto him as they parachuted down to the ground. The moment he slipped from her grasp, her heart had died. He was the love of her life, and it was hard to go on those first few days, but Gala kept pestering her to try and eat for the babies sake.

Well, eating wasn't a problem now, she was constantly hungry, and growing like a giant pumpkin. Manuel would have laughed at her swelling oversized belly, and teased her until she was boiling mad. It was what he did. He'd always made her feel special, yet embarrassed at the same time. It was a feat only he was able to accomplish.

Oh, how she missed him.

"Get your hands off of me!" Nadia shouted at the one they called Vaughn, the ugly one. He had yellow teeth and bad breath, making her gag like she did when she was first pregnant. And he wanted her to cook, after that foul breath? "I'm coming. All you have to do is say it nicely. I'll make the meal if you treat me with respect."

Nadia grinned at Gala. She taught her that. "Stand up for yourself girl," she told her after the first week of being held hostage in that crappy hunter's shack. It wasn't built for five people. She and Gala shared the living room as a make-shift bedroom. Peter had the large bedroom, and Vaughn had the small one. The unfortunate owner of the property, was forced to sleep in the closed-in porch, which wasn't very warm. At least she and Gala were near the woodstove, and that was especially a comfort on a day like today. The snowstorm was really getting nasty, and she could feel the wind-chill straight through the walls.

Gala had spent the last few months, trying to figure out how to get out of there. It wasn't even sanitary to bring a baby up in there.

Old man Wormwood stunk so badly, the little shack took on his rancid body odour smell, as well. Everything was dirty no matter how hard she and Nadia cleaned each day. And there was only so much the old man would let them touch.

He was both a hermit and a hoarder. Stacks of books and hunting supplies, made it difficult to move. Tiny winding pathways made their way around the floor space, throughout the entire shack. It made her feel claustrophobic, especially in the middle of January, with cabin fever.

She noticed the thermometer today. It was headed to minus thirty degrees Celsius again, and that was cold, even though she was use to Fahrenheit. Canadian temperatures were different, but not that different. Cold was cold. Not even a dog could live out there.

There was nowhere she and Nadia could go, even it they wanted to.

And they hadn't seen an infected person in weeks, but they were still lurking somewhere. The sickness was not as prevalent in the middle of a frozen prairie winter, but she was sure they were hiding in the warmth, where ever that was.

Each night, Gala would lay in the smelly old leather recliner next to Nadia on the couch, and look out the window to survey the landscape below. The terrain was mostly bush land, but they were situated at the top of a hill, looking down into the valley. There she could see at least two other lights flickering in the distance. The one to the far west, she was told, was what remained of the military base in Moose Jaw. Obviously, someone had taken it over after they bombed it. Last she was told, the med lab had been completely destroyed, and the place was overrun with sickness.

In these frigid temperatures, she assumed there wasn't much going on there now, except probably a back-up generator keeping the emergency beacon on at night. If anyone was still alive down there, they weren't living on the base. Besides, Vaughn and old man Wormwood, had checked it out numerous times while hunting.

Perhaps in the spring, she and Nadia could check it out for themselves, but not now, not in Nadia's condition, and certainly not in thirty below zero.

The other light closest to them, but still quite some distance away, was what Wormwood referred to as a survivalist cult. From what he told her about them, a handful of people lived there since the infection. Previous to that, it was just a quirky middle-aged couple, and their grown daughter, holding down the fort.

They set up a place *off grid*, totally self-sufficient, stocking up on food and supplies, and ammo for the apocalypse. According to Wormwood, there was no such thing as the apocalypse, and the infection was just a government conspiracy to spread mass panic. He said the base was experimenting just like Hitler did in the 1930's, and that's where the infection came from—*Man made*.

Gala knew otherwise, but then, Wormwood's ideas could be possible too. The virus was indeed a Prion attachment, like Mad Cow disease, and even *she* could manipulate the proteins. But none of that mattered now. The damage was done, and whether a person called it the apocalypse or not, was irrelevant. It had spread like rabies, and there wasn't much hope for a cure—except that Nadia was the only one immune that they knew of. That fact alone, held them captive.

Yet, Gala couldn't help but wonder what went on at the survivalist's camp. Was there hope there? Were they sane? They obviously had food, and that was a lot more than they could say for themselves. Venison was getting sparse, and rabbit stew was getting old fast. What they needed was vegetables, milk, and flour.

Gala wanted to check out the camp, but she couldn't leave Nadia behind. Besides, Wormwood warned not to go there. He insisted they were insane and he wouldn't go there if his life depended on it. They were troublemakers, and had the perimeter armed with guards, and rigged with booby traps. In fact, they'd already lost one of the doctors to their traps a few months ago.

No, Wormwood stayed clear of them, and so should she. They were troublemakers, and he suspected them for the bombing of CFB Moose Jaw. "Who else would have the capability?" He blamed.

As Nadia worked over the wood stove, warming up left-over rabbit stew again, Gala shivered as she joined her. She hunched as she wrapped one of Wormwood's smelly old sweaters around her body. Nadia also wore one, even though hers was getting pretty tight around the middle these days.

"How you feeling lately, honey?" Gala whispered, sitting down with her instant coffee, thankful for the endless supply of water from the deep artesian well under the kitchen floorboards. At least they had the essentials, even though they had to boil the water.

"Oh, I'm fine." Nadia gave a half-smile, rubbing her lower back. "The bigger I get, the more my back aches. And I sure get tired fast."

"Well, you're probably about thirty-seven weeks or so. It could be any time now. You realize that, don't you? Especially with twins."

Nadia's face fell. "I thought you said I have another month!"

"Well, that's an estimate dear." Gala tried to comfort. "With twins, you might be early."

"*I don't want to have these babies here! I told you that!*"

"I know sweetheart."

Tears started flooding Nadia's eyes as she brushed them away. It was hard to see the young girl in such a desperate needy way.

"Can't you do something?" Nadia whispered.

"Sweetheart," Gala leaned in so the others couldn't hear, "I already removed the tracking device. If we left, they couldn't find us, no matter how hard they tried. But look at the weather. If it's not one thing it's another. Either we freeze, or starve, or we get lost in a snowstorm. The weather is brutal out here. It's best to stay put right now."

"That's what you said last time. I can make it over to the camp, I know I can. I fit into Wormwood's orange hunting parka and ski-pants. I can still zip it up. And he never wears it anyway, just that dirty Camo thing. Same with Vaughn. *Please!* It's now or never. I can't wait any longer. And they won't notice that we're gone if we sneak out in the middle of the afternoon. Wormwood and Vaughn go hunting then, and Peter's good for nothing. He's always got his nose in a book, and falls asleep when they go out. It would be easy."

Gala bit her lip, and wondered the same thing. But it was so risky in Nadia's condition. What if it was too far? It looked close enough, but the terrain would be terrible—ice, fog, bitter cold winds. Plus, the sickness was still out there, even if they hadn't seen anyone with symptoms for a while.

"*Please Gala!* It's downhill! And what will Peter do when the babies are born? He's been threatening to use them for some vaccine he's been working on. He thinks their blood will be even better than mine. *C'mon!* I can't let him do that!"

It wasn't an easy decision, but Gala knew the girl was right. They had waited long enough, and even though Peter had just been scaring the girl with his threats, she really didn't know what the man was capable of, or what demented theory he was working on. With no med lab it was virtually impossible anyway, but she didn't want to leave it to chance. It was now or never. If they *were* to go, they'd have to wait until the storm broke. Visibility was down to zero, and the cold wind would freeze a person in minutes.

"Fine," she whispered in the girl's ear. "We go tomorrow after lunch if the weather clears—but you have to be sure!"

"I'm sure!"

Gala tried to force a smile, hoping she wouldn't be leading the poor girl to her death. "All right then, I guess we're leaving tomorrow."

~~~~

That night, underneath her covers, as the fire flickered in the wood stove, Nadia sobbed softly as she prayed, hoping Gala was asleep. *God, help us get out of here. Help us make it to the survival camp before my babies are born. I know I can make it there, but I need your help. Please God, even though I want to be with my husband, and I'd give anything to be up in heaven with him right now, I know I have to fight for these two little ones. It's what Manuel would have wanted.*

Then she heard Gala turning uncomfortably in the squeaky recliner again, and paused for a moment, checking to see if the woman was awake. "Gala?" she whispered against the howling wind outside.

But nobody answered.

Tears suddenly overcame her as she held her hand over her mouth to muzzle the pain. It wasn't just the loss of her husband, or the sickness, or the fact that they were being held hostage, or even that they were leaving tomorrow, but the cramping pain in her back and belly, that tortured her. It would go away like it always did, but this time it was twice as painful. It wasn't labor though, she assured herself.

It wasn't!

Chapter 2

Yah Kathryn liked him, he was the new guy, but they didn't have to be such jerks about it. The teasing was getting ridiculous. Her four brothers wouldn't stop. They joined them when the outbreak first started. The moment the Canadian boarder went into lockdown, they fled to their parent's one-thousand-acre fortress, to await the apocalypse.

And it came with a vengeance, despite what people said. *They* were the dead ones now. And Ricardo would've been one of them, had it not been for her. She dragged him in like a stray puppy.

Right from the start, he was all mysterious and everything. He wouldn't tell them his name, so she had to give him one. He was her project—a gift from heaven to replace what was lost. The boys teased her non-stop, but she just kept nursing him back to health. Mom was afraid he was sick, and the boys tied him to the bedposts, but she was sure he was fine. She didn't know how she was sure, only that her gut told her, saving him would be worth it in the end.

She didn't normally believe in love at first sight, but this was the exception. The moment she set eyes on his big muscular tanned body, and rugged good looks, she fell madly in love with him. It had been like that ever since.

Kathryn was the baby of the family at only twenty-two, but Ricardo didn't look very much older, even though he wouldn't say how old he really was. Actually, he didn't say much of anything. Mostly he'd just sulked around like he carried a chip on his shoulders. Dad said he wasn't right in the head, but Kathryn knew he was just having a hard time remembering things.

"He's not a *psycho* you guys," she'd tell her brothers when they started teasing her about him. "He just doesn't like to talk much. I got him to open up a little, and he said he feels like he doesn't belong, and wishes he could remember how he got shot."

"You sure are spending a lot of time with him Kathryn." Her mother joined in the conversation one day. "You don't need a *replacement* you know."

But Kathryn chose to ignore what her mother was insinuating. She wasn't trying to *replace* anyone's shoes. More importantly, she wasn't a baby either, even though her family still treated her like one.

She could take out a whole group of sickos with one round, kick-box her way out of anything, and still make it home in time for supper. And yes, she might look like a Barbie, but she certainly didn't act like one. Her brothers always underestimated her. Even the Asian Yamasaki brothers didn't think she could carry her weight. They were lucky her parents opened their door when they did, or they'd still be stealing food from the military.

It was her idea to bomb what was left of the base, anyway. Their experiments were atrocious, and she had to put a stop to the torture going on, that and avenge what they so heartlessly took from her. Everyone knew they were killing innocent people, but nobody had the guts to do anything about it, except her. And to think they said she didn't have it in her.

No, she wasn't a baby, *absolutely not!*

Tonight was no exception. She could do her rounds with Ricardo as usual, even in a snowstorm at thirty below. They had the survival gear for minus fifty-five and then some. A little snow wouldn't stop her, especially not Ricardo with his robust build.

"Well, maybe your lips will get frozen together this time," her brother Kiefer giggled. "We've seen what you guys do up there on the box. That's what we've got binoculars for, you know."

"Shut up you *jerk!*" she screamed, throwing a carton of shells at him. The carton opened up, and spilled all over the floor. *"Now pick 'em up and make yourself useful!"*

"No!" Kiefer teased. "Why don't you ask lover boy to do it?"

Kathryn couldn't believe what jerks they were being, *again.* It was an ongoing thing. She knew they didn't like the guy very much. Most likely, it was because he made them look puny when he stood beside them. But he earned his place in the group. He'd saved their butts plenty of times.

Nobody could say he wasn't a lethal weapon. He'd even outfought her middle brother Kipp, who used to be a firefighter. He kept himself in shape, but Ricardo still outdid him. That made Kathryn beam, every time he won the sparring completions her dad put on in the evenings.

He'd never spar with her, though. He refused every time, saying, "I don't want to hurt you, *Chica.*"

She didn't know what the whole *'Chica'* thing was all about, but she didn't mind when he called her that. It was kind of cute. Her brothers didn't like it much though, and they let him know it every time.

"Her name is *Kathryn,* bud," they'd tell him rudely, "and you'd better not hurt her if you know what's good for you. We'll throw your ugly carcass to the sickos in a heartbeat."

"*Locos*," Ricardo would always correct them, not intimidated in the least. That would annoy her brothers and they'd always walk away after that. She didn't know why he insisted on calling the sickos, *Locos,* either, but then, he was a mystery, and that's what attracted her to him in the first place. He was daring and strong, and every girl's *bad boy.* He'd take chances none of the group ever would.

If she didn't know any better, she'd think he had a death wish. But, with a little more time, Kathryn knew she'd crack his shell.

And time was all they had anymore, endless blocks of time, way up on the lookout tower they called the box, taking the night shift in a snowstorm with minus thirty wind chills.

Hardly romantic, but as long as she was with him, she didn't really care.

~~~

Ricardo couldn't shake the nagging pain in his gut, and it wasn't from the old bullet wound either. He just couldn't put his finger on it. Something seemed wrong. Ever since he woke up with a gunshot wound, chained to a bed in pain, he'd been out of sorts.

Sure Kathryn Kirkpatrick and her family took him in, nursed him back to health, helped him regain his strength, but his head wasn't right. He had headaches that lasted weeks sometimes, and the nightmares were getting worse.

If he could only remember who he was.

Sure Kathryn took a liking to him—she was a sweet girl even though she acted tough, but he didn't feel right about leading her on. Every time they kissed, he started feeling uneasy, like he was doing something wrong—and that wasn't good. What was the matter with him? He had it made—a beautiful young blonde, food in his belly, and a place to lay his head. What more could a man want in these conditions. Yet, something wasn't quite right, and it hadn't been right since the day he arrived.

What he was doing floating in their dugout, he'd never know. It was just amazing he didn't drown or die of hypothermia, especially being unconscious with a bullet wound in his gut. Kiki, the mother hen of the place, said it was divine intervention that kept him alive that night. He didn't know what to think of that. Was he a praying man? He just didn't know.

He was told the night they found him in the dugout, that the military base attacked some helicopters in the air. Could he have come from one of them? If so, where were the others? Was he the only survivor? .

All these questions ran through his mind every day, and every day he tortured himself to remember.

"Ricardo?" A cherub voice pierced the bitter cold air, snapping him out of his trance. "You're doing it again."

"Huh? Doing what?"

"Day dreaming!" Kathryn smirked. "You do it all the time."

"I do?"

"Yeah, you do!"

Ricardo looked at her in the moonlight, thankful the winds had died down and the snow had stopped. She was beautiful all bundled up in that Eskimo parka with fur surrounding her flawless face. Only small pokes of blonde hair peeked out of her hood. How could he *not* love that?

'C'mere you!" He pulled her to his lips and held her. "I've never thanked you for saving my life, have I?

"Nope."

"Well… Thank you!"

He kissed her again, and fought the uneasiness this time. He had to get on with his life, and stop wondering what was missing. Whatever happened in his old life was gone now, and he had to accept that. Life would never be the same, and he was tired of fighting his feelings for no apparent reason. The world had turned upside down, but together he and Kathryn could make it a better one.

"I hope a kiss isn't all I'll get."

He wished he could tell her, *maybe someday*, but he caught himself before he promised anything, turning it into a joke instead. "Oooo…" He laughed for the first time in a long time. "You sure are a *Naughty Nadia*."

"A what?… *What did you just call me?*

Ricardo gulped, and couldn't tell if she was teasing or actually mad. "I… I just called you *naughty*. What's wrong with that?"

"Not that… You just called me *Nadia*."

"No I didn't."

"Yes you *did!*"

"Well… It's an expression, *Chica*," he told her with a half-grin. "Don't freak out."

"Look," she said bluntly, like she always did. "You're probably from Mexico or something like that, but even so, we don't talk like that here. There is no *Naughty Nadia* expression in Canada, unless your name is *Nadia*. Do you know someone named *Nadia?*"

"No!" He tried to appease her, but really, he couldn't answer truthfully because he just didn't remember. "I don't know a *Nadia*. I told you, it's probably some stupid Spanish expression like *Chica* or something—and you like me calling you that."

"I know."

"Well then, dry those tears before they turn into icicles," he said. He grabbed her petite chin softly with his gloves, bending in for a make-up kiss. "*Ay carumba*, you get ticked off easily. I better not get on your bad side, or you might blow *me* up."

"I have four brothers, remember? It comes naturally."

Kathryn was known for her craziness, which explains her bombing the military base by herself, but Ricardo really didn't know what she was capable of. All he knew was that he wanted to stay on her good side. Besides, he knew Kiefer's threat was real, and they'd use any excuse to throw him to the *Locos* if he hurt her in any way. The brothers reminded him quite regularly. Usually, all they had to do was glare.

A long moment of silence passed as he and Kathryn re-directed their eyes to the ground below, where they should have been in the first place. They were on duty after all, and had to keep their eyes peeled for *Locos,* or anything else that looked suspicious.

He was told, an old hunter lived up in the hills to the west. One of his men got zapped by the electrical fence surrounding the second quarter. He assumed they carried a grudge because of that, so they were put on high alert ever since.

Kathryn sniffled in the silence, and rubbed her nose. "Man, my face is frozen." She patted her cheeks with her mitts. "How much longer do we have to be up here?"

Ricardo looked at his watch. "It's almost dawn," he said. "Another half hour to go."

"Good! She yawned and stretched like a cat. "I can't wait to get to bed."

"Me too!" Ricardo cringed, hoping she didn't think he was insinuating anything. He tried to change the subject quickly, before her mind went to the gutter. "I don't see much of anything down there, do you?"

"Ah...nope! Don't think anyone would be crazy enough to be out there in this."

"Except if you're *Loco*."

"Yes Ricardo." She rolled her eyes and smiled.

At least he was on her good side again.

Then, just through the clearing in the trees, as the sun came peeking over the frosty horizon, Ricardo spotted something moving. "Uh oh, we got company."

"Where?"

"Down there." Ricardo pointed. "Five hundred feet that-a-way. See it?"

"That's just a *Slow-Mo*, Ricardo."

A *Slow-Mo* was Kathryn's made up name for a frozen *Loco*. They barely moved.

"It's still a threat, *Chica*. We gotta alert the Yamasaki bothers on the ground. They can take care of it.

Ricardo worked his walkie-talkie without hesitation. "Hey bro's—you copy? Over."

No answer.

"Bro's? You copy? Over."

"Maybe their battery died again."

"I doubt it. Your old man just charged it. Mine too."

Something was wrong, Ricardo could feel it. He tried one more time, waiting for a response that didn't come. *Three strikes—you're out.* "Let's go Kat." He took her hand to help her up. "We're going down to check it out."

Chapter 3

The base was deserted except for those in charge. The bombing destroyed part of their prize medical lab. It was almost world renown. At least that's what Lieutenant Murdock liked to brag. He took pride in the work they were doing, and nobody was going to mess it up this time, not even the dumb doctors in the hills. They had tried to become part of what he was doing, but after the bombing, there was no way that was happening.

He told them the entire med lab had been destroyed. A lie, but he couldn't exactly tell them the truth. He couldn't tell them they managed to salvage a very small section of it, with minimal equipment. He could still do his work, him and the core group, that is.

They were spared.

Whoever did the bombing, must have been an amateur. The C-4 was poorly distributed, and most of the damage was only sustained at ground level. Hardly enough to knock them off their feet. To the naked eye, it would appear there was nothing left of CFB Moose Jaw, but underneath, they were alive and kicking—*even the dead ones.*

Murdock smiled at his experiments, thankful he had gathered some more non-infected lab rats for the next round.

The whole point was to find a cure, yet he'd been harassed right from the get-go. Did it really matter that his methods were classed as inhumane? The whole world was in-humane right now.

Thankfully his core group had been on his side since day one. It consisted of top military personnel from around the world: medical scientists who stood for what he did. Sure, they lost most of them, but still, six remained, and he'd fight to the death for them.

And those silly doctors from North Dakota sounded promising when they first flew in, telling him they had a live specimen who appeared immune. But he was skeptical. If they really had such a person, where was she?

"A minor technicality," they told him. But he didn't believe a word of it. He kicked them out and told them not to come back without the patient. Murdock was certain it was them that bombed their facility, and he'd get them back when the time was right.

The one doctor even had the nerve to show his face the day after the bombing. Murdock nearly shot him down, right then and there. It didn't even matter that he said he found his missing patient. By then, his credibility had been lost. If he really did have someone that developed an immunity to the virus, he wouldn't have had to beg at his door like all the rest.

But Murdock knew the man was lying, anyway. A cure was impossible. The medical community knew they could only manage the infection, not cure it. And manage it he did. He had successfully developed a drug that big Pharma would pay anything for.

The *Purge* was ready for trial.

~~~~

Bronson pretended to swallow the pill, and spit it out when the doctors weren't looking. He looked over at his younger sister, Brooke, spitting in the doctor's face. They attempted to force-feed her instead. *Make them think you took it*, he wanted to tell the innocent eight-year-old. But nothing would stop the inevitable.

He knew what it would do, slowly, little by little. The same thing happened to his older brother Bellamy. He was only twenty-one, and died at the hands of lunatics. He watched him, and all the others, bleed until there was nothing left of them. And that was supposed to stop the virus?

He seriously doubted it.

But now, it was Brooke's turn. No matter how hard he tried to protect his little sister, she still got caught. He'd done a decent job keeping her safe, until today. There was nowhere left to hide. He and his sister had been on the run since September. Their parents were killed trying to leave Saskatoon. They weren't sick, just shot for no good reason.

Circle Drive had been blocked off, and they weren't letting people through to Highway 11 South—the main exit out of town. It didn't make sense, because they were told to evacuate to CFB Moose Jaw, because it was the safe zone. Bellamy was posted there. But his parents didn't follow protocol, because Bellamy told them to ignore it and just get out of there as soon as possible.

Everyone was told to follow the phonetic evacuation procedure (PEP) but Dad said they'd be dead by the time they called Zwolski. And Bellamy had pull, so they thought they could bypass waiting for 'Z' to be called. It was just like school—always the last on the list. He sure wished he could turn back the clock a few months to his first year of high school. Cracking up in homeroom, without a care in the world except for homework, was a usual day for him. But that was a lifetime ago.

Bronson recalled the painful memories of his parent's death, and swore he'd never let them surface again, but they always popped up without warning. He remembered the road block. His parents got out of the car to find out what was going on, and were shot on site, right in front of his eyes. He choked back the tears.

After he and his little sister witnessed their parents' brutal death, he snuck Brooke out of the car, and took off on foot. They'd been on the run ever since. And when they finally made it to the military base, thirsty, tired, and hungry, Bellamy could only give them temporary refuge, because the place was so overrun.

Once the sick people took over, the three of them went into hiding with a group of his brother's friends. Then Bellamy was taken, and Bronson decided to follow them. He wished he hadn't. The memories still haunted him. It was something he vowed he'd never tell his sister. Then, the bombing scattered everyone. They lost their core group a week ago, and were caught by the regime soon after.

Now, Bronson lay strapped to the table, knowing he'd have to watch his little sister bleed out, the same way his big brother did.

~~~

Murdock realized she was the youngest patient to try the new and improved drug, and that was a good thing. His studies proved that children were able to hold off the sickness longer than grown adults. That, in itself, led them to do further research. But, it was always a challenge to find live subjects. Most of the children he found, had already been consumed by the virus, and they were worthless to him.

Yes, this little one would do nicely. He wasn't too sure about the teenage boy, but he guessed they'd find out pretty quick.

"Please dear, stop wiggling." He tried to sooth the girl with a calm voice. "Just settle down. We're trying to save your life."

But the girl was impossible. She wouldn't stop kicking, or crying, or thrashing. They had to muzzle her, just so she wouldn't spit at them again.

Murdock sighed. His co-worker, Jenkins, apparently had enough. He flew his hands up, and walked away from the girl. "You deal with her, doc! I've had enough of the brat!"

"Not a problem." He assured his co-worker that he could handle her, not wanting to exacerbate the situation any further. "I'll watch these two myself."

Jenkins stormed out of the room.

The teenage boy wasn't making trouble. He apparently surrendered to whatever was going to happen. It was the girl he was mostly concerned about. Her temper tantrum was getting on his nerves as well.

"Make your sister stop!" He ordered the teenage boy. Murdock quickly un-belted his restraints. "I want you to sit beside her until she calms down. Do you understand? And just so you don't try anything, Demitry has watch. If you do anything crazy, he won't hesitate to blow your head off. Got it?"

The lanky pockmarked teenager nodded his head like a puppet.

Murdock lifted his chin to Demitry, and the muscular security guard came right over. "Watch them! I'll be back in a couple hours. By then we'll know if either one of you is worth the trouble."

Chapter 4

The night was uneventful, and what he thought was a reason to get down from the tower last night, wasn't. The Yamasaki brothers had already taken care of the *Loco* they spotted in the snow, and that was that. No emergency. Not like he wanted one, but lately, with the cold winter, things were getting pretty boring on the night watch.

As the sun beamed in on their faces, he kissed Kathryn good night, and headed for bed. *Alone.* It wasn't what she wanted, but, he didn't feel right about sneaking around like she suggested. No, he didn't feel right about any of it.

Besides, he didn't want to get lynched by her mob of brothers.

No, he went to bed, tossing and turning between fits of on and off again nightmares. The *Locos* kept coming at him inside the plane, flying high above the clouds. There was nowhere left to run. He sliced through their heads with his machete, but he couldn't get away in time.

They were attacking Kathryn...*and the baby.*

With all of his might, he pushed toward her, through the crowd of passengers, but he was too late. The *Locos* were feasting on his new bride. She was down on the ground, struggling, while they ate away at her neck.

And the baby cried.

Where is it? Where is the child? He couldn't find it anywhere. All he could hear was a screaming, gurgling sound.

It was too late.

The sound was fading fast. Ricardo shoved the *Locos* out of the way, using his machete again. In a panic, he hurried seat to seat, but still found nothing. Then the crying stopped. The *Locos* were dead, and so was Kathryn.

Would he ever find the baby?

Hopeless, he fell to his knees and began to cry. "Help me! *Please God!*"

But instead of God, a serpent slithered through the seats! "God will not help you, you fool, but I am here. Reach out to me," it said. "God has forsaken you. That is why you don't remember." Then, with a striking force, it stung him with a crimson tongue.

Ricardo dropped to the ground, and the serpent laughed. "Your wife and child are dead to you now! Surrender to me, and I will make you the *living dead!*"

~~~~

Ricardo woke with a start. Sweat dripped down his entire body, and his heart palpitated in his chest. Was he married? He checked his ring finger. No ring, not even evidence that he once had one. And what about the baby? Was he a father? He couldn't remember. Why couldn't he remember?

Had God really forsaken him? Is that why he couldn't remember anything? And what was the snake about?

His dreams were getting worse, and he had nobody to talk to about them. Kathryn was always there, but he had to watch how much he told her. She had demons of her own, even if she never spoke about them. It was the little things he picked up on that told him she had recently been hurt by someone. An old boyfriend perhaps?

Or, he could be wrong. It could be the same thing that bothered them all. Everyone was having a hard time wrapping their heads around what was happening out there. People eating people, wasn't your normal turn of events. It was like watching mini wars erupt in your own back yard.

And this was no normal back yard.

The Fortress they called it, consisted of a pentagon of large shipping containers put together. There were approximately ten containers in all, stacked in two levels on top of each other. The empty middle section was converted into a main living quarter, with a kitchen and lounge on one side, and an open area used for sparring on the other. The entire middle pentagon, had an impenetrable sheet metal roof.

The place really was a fortress.

There were no windows to be had, only peep holes. He guessed they thought it would be safer, but that depended on the circumstances. It didn't exactly meet code, but Kevin, the dad, didn't care. He made it to keep the bad guys out, as he put it. Ricardo figured it would be a firefighter's worst nightmare. He wondered why Kipp, being a fireman, wouldn't have mentioned this to his dad. They actually needed emergency exits in the event of a fire. Sure, they had hidden cubby holes they could wiggle out of, at the top of each container, but that wasn't enough. If there was ever a fire, they'd all be toast.

But then, what did he know. He wasn't a firefighter. Yet, something told him that he knew what he was talking about. He just didn't know why.

Ricardo wiped the sweat from his brow and figured he might as well get up, even though it was only eleven o'clock in the morning. Only two hours of sleep, but what could he do? He couldn't stand the nightmares any more. He had to get up and take his mind off the snake thing that kept popping into his dreams.

~~~~

Kathryn tossed and turned.

Ricardo's reaction still bothered her. One minute he seemed interested, and the next, he gave her the cold shoulder. What guy wouldn't jump at the chance to sneak around with her? Sure, it probably wasn't wise, but Kathryn didn't care at this point. She was tired of being lonely.

Tired of an empty bed.

Maybe he was the kind of guy who saved himself for marriage? Probably. With her luck, Ricardo was already married. That would explain a lot. She'd heard him more than once, refer to her by someone else's name: *Nadia.*

Who the heck was Nadia?

Kathryn lay on her back and sighed. Sleep wasn't coming anytime soon, especially with Ricardo on her mind. And even if he was married once, his wife was probably dead already, and wasn't a threat to her relationship with Ricardo at all.

Still, she felt jealous.

This Nadia must have been quite the woman. Obviously, Ricardo was still in love with her, even if he couldn't remember her. Hopefully, he never would. Kathryn didn't need another heartache.

One was enough.

Even now, memories flooded in. He was going to propose. They talked about it all the time when he got transferred to CFB Moose Jaw. It was a dream come true. A long distance relationship was hard, yet, she had dated him for a year while at the U of R in Regina, so that made it a little easier.

But, things didn't go exactly as planned. She moved back home when the love of her life went away for basic training. She never expected him to join the military. But then, his father had suddenly lost his business in Saskatoon, and couldn't afford to continue paying for his education. So, joining the military, was a way to get it paid.

She thought she'd die without him.

"I don't want you to join!" Kathryn screamed at her boyfriend one night.

"Calm down! We're not breaking up!"

"Well, it feels like that!"

"Oh Kit-Kat."

He was the only one that could call her that. She wouldn't let anyone give her a nickname now. Only Kat or Kathryn.

She felt like she was putting her own life on hold while he skipped off to Cornwallis to complete his basic training. At the time, she was still enrolled in the U of R, and had a part-time job in the Tunnels of Moose Jaw. She got an actress part, playing Miss Kitty, the tour guide. It was fun, but she didn't want to spend the rest of her life doing that, or going to school for that matter.

Now she didn't have to.

The day he got his posting, she quit school, and lost her job, all in the same breath. When he told her he was going to Cold Lake, she cried all afternoon, and just didn't show up for work. How could she, with big puffy eyes?

That's the day she moved back home.

The love of her life had abandoned her for over a year, and all she could do was reek havoc for her parents. Almost daily, she hung out at the bar, and didn't come home until the wee hours of the morning. *Drunk!*

"You can't keep this up," her mother told her one night.

"I can, and I will!"

But then her brothers held an intervention on a chilly Thanksgiving weekend. They all decided to come home for the holidays, which was very unusual. Little did she know, that they had come home for *her*.

"We're all concerned Kathryn." Her oldest brother, Karson, told her as they forced her to sit down with them in the living room.

"Leave me alone!"

"We're not leaving you alone!" Kipp blurted out. "If nobody else is going to say it, I will. You're acting like an idiot, Kathryn. Stop moping about your boyfriend, or I'll kick your butt!"

Leave it to Kipp, to tell it like it is.

"Oh really—*let's go then!*" She put her fists up, ready to fight. Her years of self-defense and Taekwondo classes, told them she could do it.

"Enough!" her dad yelled. "Nobody's fighting anybody. He stood up, holding both Kipp and Kathryn off. "Seriously! Are you really my little girl? —cause you're not acting like her. I don't even know who you are anymore."

"I'm *me* dad!"

"Then act like it," he said. "You can either spend the rest of your life crying over something you can't control, or—you can suck it up like a man."

"Oh—*thanks dad!*"

"Kevin!" her mother scolded.

"Well…you know what I mean, dear."

The brothers roared with laughter, with her mother caught in the middle, trying to shush them all. "Stop it! All of you! You promised to help. This is not helping."

"Look, Kat." Korwin, the second oldest piped up. "We all care about you, kid. But you need to stop trashing your life over a boy. If he loves you, he'll be back. If not, you gotta move on."

Kathryn sobbed then, realizing they were right. She promised to move on with her life, and stay out of the bar. In fact, she signed up for college again. And then he came back, just like that.

She didn't know how one boy could turn a girl's life upside down so easily. But she didn't complain. No, the moment he told her he got a transfer to CFB Moose Jaw, she welcomed him back with open arms, dropping all of her silly ideas of college immediately. *Who needs an education anyway.*

Her parents were disappointed, but happy that she was happy again. Her brothers just rolled their eyes. Kathryn didn't care. She had her sweetheart back. And she knew it was only a matter of days before he would propose.

And then the world turned upside down.

Kathryn brushed away the tears, remembering how they killed him so brutally.

Why did you leave me, Bellamy Zwolski?

Why?

Chapter 5

Murdock couldn't figure out what kind of game they were playing.

The boy didn't seem to have any signs of *Purge* at all. Maybe that was a good thing? If the drug had no effect, he would up the dosage.

"I see you had a good night," he told the kid.

The pocked-marked teenager scowled. "*She* didn't."

The two of them observed the young girl, feverish and lethargic. Blood had already started trickling from her nose and mouth.

"It's supposed to be like that. That's why it's called *Purge*."

"You're a murderer."

Murdock smiled sympathetically. He realized the boy was just worried about his sister. "On the contrary. I happen to know, this method works. Phlembotomy therapy has been around for 3000 years.

"You're a quack!" The teenager turned away in disgust.

"You'll see, young man. This time it will work. I know you've nosed around and seen my failures, but I've improved the drug immensely. The bloodletting will last approximately 24 hours. During that time, she may become severely weak, but she will pull through. She's young."

"And how's this supposed to help her?"

"Simply put," Murdock tried to explain in layman's terms, "Her blood volume will deplete. Then, the drug will feed an immunity directly into her DNA. If she's strong enough, her body will start making new blood, and she'll be our first ever specimen to go forward to the next trial."

"And what's the next trial?"

"To expose her to the virus of course."

The teenager bolted toward the doctor, swearing and clawing. Security thankfully apprehended him immediately. Murdock couldn't let this kind of behavior go unpunished. The boy was unpredictable, and was a threat to the project.

He may have found a way to evade the drug's potency for now, but not for long. Like his sister, he would be prostate on their table, bleeding out by nightfall.

"Take him to a cell."

"NO!"

Demitry held him tight while he squirmed, and fought against him. Obviously, he wanted to sit beside his sister forever. But Murdock couldn't have that, he only needed him to calm her down. Reality was, the young girl may not even survive. In fact, she would probably be dead in a few hours. Then he would need the scrawny teenager even more.

But Murdock hoped she'd pull through. He was tired of experimenting. He needed success, now. He had to come through with his promise. He'd already told *The Elite* that he had a finished product. If he didn't have anything to show for it, they wouldn't pay.

And *they* were scheduled to arrive in a week's time.

~~~~

Bronson rubbed his bloodshot eyes.

It was hopeless. He had tried everything to prevent Brooke from getting the virus, and now, because of it, she was their next experiment. It was only a matter of time before she would die like Bellamy.

He had to do something! Bronson hammered his fists against the bars, and cried in agony. He didn't care if the stupid security guard was listening. How could he be so heartless, knowing his sister was in the other room dying?

If he could only get the key.

"Hey goon..."

The security guard turned his head, and spit on the floor. "What?"

"C'mere."

"I don't got time for this kid. *Now shut your hole.*"

Bronson began shaking the bars like a caged monkey. He screamed to the top of his lungs, and hit his head against the bars. *Not the best idea.*

"Kid, you're gonna give yourself a concussion."

"So! I'd rather die, than let you guys use me for your experiments!" Bronson screamed to the top of his lungs, trying to get the guard to come over. The goon wore the keys around his neck. If he would only move closer, it wouldn't take much to grab them.

Suddenly, the guard stood right beside the bars, and told him to stop. "Look," he said. "I get it. Your sister's in there, and you want to help her. But seriously dude, the best way you can help her, is to shut up."

"Fine!" Bronson immediately stopped, hoping to trick him into inching a little closer. "So... What? Your names Demitry, right? Where did you come from?"

"I ain't telling you squat."

"C'mon. If you want me to calm down, then that's how I'll calm down. Get my mind off of it. *Please!* My sister's in their dying, and I don't want to think about it."

Demitry sighed, inching closer to the bars. He wasn't very bright. But personally, Bronson didn't care. All he wanted, was to get the keys, anyway he could.

"That's better. Now we can talk." Bronson rubbed his temples. "How did you get caught up in all this, anyway?"

"I didn't get caught up. *I volunteered.*"

"Why would you volunteer?"

"Cause that's what *men* do."

Just a little closer. The guy was playing right into his hands. A few more inches, and Bronson would have him by the throat.

"So, are you insinuating that I'm not a man?" Bronson tried to pick a fight. He knew it was the only way. Reel him in like a fish, just like the last big Jackfish he caught with his dad at Meeting Lake last summer.

"Hey, I just call it like I see it, *little girl!*" Demitry laughed.

Bronson gulped as the big ape shook the bars. "I'm not a— *a girl!*"

"Fine then—you're a *retard!*"

But Demitry was the retard. Bronson grabbed the dangling keys that hung around his big square neck, and pulled his face into the bars.

Got my fish.

Bronson looked into his deep brown eyes, as he twisted and turned. He had never done anything like this before. But to his surprise, it almost seemed natural. Within seconds, Demitry's face turned red.

The veins in his neck started to bulge, and then everything turned blue.

It wasn't that Bronson was stronger, that made him overpower Demitry, it was the predicament, and the angle he was pulling. Bronson's scrawny body had an advantage over the brute, by mere gravity.

All Bronson had to do was pull and twist, until the lifeless body collapsed.

Stunned, the teenage boy looped the keys around the dead body's neck, to retrieve them. With shaky hands, he found the right key and unlocked the cell, sliding it open. He paused to look at what he did, and felt his stomach churn. In seconds, he vomited beside the strangled man's bulging eyes.

It had to be done.

But for some reason, Bronson knew it didn't. He wasn't a murderer. He was a vegetarian. He was an animal rights activist for crying out loud. This city boy who most people called a wuss, had just killed another human being with his own bare hands.

Bronson even had a hard time killing fish, but got used to it in time. He wondered if he would get used to this in time. He hoped not. Yet, it wasn't exactly the first time he encountered death. There was too much of it since the outbreak. Usually, other people did the killing, *not him.*

Slipping on his own vomit, he fell to the floor and sat there for a moment. His head throbbed, and his heart beat wild in his chest. He didn't have time to deal with these strange girlish emotions. He had to get to his sister.

C'mon—be a man!

To continue reading BLOOD PURGE please purchase it on Amazon.com.

ABOUT THE AUTHOR

Award-winning author Kathleen Morris has written numerous articles, poetry, and short stories published in various Saskatchewan newspapers. Her poem *Refuge* is published in a book anthology titled *A Golden Morning.* She has written many plays and skits including her play titled *Gotta Love It,* winner of Dancing Sky Theatre's rural writing contest in 2001 where it was also performed by the theatre troupe in Meacham, Saskatchewan.

Deep Bay Vengeance is Kathleen's first novel followed by its sequel *Deep Bay Relic,* and final book in the trilogy, *Deep Bay Legacy.* She also writes non-fiction inspirational books about funny stories from her own life. Her latest novel is called *The Prion Attachment,* first book in the *Blood War series,* followed by the sequel, *Blood Purge.* When she's not writing, she enjoys spending time with her husband Barry and their three grown children and grandchildren at her home in Saskatchewan, Canada. For more on Kathleen Morris please check out her author page on Amazon.com.